Common Bonds

SOUTHWEST LIFE AND LETTERS

A series designed to publish outstanding new fiction and nonfiction about Texas and the American Southwest and to present classic works of the region in handsome new editions.

General Editors: Suzanne Comer, Southern Methodist University Press; Tom Pilkington, Tarleton State University.

Common Bonds

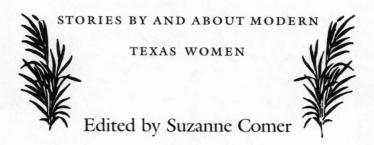

STORIES BY AND ABOUT MODERN

TEXAS WOMEN

Edited by Suzanne Comer

Southern Methodist University Press
Dallas

Library of Congress Cataloging-in-Publication Data

Common bonds: stories by and about modern Texas women / edited by
    Suzanne Comer.—1st ed.
        p.   cm.—(Southwest life and letters)
    ISBN 0-87074-287-6—ISBN 0-87074-288-4 (pbk.)
    1. Short stories, American—Texas.   2. Short stories, American—
Women authors.   3. Texas—Fiction.   4. Women—Fiction.   I. Comer,
Suzanne.   II. Series.
    PS558.T4C65   1990
    813'.0108352042—dc20   88-43251
                                                                                                          CIP

Grateful acknowledgment is made for permission to include the following stories:

Gail Galloway Adams, "The Purchase of Order," from *The Purchase of Order* by Gail
    Galloway Adams, published by the University of Georgia Press. Copyright © 1988 by
    Gail Galloway Adams. Reprinted by permission of the University of Georgia Press.
Karen Gerhardt Britton, "Infections," previously published in *Sands*. Copyright © 1985 by
    Sands. Reprinted by permission of Karen Gerhardt Britton.
Pat Carr, "Hitchhikers May Be Escaping Inmates," from *Night of the Luminarias* by Pat
    Carr, published by Slough Press. Copyright © 1986 by Slough Press. Reprinted by
    permission of Slough Press. (First published in *Women's Quarterly Review*.)
Elizabeth Davis, "The Hawk," previously published in *Gulf Coast* and the *Houston Post*.
    Copyright © 1986 by Elizabeth Davis. Reprinted by permission of Elizabeth Davis.
Bobbie Louise Hawkins, "This One's for Linda Joy," from *My Own Alphabet* by Bobbie
    Louise Hawkins, published by Coffee House Press. Copyright © 1989 by Bobbie Louise
    Hawkins. Reprinted by permission of Bobbie Louise Hawkins and Coffee House Press.
Shelby Hearon, "The Undertow of Friends," previously published in the *Chicago Tribune
    Magazine*. Copyright © 1984 by Shelby Hearon. Reprinted by permission of Shelby
    Hearon and the PEN Syndicated Fiction Project.
Mary Gray Hughes, "Luz," from *The Calling* by Mary Gray Hughes, published by the
    University of Illinois Press. Copyright © 1980 by Mary Gray Hughes. Reprinted by
    permission of the University of Illinois Press. (First published in *Southwest Review*.)
Beverly Lowry, "Class," previously published in *Houston City Magazine*. Copyright © 1978
    by Beverly Lowry. Reprinted by permission of Beverly Lowry.
Carolyn Osborn, "The Apex Man," from *A Horse of Another Color* by Carolyn Osborn,
    published by the University of Illinois Press. Copyright © 1966, 1977 by Carolyn Osborn.
    Reprinted by permission of Carolyn Osborn. (First published in *Red Clay Reader*.)

(The following page constitutes an extension of this copyright page.)

For my parents and Ernest
In memory of Gan

Contents

Acknowledgments

This book began with a conversation between Keith Gregory, director of Southern Methodist University Press, and me in the winter of 1986. As senior editor at the press I often have conversations with Keith about the ideas for books we hope to develop, but they do not usually lead to projects that are as personally involving as *Common Bonds* has been. I have been a behind-the-scenes editor for a decade now, but this book represents my first "up-front" appearance, with name on cover, responsibility for contents, and all the joy and terror that those things imply. Keith is an immensely supportive person to work with—"the best boss a gal could ever have," as Roz Russell might have said in one of her working-girl films—and his generosity of spirit and belief in encouraging his staff to exercise the full range of their talents and to grow in their work have made this book possible.

My experience working with Don Graham on his collection *South by Southwest: 24 Stories from Modern Texas* while I was editor at the University of Texas Press also fostered this book, because through that experience I came to know many of this state's finest writers of fiction. Don's respect for my opinion and willingness to allow me to work closely with him in selecting stories for his anthology strengthened my confidence and gave me one of the most enriching experiences of my career.

My own "second reader" for this present anthology has been my friend Tom Zigal, himself an accomplished writer as well as former editor of *The Pawn Review*, that literary journal which nurtured the talents of so many Texas writers. With his customary kindness and magnanimity Tom suggested writers to me, then read story after story that I sent to him, thereby giving me a keenly perceptive person with whom to discuss much of the work submitted for consideration. Even when we disagreed, Tom's opinion was always an intelligent one, much valued by me. I thank him most sincerely for all his help along the way and for his critique of the finished manuscript as well.

I am grateful also to Rosellen Brown and Marshall Terry for their evaluative readings of that next-to-final version of this collection. Their compliments were extremely encouraging, their criticisms genuinely helpful. To Rosellen I owe my awareness of Sandi Wisenberg's wonderful "The Sweetheart Is In" and to her too I owe lasting appreciation for the impetus to make a final push to expand my selection of stories and thereby better this book.

Sandra Cisneros, Nic Kanellos, and Phillip Lopate graciously shared with me their excellent suggestions of writers to contact. Sandra and Nic introduced me to the work of numerous talented Chicana writers, among them Adela Alonso and Carmen Tafolla, whose stories appear here. A brief letter to Phillip, whom I had never met, netted two pages of handwritten names and addresses—and, ultimately, the stories by Elizabeth Davis, Lila Havens, and Elizabeth McBride that I selected for this volume. Lou Halsell Rodenberger, whose *Her Work: Stories by Texas Women* was predecessor and role model of this book, shared with me her vast expertise of Texas women writers and gave her support to this project from the start. When I began work on *Common Bonds,* I wrote Lou a timid letter telling her of my plans for this book and, in effect, asking her forgiveness of my temerity in planning to edit a collection like her own. Kind lady that she is, Lou wrote immediately to offer the first of many encouraging words.

In the course of putting together a collection such as this, one must become a detective, I think, scouring the review media and the bookstores for writers from whom to invite work and, most important, counting on the tips of those who are "in the know." Among my best tipsters in this instance were writers whose work I invited and who suggested other writers to me. It was Karen Britton, for example, who advised me to contact Lianne Mercer, and Carolyn Osborn (as well as Tom Zigal) who suggested I contact Annette Sanford. Harryette Mullen (with Eleanor Crockett and Joanie Whitebird) led me to S. E. Gilman, a Texan moved to New England. Other excellent suggestions and information came from Gloria Anzaldúa; Denise Armstrong; Susan Baugh; Jerry Bradley; Sidney Brammer; Jo Brans; Eloise Burrell; George Christian; Betsy Colquitt; Bob Compton; Laura Furman; Leticia Guillory; Dave Hickey; Sabine Hilding; Vivian Johnston; Peggy Little; Betsey Mills;

Richard Oram; Judyth Rigler; Margaret Roberts; Rebecca Tillapaugh; Celeste Walker; Barbara Wedgwood; Eddie Weems; Stanley C. Williams; Jane Roberts Wood; and Peter Wyckoff. I name these names with gratitude and anxiety, since I am certain that I am inadvertently omitting someone whose advice I also benefited from. To any such unintentionally neglected advisors I give my sincere apologies and thanks.

In selecting stories for *Common Bonds*, I found that work by many extremely accomplished writers could not be included for various reasons, some of which I have discussed in my preface to this collection. My deepest gratitude, then, must go to all the talented women who shared their stories with me as I put together this book. I can only hope that I will have an opportunity to publish work by many of you in another book, or books, in the future.

Three women are responsible for the handsome appearance of this book, and I would like to thank Joanna Hill for her elegant and appropriate design; Barbara Elam for creating the beautiful, iconographically rich intaglio print that appears on the cover of this book; and Carolyn Lowrey for her help in introducing me to Barbara.

This book is dedicated to my parents, Mildred S. Comer and Jack Comer, and my beloved grandmother, Mabel Stinnett, who died at the age of ninety-six just a few months after I had begun work on *Common Bonds*. And it is dedicated as well to my husband, Ernest Sharpe, Jr., whom I thank here for the laughter, understanding, and love that he brings to my life.

Preface

 The myth of Texas is undeniably masculine. Say "Texas" and what comes to most people's minds is cowboys and Indians—lusty trail drivers of the sort depicted by Larry McMurtry in his Pulitzer Prize–winning novel *Lonesome Dove*—brawny oil field workers yearning to "bring in a big 'un"—football players giving their all for the glory of the team. As historian Celia Morris has wryly observed, "Texas is best known for the things men do outdoors—by wars in its early days, gradually by cattle, subsequently by oil, and now by football." As a result, the subject of most Texas fiction is also men and men's doings. At times it seems as though writing itself is a man's job in Texas, something men do, presumably, indoors. Say "Texas writer" and many folks in the state will either draw a blank or name McMurtry or perhaps A. C. Greene or John Graves or maybe, in the confusion of the moment, Texas songster Willie Nelson. If those queried aren't familiar with authors' names, plots may come to mind all the same, stories about ranching or cowboys or coming of age in a West Texas town where one's chief learning experiences happen with whores on the border or "bad girls" from the high school.

Small wonder that many women readers in the state have come to view Texas fiction and discussions of the Texas literary scene as the same old same old. I didn't grow up here but I have lived in Texas for twenty years now and been friends with many a Texas man and woman, and it seems to me that the traditional images of Texas may have had some influence, as mythology to live up to, on the Texas men I have known but little on the Texas women. In putting together *Common Bonds,* then, I thought it would be valuable not just to bring together a set of stories by women but specifically to bring together stories about women's lives in this century. What we write about when we write about ourselves, so to speak.

Writing in the *Texas Observer* in 1982, novelist Kathryn Marshall bitterly described the Texas literary scene as "a letters that doesn't really believe women in general, and women writers in particular, exist." I wouldn't go so far, though I understand Ms. Marshall's anger and have shared it at times. One problem may simply be that many women writing in Texas are writers of short fiction and poetry, neither genre as likely to draw attention as the novel. Another problem may be the lack of a statewide community among writers in Texas. In gathering suggestions of writers to contact to submit work for *Common Bonds,* I was advised by two book reviewers in the state simply to check the Texas Institute of Letters's membership list. I had already done so, and now wish to point out that fewer than a half-dozen writers included in this volume are members of TIL. I call attention to this not to criticize the Institute, which by its nature has a limited membership, but rather to emphasize how many writers in the state—surely men as well as women—are not included within the established organizations. And therefore, as I now know from experience, are not always easy to find!

In any case, my belief that women writers are given short shrift in the state's conferences and in Texas readers' awareness of their literature was reinforced when I read the results of a poll taken in the spring of 1988 by Patrick Bennett and Chris Willerton of Abilene Christian University. The poll's subject was the future of Texas writing, and among Bennett and Willerton's questions were these: Who are three established Texas writers whose work will endure into the twenty-first century among serious readers? What three Texas books (current or classic) will help initiate a present-day newcomer into the Texas experience? What three Texas books (current or classic) will be influencing Texas writers in ten to twenty years? Of the twenty-seven established writers whose work was most often cited as enduring into the next century, only three are women. Of the twenty-eight Texas books most often named as helpful to initiate newcomers to the state, only one is by a woman. Of the thirteen Texas books most often named as influencing the state's writers in the next two decades, none is by a woman. An encouraging note is struck by the fact that seven of the twenty emerging Texas writers named by respondents to the poll are women. Increasing awareness of Texas women writers' work is surely traceable in part to the publication in 1983 of Lou Halsell Rodenberger's landmark collection *Her Work: Stories by Texas Women.* Rodenberger's anthology brought before Texas readers a wide selection of classic and contemporary Texas women writers' work and certainly deserves to be listed both among those books helpful to newcomers to Texas and with those most likely to endure into the next century.

As I planned *Common Bonds*, I of course had *Her Work* as an important model. I also wanted to contribute to Texas letters by presenting not only stories about women but also stories by lesser known writers whose work had not been showcased before. I was curious to learn what women in the state *are* writing today and whether the Texas myth described above plays a part in their work. I wanted stories by women whose association with the state was longstanding enough to assure that they "understood" Texas and could write from a sense of what the state really is. Primarily I was looking for stories with aesthetic merit—including credibility and consistency of characterization, dialogue, and narrative—but I was also eager to gather stories that explored a variety of experiences common to women.

I began inviting submissions in the spring of 1987 and ultimately contacted more than two hundred writers, from whom I received 356 stories "about women in twentieth-century Texas." Besides those writers with whose work I was already familiar, I sought out others by asking suggestions from book reviewers, teachers of creative writing and Texas literature, bookstore managers, and knowledgeable readers, and I kept a constant lookout for reviews of new books by Texas writers, then contacted them to invite work. I found that some of the writers whose work I fully anticipated including in *Common Bonds* simply did not have on hand stories that fit the book's theme, or whose stories were committed elsewhere. Hence this collection does not claim to present stories by all the most important women writers in the state. Several of my own favorites are missing, in fact.

In reading the many submissions, I learned two things. First, the women who sent in work rarely wrote about rural Texas, choosing instead to write about the state's urban and suburban areas. When they did write about rural happenings, they often wrote stories based on tales they'd heard about their mothers' or grandmothers' lives rather than their own or their contemporaries'. Second, "Texas" either as a literal place or as a set of myths played little part in their work. When the myth appeared, it appeared very much as it does in the lives of myself and many other women I know—satirically, as when Diane Payton Gómez dresses her "bad-news man" in cowboy/outlaw gear or when Mary Flatten has her wry narrator try to summon her lover back to her arms by crying out, "Shane! Come back!" I had thought about some of the sociological "truths" (or quasi-truths) that might show up in the stories—Texas women as daddies' girls; Texas women as variants of the Southern belle;

Texas women as hardy daughters of pioneer stock, more liberated than most because their daddies taught them to rope and ride with the men. But these "truths" were evidenced in no more than a half-dozen or so of the many stories I read. I found that the women who sent me stories, then, wrote most often about relationships—with other women, with men, with parents (mainly mothers) and siblings and grandparents (entirely grandmothers), occasionally with children. I saw no stories about women's work lives and only a couple of stories (heavyhanded ones at that) about women's involvement with larger political issues. None of this is to say that those stories may not be out there, somewhere, or that women in real life are not actively involved in their work and often also committed to larger causes. This is just to say that the women in the state whose writing I read do not seem to be addressing these matters in their fiction.

Because so many of the stories focused on relationships and spoke of shared female experience—experience that is at times inhibited because the experiencer is a woman—I chose the title *Common Bonds*. I hoped to suggest relationships, shared experience, and restraints all at once.

Writing the notorious "Ever a Bridegroom: Reflections on the Failure of Texas Literature" in the *Texas Observer* in 1981, gadfly Larry McMurtry urged Texas writers to turn away from the rural myth of the state and write instead about how Texans really live today, when the vast majority live in urban areas and seldom think of the frontier past. Perhaps McMurtry did not look far enough in his quest for such writing, for in these varied stories of women's lives in today's Texas we do see real contemporary life depicted, without reference to the myth of Texas. If that myth or a strong sense of Texas as place is missing from these stories, or if the women's experience depicted is in almost no way *particularly* Texan, that is because the work I read did not suggest that women writers here think much or often of their "Texanness" as they write, choosing instead to think of their womanhood or, more frequently, their shared humanity.

Suzanne Comer
Dallas, Texas

Return of a Bad-News Man

DIANE PAYTON GÓMEZ

When Gaylene sees the man in black she is in the produce section of Safeway weighing Ruby Reds, trying to decide if she wants out-of-season grapefruit badly enough to pay an outrageous price. The man is wearing a western out-fit that, even by Texas standards, is quite an eye-catcher: villain black from the top of his enormously brimmed hat to the pointy tips of his boots. Looking at him, she gets a vague impression of his face without the shoulder-length hair and bushy mustache. Suddenly, it flashes in her memory. She can't remember the name, but she knows that she has slept with him.

Running into an old lover is awkward. One whose name she can't recall, dressed up like Willie Nelson's drummer, is worse. Gaylene hurries her cart down the aisle, leaving the Ruby Reds dangling in the scales. In the dairy section she hears his spurs clanking accompaniment to a slow Muzak rendition of "What's New Pussycat?" Dropping a package of Kraft Singles into her cart, she sneaks a peek from the corner of her eye. He is in the middle of the canned meats aisle and looking her way, but he appears to be glancing over her shoulder. Though she recognizes those baby blues, the only name that pops into her mind is Jules Verne. That's ridiculous, she thinks. Gaylene trots her cart around the corner out of his viewing range.

Abandoning shopping, she hurries to the checkout and hides behind a movie magazine. When she focuses on a photo of Penny Marshall, the name comes to her: LaVerne. LaVerne Weatherby.

On the way home she sorts memories of past relationships until she finds LaVerne. She had met him several years ago when she worked for the State Comptroller, where he had applied for a tax permit for his new business, The Organic Camera. He took candid shots of people grinning in fields of bluebonnets or trying to look natural standing in front of the artificial waterfall at Zilker Park.

He had come on strong from the very first. His hair was a tad long then, too, but he wore a reassuring plaid Madras and Weejuns without socks. "I don't go out with hippies," she had said, eyeing the fringe edging over his collar. But she did go out with him, and he took her to a French film that didn't make a lot of sense to her, even with subtitles.

Later that evening he nibbled her fingers and declared, "What sensitive, artistic hands you have. You must be a very creative lady." She thought that was very perceptive. She hadn't mentioned that she had made all the macrame cluttering her apartment, or that she had recently completed a course in Stretch & Sew. Making love on the mattress sprawled on LaVerne's floor as a fan turned slowly overhead seemed to Gaylene slightly Bohemian, but not entirely uncivilized.

From the beginning LaVerne pushed her tolerance. He was always late for their dates. Just as she would decide he had stood her up, he'd finally arrive with a three-dollar bottle of wine or an apologetic handful of dyed carnations he'd stopped off to buy. In scarcely five weeks, the relationship had run its course and LaVerne dropped out of her life as suddenly as he'd appeared. When she found out from his landlady he'd gone off to New Mexico she downed a whole box of Dunkin Donuts and a sixpack of Lone Star, and spent the evening throwing up.

No, Gaylene doesn't want to face LaVerne after all this time. She wouldn't know what to say to him. Nevertheless, she is glad she is wearing a tennis outfit that shows off her shapely legs and nice tan. At thirty-two, she feels her figure is as good or better than it was when she was twenty-two. She takes tennis lessons on Mondays and Wednesdays, and goes to Jazzercise on Tuesdays and Thursdays.

Gaylene thinks it would be a hoot to tell Bert about seeing this eccentric man from her past if he wouldn't be a horse's ass about LaVerne being an ex-lover.

Bert is a real go-getter. He owns an appliance dealership and has plans to open a second in the near future. He likes to refer to himself as upwardly mobile—like a just-launched rocketship, Gaylene thinks. He says he could sell paint-by-number kits to the School for the Blind. Gaylene believes him. When little Bertie was born last year, Bert sold her on the idea of quitting her job to raise their family and lead the life befitting the wife of an upwardly mobile young businessman.

As Gaylene looks into the rearview mirror to change lanes, she sees that the driver of the blue pickup behind her is wearing a large western hat. Her heart skips a beat. She steps on the accelerator and quickly gains some distance between her and the truck. When she turns into her sub-division she sees the truck flash on by. Ninnyhead, she thinks. She couldn't tell if it was LaVerne, and if it was, why would he be following her? She isn't even positive he recognized her in the grocery store. Gaylene opens her front door and nearly falls over little Bertie, who is crawling on the floor. His tiny crew socks droop off the ends of his feet like elf shoes. He gives her a sparse-toothed smile and reaches for her.

"Hi, punkin," says Gaylene, setting a sack of groceries down and lift-ing the baby up. "How'd it go today, Myra?"

A pixie-faced Black woman with a short Afro sits on the couch watch-ing "All My Children." "You're here early," she says, her eyes riveted to the set. "It's just started. Looks like Erica's up to her old tricks again."

"Not the program. How was Bertie today?"

"Oh, he was fine 'cept he rubbed Velveeta all over my shoe."

Gaylene holds Bertie in one arm and puts some things away in the re-frigerator with her free hand. Then she sits down by Myra to watch their soap. Bertie wriggles off her lap and scampers across the carpet on all fours.

"Looks like Tad's going to get hisself in some more trouble," says Myra, turning up the volume of the TV with the remote control. At thirty-five, Myra is a grandmother with a teenage figure. She wears three pierced earrings in each ear, several rings on both hands, and has a gold front tooth. She babysits every weekday morning for Gaylene and spends most of the money she makes on trendy clothes, even though her old converted postal jeep is in such bad shape that half the time she can't get it started and Frank, her third husband, has to drive her over to Gaylene's.

The two women are close. Besides their noon soap, they share thoughts and ideas on cooking, clothes, kids, working away from the home, mar-riage, and men in general.

Sometimes Myra stays for lunch, but today she is anxious to leave and so Gaylene doesn't get a chance to tell her about LaVerne.

"I'm going shopping out to the mall and get me a Belle France dress they got on sale at Foley's. Tell me tomorrow how the rest of 'All My Kids' turns out," Myra says, scurrying out the door.

Later, Gaylene sets a jar of sun tea on a flat rock by the nasturtium bed. There is always a steady, though not heavy, stream of traffic on her street, and she looks up slowly when she hears the light squeal of tires nearby. By the time she realizes what she has seen, the blue pickup is out of sight around the corner.

All afternoon forgotten details of her relationship with LaVerne have surfaced before her like snatches of an old movie that got bad reviews. Now it bothers her that not only is he intruding on her thoughts, but he may intend to make some sort of personal appearance as well.

Gaylene goes back into the house and locks the front door. She checks the locks on the back and side doors and lowers the miniblinds. She is not so much disturbed by the possibility that LaVerne could make trouble for her as she is by the twinge of exhilaration she feels as her heart pounds. She opens the kitchen blinds a crack to keep an eye on the street while she tries hard to think only about fixing supper.

She is making a meat loaf with dried onion soup mix. She shreds bread crumbs in her new food processor. She also has a new gas range with a self-cleaning oven and a built-in wok. She hasn't the faintest notion of what to do with a wok—doesn't even like Chinese food. She doesn't like the self-cleaning oven because the heavy insulation makes it hardly bigger than a rural mailbox. She prefers the original stove they had when they got married. That was at least three stoves ago.

Bert changes appliances like Gaylene used to change lovers. Last month he brought home a convection microwave with a carousel interior and as many buttons as the First Methodist Church organ. While she cooks, Bertie is at her feet taking baking pans, muffin tins, and assorted Tupperware out of a cupboard. He tosses them to and fro, licks their interiors, and clumsily tries to put them back on the shelf.

The four digital clocks in the kitchen say it is somewhere between 5:53 and 5:58 and almost time for Bert to leave the store. Gaylene calls him and tells him to stop on the way home to buy kitty litter, milk, and Huggies.

"Hi, honey, your handsome hunk is home," says Bert as he comes through the door.

He has a good self-image and, indeed, he looks fit and trim (he works out at Nautilus three times a week) in his creased Calvin Klein jeans and laundry-starched shirt, still crisp after selling appliances all day.

Bert always tries to look his best because he considers himself an Austin celebrity since he started doing his own television commercials. Delivered in a nasal twang through a grinning mouthful of gleaming choppers, he ends his thirty-second spiel, "Come see Bert Pope for a wide range of appliances." When he says "wide range," he makes a sweeping gesture toward a row of sparkling new ranges.

Gaylene takes the grocery sack from Bert and he picks up little Bertie. "I swear, Bertie, you're sure growing. Getting heavier'n pig iron," he says, tossing his son into the air.

At first Gaylene is glad to see Bert. She rubs up against him and he puts Bertie down and gives her a hug. She feels relieved and protected now that he's home. However, as soon as she begins taking his purchases out of the sack her jittery irritability flares up again.

"These aren't Huggies, Bert. I told you to get Huggies."

"I can't remember what kind of diapers he wears," says Bert.

"I didn't say get diapers, I said get Huggies. He never wears anything but Huggies."

"I'm sorry, honey," says Bert. He opens the door of the refrigerator. "God, this is a fine model. Removable egg racks, even." He pulls out a can of beer.

"I specifically said Huggies," says Gaylene, banging a pan down on the stove.

"Careful. You don't want to scratch the chrome finish." He gives the stove a loving stroke then pats his wife's behind. "I thought you were going to the store today, anyway."

"I told you, I forgot some things when I went. And I said to get Huggies. Huggies." She takes the meat loaf out of the oven.

"The house smells like cat shit," says Bert.

Gaylene stops what she is doing, picks up the bag of kitty litter, sticks it in front of Bert's face, then slams it down on the counter. She goes on preparing supper. Bert drinks his beer in silence while Bertie drops his socks into the empty sack, then fishes them out again.

Late that night Gaylene lies in bed awake. Bert is snoring softly, making little "pooh" sounds with his lips when he exhales. But that is not what keeps Gaylene awake. She is worried about why LaVerne Weatherby would want to follow her. She is even more concerned about what his next move will be. No telling what kind of scene he might cause that would embarrass her in front of Bert. And why is she more excited than terrified by the thought of it?

Suddenly she hears a clattering noise outside, followed by a papery rustling sound. Someone is on the back patio! Bert doesn't stir. Gaylene slips out of bed and, weak-kneed, tiptoes to the den. She takes a deep breath and pulls the draperies aside a fraction of an inch to peer out onto the moonlit patio. It's only a possum rummaging through a trash can. His fur is spiky and sparse like a punk rocker's hair and he hunches his body so low it appears to flow rather than move on legs.

Even when she turns on the patio light, he boldly goes about his scavenging before finally meandering off into the darkness. The possum is hideous and yet almost cute, like E.T. or a gremlin, she thinks. Bert would shoot it if he knew about it but Gaylene won't tell him. She may even put out some scraps to lure him back. With a mixture of relief and disappointment Gaylene turns off the patio light and returns to the bed to wait for sleep to come.

The next morning Gaylene goes to her Jazzercise lesson and when she comes out of the building she sees a blue pickup parked in front of her car. She looks around but LaVerne is nowhere in sight, so she cautiously peers into the cab. On the seat is a black case whose size and appearance tell her it surely contains photography equipment. Also on the seat is a black western hat.

She drives around the block three times to see if LaVerne will come out to the pickup and follow her. She sees no one and slowly drives home, checking her rearview mirror all the way.

"The nut is obviously following me around and I don't even know what he wants," says Gaylene, reaching for a chunk of piña colada cake. The TV is silent and Bertie is down for a nap. The two women have just finished off Gaylene's taco salad while she tells Myra the story of LaVerne.

"I kinda get the feeling you're getting a thrill from all this," says Myra, licking the icing from her fingers.

"Thrill? Are you crazy? I never liked LaVerne much back when I had him."

Myra narrows her eyes at Gaylene. "Maybe you weren't crazy about him, but like you said yourself, he up and left you. Now here he is again and it sounds like he's looking wilder and weirder than the first time he got your blood a-boilin'—might be fun to talk to him again."

"Oh Myra, don't be ridiculous. It's his nature to run after women. He told me that one time he tried to pick up a bus girl at a cafeteria because she had this gorgeous waist-length hair. Another time he followed a woman out of a Stop-N-Go and introduced himself in the parking lot as a member of the Society of Pineapple Yogurt Lovers just so he could talk to her." Gaylene paused and added almost wistfully, "He was really outlandish . . . And I couldn't count on him for nothing. Anyway, now I'm married and I just want him to leave me alone."

"Then why did you drive around the block three times to see if he'd follow you?"

Gaylene twists her big diamond around her finger. Finally she says softly, "I don't know. I don't understand it myself."

"Well, I'll tell you why. We women have a different place in our hearts reserved just for bad-news men. When one of them good-lookin' lowlifes comes along we open that different place up and say, 'Come on in, honey, and cause me some pain.' After he does his stuff and runs off, we try to convince ourselves we was going to kick him out anyways. Then we close up that place in our hearts until another bad-news man comes along."

Gaylene can't help but giggle. "But what about Bert?"

"The most exciting thing that husband of yours ever does is bring home a different stove, refrigerator, or digital clock every other week. Most of your heart is happily lolling around in all that security but that different place is just beggin' for danger."

"But Bert is the jealous type and he'd plumb go crazy if I was having anything to do with an old lover."

"Makes it even more tempting, don't it?" says Myra.

Gaylene doesn't answer.

It's Bert's afternoon off and he and Gaylene go shopping to find a new dress for a big party they're attending in the evening. Bert wants Gaylene to look as glamorous as possible, since it's the kind of affair where there will be a lot of Bert's contacts.

"I love to show them contacts that I not only have got the boomingest business in town, but the classiest woman, too," he says. He follows Gaylene with her purse hung over his arm as she sorts through racks of gowns in a ritzy mall boutique.

She doesn't find what she wants there so they head off toward a large department store next door. Gaylene tells herself she's glad there has been no new development regarding LaVerne the past three days. She can't figure out why she's become increasingly cranky, though.

On the way to the escalator leading up to women's apparel, Bert pauses to admire some expensive enamel cookware. "Look at these boogers, sugar. They got flowers painted all over the sides. Wouldn't they look nice on your new stove?"

"My Teflon II's suit me fine, thank you. Don't get it into your head, Bert Pope, that I want to start cooking in pots and pans too heavy to lift and impossible to clean, just because they look good," she snaps.

"I swear, Gaylene, if you get much crabbier, you're gonna end up bitin' yourself."

"I'm sorry. I didn't mean nothing by it. You sure are sensitive lately," she says defensively.

Bert puts down the saucepan he's been caressing and starts to usher her onto the escalator.

Gaylene catches her breath. LaVerne is just a few steps up the escalator. She can't see his face, but that monotone black! When he turns his head in profile there is no mistake who it is.

Gaylene almost knocks Bert over backing away from the escalator.

"Ow, what's the matter with you?" he yowls at her as a miniskirted teenager behind him steps on both his ankles.

"I just remembered, I don't like to shop here. They have snotty sales-girls," says Gaylene, trying to push Bert around the corner. LaVerne peers over his shoulder towards the commotion just as the escalator moves him out of sight.

"Well, let's go somewhere else, then."

"I think I'll just wear my Mexican wedding dress. I'm not in the mood to shop right now, okay?"

"Everybody wears Mexican wedding dresses. I wanted you to wear something different," he says, reluctantly following her long strides out of the store.

"Look, if we hurry we can get home in time to watch Firestone Championship Bowling," she says.

At 6:00 they sit down to the dinner of tuna quiche and onion-garlic tomato soup Gaylene has prepared.

"Hoo boy, this tastes real French!" he says after he sips a spoonful of the soup.

He is humoring me, she thinks. She knows Bert is eyeing her, confused when she snarls at him one second and giggles uncontrollably the next.

She also realizes that this was the wrong time to make this dish. At the party, they are going to reek of enough garlic to scare off a pack of vampires. Gaylene eats hers anyway as if to punish herself for her behavior. It won't matter to Bert if his breath is offensive; as long as he feels dressed to kill, he'll have a good time.

On the way to the party Gaylene tries to imagine sleeping with La-Verne until she recalls a scandal sheet headline that read "How Can I Tell My Lover I Have AIDS?" It was a weak fantasy anyway. She can't re-member what it was like when she actually was with him.

She has a good time at the party in spite of her near-hysteria earlier that afternoon. She wears a lime green Mexican wedding dress covered with red orange embroidery and with little puffed sleeves. It is offset by her Anne Klein espadrilles, gold add-a-bead necklace, and gold "shrimp" earrings.

As she recites her Five Cup Salad recipe to a woman she calls Miss Sugary Socialite behind her back, she sees the crown of a black western hat bobbing among the heads in the crowd.

"One can of fruit cocktail, one carton Cool Whip—" she says, experiencing a variety of sensations, the strongest probably akin to falling off a very high building.

She decides there is no alternative. She excuses herself and begins to weave her way through the throng of partygoers. She is only faintly aware that her concern over her garlic breath is interfering with the sense of drama she feels pulsating through her body like an electric current.

LaVerne is involved in an intense conversation with a thin bald man in a pinstriped suit and doesn't notice her approach. She hovers around them a few seconds, clears her throat loudly a couple of times, which doesn't seem to register over the din, and finally touches the bald man's elbow (she can't bear to touch LaVerne).

"Excuse me, I have to talk to this man alone for a few minutes."

Both men raise their eyebrows to her, then the bald man leaves, mumbling something about refilling his drink. They are alone. Face to face.

"Well," Gaylene says. Her chin trembles slightly.

LaVerne cocks his head and regards her with a bemused smile. Finally he says, "How do you do?" in the same distant, polite tone she has seen Bert affect with customers.

"What are you doing here?" she asks firmly. She hopes the direct approach will catch him off guard and give her the upper hand.

"I beg your pardon?" he says, his lips still holding the formal little smile.

"I want to know what you're up to," insists Gaylene.

LaVerne snaps his fingers. "Wait a minute—I know you, don't I? I remember now—the cheerleader from Thornton?"

"No, twirler from Taylor," says Gaylene. This is confusing because she did not expect LaVerne to deny remembering her.

"Gayle, isn't it? You work for the state."

"Gaylene. Used to work for the state. I got married and quit."

"Gaylene!" he says, slapping his forehead with the palm of his hand. "God, I remember—it's been years, hasn't it? Why, you haven't changed a bit."

"Well, your hair didn't used to be that long and you've grown yourself a mustache."

"Yeah, and how do you like my new image?" He fingers the curlicued piping on his shirt and pats his shield-like belt buckle.

"You never were too conventional, LaVerne." Gaylene tries to control the sarcasm level in her voice until she figures out what's going on.

"It's all part of the gimmick," says LaVerne proudly.

"Gimmick?"

"I do western-style photography shows in malls, featuring different artists' work, and then I have a little setup where you can have your picture taken in a Wild West costume. I'm here to promote my show."

"You don't live in Austin, then?"

"Phoenix. I'm just here for two weeks."

"I thought I saw someone dressed like you in Safeway on Monday."

"I was in Safeway on Monday! I didn't see you. Why didn't you come up and say something?"

"I didn't know it was you," says Gaylene coyly. "I just remembered I'd seen someone in that costume before. I also thought I saw someone in that costume wandering around the mall earlier today, only I didn't see any photo booth."

"Hey girl, what are you doing, following me around or something?" He scrunches his eye into what is probably a wink but looks more like a tic to Gaylene.

"Not hardly," she says, rolling her eyes and crimping the edges of her mouth in disgust.

"How'd you know it was me here?"

"I got a better look at you. And I, uh—saw you get out of your pickup tonight."

"Pickup?"

"Don't you have a blue pickup?"

"Gosh, no. I couldn't carry diddly-squat in an open truck. I got me a white Ford van. Don't tell me someone else here is dressed like this. I didn't know I had competition." LaVerne looks around in mock horror.

"I reckon I made a mistake," Gaylene says tonelessly.

"So what have you been doing besides getting hitched?"

"For one thing, I got me a baby now." Her voice shifts gears into a lilt.

"How about that. I got me a wife and two babies back in Arizona."

"My boy is beautiful and smarter'n all get out."

"I got two pretty girls, ages two and four."

"My husband owns a big appliance shop. We're getting ready to open another outlet."

"My wife is half Navaho Indian. Her uncle is a chief!"

Gaylene finishes the one-upmanship. "My husband does his own commercials on TV. See, he's that good-looking guy over there in the pink shirt talking to that homely red-headed man."

On the way home, Gaylene says to Bert, "Did you see that cowboy in black talking to me?"

"No—I was wondering where you were at. Were you making eyes

with someone behind my back?" His tone is jovial but Gaylene senses the underlying insecurity.

"Naw. He used to go with someone I knew a long time ago."

"Not that I mind you looking. I don't care where you get your appetite as long as you eat at home."

"I just wondered if you saw him. I thought he looked sort of dumb, myself."

"You been so crabby lately I don't know who would hardly want you anyways," he says.

Gaylene studies Bert's silhouetted profile in the dark car. Without turning his head he pats the space on the seat between them. Gaylene scoots over a little and he puts his arm around her. She cuddles against his shoulder and rests in the smell of his cologne and starchy shirt. "You know, I oughtn't to have put so much garlic in that soup," she says.

"Tasted good to me." He pauses then says, "You know, there's a new model freezer out that makes ice cream. I've been thinking about bringing one home to try out. What do you think?"

Gaylene doesn't answer him but she smiles and gives him a tickly poke in the ribs.

"Better watch out, girl," he snorts. "I feel a bout of nastiness coming on fast."

He suddenly swerves the wheel to avoid running over a dead possum lying in the road and Gaylene is jerked heavily against him. She pokes him again and Bert answers by squeezing her breast with his right hand dangling over her shoulder. She is not unaware that Bert's advances would have made her want to whack him one if he'd done that before she talked with LaVerne. Now, in the dimly lit car, Bert looks better than ever to her.

Still, Gaylene feigns protest by twitching her shoulder under the weight of Bert's arm. She looks away so he can't see that she's smiling.

"Turn up the radio," Bert tells her. His arm stays put.

On the radio Eric Clapton is singing "Lay Down Sally." Singing along when she can remember the words, Gaylene places her hand lightly as a gnat on Bert's knee. The smile is still on her face when they arrive home.

Roberta

LISA FAHRENTHOLD

Everything was nice and easy most of the day, those days our new maid Roberta came. Then in the afternoon when my brothers got home from their jobs, all hell would break loose. So Mom told them they couldn't come home until they saw us pulling out of the driveway to take Roberta to the bus stop. Roberta simply threw down her rags and ran to the back of the house if there was any boys around.

I turned thirteen at the beginning of that summer, and Mom had started letting me drink coffee, which I decided I'd always and forever take black. One morning, bending over my cup, I blew away the steam. In the smooth black, I studied my reflection for a long time. Then, breaking the spell, I scattered starry grains of sugar, slowly, like a blessing, turning my ear to the hiss. I stirred in the sugar, then held my spoon up like a cigarette. My sister banged the table leg and gave me a bald look. My cup trembled, but I hadn't been telling on her.

Through the kitchen window, morning light flashed in and out of the trees, and if I moved a certain way, it was like being photographed by lots of exploding bulbs. "Thank you, gentlemen, that's all," I whispered into my cup, practicing for when I'd be a famous movie star.

"Hah!" my sister snorted. "Never heard of a movie star wearing a training bra."

In my mom's house, they not only eavesdropped, they uncrumpled personal notes balled up in the trash and read them out loud. They came up behind you when you dropped something, 'cause even the stenciling on your thrown-away candy wrappers held microdots or some secret code.

That morning my sister, the chief spy, was reading a newspaper propped up on a porcelain cow that had a belly full of napkins. She was sitting just so with her legs crossed, jiggling one foot like crazy, and blowing on her pearly fingernails.

"I don't see how you girls can just sit around drinking coffee. It's too hot."

That was my mom saying get to work.

The vacuum cleaner, propelled by our maid Roberta, was screaming in the back of the house.

My sister lifted her hair off her neck and, yawning, said, "It *is* hot. I'm gonna go take a long, cold, bubble bath," and shimmied off with the funny pages.

So it was "go help Roberta" for me.

The summer before, when I was twelve, and Mom wanted me out of sight, she'd hand me a bucket and say, "Go pick some dewberries and I'll make us a pie." Or me and my friends, we'd race our bicycles deep in the ditches so we'd pop out and fly; or laze around on the porch, pulling the legs off the daddy longlegs and spider hawks that did their stilt-walk up the brick of our house. We'd feed horny toads some pistol caps and watch 'em explode; dress up like gypsies, or steal the cigarette butts from my sister's scrapbook, where they were labeled "Mike at Prince's," "Terry at the Palace," and "George, Eddie, Bets and me—on the ferryboat to Pelican Island." Deep in the woods, we'd smoke them down till they quick-burned our lips.

But that summer I was thirteen I hated everything, especially my friends. Anyway, I knew I needed to keep real, real still, 'cause a ghost had taken over my body. Every time I tried to stand up, *he* decided to sit—I could feel him pulling me down. On hot hot days when I tried to get out of bed, he put a tingle on me that knocked me back out, till my mom turned the stereo up full blast to marching music, then we both shot out of bed. I said, "Mom, there's this *ghost* . . . ," and she put a torn pair of Daddy's underwear in my hand and said, "Can he dust?" and disappeared.

In the bathroom, Roberta considered me with her yellow eye. She took two steps back and one to the side—like a goat dance—then stuck a toothbrush in my hand. We huddled in the shower stall, the milky glass door sealing us in. A long wordless time passed while we practiced dentistry on the mold in the grouting. And then—"Mo' that Bab-O"—a brilliant echo, startling the faucets silver, shocking the pink tiles pinker. I handed her the can of scouring powder; her black prehistoric fingers wrapped around it; green smoke leapt out of its holes. I wanted to make an echo in the shower too but was too scared. I thought for sure she was the devil.

But, I thought, leaning back on the cool tiles, if she's the devil, maybe I can tell her my sins. Mom wasn't someone you could talk to anymore. The new baby and remodeling the kitchen had made her crazy. Her eyes moved like searchlights in a concentration camp. I could've kept a diary, if you could please explain to me how in a place that's crawling with spies. Roberta never talked, not *to* you anyway, and her voice came out like cranking up a car that's already running.

"Roberta," I said with an echo that had God or the devil behind it.

She scrubbed as if digging an escape; the wet kinks at the back of her neck shook like a string of bells. That was about it for her hair; what was left was gray and in patches.

"Are you listening?"

"Po' chile. Lord God Jesus, God's little chile."

Roberta had whiskers, too, some white, some black. Short, stubbly ones, that worked when her chin worked. Above them an old mouth was quickly sinking in.

I tried out my first confession.

"If Mom thinks I'm gonna get a summer job at that fast-food place, she's crazy," I announced. "When I applied, I told 'em I was pregnant. You don't think they can tell by just looking that I hadn't got my period yet, do you?"

"My, my, best call dem police," said Roberta.

"Well, I'm not going with Nanna either to the Grand Canyon."

The shower made better echoes anyway, spilling sound out endlessly like the inside of a cathedral bell.

Roberta shook her head. "It don' matter," she whined.

"Trouble is, Mother, I think you favor a crazy maid," said my sister, who was on her knees in the closet, holding a single red shoe in the air. "Face it, you like the excitement."

The bottom of my sister's closet was lined with shoes, and on the shelf above the dresses were just as many purses, and everything as many colors as there are colors of cars. I always stole the change from the bottoms of the purses, which were crumbly with forbidden tobacco.

"She's not crazy, she just talks to herself. It's not the same thing," said Mom, eyeballing the closet floor for the red shoe's mate. "Why, St. Thomas has her every Tuesday morning for the altar guild. I mean, it's *Roberta* that irons the altar cloth."

"Mom, if Roberta's not as nutty as a Pay Day, then let God strike me dead." My sister hung her arms out in space as if she was being crucified. When a lightning bolt didn't crash through the ceiling, she widened her eyes at Mom and went back to rummaging through the closet. Then she dragged a huge doll out and pitched it on the bed next to me.

I had inhaled her sweet plastic skin, soaped her when she got smudgy, kissed her hard on her hard lips, and wept into her hair. With her gauzy, stiff, now yellowed net bridal gown scratching my cheek, I had fallen asleep night after night after night with—Belinda, I'd named her—for five years.

But when my sister, popping her gum, said, "That yours, kiddo?" I denied her.

"You got *another* weirdo on your hands, Mother dear. Kid cuts all the hair off her dolls' heads."

Mom was leaning on the doorjamb, absently patting her own black, gleaming, bobby-pinned head.

"I don't play with dolls anymore," I asserted, surprised because this resolve was newborn the instant I said it. "I'm only saving this one for when the baby gets older."

"Why wait, when they have so much in common now? Baldness and everything."

"Now, girls," Mom singsonged.

Belinda jumped into my hands and, entirely beyond my power, launched a superhuman flight across the room, missed my sister by a billionth of an inch, then bounced off a smiling poster of Johnny Mathis before sacrificing herself on the bedpost.

Mom ran her hand over the doll's stubbly head. In the third grade they make you draw planets and their orbits. That's how the doll's hair was stitched on—circles inside of circles. Mom was taking all this in, crouched down in her day clothes, which were Daddy's torn golf shirt, and Daddy's old paint-splashed shorts, which didn't hide her varicose legs all knotted up and blue.

My sister found the other red shoe, so now she was standing on the chair to her vanity table, primping her feet for the mirror.

"Bride doll, hah!" she smirked. "You blew it for her, sister. No boy doll alive would marry her now."

Mom was trying to fluff out the bride doll's gown, which was row on row of ratty yellow lace. More to herself than to us she said, "Her husband was killed."

"Forget it, Mother," said my sister. "Roberta's too busy baying at the moon to know where her tail is much less what made her crazy."

So that was the discussion all summer long. Should we keep Roberta or not? Was she dangerously crazy, or just a little bit off? I didn't care one way or another, long as we got to keep her around. I'd figured something out. If I hung around Roberta, my mom wouldn't put me to work. You shoulda seen that lady clean. All's I had to do was climb in behind her wake and hang on—she was the powerboat and I was waterskiing. It put one over on Mom. She'd come flying through the den with her wallpaper book on the way to the nursery, waving a friendly diaper.

So when Mom got busy I'd turn up the stories on TV, Roberta would slow down on her rubbing, and we'd get under the spell of that syrupy music. One time when Jessie, the head nurse on TV, opened the narcotics cabinet, machine gun fire blasted out, scaring me and Roberta out of our skins. But Jessie had only reached for the medicine bottle. The machine gun fire was the kitchen being remodeled. It ruined our stories but we couldn't say anything. Everybody was barred from the kitchen. My mom said it was 'cause the sight of men put the spooks into Roberta, but Mom was the one who acted like the carpenters all had snakes growing out of their foreheads.

One day when Mom didn't shut the door to the kitchen hard enough it creaked back open. Smoke swirled around in there like a white hell. A man with huge goggles drove a drill into a slab of wood, sparking up splinters. Two others busted holes in the wall, taking it down to its natural wool. Then, out of the smoke, a steel snake shook itself down at my feet. When I looked up there was a young man at the end of the measuring tape, and he looked at my surprised face as if it was perfectly natural for a man to shake steel right out of his hands.

I backed up and he stretched the end of the tape to the wall.

"Ninety-five, give or take," he said over his shoulder, and then looked down at me as if I was a piece of crooked iron you might want to twist back into shape. He dropped the tape down to the floor with a shattering sound, then stepped on the end-hook with his boot.

"Okay, shrimp, let's see how you measure up," he said, motioning me towards him. "We'll see if you grow any this summer."

As I turned a circle underneath him to put my back up against the tape, I held my breath. I thought: *If I have to say something, I'll die.*

"Fifty-two. Hell, we could lay three of you across this kitchen."

That was a funny way to think about people—in lengths. His skin was the same color as the iron ore in our driveway. He patted himself all over his white tee-shirted chest, even though he didn't have a pocket, then pulled a nail out from behind his ear.

I pressed the tape against the wall to hold the measure, and he tapped the nail into the sheetrock.

"Now you can measure yourself," he said. And then when he said, "So who're you?" a terrible thrill went through me. An awful miracle was taking place; someone had asked me the simplest yet the most profound question I'd ever been asked. Yet he looked down at me matter-of-factly, with eyes that shone like iron painted black. But they were funny, different, not right; they were eyes that saw back in on themselves, not *out* the way girls' eyes did, but *in,* back in on something, and this was so alien to me it made me a little bit sick. Then all of a sudden my mom whipped me around and slammed the kitchen door shut.

"Did he say anything to you?"

"Who?"

Her eyes, frantically searching my face, shot off tiny white stars of worry, which darted in and out between us.

"That man, the journeyman."

Journeyman: that was a name out of a fairy tale. He might wear layers of rough wool and carry a staff and sleep under the stars and drink heartily from a wooden bowl. When he made his way through the forests, witches would help him if he could make a magic symbol with sticks, an old man would pack him a leather bag of food, and wolves would eat from his fingers. Under a mound of pine needles he'd find a baby with a pig's head, and if he followed a trail of pine cones he'd—

Mom was shaking me by the shoulders. Her breath smelled rotten from tasting baby food.

"The journeyman! I heard him ask you your name."

I started to say what I always say, "Oh, Mom, I don't even like boys yet anyway," but the ghost inside me chuckled and I stopped.

Hush, I told that ghost.

"No, Mom, who're you talking about?"

One afternoon I found Roberta in my brothers' bedroom, tiptoed up on a chair. Her black hands combed cobwebs out of the air-conditioning vents as if they were a fine wool she'd been spinning all her life. When I shut the door she took to slapping the vent with a whisk broom.

"Roberta," I whispered.

Her shoes were laced tight, with little white anklets coming out of them bordered with purple lace.

"Miss Ro-ber-ta?" I sang, tugging on her patchwork-quilt skirt, its stuffing coming out. It ballooned out over skinny legs that were too old anymore to grow hair.

"Like your underpants," I said, which were purple polka dot.

"She don' know anythang" came out like I'd accused her of murder.

Roberta stepped off the chair and I plopped down on the bed and spread my arms wide.

"Roberta, do you think movie stars and carpenters go together?"

"Jus' an ole nigger woman. Jus' mindin' her own." She shook her head back and forth, then spanked some dust out of a football pennant.

"Carpenters can build movie sets, can't they?" I asked.

The intermittent shower of Windex on the mirror stopped.

"I may be running away to Hollywood, California."

"Don' mount to nothin'," said Roberta, the rag wiping away her yellow-eyed face in the mirror.

In a corner outside, two brick walls, partly the kitchen and partly the den, met at a right angle where a big pecan tree hovered and a faucet dripped. That was my mom's mint patch.

One day the ghost had me pinned on the couch and my mom ran through the den. She said, "What if we had some mint for our tea tonight?"

"The world would come to an end," said my sister, falling on the floor and strangling herself. "Help me, I'm dying."

The mint patch was dark and cool. The mud black and shiny as Roberta, the greens wavy like when sunlight bounces off water and back onto trees. And little things growing everywhere, for instance little white flowers with brown centers coming out of cracks in the brick. When I bent down and breathed, the mint made my lungs cold; it was a drug that said, "See, you can be happy." The long stalks shaped themselves around me. I snapped the prettiest triangle of leaves from its stalk, then felt the shadows deepen.

Behind the window curtain, the journeyman stood, his arm out-stretched, offering a grease-blackened palm to the sun. He picked a little metal circle out of his open palm and squinted through it. A rag flew through the air and as he turned to catch it, the sun turned his hair the color an electric burner shoots off when you sprinkle pepper on it. Fire on fire. Then, frowning, he turned full around and spoke. I put my finger on the pane to feel the tremble he made.

I sank down into the patch. This was terrible; why was my stomach a fish jumping out of water? He was nothing but a scrap heap: iron ore and copper and steel and a big eagle belt buckle made of beaten silver. He was just a boy; he could be junked.

I eased up out of the patch and put my chin on the windowsill. Oh no, he was a man, a man of metals, an earth magician. At night, he stepped down a long staircase of dirt stairs and disappeared into the earth. In the morning, he carried up to the surface undiscovered metals. He was talking still, the veins in his throat working. His throat, full of something that wasn't there when I put my fingers to my own throat, was wide with veins, like the larger ropes that ran all through his arms. Wires and ropes: that's what men were made of.

One of the carpenters handed him a sawed board to inspect. He ran his finger in the groove and looked deeply into the wood grains. Then the strangest thing happened: it seemed the life of the wood traveled through his fingers and on up until it reappeared in his cheek as solid muscle. I pulled back as I watched that cheek hardening; it made a wall, a boundary of something. How could you hate someone and love them and not even know them? It made my stomach hurt, so I leaned back against the cool brick wall and closed my eyes, counting the faucet drips.

I never did feel better but got up 'cause something made me think about Roberta, so I went back inside.

In the nursery, Roberta was standing over the crib pulling on her chin hairs, one eyebrow up and one amazed eye bulging.

"Oh, Roberta. You scared me," I whispered, leaning back to shut the door. "I couldn't find you."

The vacuum cleaner at her side was a pet robot.

"Listen, I want you to know—don't you ever worry about your job, I'll take care of you. I'll stay home and help you."

"Look at dat, black bitch. Look what you done," said Roberta in a low voice. She aimed her yellow eye at the small heap that was the baby curled up in the crib.

"Roberta, I'm trying to tell you. You can stay as long as you want. I've just decided: I'm not going to high school. It's stupid; I don't wanna go. Everybody's gonna be like my sister—painting their fingernails and chasing after the guys. It's stupid."

"Witch. She-devil," hissed Roberta.

"They can break my legs or put razor blades in my food—I'm not gonna go. You hear me, Roberta?"

"Done killed her. Done killed my little angel girl when I was asleep."

I rushed at Roberta and flung her out of the way. I rolled the baby over and it coughed twice, bared its mute gums at me, then started howling. When I could breathe again I saw that Roberta hadn't done anything; the baby was only asleep. But I'd pushed Roberta out onto some ledge: she was all scrunched up in a corner trembling, pulling on the few curls she had left.

I held the screaming baby up. "See, she's okay," I said, and Roberta started howling too. I kicked the vacuum cleaner up to high like I always did until both she and the baby softened down like whistling teapots cooling on the stove.

Near the end of the summer one day—it was one of the days Roberta didn't come—we all had a powwow in the bedroom about what to do about her. I was divining my life in the girl who looked back up at me in the black sea in my coffee cup. *Movie star, movie star,* I chanted in my head. Not something you painted on out of a smelly makeup kit, but something far purer, that shines out of a face just splashed with water drunk from a garden hose. The kind of pretty that makes a cat stop in his tracks and come over to talk. That looks good rolling in a field of weeds as high as a man. There were movie stars like that, weren't there?

My sister at the vanity mirror drew the skinniest line of eyeliner ever drawn in the whole world. Her eyelids were puffy and red, 'cause she'd drawn it about a hundred times. The afternoon was filling up with the smell of cigarette smoke and home permanents.

Having just put the baby down, Mom was sprawled in the rocker, rocking the baby's ghost and staring up at the ceiling. Too tired to puff, every now and again she'd tap cigarette ashes into a little tea saucer she had balanced on her lap. This made saliva build up in my sister's mouth—I could tell by the wrinkles in her chin. When she turned to my mom, her nostrils widened a little, taking the good smoke in.

"I say, get rid of her," she said.

I sat up on the bed, waving away a trail of smoke. "I don't see how y'all can stand that stuff, it makes your teeth yellow."

My mom's tired eyes flicked at my sister.

"Listen to Marilyn *Mon*roe," said my sister quickly, aiming a glittering emery board at me. Then she turned around and sprayed a cloud of poison on the intricate beehive of her hair. I watched morbidly while it turned stiff. When my sister caught my reflection holding its nose she said, "At least I don't smell like the septic tank and the mint patch all the time."

"I just can't make up my mind," said Mom, crushing out her un-smoked cigarette in a pile of bullet ashes.

"Mother, her little episodes are tearing my nerves," said my sister, who thanks to me and a new high-powered Hoover had not heard one-tenth of them. "I mean, after a while, it interferes with production." This was spoken by a person who had not worked a minute of her life.

"If the postman or the mailman or the TV repairman come to the door, she crouches in the closet, smashing the life out of every last pair of my pumps."

"I like the way she does the blinds," sighed Mom. "You know the little circle where you thread the cord through? Roberta can even get *that* sparkling clean. And I've never seen anybody quite go after a corner like she does. She's a wonder."

My sister slammed down a bottle of fingernail polish. "Look, Mother, I don't know how many phone calls I've missed 'cause Roberta just picks up the line and whines out all that devil talk. Why, it's nothing but gibberish. Wouldn't *you* hang up?"

Now we were getting down to it. I leaned back and drummed my fingers on the windowpane, where most nights out of the week her boyfriend would tap out a signal, and my sister would lift up the window. The slobber noises they made were sickening and wet. I put my lips together in a big kiss and showed them to my sister, but she shot me a look that said, "Go ahead and tell. I don't care." She really did want Roberta gone. Who did she think tried to call her—Paul Newman?

"And she does all that fabulous ironing," Mom said. "Why, the pope would be proud to wear clothes ironed by Roberta."

"The pope would not wear holy vestments pressed by a witch, no matter how clever she is with pleats. Can't you hear her? She speaks in *tongues* for Jesus Christ Almighty God's sake. *Mother,* look how she's turned the household upside down. You won't let the carpenters use the bathroom 'cause she goes ape-shit around guys, and my own brothers can't come home till she's gone. She's Looney Tunes."

For weeks I either slumped around after Roberta, or sat on the floor trying to beam myself into the TV. I liked the black and white world in there, it was simpler. Here was a shadow, there was an edge. You were a gangster, or you were a priest. A whore or a hospital nurse. I wanted all of it but was too scared. To hurl a wine glass across the room and absorb its shatter; to troop across snow to collect the dying soldier; to feel the kickback current of the pistol that laid the gangster down. The color in the world was too bright, too pretty, too startling, too full of choices. It asked too much. With the TV, you could slip between the blue dots and no one would notice. It shed a peaceful gray rain down on me and Roberta.

It was so hot we shut up the house and drew all the curtains to stay cool, so it was almost like night in the middle of the afternoon. My sister was outside in a lawn chair in her kitty-cat sunglasses catching some rays, and Mom was back with the baby. Roberta was ironing, the starch floating towards me, a saint's perfume. I was curled up on the couch, memorizing the way the TV, when it changed scenes, changed the shades of the blue and gray shadows on my bare legs. This particular collection of patterns was "The Loretta Young Show."

Roberta's back was stiff with listening as she nosed the iron across the neck of my daddy's white shirt. Loretta said: *Why, hello, Pete.* Roberta wagged her head. The TV phone rang; Roberta said, "Won' talk to that thang."

Roberta had set the ironing board up by the window seat. Hooked onto the moulding above hung white after white after white starched shirt, belonging to the four men in my family. In another basket was a pile of their big underwear to be ironed. The bump of the iron putting down, when it met with the steam hissing up, and the tick-tock as she coursed around a button, was a lullaby to me, it almost put me to sleep. Beyond the kitchen door, fans thrummed, and there was the soft slap of paint as the workers put the finishing touches on my mom's kitchen.

On the TV screen, Loretta leaned her dark head against a wall and closed her large eyes. She said: *I can't tell you, Pete.*

In the kitchen something dropped, and then came a man's voice: "Stupid nigger!" Then laughter so hard it was almost like hitting.

Roberta set the iron down very slowly at the end of the board, near a tower of crisply ironed handkerchiefs. She sat down on the window seat, and out of a large plastic bag shook out wet shirts that had been rolled into a ball and frozen. She laid her black hand on the bundle, started to whine and then just as abruptly stopped. She raised her head slowly, and when it was even with mine, she let her big lip curl up to show me pink gums which were dark brown where the teeth should've been.

"Please . . . don't . . . Roberta," I whispered, glancing around for the vacuum cleaner.

Roberta pried a shirt sleeve away from the frozen ball, then looked up at me—directly, she'd never looked at me directly—with a yellow eye that was brimming over with love.

"*Crazy,*" she hissed.

A man's back in a dark suit was moving towards Loretta pinned up against the wall. I myself couldn't move. The shirt was being skinned alive off of that frozen ball.

"Crazy, crazy!" Roberta shook her finger at the man who had taken Loretta by the arms. He was bending towards Loretta when my mom's baby back in the bedroom screamed. Loretta's wide dark mouth parted for a sigh as it took the crack of the frozen white shirt. When the shirt fell away from the channel knob, the sigh had changed into the screech of Olive Oyl escaping from the clutches of Bluto.

Roberta's eye burned gold; it bloated at Bluto swinging his caveman stick. Then her sunken mouth stretched into a smile, as if she'd suddenly figured out something marvelous, as if she was finally free.

"Crazy nigger *man!*" she shouted, whipping the white shirt over her head, the shirt cuffing the iron away from the ironing board and dropping it on the floor. Roberta with open arms was praising the rack of shirts with unspeakable joy when the kitchen door opened and my paint-dappled journeyman appeared. Roberta gathered up all the stiff white shirttails in a bunch and was hugging them when the journeyman said, "Got a molly bolt?"

Roberta dragged the shirts across the moulding to the edge and they fell off singly, like assembly-line ghosts quitting work. The wide grin she gave the journeyman was unhampered by teeth.

"*Crazy!* Dat baby's alive!"

"It's a bolt that's got these clamps like an alligator mouth," said the journeyman.

Roberta suddenly retreated back into her old, tiny, shy, desperately wrinkled self, gathering up her quilted skirt and fingering it like mad. She tugged on whatever of her hair was left. Her goat dance carried her to the back of the house.

The journeyman's eyes surveyed the room, and when they landed on me he said, "Get the iron," so that when I leapt up I almost flew to the ceiling.

The door to the back porch popped open and my sister, her sunsuit straps off her shoulders and bending the spine of a thick paperback book, put her hand on her hip, tsked her tongue, and, looking at the heap of white shirts, said, "I told Mother to buy that new polyester blend. Nobody wants to iron that many 100 percent cotton shirts."

The first thing Mom noticed when she came running in with the baby flopped on her shoulder was that the journeyman had escaped from the kitchen.

"Outside, please," she said, shooing him away with a baby blanket.

The vacuum cleaner screamed in the back of the house.

It was a long quiet time and then the three of them, arm in arm, strutted into the den. I was Roberta's best friend in this nest of spies, but of course I wasn't allowed. Roberta's washed-out yellow eyes were tinged with red, and her polka dot scarf—which only I knew matched her underpants—was tied tight at her chin. She was clutching her purse, which my mom, her hair half out of curlers, was trying to stick a few extra dollars in. They'd broke her down with their searchlight eyes and their witch-burning threats.

"Now, now, you're all right"—my sister tied Roberta's scarf knot tighter and unrolled her blouse collar—"but I sure don't blame you for not liking those mean old things." My sister tossed her head to indicate the carpenters, who had been ordered outside. "Scaring you like that"— she pulled the quilt skirt around so the zipper was in back where it belonged—"such a delicate little lady." My sister sighed, patting Roberta on her whiskered chin. She started to go for the anklets that had fallen into the shoes with untied laces, but Mom grabbed her up. I wished I could've fixed Roberta's shoes so they were electric, like when the witch got fried on Dorothy's ruby slippers.

"Think Roberta might like some leftover ham?" asked my mom. "It's got that honey glaze. Sweetheart, why don't you fill up that empty butter tub with black-eyed peas."

While my sister was filling a grocery bag in the kitchen, Mom went back to the bedroom to "get ready for when your father gets home," 'cause by the time she got back from the bus station Daddy would've come home from the office.

In the dark utility room Roberta stood with her back up against a door whose curtained window brimmed with light, a light which illuminated her proud, outstretched, silky lip. While I was thinking what to say, something caught onto my lungs. The smell of chlorine drifted from a clothes hanger above the washing machine. Doubled over the hanger's spine was the ratty, now too-white wedding dress of my bride doll, who sat naked, spread-legged and bald on the shelf with the detergents and bleaches. The way her arms reached out and her bright, sleepless eyes retained their enthusiasm made her look as if she was trying to sell all that cleaning stuff for a TV commercial.

The dryer ticked as it tumbled the snaps on the baby's pajamas. In that hot room, staring at Roberta, I found myself in the dark middle of something. Before, I could've put my face in her quilted skirts and hugged her without saying a word. If I was my sister's age, I could say silly things and nobody would mind. There were hot things in my throat, but they weren't going to make it up into words. So I only stood there, with my tongue cut out and my hands cut off, a headful of magazine dreams and scissored doll's hair, until my sister came around the corner and pushed us both into the carport. As soon as the door shut I thought: *I could've tied her shoes.*

My sister hopped in the car with the grocery bag and the baby, but Roberta stood outside, holding her umbrella up against a sunny sky. Red smoke from the iron ore driveway swirled around her. In the backyard the carpenters were playing touch football. All except the journeyman, who stood apart with one arm outstretched saluting the sun. His head was cocked funny; he was scratching the paint flecks off his arm. I picked up a handball from the carport floor and slammed it up against the wall.

He looked up at me, red with white paint spots, like a new ore that would be discovered against a flat green lawn and an unbroken blue sky. He was serious, there was that hard muscle in his face, streaked with paint, and I saw that it was too strong, it would come between us. It was like the line on a map of a highway you'd someday take, but now it was dangerous, far off, not to be traveled.

As soon as the handball got a rhythm up, words flooded back into my empty head. Just as Roberta closed her umbrella and got into the car, the ball bounced out the words I'd longed to say in the utility room: *don't leave me with them, don't leave me with them.*

On the blinding, white-lit threshold of the carport Mom stood, all done up: black hair in curls, red earrings, a dark blue dress. She brushed a puff of white powder off her shoulder, then drew in her lips with lipstick.

Why did this sting? Why was this another betrayal? She rubbed her lips together and clicked her compact shut, and when she stepped down into the deepest shadow of the carport, all her colors sucked out, and somehow, God, I still don't understand why, I hated her, and I felt relieved. She said, "You coming, honey?" with lips that were such a dark red they weren't red anymore, they were black. To me beautiful, beautiful, there in the blackness: black as the lips of the movie stars on our black and white TV, black as my coffee, black as our ex-maid Roberta.

Federico y Elfiria

CARMEN TAFOLLA

 Pos, he liked her jus' 'cause of that—no le hacía—que era muy ranchera y nunca había visto más que su casa— She was a good girl, which is like saying that she wasn't a bad girl, or not even a little bad, y'know?

The first time Federico started liking Elfiria was the day Chato and Manuel were teasing him and said that Federico se vestía muy galán, that a lo mejor he was trying to impress the girls . . . and then Manuel said that a lo mejor there was somebody he was already talking to a las escondiditas and Chato (to impress Manuel) said he'd seen Elfiria writing notes with big hearts that said "Federico plus Elfiria." And they both laughed a lot at Federico and Federico got red. He knew that a lo mejor Chato was just making it up but de todos modos he wondered. I mean, it was real embarrassing. I mean, Elfiria was the kind of girl that didn't "like" nobody—she just went home from school and did what her parents said. And she wasn't the kind of girl that anyone went around "liking" either. I mean she was just somebody who sat in that desk and whose name got called two before his on the roll, and that's the only way anyone thought of her, y'know? But just the same he wondered.

And I mean she'd never had any boyfriends or anything and you knew she was a good girl (which is to say, not a bad girl).

Well, the next day Manuel and Chato were talking about the baseball game with Concho Mines High and wondering were they gonna lose now that Pato had joined the air force, and they had forgotten all about the love notes and the teasing. Federico remembered, but he wasn't gonna say anything. And then he started noticing how Elfiria always had her hair so neatly braided in a trenza and none of the hairs ever loose and it always fell right down the middle of her back between her rounded shoulders. Well, he didn't know for certain if they were rounded but he'd read something like that once and they looked kind of round (como estaba ella media llenita, but that was okay because everybody always made fun of guys that went with girls that were flacas and called them "Bone Chompers," and things like that. And I mean, nobody was gonna call her "La Gorda" of the class 'cause that was María de los Socorros and there were lots of others almost as fat. Besides, good girls were supposed to be a little llenita so they wouldn't look like those mujeres in the movies who were definitely *not* good girls).

Still, he wondered. And once, when he was home alone and no one was lookin', he drew a little heart (in the corner of an old homework paper that he was going to throw away) and wrote "Federico + Elfiria" on it. And looked at it, just to see what it looked like (if she had done it, which she probably hadn't, 'cause she was a good girl), and he liked the way Elfiria had an *F* and an *R* in it, just like Federico. And he noticed how, when the teacher had them check each other's papers, she made her *F*'s kinda nice and open, even when they were *F*'s on somebody's paper. And then—one day Elfiria started looking at him. (Yeah, he looked at her lots, but he only did it when he was sure she didn't see, so it couldn't be that.)

Pues llegó summer. Y se casó Manuel. Y Chato se fue al air force, y en la boda de Polos, éste le dijo, "Ahora solo quedas tú. You're the only one left, buddy."* So he started going to Elfiria's house . . . y después de rato, se casaron.**

About a year after they were married, he saw this movie. Not *dirty* dirty, tú sabes, but it had lotsa good parts in it. He came home all excited. Elfiria estaba lavando el piso and he could see her nalgas pointing at him y también esas cosas hanging down. Pos, que se reventó el globo, and he was all over her. And him going for her and her fighting him off, kinda (in her feelings), but not saying "no" ('cause she was a good girl and s'posed to let her husband do things like that), and he was real excited, 'cause he knew that's what good girls were s'posed to do (but not

* *Pues llegó summer. . . . solo quedas tú.* Well, summer arrived. And Manuel got married. And Chato went off to the air force, and at Polos's wedding, Polos says to him, "Now, you're the only one left." [Spanish-language passages whose meaning is essential to understanding of plot are translated here in asterisked footnotes. Most of the remaining Spanish in this story, "*Sabor a Mí*/Savor Me," and "Enedina Pascasio" is translated in a glossary that appears at the back of this book.]

** . . . *y después de rato, se casaron.* . . . and after a while, they got married.

do) if they were married. And he started kissing her lots, just kinda forgetting himself. And she even quit making faces for a while. And he was real excited and breathing on her neck hard, like when he—well, you know, did it—an' pos, they did, an' just when he was about to—well, you know, venir—he just grabbed her neck and kissed it with his teeth and tongue, sucking hard. I don't know why, maybe it was just seeing it in the movie that made him do it, but he didn't do it on purpose. And then he—pos estaba viniendo—and she could feel it, you could tell, and she did something that really surprised Federico—she grabbed his head in both her hands and kissed him real hard on the lips.

Well, they were both real sleepy after that and didn't think too much about it that night, but the next day, Federico was still turning this over in his head. I mean she'd never acted like that before. (He hadn't either, but then he'd seen this love movie, so that was why.) And then he started wondering if maybe she'd seen a movie too or something. I mean, she was supposed to be home during the day and he hadn't heard nothing about her going out to movies. And this started to get his little hairs on his neck up and prickly until he realized she didn't have no way to get to no movie. And then he relaxed.

But then Elfiria got up and started to get dressed and when she took her robe off, the most horrible thing happened. Right in front of him there was this dark, dark blue mark on her neck and he *knew* what it looked like.

He'd seen those before (at school) but only on bad girls. It looked every bit like a hickey.

And I guess it was okay, what with his being her husband and all, but still—it looked funny and it bothered him. Manuel had always said, "Any girl that lets a guy give her a hickey is una *desas*." That night, Federico was still feeling bothered by it and for some reason didn't feel like going home right away. I mean he wasn't angry at her or anything, he said, he just wanted to stay out late. After all, he was a man, he could do that if he wanted. It was her business, cosa de viejas, staying home, and he went over to the cantina. He didn't go in, 'cause he didn't have but forty cents on him and that was for a Coke to go with his taquitos tomorrow lunch, but still he went to the cantina, and he parked outside in the troquita his brother gave him, and he just watched from the dark. And when it was real late, he went home.

But she was still awake and that pissed him off. And worse, she was looking at him nice-like, and like she wanted to do something. He just went around the bed, the other side, quitó los zapatos, and took his shirt and pants off quick, leaving his camiseta and underwear on, and slipped under the covers, facing the other way and looking asleep. She was in her gown and she curled up right against him (¡Ingrata! So he could feel her!), and his heart was going double but he didn't move a muscle, except for squeezing his eyes more shut, to look more asleep.

Pos, if esa ingrata doesn't squeeze up against him even more, like hinting. And she stays like that, several seconds (or maybe hours), and he's so he can't take it anymore and finally—all angry—he shoots off, "¡Cabrona! ¡Qué I'm asleep!" And she's so scared, 'cause he's never called her anything like that before, that she doesn't know whether to move away or how, and so she just stays absolutely still. And he's so mad that he had to speak that he keeps his eyes even more shut and his body even more still (so she can't say he's awake). And they stay that way the whole night— scrunched up against each other, his eyes squeezed shut, hers scared open, both of them scared to move an inch, and him with a hard-on and her hungry.

Bueno, that kind of did it. I mean, a man can only take so much, you know? I mean, a wife is s'posed to respect him, do what he wants when he wants, and not go bothering him otherwise, y'know?

And for the rest of that week, Federico went to the cantina every evening after work and stayed outside, parked in his troquita, and came home late and slept in his underwear, and Elfiria went to bed quietly, with her eyes open all night long.

Well, by the end of the week, they both looked pretty bad, but Federico looked the worst. Missing supper and not getting much sleep was really draining him. And Elfiria was lookin' okay, but pretty sad, and never said much—even more so than usual, and she usually didn't say much.

So one day, Federico thought, "Forget the cantina, I'm going home for supper." And Elfiria was so surprised, she ran around fixing supper as quick as she could, and they both ate, and without a word, he just went to the bedroom, pulled his clothes off (even his underwear—¡ya le calaba!), and went to sleep. She did too. And they slept kinda comfortable. I don't know why, but maybe they were just too tired to care about the rest.

The next day was Saturday and things felt okay. I mean, really quiet, but they did the work they needed to do and then, come evening, ate and Federico went to bed early again. He lay and thought for a while, and wondered about that hickey of Elfiria's, but when she finished the dishes and came to lie down too, he noticed that it had faded almost away, and that made him feel better, so he drifted off to sleep.

Elfiria was really worried about Federico. I mean, she wanted to be a good wife and she sure didn't like this business of him being angry, so she resolved to try not to do anything to upset him anymore. Still, she thought about that one night lots, and how she had felt hot and shivery all over, and she tried not to think about it too much, but she fell asleep thinking about it anyway.

It was maybe 2:00 A.M. and they'd slept for several hours already when suddenly Elfiria found herself dreaming half-awake and hungry and felt him hard and, just tired of waiting, she pushed herself up against him and helped it along. And when Federico woke up, her hand was pushing his mouth against her neck and her—well, all the different parts of her were rubbing against him, and it all felt real good, for about twenty minutes, until he came. And then, he started realizing—well, he wasn't too certain what, but realizing it anyway.

An' he looked real quick to see if she had a hickey. And she didn't (or not that he could see in this light anyway) and that made him feel a little better.

But *still* . . .

And he fell asleep, but the next day he was worse upset than ever, and made her go to misa, while he stayed home and thought. Pos then if she doesn't up and hit him that week—right in the middle of all his confusion—con que she's pregnant. At first, Federico was even more confused—and irritated que la ingrata had gone and gotten herself that way right now, when he was trying to figure something else out. But then, when everybody found out, and all the guys patted him on the back and said que ya era tiempo and Polos said his wife was expecting their second, and they all congratulated him, Federico felt pretty good. But still, he wondered. And the next day, he stayed away from work so he could watch the house from behind the bushes, to see if somebody else was coming to visit her.

The sun got pretty hot, y ya le andaban las moscas y el polvo, but he was determined to find out once and for all whether she was a good girl. Pos if he didn't end up staying there hasta las 2:00 de la tarde, y lo único que vió was that Elfiria hung all his clothes on the line first, and then the toallas, and then her clothes. And then she gave the sobras al gato vecino. But most of the time it was just him and the moscas, sufriendo del calor. At 2:00, he decided that she wasn't gonna do anything anymore porque a esa hora she listened to her novela and if she was gonna do anything, she wouldn't have made it at that time, 'cause she'd miss "Amor de Lejos." So he decided it was his baby, and, relieved, he left, sin decirle nada.

He began to feel real good about her being pregnant, and as she got bigger each month, it made him feel more like uno de los hombres que eran middle-aged y bien-respected. Y ella se portó bien también, nomás que around her fifth month she started getting real wet and hungry at night, e ¡híjole! pregnant y todo, qué desgracia, pero what could he do? I mean a man can only hold back so much, and there she was, *pushing* him to do it!

He didn't like the idea and he didn't *agree* with it at all—pero he was just too tired and turned on to fight it all the time. So he'd go ahead and do it, and just agree with himself in the morning that it shouldn't be that way, you know, and that it wasn't his fault.

When the time came for him to take her to the hospital, she was screaming and all that woman kind of stuff. Federico tried to be strong for her, but then as they were walking in the door, her water broke, y se mió allí, a chorros. "Elfa, can't you wait?!" le regañó in a whisper, embarrassed that the nurses should see his wife letting it all go like that. I guess Elfiria didn't hear him, 'cause she kept right on doing it, and her dress and the floor were all wet. And then he realized it had nothing to do with her going to the bathroom, and the nurse called for a wheelchair, and Federico's stomach felt funny (probably from the leftovers at supper last night) and he slumped onto the check-in counter with a color on his face Elfiria had never seen. For a second, Elfiria forgot her pains and just stared at him in shock, then she caught him just before he went to the floor, and pushed him into the wheelchair, saying to the nurse, "Cuídamelo."*

When he came to, she had already been taken in, behind those doors, and the nurse just smiled and said, "We'll let you know when you can go in."

Federico looked at the man in the wheelchair next to him, a viejito in his eighties, with an oxygen tube taped to his nose, who said to him, "Hijo, what are you in for?" It took Federico a few minutes to comprehend the question, but when he did, he scooted out of the wheelchair as fast as he could. Finally, they let him into Elfa's room, and it was real tough with her screaming and sweating and all, but Federico was real brave about the whole thing.

Sometime around midnight, the doctor came in to both of them, a yawning old man with a look como si había comido algo that didn't taste good, saw her still in labor and said, half to the nurse and them and half to his clipboard, "Let's quit all this nonsense and get that baby out. I've got a golf game early tomorrow. She's been in labor five hours already—prep for a C-section." Federico was about to feel fear coming on when he was interrupted by this loud voice, strangely familiar, yet totally alien.

---

* "*Cuídamelo.*" "Take care of him for me."

"¡NO SEÑOR!" It was Elfiria! Talking to the doctor like that! "If you can't help me, then go home and let my mother come!"

It was a boy. Named after him. Federico was in shock. He'd thought about her being pregnant, but he'd never really thought about the baby! Su hijo. Claro que era su hijo—he was named Federico, Jr., wasn't he? And when he looked at him for the first time, and saw this little person, all alive y pataleando, he just said, "I did that?!" and melted into a little pool of pride and tenderness.

Manuel had come pa' estar con él. "How ya doin', man? ¡Compa'! *¡Papá!*"—and saw Federico's eyes water up as he answered, "God, I feel . . . good." Manuel, smug over the birth of his own daughter two months earlier, smiled, muy compañero, and teased, "You feel good, huh? Oh, and it gets *better*, hombre. M'ija 'ta más chula . . . And you feel good now? Just wait till Elfiria gets all healed up and starts *wanting* you again—¡uy!" He laughed and nudged Federico. Federico laughed, but it was only from the face out, porque what Manuel had said had really bothered him. Y ni le dieron the time to absorb that when Elfiria was back in her room and ready for company . . .

Fred Jr. kept them both so busy that Federico didn't have much time to think about his earlier problems with Elfiria until one day, about seven weeks later, when she comes up to him, real suavecito-like, y'know, and says, "Hace mucho tiempo. I'm healed now, tú sabes, down there . . ." Federico was touched, but, muy caballero, comforted, "That's okay, honey. I don't need it. I can wait some more." The dam burst, and Elfiria, tired and glad the baby was finally asleep, burst too. "But *I* need it! *I* can't wait some more!"

Federico was stunned. "But . . . you . . . ¡Hombre! . . . I always thought you were . . ."—he gulped and said it directo—"a good girl."

"¡Ya para con estas tonterías! Of course I'm a good girl! I'm more than that! Soy una madre—the mother of our *child*—y soy tu esposa—*wife*, you know. Like, *married?*"

Federico had never thought of it that way. He had always heard of—pos, tú sabes—*desas*, bad girls, y también of course de good girls—but of someone being a good girl plus more? Maybe that explained it. Maybe eso de ser mother and wife let her do these kinds of things *plus* be a good girl. He hadn't figured it out completely, pero Elfiria interrupted him and said, "¡Ya olvídate de esas cosas! Let's go to bed!" And they did, and pos, tú sabes, a man can only do so much all by himself.

The Ride

ALMA STONE

She was a trim, spry old lady and as she came through the gate now, swiftly, smiling, to meet her son, she felt a quick, almost foolish little ripple run up her spine. "Goodbye, cat," she said, and pushed the half-grown kitten back through the crack in the gate. And because she was happy again at the sight of John Edward, because this nightly visit with John Edward was a thing that she had looked forward to all day, she smacked the kitten playfully on the rear. "Scat, cat," she said, and looked up at John Edward.

"Look like she wants to come with us, Mama." John Edward was bare-headed. She could see on his forehead where his big Stetson had set in the sweat.

"Wanting's not getting," said the old lady, noting with pleasure that Katie D. had not come tonight. She often said it, and right in front of John Edward, that the best day's work he'd ever done in his life was when he got Katie D. Fletcher. All she hoped was, she said, Mrs. Fletcher could say the same about him. You mighty right she could say the same about John Edward, said Mrs. Fletcher, he was just like one of her own.

As she walked with John Edward toward the car now she could almost hear Katie D. saying, "Oh, take your mama by yourself, John Edward. Give her a chance for a little visit with you. Take Arleen, though, it's the only chance she gets to see Arleen." So of course he had brought Arleen, thought the old lady indignantly, some of her pleasure at the prospect of the ride going sour at sight of the little girl. Why in the name of time they didn't leave that youngun at home was beyond her. Nobody was going to kidnap her, sure thing.

"Now, Miss Priss," she said, "you just politely shift to the back seat with Spot. I'm sitting up front with John Edward tonight." She looked a moment into the cold gray eyes of the little girl. If they did kidnap her, she thought, they'd turn her loose pretty quick.

The little girl, thin-armed and scrawny-headed (old Mrs. Fletcher to a T), slid reluctantly over the front seat to the back, skinny legs waving in mid-air, defiant.

"Do like Grandma tells you, Arleen," said John Edward. "Set back now and keep an eye on Spot. See old Spot don't fall out and crack his noggin."

The little girl drew her legs down and joined the bird dog on the back seat. She said nothing.

"We gonna hold her responsible if Spot cracks his noggin, ain't we, Mama?" John Edward shut the door behind the old lady and oozed in under the wheel on the other side. He could barely make it for his stomach. "Well, where'll it be tonight, Mama?"

"I leave it to you, John Edward," she said, and hands clasped in the lap of her white lawn dress, she sat looking through the windshield, waiting for the ride.

"I believe long as you're riding, Mama, you don't care where you're riding to." John Edward looked down at her and smiled and the old lady tried to catch the smile and hold it, but John Edward had turned back to the engine.

"Long as I'm riding I'm happy," she said, thinking he looked tired and fat. John Edward was just forty-two.

"Well, let's us just go out this way then and see what we can see," said John Edward, and he headed the Ford out toward the Newton Highway.

For a few minutes as they passed through town, by the post office and the courthouse, they sat in silence. The sun was nearly gone, but the steam still rose from the dusty road and there were late shadows on the courthouse lawn.

"Yessir, we'll just see what we can see," said John Edward, when they were out of town. "They never had cars when Grandma was a little girl, Arleen," he said. "Reason Grandma likes to ride so much. Sure building up out this way, ain't they, Mama?"

Every night John Edward would say how things were built up out this way, that he honestly believed things were built up more out this road, look at that new little bunch of houses there, than they were on the Fish Hatchery Road even. The old lady, trying to make a real conversation out of it, would agree. "It looks like it, Brother." They had called him Brother at home, though he had been an only child, and she still loved to call him that. She would use it whenever she could without seeming to just drag it in. "It strikes me that way too, Brother. But then the whole world is growing, Son. We are living in a wonderful age of growth and knowledge." Then she would wait, hoping, thinking oh, Brother, let's talk, let's discuss something, hon. But to hear John Edward you would think the entire world and all it stood for was right there on that Newton Highway, in that little squat of mill houses. One night she had said, "We are part of the whole world, John Edward. Not just these little houses the mill has put up out here on the highway." John Edward had looked at her peculiar. "I reckon we're all part of the same old world all right, Mama," he said. She had waited again, hoping this time John Edward would say more, would discuss a real topic of conversation. "Look at that little house over there, Mama," he had said, and stepped on the gas. "Look how they building up." After that she just agreed it was like a miracle the way things were built up. Looked big as Beaumont.

Tonight, however, riding by John Edward's side as he called attention to each little house they passed, she was conscious of a strong impatience with him. Then at once, looking up at him, she thought: now don't you go lose your patience with Brother.

"Hard to realize they're building so, just sitting up in that little house all alone talking to the cat." This was to make John Edward feel good, to let him know how much he was doing for her. Sometimes, though, she thought, it looked like she and the cat could find more to talk about than she and John Edward could.

"Look over there, Mama, got a little ranch house going up. Look, Arleen, kind of shaped flat like a ranch house, hon."

Ahead of them, beyond the sawmill and the mill pond, the old lady saw the Rutherford place coming up, and got ready, trying a stunt she pulled ever so often, trying to will him to go farther. Go a little farther, Brother, don't turn here. Make it last, hon. And tonight she added, let us see if we can figure this out together, how we lost touch with each other, John Edward. Go on farther, hon, give us a chance, give us more time to work on it. She kept thinking John Edward, John Edward, John Edward, holding his name in the front of her head there, making it easy for him to get the message. He looked down at her once, funny, like he had almost got it, too, but just at the moment when it appeared that for once he was not going to turn the Ford around the Rutherfords' old chinaberry tree, John Edward swerved quickly on screeching wheels, kicking gravel into the gully, almost losing Spot, the bird dog, out the window.

"Look there, Mama, she almost let Spot crack his noggin," said John Edward. "She don't believe that about us gonna hold her responsible if

Spot cracks his noggin. Look, Arleen, over there. Mr. Rutherford using a bedspring for a gate. Got a old bedspring turned upside down and using it for a gate to his lot."

There was no answer from the back and John Edward half-turned in his seat. The old lady, her breath still coming in quick snatches, would not look but could imagine too well the thick curtain of boredom that masked the thin, indrawn features of the little girl.

"I seen it last night," said Arleen.

"Saw, hon," said John Edward. "You saw it last night."

"You may have saw it," said the little girl, "but I *seen* it."

"Don't get sassy now, young lady," said John Edward, and the old lady thought hooray, give it to her. Sometimes when John Edward looked like that it was too plain that he was thinking Jesus Christ God A'mighty, but then he told himself it was one of the few pleasures Mama had left. This little ride every evening after supper meant a mighty lot to Mama. They lived on the other side of town from Mama and it was the only chance she got to see Arleen. He turned, smiling, to the old lady now.

"I call her my old pardner-wardner, Mama."

The little girl was leaning over the seat now, watching.

"I call her Miss Priss," said the old woman coldly.

"Is that what you call her, Mama?" John Edward turned to the back seat again. "Whose old pardner-wardner are you back there?"

The little girl stared straight ahead. John Edward passed by his filling station to see if everything was all right, then took the red clay hill to Miss Til Hamilton's. Forgetting the little girl for the moment, the old lady waved, shy and pleased, as Miss Til, her friend, called to her from the front gallery. When Miss Til quit looking the old lady turned back to John Edward. John Edward poked the car along.

"Gonna poke along here a minute, Mama, for Spot. Spot and old Jessie there cousins. Look, Arleen, old Jessie running alongside the car. Speaking to her cousin."

"Quit poking," said the little girl.

"All right, pardner-wardner." John Edward put more gas to it, leaving Jessie behind as they took the street to the cemetery.

"Want to get out, Mama?" John Edward stopped under a big pecan tree.

"Might as well, reckon." John Edward expected it. "Reckon it won't do any harm," she said. John Edward opened the door and helped her as they walked among the graves, touching her arm carefully as they crossed the live oak roots, as though soon, too soon, he would lose Mama to the live oak roots and the Cape jessamine and the althea. Too soon, Mama would be gone. As they did each night, they stopped at a tall stone marker. "John Cooper, 1875–1920. Doctor and Benefactor." Stooping, she picked a few grass sprigs from the corner of the iron fence, remembering again the kindness, the goodness, of the man who lay beneath the shaped earth.

"Here's where Grandpa's buried, Arleen," said John Edward.

"I know it," said the little girl. "I seen it last night."

"Saw it last night. That's why Grandma likes to come here. Grandma likes to come here because it's like a little visit with Grandpa."

"She don't like to come here," said the little girl suddenly and watched Spot digging, hoping he would dig up a dead person. A dead old lady.

"Don't be sassy now. Don't be sassy to Grandma. Grandma's tired," said John Edward. "You'll be tired too when you're old as Grandma."

The old lady was already leading the way back to the car. She could snatch John Edward baldheaded when he acted so dumb. There was no sense in a grown man acting so dumb, always trying to explain things to kids. Tell 'em to shut up was what he should tell 'em. Shut up and let grown people talk.

"Come on, Arleen, we'll stop by the drugstore and get us a treat. First one that gets back to the car gets a treat free. Look here," said John Edward. "Spot's beat us all. Spot's gonna get the treat."

John Edward, thought the old lady, was too young a man to have begun talking like that, repeating the same words like an idiot. If he felt like he had to fill up the conversation with something, fill it up with something worthwhile. Discuss politics, talk about world events. She might be an old, tired lady, ready for the graveyard, but she could keep up her end of it, all right, she read the paper, she listened to her news events, she didn't spend all *her* time at that darn filling station, drinking beer and throwing horseshoes, never reading a blessed thing but those darn comics. The world was in danger of another war at any moment and John Edward couldn't find anything to talk about. A young man on the radio last night had said the greatest crisis in the world's history was going on, and John Edward was so darn desperate for a subject for conversation with his mother, he had to talk to that darn youngun all the time. It made her sick to think of a fine boy like John Edward letting himself go like that, giving up the idea of being a doctor like his father, and getting that darn filling station instead, thinking that darn little building going up on the Newton Highway was the only thing to talk about. It made her feel sick all over. She couldn't lay it onto Katie D., either. Katie D. didn't have a darn thing to do with it.

"What you gonna have, Mama?"

John Edward pulled the Ford up to the curb at Bailey's Drugstore. Next door the Six Flags Theatre had just turned on its lights. A few couples stood in front, fanning, waiting for the doors to open. The old lady watched them, her indignation temporarily spent, thinking: the ride is nearly over.

"Taking your evenin' ride, Mrs. Cooper?"

She looked up at Chet, Ed Bailey's son. "Yes, had a real nice ride," she said.

"Hi there, little sweetheart." Chet had turned to the back. "Who's that little sweetheart back there, John Edward?"

"That's my pardner-wardner, man."

"Strawberry cone," said Arleen.

"Unh uh," said John Edward. "Spot gets to say first. Spot won the race back to the car. Tell old Chet what you want, Spot."

"Strawberry," said Arleen, unamused.

"You got any strawberry, Chet?" asked John Edward, and winked at Chet.

"Nossir, ain't got a bit of strawberry, John Edward."

"Chocolate," said Arleen, her thin lips set.

"Fresh out of chocolate, ain't you, Chet?"

"Just that second sold the last drop, John Edward."

"Well, I swan, looks like we gonna have to go home without no ice cream." John Edward started the engine of the Ford.

"Vanilla," shouted the little girl. "And I seen you winking."

"Saw, hon." John Edward shut off the motor. "I got a smart little old sweetheart back there, haven't I, Chet?"

Chet said boy hidey he sure did and John Edward said, "How about you, Mama?"

"Vanilla," said the old lady. The ride was nearly over, all right. When they got to the ice cream discussion, was chocolate in, was strawberry out, what was old pardner-wardner gonna have, the ride was nearly over. The ride was through.

Licking their cones, they rode on up the road back to the little house.

"Well, we had a good old ride tonight, didn't we, Mama?"

"Yes, but we'd a-had a better one if Miss Priss here had stayed at home." She couldn't keep from saying it.

"We'll leave old Priss at home next time then, Mama." He said it in a big, good-humored way, humoring them both. "So you say don't bring old pardner-wardner tomorrow, Mama?" He winked at her broadly over the little girl's head.

"I say leave Miss Priss at home," she said and got out of the car, thinking when John Edward couldn't figure out anything else to fill up the conversation with, he winked.

"Be around to take you tomorrow evenin', Mama."

"All right," she said. "I'll be waiting, Brother."

John Edward looked tired and whipped, leaning there on the gate. He had a look almost as though he wished he had more to say, he wished things had come out different, and for a moment she was sorry she had spoken up so plain about Arleen. John Edward had gone to a great deal of trouble to think up things to say, to point out spots of interest along the way, trying to make things nice. If he'd just leave that darn youngun at home, she thought.

"Your yard sure looks pretty, Mama." He said it like he was trying to make up for something. "Got old Katie D.'s beat."

"Katie D.'s got a good yard," she said. "Get out of my verbena, cat."

"Come on, Arleen," said John Edward. "You can get up front with Daddy now. Tell Grandma you'll see her tomorrow."

"I ain't coming tomorrow," said the little girl.

"We'll see about that, won't we, Grandma?" Then John Edward without looking back turned the car around, anxious, she knew, to get home to a nice cold bottle of beer. The little girl stuck her head out the window watching her. And for the first time that day she saw the thin lips of the child spread into a smile, old, devilish. Looking at her, seeing that smile grow dimmer and dimmer as the car disappeared in the dust, the old lady, alarmed, swayed against the gate. Suppose he didn't bring Arleen? Suppose she refused to come? (It was in the smile.) Suppose they were left alone together, she and this heavy-cheeked, blare-bellied son of hers who had lost touch with each other, who were strangers?

She stood waiting as she did each night till the car was out of sight, getting her last look at Brother for the day. Then slowly she opened the gate.

"Come on in here, cat, out of my verbena bed," she said, and the gray kitten followed her into the house. Suddenly stooping, she scooped the kitten into her arms. "Don't worry," she told the cat. "He'll bring her all right."

The Ninth Day of May

NJOKI McELROY

 *Thursday May 4, 1930*
We ate our corn cakes without syrup this morning. Mama sent Buddy to ole man Grimes store for a can of syrup. Buddy comes back empty handed. He tells Mama that ole man Grimes said he had only one syrup now and that was Nigger in the Cane Patch. Buddy says Mama, I just couldn't bring myself to say Please suh give me a can of that Nigger in the Cane Patch syrup. Mamas shoulders slumped a little bit. She didn't say anything. She pulled up her apron, wiped her hands and found a jar of her homemade pear preserves.

Last night Mama asked me—every night she ask the same thing—Have you seen anything yet? Sixteen years old. You should have come around by now. I wants to know if you been fast and if you've been pulling up your skirt. Me and your papa wants you and Buddy to get more education than we were able to get. I don't want you to end up busting suds for white folks.

No Mama, I says, I haven't seen anything yet but you don't have to worry I haven't done nothing wrong. I feel like a freak cause all the girls in my class came around three or four years ago. Mama says that Saturday she is going to get my graduation dress out of the lay away. She is paying the last dollar. Every week for twelve weeks Mama's paid a dollar from her sudsbusting money to the Clark Brothers department store for my dress.

Saturday May 6, 1930
On our way to Clark Brothers we delivered Miss Joiners laundry this morning. We had on our going to town clothes. Miss Joiner counted out her $1.50 to Mama. She had a look of pain on her face. She looked us up

and down and says to Mama—Sadie, how do you colored people live so well? You have nice clothes and nice homes. I want to know just how do you do it? You colored pay more and make less than we do and we can just barely make it. Mama said Miss Joiner, we've always had it hard. Its always depression for us. But God takes care of us. Yes mam we are in Gods care. We are still on our knees to Him.

Mama paid the last dollar to Clark Brothers for my graduation dress. It is some pretty—it is pink Spanish lace and chifon—has a sweetheart neck and the flounce at the bottom has points all around. I couldn't try it on at the store, but the saleslady measured me with the tape and she said it would fit just fine and it does. One more week until the graduation reception.

Next Tuesday is the day they are going to take John Hughes to trial. All the white folks looked meaner in town this morning and all the colored folks looked worried.

Monday May 8, 1930
After supper Papa, Mr. Walton, and Mr. Gaston were talking about the John Hughes story. John Hughes is the good looking colored man who worked on a farm over by Honey Grove. A few days ago they brought him here to Sherman and put him in jail. He was in there two days before they said he had raped the farmers wife. The woman said that John Hughes pointed a shotgun at her when her husband was gone. He told her he was raping her cause whites had taken everything from him and he was getting even.

Papa and his friends say they heard thru the grapevine that John Hughes and the woman were lovers. That the woman liked colored men. Mr. Gaston said I know from experence what these white womens is like. I wuz working on a farm over by Whitesboro. The farmers wife started giving me the eye, rubbing up against me. My brothers I saw the handwriting on the wall, the noose around my neck. I knew what time it wuz. It wuz time for the sun not to go down on me in Whitesboro. I left and I didn't even bother to collect my pay.

Papa says a mob of crackers were up at the courthouse this morning. They shouting threats. They say he don't deserve a trial and that they will show him and all the uppity niggers around here that they better not mess with their women.

Thursday May 11, 1930
It may be a long time before I can wear my pretty pink graduation dress. Its hanging where I see it the first thing in the morning and last thing at night. Frederick Douglass Memorial High School is closed. The Texas

Rangers and the troops who came to town yesterday the day after the riot have set up there. Where were they when we needed them on the ninth day of May?

On the ninth day of May the whites came to John Hughes trial. They acted so wild that the judge dismissed the jury and left John Hughes in the vault. When the courthouse closed for the day the mob came back. They threw dynamite into the vault. They dragged John Hughes body out of the burning courthouse. Then they tied his feet and legs together and tied him to the back of a car. They dragged John Hughes body up and down our street, Brockett street, Montgomery street. When they got to Mulberry street they set fire to our whole business area and all the homes on Mulberry. They burned down Dr. Porters office, both of the dentist offices, lawyer Grahams, the two cafes, the picture show, the insurance office, Millers drugstore, the funeral parlors, Bishop Allens big white house.

Papa and his friends stood watch at the upstairs windows. He supplied them all with his pistols and shotguns and boxes of shells. Papa said By God if those devils try to take this house they will take us all. We gonna die right here before we let go. And we gonna take some of them with us.

The women and children stayed downstairs. The women took turns praying, singing hymns and cooking. I kept wondering where was that God that Mama said would take care of us. Seemed to me that he had forgot all about the colored folks in Sherman. There were college boys and girls, women with babies in their arms—Buddy said he even saw ole man Grimes and his demented son in the mob. They hooted and howled and sang

> Happy days are here again
> The skies above are clear again
> Happy days are here again

The mob gathered around a big tree on Mulberry street. They hung John Hughes battered body on a branch. They cut off his privates and passed them around on a piece of paper. Then they set him afire and sent his soul to Jesus.

Its been raining every since that night but the tree keeps burning. The smell of the smoke is in my nose and in the water I drink.

When I stand up, the blood flows like a river. Mama says it was the shock of the riot. Shock finally brought me around.

> Smoke is in the air. Rise up
> Smoke is in the air. Oh rise
> And take my soul to Jesus.

Hotter Here Than It Ever Was
in New Jersey

LEE MERRILL BYRD

The lady who said she was from Tupelo wore pink bedroom slippers and a too-short dress stretched taut and ragged across her swollen knees. She was rehearsing the recent agonies of her granddaughter for a woman who sat across from her in a close and narrow waiting corridor, a woman with brown hair who said she lived in El Paso but took pains to note that she had not been born there but was born instead in New Jersey. NEW JERSEY, she said twice.

Not interested in where the brown-haired woman came from or why it was important for her to mention it more than once, the lady from Tupelo labored through the details of her granddaughter's ordeal in a drawl as flat and indifferent as if she were talking about the offspring of some Chinaman who lived in the furthest reaches of Siberia and not her very own flesh and blood. She punctuated the more gruesome items with a tap-tap-tapping from an umbrella she held in her left hand, a ruffled black taffeta affair that had long ago lost its shine and many of its spokes.

Beside her in a chair at either bulging arm sat a vacant, rawboned couple, a man and woman whose complexions were as pale and ashen as cooked pork. Both of them were preoccupied with smoking.

The sun outside the thin hospital window was set for noon in May, pitched directly overhead, hard and yellow. The narrow waiting corridor baked in its glare and reeked of the dark secret odors of hidden unwashed flesh and greasy food which for the woman from New Jersey most assuredly constituted the very essence of Tupelo.

I went to town, was how the fat grandmother from that city had opened suddenly, immediately after she and the New Jersey woman had established their respective places of residence and birth. It being the first of the month and her daughter eligible for welfare and food stamps.

Had to go. Couldn't trust them to go alone, she said, squinting narrowly at the woman with the brown hair so as to shut the rawboned couple out of her vision. The boyfriend was no good. Had been in jail twict and couldn't be trusted with money. Her own daughter didn't have no sense. The things she could tell. Tap. Tap. Tap.

She sighed. They left the granddaughter at home alone. She was seven. Plenty big enough to be left alone. Plenty big enough to know how to cook. Big enough to know how to turn on the oven by herself.

Anyways she was sick with a fever and the chills. She stayed in bed. She had on her pink nightgown, the one they give her for her birthday, from the K-Mart.

They had them this lady next door. A nigra woman with a big mouth. This nigra woman had a big black buck who come and beat her up a few nights a week. Tap. Tap. Tap.

They both was in the house next door at the same time that the granddaughter stood up to try to warm herself from the chills in front of the oven in her pink nightgown.

The woman with the brown hair who was born in New Jersey did not quite see the relationship between these two events. She scowled.

The Tupelo lady said that it would be a matter for the police to be investigating. As soon as them doctors found out for sure whether the girl would live or die they were going to look her over to see if that black buck had touched her. Tap. Tap. Tap. Because from what the nigra lady said, it had been the black buck who first seen her come out on the front porch of their house, spinning and screaming and all on fire. That's what the nigra with the big mouth told the police. But there weren't no black buck around anywhere by the time the Tupelo lady got home with her daughter and the daughter's worthless boyfriend and the four sacks full of groceries. And the granddaughter couldn't tell them nothing. She was half burnt to death.

The lady from Tupelo wiped her face off with a dirty piece of Kleenex she held tight in her hand.

The nigra next door was the stupidest nigra the Tupelo lady had ever met. When her and her daughter and the daughter's worthless boyfriend had come back from town, the nigra could hardly tell them what had happened or where the granddaughter had gone or why the house smelled like smoke.

She's gone, the Tupelo lady whined, imitating her stupid neighbor. Your girl is gone.

Where's she gone? they demanded of her.

Don't know, the nigra had wailed. Didn't tell me, but she gone. Gone in the am-bu-lance.

They called the police and the police finally come and took them to the hospital. They had the si-reen on. The umbrella struck the floor while the fat lady from Tupelo raised her neck and howled to demonstrate the truth of that very fact.

There was a bunch of doctors. One after another. There was a little-bitty doctor who had no hair on his head and he said the granddaughter was burnt inside and out.

There was one who was a Jap and he said she was going to die that day. Said she was burnt 36.

There was one even who was a nigra. A fe-male! And she said they were going to have to fly the girl to the charitable hospital for burns in Galveston, Texas, in whose sweltering third-floor waiting room they now all sat. The lady from Tupelo and her daughter and the daughter's worth-less boyfriend. And the woman with the brown hair from New Jersey.

But they didn't fly the girl that same day. Mostly what they did was to keep them all sitting there in that hospital in Tupelo way past supper-time. And they were getting tired, too. The grandmother got aholt of the Jap and told him about being so hungry and so tired and having nothing but food stamps for money and he took them down to the cafeteria and bought them some supper.

She didn't care what they said about Japs.

Fried chicken and ladypeas and mashed potatoes and black bottom pie for dessert. And then he called the police and they come and drove them home. And hardly before they even got to sleep, the police car come back to get them and take them to the airport. Dark it was and still nighttime and them with just the clothes they had on and a change of underwear and a couple of sandwiches in a paper sack. And the frigerator back in Tupelo full of food from the food stamps and them not having any idea how long all this would take.

One of them private jets flew them all down to Galveston. The grand-daughter had a nurse. The girl was wrapped in white bandages all over. All over her hands and her legs and her head and her face. And she smelled. Lord. Gawd. The whole airplane was filled with her smell.

The umbrella clattered to the floor. The lady from Tupelo shut her eyes and stopped talking as abruptly as she had started.

The woman with the brown hair who was born in New Jersey tapped her faded red sandals impatiently on the floor. She fished around in the bottom of her purse for an old wristwatch she always carried that had no buckle on the strap. A quarter to one. In ten minutes she could go to her son's room and take him out on his first pass, but for now she would have to sit here. There was no point in going somewhere else. Though she might have chosen different circumstances for herself than the ones that presently surrounded her.

The hospital cafeteria was on the next floor down. She could probably go there if she really wanted to get away. But it was closed already. She wasn't hungry anyway. And she'd already drunk enough coffee to sink a ship.

She could go down and talk to the psychologist.

But there was nothing really to talk about.

Now there definitely had been a time when there was PLENTY to talk about. She would be the first to admit that. PLENTY. And she had talked and talked and talked and talked. But that time was past. She had accepted the fire completely. She knew that the next step was to stand beside her boy while he faced the world. And since she was right now on the very brink of that next step, there was really no place else to go but right here, exactly where she was, whether she happened to care for the circumstances or not.

She eyed the strange trio sitting across from her. The grandmother looked like she had fallen asleep. That was fine with the woman from New Jersey. She had no desire to hear any more about the Tupelo granddaughter. And the vacant couple was so intent on smoking they didn't even notice her staring at them.

Trash, she thought, pursing her mouth up. This hospital was full of them. Poor. Slovenly. Stupid. Wondering whether a black man had touched their child when the girl was half burned to death. Worried about the food in their refrigerator and how long all this would take.

Soon these people would be just like the rest of the trash here. Fascinated by the details of each case on the Acute Ward. Sitting around all day and talking. Talking in the halls. Talking outside the rooms. Talking in the elevator. They always took the elevator.

That kid there been burned all over his body. Ninety-two. Should of died. Nurse said so.

You seen that little niggah boy? Don't have no mama. Mama done left. The daddy's girlfriend stuck that kid in a tub full of boiling water. She in jail for the reeeest of her life.

See that little-bitty baby. You seen that poor little baby by itself in the big room? Bless its heart. Its mama and daddy take drugs. Nurse said so.

The woman from New Jersey glared at the Tupelo contingent, tugging at the strands of washed-out red glass beads around her neck. That was exactly the sort of thing they'd say, exactly the sort of thing that would occupy them for the next however-many months, while the food rotted in their refrigerator in Tupelo. Where do these sort of people come from? she thought to herself. They are so stupid. They don't understand anything.

Suddenly the grandmother's eyes popped open and she began again. She smelt like burnt meat, she said. That whole airplane smelt like burnt meat. I got sick, couldn't hardly stand it. Later I seen her chest, looks like a slab of raw beef. She got fire on her face, too. Doctor says she going to have scars all over her. Ain't no man ever want to touch her, that's one thing.

The woman from New Jersey looked away, out the window. The lady from Tupelo made her sick. She was fat and she smelled. The daughter and her worthless boyfriend made her sick, too. The hospital made her sick. The blue and yellow rooms. The close waiting corridors. The smells of dressings and diapers and flesh. The halls always full of burned children, racing up and down, dirty and unruly. As if they'd given up caring what people thought about them. As if their lives were over. As if now that their lives were over they could do whatever they damn pleased. Spoiled! Rotten! Just like that food in the refrigerator in Tupelo would be by the time these people got back. Just thinking about it made the woman from New Jersey sick.

Her boy was not spoiled. Not her boy. Not her Carl. Burned or not, he was different. Had been different before. Was going to be different. Not like the rest of them.

Carl was well-mannered and polite. He was always clean. The woman from New Jersey saw to that. His clothes were going to be brand-new. Though they might have to go in debt to get them. She touched the shopping bag beside her chair. It was full of boxes. New slacks. A new shirt. A new pair of socks. And new brown shoes. It would be obvious to people what kind of boy he was. Anyone that tidy was a good boy and a nice boy and people would like him for that. He would not get treated like the rest of these children were bound to get treated. Oh, she knew. The psychologist had spoken to her many times about how burned children were received out in the world. Yes, she understood that. She had come to terms with that. She knew there might be some difficulty. But she was also confident that, with her help, Carl would fit right back into things nicely.

Now the rest of these children. She couldn't answer for any of them. They may have been bad children to start. Bad children from bad and broken homes, where their parents, if they had any, didn't give a fig what they did or who they played with. If they had cared, their children never would have gotten burned.

Carl never would have gotten burned if their garage hadn't caught on fire. And he wasn't the one who set it on fire, she said to herself slowly and mechanically, as she had said before a million times to what seemed to be a million inquiries. It was nobody's fault. It was an accident. He doesn't play with matches.

She was not like these other parents. These other parents obviously didn't love their children. They just left them to raise themselves. Now all of a sudden all they could think about was how their kids looked. Why, just this morning in the parents' weekly conference with the doctors she had heard a mother—a scrawny unkempt girl whose sweat smelled as if she'd been taking drugs—ask in a thin and whining voice where her boy could go to school now that no one would look at him anymore.

God! She tugged at the end of her fingernail with her teeth. This is 1981, she said, lecturing to the whole lot of these foolish parents in her imagination. This is 1981, not the Dark Ages. You don't need to hide your children. Times have changed. If you will just change your own attitude. If you will just look and see that you have not raised your children properly. If you will just tidy them up, keep them presentable, teach them to be well-mannered, and change your own attitude . . .

She considered again the roster of things that she had planned for that afternoon. It would make a good example—if anyone cared to listen—of the sort of thing these people could do to help their children toward recovery. It was a good idea, this pass, and was highly recommended by the doctors and psychologists as very very therapeutic. An opportunity to get out and test your wings before you were actually released from the hospital for good.

First she and Carl would walk down the three flights of stairs. That would be good exercise for him, as it was for every person here, a healthy alternative to the elevator. They would stop at the front desk, to show the receptionist how nice he looked in his new clothes. The receptionist was a lively young college girl who was always asking how Carl was doing.

From there they would walk to Baskin-Robbins for an ice cream cone, then on to the beach and a possible stroll down beside the water. Then home to the apartment she had rented so that Carl could see where she had lived these last three months.

Now these were the kind of wholesome activities that a child who had undergone so much . . .

What's the number of your kid? asked the lady from Tupelo, leaning forward.

The woman from New Jersey frowned. She had almost completely forgotten the flesh-and-blood fat lady across from her while she'd been delivering her little talk to her and others like her in her imagination.

You got a kid here, said the lady from Tupelo. I seen you here this morning.

Yes, said the brown-haired woman. She folded her hands together on her lap and tapped her red sandal on the floor.

Do you mean what room is he in or how much percent of his body was burned? That's what you mean, don't you? It's called the percentage. How much percentage of his body was burned? she said, talking very quietly and carefully.

The lady from Tupelo blinked.

My son, continued the woman from New Jersey, was burned over 62 percent of his body.

Yeah? said the lady from Tupelo. My granddaughter got 70.

The woman from New Jersey crossed her arms over her chest. I thought you said it was 36 percent, she said.

Yeah, said the Tupelo lady.

Well, what is it? Is it 36 percent or 70 percent? Because there's a big difference. The brown-haired woman sat up very straight in her chair. Is it all third degree?

It's bad, said the Tupelo lady.

The woman from New Jersey fussed with the creases in her seersucker skirt, pushing at them nervously with her hand. Her ankle wiggled of its own accord. A single thread of sweat unexpectedly made its way down along the underside of her arm.

My son is burned almost entirely third degree, she said suddenly, the words exploding from her. She glowered at the lady from Tupelo, trying to hold that person's watery eyes with her own, but the lady from Tupelo looked right past her. That's the maximum amount of burn there can be, she pushed on, but deliberately now, precisely. That's all three layers of skin. Sixty-two percent. Now that's bad.

Yeah? said the lady from Tupelo. She shut her eyes.

He is burned on the top of his head, continued the woman from New Jersey, on the left side of his face, on his left arm, on his back and on his chest. He lost his ear and three fingers.

The Tupelo lady's head slipped forward a little, as if she were just catching herself from falling asleep.

He's bad, said the brown-haired woman, just a little louder than she had intended to before. She tried to get the attention of the daughter and the daughter's boyfriend, but their eyes wouldn't connect with hers.

Sixty-two percent, all third degree, is bad, she said again. He's been in the hospital for three months. For over three months. And I've been here with him the whole time. I had to leave my whole world behind me.

No one seemed interested. The daughter's worthless boyfriend put his hand in his breast pocket and took out another cigarette in a motion so slow that the brown-haired woman was arrested by it. When he finally lit the match, she felt as if he'd struck it on her insides, it surprised her so, and she jumped and pushed ahead, now fully irritated.

I went in to see him right away, right after the fire, long before they flew him here in the private plane, she said. My husband—she said it emphatically as if the word might have no meaning to her audience—was with me that whole first month. Then he had to go back to work. We just could not afford to have him out of work for more than a month. He works, she said pointedly. In El Paso.

When I first saw my son, his skin was falling off in strips and it was yellow. And when they took him into the tubs to take the skin off, I could hear him screaming. Now he was one they thought would die. He was bad.

The woman from New Jersey took a long, deep breath. She rubbed her face with both her hands.

But your granddaughter, she said finally, if she is indeed burned over 36 percent of her body, is going to be fine. Thirty-six percent is nothing.

But they didn't seem to care. The vacant couple kept on smoking. The fat lady was preoccupied with the Kleenex she held clutched in her hand.

The brown-haired woman lay her head back against the wall. She shut her eyes, exhausted. And dozed off, or must have. Carl's face flew before her sleeping mind, the left eye drawn down to his chin, the mouth twisted up by his forehead. No! She woke up suddenly, sweating. That's not what he looks like!

Which one is he? The lady from Tupelo was asking her a question. She was leaning forward and squinting at her out of one eye.

The brown-haired woman looked out the window, across the street, trying to get her mind settled, trying to figure out where she was and what this lady across from her wanted. Finally it all came into focus. He's in the first room, she said slowly.

Yeah? said the lady from Tupelo.

His name is Carl, said the brown-haired woman after a while.

Yeah? said the lady from Tupelo again. She dabbed at her lip with the rumpled Kleenex. He the one that wears that thing over his face? Just sits there on the end of his bed? First room?

Yes, said the brown-haired woman. She sat up straight. Only he is not just sitting there. Sometimes he watches TV. He watches many educational programs. You can't see the type of show he is watching from the hallway.

Why's he wear that thing? asked the Tupelo lady.

That's a mask. All the children wear masks if they are burned on their faces. Haven't you seen any of the other children wearing masks?

The lady from Tupelo sniffled.

Well, said the brown-haired woman, the masks are a major breakthrough in burn care. A very major breakthrough.

The Tupelo lady looked at her sullenly.

Your granddaughter will have to wear a mask, said the woman with the brown hair. She tried hard to look very serious. Just like my son. Just like everyone else.

That so? said the lady from Tupelo. She crossed her arms up over her chest. She didn't say anything at all. And then, suddenly, How'd he get burned?

The brown-haired woman sat back in her chair. He was in a garage fire, she said. It was nobody's fault, it was an accident.

My girl wasn't playing with no matches, said the Tupelo lady. She knows how to light the stove.

Well, said the woman with the brown hair. My boy doesn't play with matches either.

The two women stared at each other.

The lady from Tupelo spoke first. Nurse said this morning that a little boy died here awhile back. She sat up particularly straight. Didn't die from no fire, just died from being here. Nurse said onct an infection starts can't nothing stop it. Kills people. Everybody dies, even the doctors.

The woman with the brown hair scowled at the Tupelo lady's pink bedroom slippers. Her toenails were yellow and dirty and long.

The Tupelo lady sighed, an enormous sawing noise. I got a bad heart, she said. Had a heart attack last year.

The brown-haired woman's red sandal slapped against her foot.

My girl here can't work. She's got to take care of her kid. They're giving us a room in the Holiday Inn and giving me and the girl seven dollars a day for food. They got king-siiize beds over there and a twenty-four-inch color TV. Don't know what they're going to do about *him*. Said they couldn't pay for more than me and the girl because we're kinfolks.

Well, said the brown-haired woman.

A door across from the narrow waiting corridor opened up. A nurse dressed in a pink uniform looked at the woman from New Jersey and said, Your son is ready for you now.

Well, said the brown-haired woman, standing up. I have to go. My son is ready for me. They're giving him a pass today so he can go outside for a while and see what things are like. He hasn't been outside for three months.

She picked up the shopping bag full of new clothes. I guess I'll be on my way, she said. We're really going to go out on the town, she said a little too gleefully for her own comfort. The ice cream parlor. The beach. Walking down the seawall. My apartment. I better get going because we've really got some things to do, she said.

But instead she stood in the corridor for a minute longer, biting on her lip.

The Tupelo lady dabbed at her face with the last worn bit of Kleenex and stared at the floor.

I think your daughter, your granddaughter, will be fine, said the woman from New Jersey, feeling for a minute as if she had been unkind to these people. I think that the first couple of weeks is the worst, she went on. I remember that my first couple of weeks here were the worst I'd ever spent. I didn't know if Carl would live or die. But it gets better.

They could hear a door down the hall opening and shutting impatiently.

Well, let me qualify that, said the brown-haired woman quickly, her eye on the hallway. It gets better until you realize that your child will have scars. Her voice got lower. Now that is really the worst part. But even that gets better. You come to terms with it. You accept it. You get a handle on it and after a while it hardly bothers you anymore.

The trio from Tupelo listened to this extraordinary capsulization of the New Jersey woman's experience without showing any sign whatsoever of having heard or understood it. She waited for them to comment, but they didn't say a word.

Well, okay, she said finally. She stood staring down at them for a minute and then turned and made her way along the hall toward Carl's room very slowly, feeling dizzy and not even half as eager to take him out on a pass as she had felt before she had met the people from Tupelo.

Suddenly the trip seemed absurd. Two hours out in the hot sun with a boy who was wearing a mask? Who had been lying in a hospital bed for three months? Just so people could see him? It didn't make a single shred of sense.

She leaned against the wall just outside of Carl's room. The blinds were drawn on his door, but she saw him peering through them looking for her.

Mom? she heard him say. And there he was, standing at the door. He was wearing only underpants, his legs and arms wrapped with Ace bandages, his hands swaddled in splints and more bandages, his head covered with a tight brown hood, like a stocking, that held a white life mask in place. With the mask on, she could only see his eyes and his mouth. His lips were swollen out from the pressure of the mask on his face. The sight of his frail, broken body, now just barely seven years old, struck her with such an overpowering measure of pain that her eyes filled full of tears and her heart felt as if it would burst loose from her. But he did not notice.

Did you bring my clothes? was his first question. And his second, right behind the first, Did you buy the shoes I wanted?

The questions brought her back to the trip at hand. She walked swiftly across the room, putting her shopping bag down on his bed. The room was empty, except for the two of them, the other children—older than Carl—having been allowed to forego their afternoon naps in favor of a game of pool in the playroom down the hall. From Carl's room, she could see past the nurse's station to the rooms opposite his. Younger children lay sleeping in their beds and in their cribs, shrouded in white sheets. In one room, white curtains surrounded a single bed. The lights were dimmed and nurses and doctors were going in and coming out. A new case. An acute burn. Probably the Tupelo lady's granddaughter, the New Jersey woman concluded.

She and her son spoke in whispers, even though they were alone. Here is a new shirt, she said quickly. I just went to the department store in the Holiday Mall and bought it this morning. Green and blue check. You always like green and blue.

A new shirt! He sank down on the bed. What about the one I asked you to bring? What about the one Dad was going to mail over here?

Look, she said. Don't start that. Your father didn't have time to mail it or any of your other clothes. He has to work. And even if he had mailed it over here, it wouldn't be right. This is an occasion for a new shirt, no matter how much it costs. Although I did get this one on sale.

He stood stiffly while she pushed his arms into the sleeves. Your first day out of the hospital, she cooed. Don't you want to look nice?

It's too small, he said.

No, she said. It's just right. And here are the pants. They were dress pants, made of polyester, in a gray blue to pick up the blue in his checkered shirt.

He groaned. Couldn't you have asked Dad just to mail my old jeans?

You have gotten fatter, she said firmly. You wouldn't be able to wear your old jeans even if your father had sent them. Now stand up.

Why didn't you buy me some new jeans then?

These are just like new jeans, she said, touching his leg so he would raise it.

New jeans! he sputtered. These are like something you go to church in.

Well, she said, pursing her mouth together. This is a special occasion. Like going to church, she added, grimly. I want you to look nice. Don't you want to look nice?

I don't look nice, he cried. I'm not going to wear this stuff.

Yes you are.

I'm not going.

Listen, she said, grabbing onto his shoulders. When you leave this hospital, you are going to go out looking decent. Do you hear me? She shook him. You will not look sloppy. You will not look poor. You are not poor, do you understand? Your father is working hard to make a good living, she said, forcing the shirt into his pants. She snapped them shut and zipped the zipper. There. We may not have a whole lot of money but we are not poor people, she said. Now sit down while I put your socks and shoes on.

The socks were dress socks, and the shoes were brown. He had wanted sneakers and gray athletic socks, and they argued again. He cried until the eyes of his mask were wet.

The woman from New Jersey sat down on the edge of her son's bed. She felt so tired. This trip made no sense at all. The boy cried on and on. Her nerves were sore and aching. She wanted to scream. She couldn't go anywhere like this. Maybe she could just lay back and shut her eyes for a minute, just to collect her thoughts. He might not even notice.

Her head hit his pillow and she was asleep, resting there in the dark cool room until the noise of his crying stopped and was replaced by his voice talking. He was telling himself things—this and that—walking around the room, suddenly entranced by the fact that he was alone there in that place that was usually occupied by four other boys vying for the TV and the nurses' attention. But not entirely alone. His mother lay asleep on his bed.

Here is Ronnie Tate's bed, she heard him say and she could see him even as she slept, as she knew he would be, standing reverently at the end of the bed of this young black boy who had not ceased to receive the weekend adorations of his many aunts and uncles since the day he arrived. They had come bearing silver dollars and baseball cards and bags of candy and movie magazines and pinup posters and comic books. And now the time was ripe for a close look, the room empty and Ronnie Tate safely down the hall, playing pool. Carl must have moved up by Ronnie

Tate's nightstand for here the catalog began and she could hear it, just faintly, like soft music, like a list of things she had always wanted.

Here is the jar of money. Silver dollars. Dimes. Quarters. Nickels. Pennies. Almost full. Hmmm. Here are the baseball cards he got last week. A baseball. Signed by the Dodgers. Wonder Woman. Batman. Michael Jackson.

The woman from New Jersey was rocked into a deep sleep by the sound of her son's voice as it moved all along the edges of that room. Here is Carnell Hughes's bed. He has surgery on Tuesday. He says he doesn't need it. Hmmm. Trays from lunch. Ronnie didn't eat his apple.

She had a dream. Her husband was secretly building her a new house even while they were still living in their old house. She said she didn't need a new house, but he said that the old house was ruined. It was no longer useful, he told her. He took her to see the new house and it was almost finished, down to the curtains and the furniture. But it was odd. She didn't quite like the fact that it was way way out in the middle of the desert, a place that was all flat empty desert and dark gray mountains. But even there, even way out there, there were many strange houses crowded up against it. And no wonder! The house was purple and orange. She wanted to look inside, just like everyone else was doing.

As she pressed up against the front windows, she saw that there at her dining table—which was just like the tables in the cafeteria across the street from the hospital—were three men in pinstripe suits and white shirts and shiny dark silk ties. They were the same men who sat in the cafeteria every morning when she ate her breakfast. They were staring at their shoes and they were all three of them dead. You could tell. You could just tell. The black waitress who worked in that same cafeteria was waiting on these dead men. She came over to the table with plates of biscuits. One of the dead men grinned and said, Ain't no man ever going to want to touch her.

And then one of the other ones said, We can't hire him. I don't care how smart he is, or how much better he is than us. We can't hire anyone with a face like that. The third dead man stared down at his polished shoes and said, Not with a face like that. He might as well be dead.

The woman from New Jersey groaned in her sleep, sweating, trying to get inside that new house that her husband had built her and tell those dead men that they were dead, tell them a thing or two about her son's face, but she could not get in at all and they just kept right on talking as if they were absolutely and positively the only ones who had the answer. And then she heard her son's voice again, was aware of it, going over and

around the dream and he was still cataloging things but they were different now, not other people's, but his own.

This is a mask, he was saying. Here is my ear. She opened her eyes.
He was standing by Ronnie Tate's nightstand again and he had found
a mirror.

Yes, he was saying, I have lost some hair. Third degree. Yes, second
degree. It was swollen shut and I couldn't eat. My ear is gone too. And
some fingers.

Carl? she said. He turned to look at her.

Are you ready? she said. The short nap had given her new energy. It
would be all right to go ahead with this excursion, to go on out and see
what it would be like. After all, it was just a mask.

Why, we all of us walk around wearing masks, hiding from each other!

And he had just been in an accident and he just needed to wear the
mask so that his skin would stay smooth. That was so easy to understand.
Everyone would. And he was going to get better, much better, and his
face would be normal and people would accept him and he would grow
up and go to college and get a job and get married, just like everyone
else, and no would ever know that anything at all had happened to him.

And really, his face hadn't been burned half so bad as some of the kids
she had seen. He looked pretty good in comparison to them. She sat up.

And really, it wasn't all that hot outside.

Ready to go? she said cheerfully. Don't you think we ought to go?
Have I been asleep a long time? She got down off the bed. We're going to
have fun. Ice cream and a walk along the beach. And you get to see my
apartment. And you get to go outside and feel the sun and the air and see
the ocean.

Do we have to walk?

Of course we have to walk. What do you think we are? she teased him.
Rich? Do you think we have our own chauffeur-driven Rolls-Royce?
Huh? And look! You have new shoes.

They hurt.

Of course they don't hurt. I matched them up exactly against the picture I drew of your foot, she said, although that wasn't exactly true. She
had matched them up exactly against the picture but she hadn't even considered the Ace bandages that were secured under his feet.

The socks are too thick.

She hadn't thought about the socks either.

It's too hot, he said.

She was quickly losing her resolve again and it irritated her. It is not
too hot, she said in a much too patient voice. Your shoes fit and so do

your socks. And you stop this right now! You're acting like a spoiled brat. She walked around the room gathering up her purse, putting away the boxes and paper sacks. She went into the bathroom to fix a cold rag to wipe his face after he took his mask off at the ice cream parlor. She wrung it dry and put it in a plastic sack and tried to imagine that things would be okay. *If* she just kept on getting ready. *Despite* the fact that his shoes were too small and his socks were too thick and the sun was too hot. Despite the fact that the clothes and the bandages would suffocate him. Despite the fact that the trip, the trip itself, would take them—in those too tight shoes and too thick socks—forever.

He was sitting on the bed with his shoulders slumped when she came out of the bathroom. She could feel sorry for him but if there was one thing she would not stand for, it was for him to feel sorry for himself.

Come on, she said, jerking him up by the elbow. We're going, heat or no heat, shoes or no shoes. We're going if you have to go barefoot.

His slender body stiffened under her tight hand.

Get going! she said, pushing him. I haven't got the time to fool with you. He began to cry again and it made her even more angry. She shoved him across the room and out into the bright, sunlit hallway and it was there that she heard the flat lifeless drawl of the lady from Tupelo once more. She remembered her and the vacant cancerous pair as if she had met them many years ago in a dream.

She pressed her nails into Carl's bony arm so hard that he winced. You straighten up, she whispered loudly. Do you hear me? Now there are people down the hall, and their granddaughter was just in a fire. They don't understand what's happened to them. She put her hand in the middle of his back to keep him going in the right direction.

You be nice to this lady. She's big and fat. And the people she's with are very strange. And don't you dare stare at them or say anything at all about them. Do you hear me?

He nodded solemnly, unable to say a word. The eyes of his brown hood were rimmed with tears.

Take a deep breath, she said.

The woman from New Jersey gave her son Carl a final push down the hallway toward the narrow waiting corridor, gritting her teeth tighter and tighter as they drew nearer to the monotonous voice of the lady from Tupelo. Then they were there, standing right in front of them.

Hello, said the woman from New Jersey. She smiled carefully. Here I am again. And here's my son, Carl. She put her arm around him.

The people from Tupelo leaned back, leaning away from them. Not all at once. Not quickly. But ever so slowly. And their eyes grew bigger the further away they got. The woman from New Jersey couldn't believe how frankly they stared. Here he is, she said again. This is Carl.

They did not say a word but only sat there, gawking. It confused the woman from New Jersey so that she suddenly felt like she did when she drank more than three cups of coffee before breakfast, like she couldn't figure out what she was thinking, like she couldn't make any sort of decision of any kind. She gave her head a little quick hard shake and pressed ahead, hoping for some response other than the one she was getting.

Carl, she said, very politely, this lady is from Tupelo. That's in the state of Mississippi. Her granddaughter was in a fire. Yesterday. Yesterday? Is that correct?

The fat lady didn't answer. She kept squeezing and turning the dirty Kleenex in her hand.

You going to let him go out with that thing on? she said suddenly.

The woman from New Jersey winced. This is his mask. She tried to whisper, thinking that this was really something she didn't want discussed in front of Carl, but he was peering up at her and not missing a word.

Don't you remember that I was telling you about it? she asked them. Your granddaughter will wear one of these too.

Their eyes roamed over every inch of Carl's body, from the top of the brown hood to the flat red emptiness of his missing ear to the piece of matted hair that stuck out from behind the mask to the splints that covered his hands, down over all his new clothes.

The woman from New Jersey watched them stare at Carl with a sort of fascination, looking therein for some understanding. And then she had it. She was suddenly absolutely certain that they did not understand about the mask. That was it. It was just the mask that frightened them. It was the mask that horrified them. Not Carl. Her stomach was filled with excitement. Though perhaps it wasn't the right time to do it, nor really the right place, neither was it anyone's business—especially the business of the people from Tupelo—she felt uncannily certain that they ought to see the face beneath the mask. Then they would see how good he looked. And they wouldn't be frightened anymore. They would stop staring and she and Carl could go on.

Her fingers reached up toward the back of Carl's head, shaking, to the velcro closing at the back of the hood, and pulled it open hard. It startled the boy and he cried out. She turned him around toward her and said, Ssshhh, ssshhhh, and whispered, I just want to show them your face, how good it looks. And pulled up on the hood and then it was off. She leaned in and looked at him hard.

The boy rubbed his eyes, as if he'd been asleep beneath the mask all that time. The woman from New Jersey brushed his face free of little bits of hair that clung to it and took the edge of her sleeve and tried to dry the sweet sickly smelling sweat off of it. And then turned him around so the people from Tupelo could be reassured, turned him around so they could see him in the full light of the corridor's window.

Now, she said. See how wonderful he looks. Can't you see how wonderful he looks? she said, addressing the wall above their heads, not quite looking into their eyes.

The fat lady sucked in hard.

Gawd, she said.

Why, you can't even imagine how he used to look, said the woman from New Jersey very very quickly. He was beet red. And now he's not. And his skin was so bumpy. But now! See! See how flat his skin is! Her eyes came away from the wall to meet the astounded and uncomprehending glares of the family from Tupelo.

The worthless boyfriend mumbled something to the fat lady.

The woman from New Jersey peered at him. What did he say? she asked the grandmother.

He wants to know what happened to your kid, she said.

The woman from New Jersey screwed up her face in disbelief.

What? she said.

He wants to know what happened to your kid, the fat lady repeated.

What do you mean? said the woman with the brown hair, owl-eyed with rage. He was burned! Everyone in this hospital was burned! Your granddaughter was burned! She's going to look just . . . just like . . .

She searched the whole corridor for a word but there was none anywhere to end that thought with. And Carl was tugging at her skirt, wanting to go on.

Just you wait a minute, said the woman from New Jersey with the brown hair, pushing her son's hand away from her. Just wait a minute, she said. Everybody just wait. She put a strong hand on his shoulder and took a deep breath. I have to say something, she said to him.

She turned to face the family from Tupelo, but even her anger could not force them to look at her. They still stared at her son.

You don't seem to realize what this boy has been through. She pushed her hair back off her face. He's been burned. He almost died. I mean, you haven't seen half of these kids here. Some of them don't even have noses. Some of them have lost their mouths. They're blind. And they can't hear. He looks very good. They can fix . . . they can do plastic surgery. He looks very very good. You just can't see it.

Her eyes were full of tears, she was so mad. This wasn't at all what she had intended to happen. But she couldn't drop it.

Your granddaughter's going to . . . she's going to be . . .

She bit her lip. She pushed her fingers into her eyes to try to make the tears go back. But it was no use. The people from Tupelo sat with their mouths open while she cried and Carl cried and the hot Galveston sun glared down with equal lack of sympathy on them all.

The woman from New Jersey finally composed herself somewhat, at least enough to take a long look at the ragged family from Tupelo, squinting at them through her tears as if they and not the sun outside caused the heat and the glare. She blinked again and again, but what she saw there was harder to bear than the hot sun ever would be. No longer the bloated grandmother or the pink slippers or the gray vacant faces of the lady's daughter and her daughter's worthless boyfriend, but now only the reflection of her son in their eyes.

Her stomach gave way, a deep dropping down of her bowels that opened to hunger and emptiness and caused her to tremble. She turned to look at her son, to look at what had so horrified them and was able, finally, to see him.

The left side of her boy's face was a flaming red. The skin there was hard and shiny and unnatural, wrinkled like the bottom of a riverbed when the water has dried up off it. His left eye was drawn down by the contracting of that skin nearly half an eyeball below his right. The left side of his lip was swollen up, frozen in an ugly sneer. That side of his head mocked the other, the right side perfect and freckled and unblemished, the left side having slid beneath it, like mud on the side of a mountain. Dull tufts of hair clung to his scalp. His ear was gone.

The woman from New Jersey slumped down in the chair she had occupied earlier in the afternoon. Oh God, she said.

Lord have mercy, said the lady from Tupelo.

Carl came and sat down next to his mother, tugging on her sleeve, but she was too stunned to move.

The worthless boyfriend lit up another cigarette, then leaned over and said something to the fat lady from Tupelo. She mumbled a reply and he answered and the fat lady's daughter acquiesced with a nod. The woman from New Jersey watched their conferring with only half her attention and waited to hear if it would mean anything to her.

The fat lady from Tupelo turned in her direction. He says you need something to cover yourself with, she said.

What? said the woman from New Jersey, dully. She studied them, trying to make out what it was they meant.

Yeah, said the fat lady. You can't go out there without something to cover you. Because it's going to be hot, she drawled. It's going to be hotter here than it ever was in New Jersey.

Although the woman from New Jersey could not make sense of what the Tupelo people thought she needed, she realized that the suggestion was made without malice of any kind.

I always cover myself, the fat lady went on. Keeps me from the sun.

There was a leaning forward of the fat lady's daughter, then a shuffling around with her hand on the floor. She brought up the ragged black taffeta umbrella. She handed it over her mother's stomach to the outstretched hand of the worthless boyfriend and then he, cigarette in mouth, eyes narrowed against the smoke, pushed it up its handle until it opened, limp and spokeless in places, but still serviceable. He passed it back to his girlfriend's mother and she took it and held it out toward the woman from New Jersey.

This'll cover you good, said the fat lady, almost tenderly. It'll cover both you and him.

The woman from New Jersey blinked. I can't take that from you, she said.

Well, you better, said the fat lady. We're the only ones here that got one.

The woman from New Jersey could not move. She could not even imagine touching the black umbrella that the fat lady in her own way held out so graciously toward her.

And the two of them would have hung suspended there a long time, held by the one's insistence to give and the other's inability to accept the gift, only the boy stepped forward finally and took the ragged covering from the Tupelo lady. Thank you, he said carefully.

He picked up his mask where it lay on his mother's lap and got the purse that sat beside the chair she had slumped into. He pulled at her hand to indicate that it was time they should set out and she obeyed, rising up and letting him lead her out and away from the narrow waiting corridor, away from the fat lady from Tupelo and her daughter and the daughter's worthless boyfriend. And then he brought her down to wait at the end of the hall in front of the elevator, even though he knew that she never took the elevator if she could help it.

A Spell without Books

PAT ELLIS TAYLOR

Austin is built on a series of crisscrossing fault lines, the intersections of which cause parts of the city to sag into what might be called "seeps," or "sucks"—places where the earth breathes in and out, sometimes seeping and sometimes sucking, heaving whole populations of students, legislators, construction workers and cosmic travelers in and out of itself at regular seasonal intervals. The largest expulsion comes regularly at the beginning of the summer, when forty-five thousand students leave all at once, stuffing aluminum-tube armchairs and whole bedroom sets, soufflé pans and art easels, textbooks and binders into the Longhorn disposal bins in the alleys, to be scavenged by dumpster divers who take the stuff home to be incorporated into low-income households or peddle it to secondhand stores which can sell some of it back after the great pause of mid-summer, when the outgo stops and the inflow begins and people start getting sucked back into town again. First the heave, then the suck, then the stew and the steam swirling up off of so many bodies, as if the Great Goddess of Liberty perched on top of the state capitol dome is a giant cook stirring up the juicy essences contained in the soupy Austin air along with the bats around her head, using her torch as a spoon.

And it is in late September after the incoming students and professors and travelers have begun to make my bookstore hours busy again that a wisp of a woman blows into the front door, stirred and emotional, while I am sorting books at the counter. My mood at the time is less than cordial, since I have only been in Austin a little over a year and haven't gotten used to the somewhat swirling rhythms of the city, having sucked, so to speak, instead of heaving at the first of the summer when all the city's readers had begun dumping their books at the store, and me somehow at the bottom of the pile when I realized it was time to get out, and by the time I had extricated myself and tried to run out to the country, the foreign lands, Galveston or Disneyland, it was too late, my brain had already begun to boil in the sloughy heat, so that by the end of the summer I had been spending many of my hours in the bookstore basement feeling like the burnt-out scum on the bottom of the Austin Pan of Life.

So this woman is smiling very widely at me and is wringing her hands, and her eyes are wide behind her plastic frames and she says, "Well my name is Carolyn, and my angels have brought me here to see you today. Wow!" She shivers. "Can I give you a hug?"

Just a week before this an ex-Marine lesbian had stepped in back of the counter without warning and had begun to massage my neck while locking both of my arms with the other of hers like a vise and exhorting my stiffness to snap under her pinching and pummeling. So this Carolyn now sees my hesitation at her suggestion of physical contact. "Oh!" she says. "I mean . . . well I just feel that . . . well . . . do you know a woman in New Mexico named Andronica?"

"Oh yes, except that I knew her as Vicky Vandorf when she was still in Tyler."

"Yes, well I met her as I was traveling through the Southwest, and she told me to be sure and get in touch with you when I came to Austin." She turns and looks around the room at the shelves of books, then turns to me again with an excited shrug. And she begins to tell me how she wants to go into a trance for me; in fact, she says that just looking at me, or even standing in the middle of this bookstore not looking at me but just experiencing the total amount of vibes ricocheting off of all the used books, almost makes her want to swoon into her trance state on the spot.

So. A trance medium. Now I do believe that Austin, maybe because of its unique breathing geography or because of its Goddess constantly stirring the stew, is one of the witch capitals of this continent, full of lesbians, practicing witches, goddess worshippers, feminists and entrepreneurs, burnt-out Berkeley street women showing up on Congress Avenue broke drunk and waving wild blonde hair a yard long, and wild girls coming in from the Baptist East or West Texas ranching families, declared defective socially because of too much love for sex and lust for drink and drugs. And some of them live in the city most of the year, but some of them, as I suspect of this little blonde woman, are restless spirits flying from the East to the West Coast of America and only accidentally getting caught up in the Austin Suck for a week or a month or more, long enough to peddle some marijuana or to get laid by some macho/macha Austin poet or cowboy or garage mechanic, whoever might come along with a beard or a certain string of pearls, and they wreak havoc with wives and previous lovers and take jobs and leave them after the first paycheck and hold workshops in tarot divination and massage and altar-making. And at some point in their struggle to lift up again out of the city's currents, many of them come into the bookstore since it is downtown, looking for a way to use its space to their advantage, or to peddle their various services.

"So how much do you charge for one of these trance sessions?" I ask her.

She staggers back and touches her fingers to her throat and opens up her eyes even wider and says, "Oh no, oh no, I don't mean you *pay* me, it's for love for free for the Lord for the sake of Jesus, because I love to go into a trance, because of a *healing* . . ." And she tells me all about the angels, et cetera, et cetera.

So okay. There is a little room nobody uses too much in the store, just a refrigerator in it to keep John-the-Boss's Diet Pepsis cold. It seems to me to be a place where angels might like to congregate, so I tell her she can go into a trance for me in that room when I get off work.

She rolls her eyes and wrings her hands together, alternately thanking me and Jesus. She goes off then, but that evening just when I am turning the key to the cashbox over to John, who is working the next shift, she comes in the door again. And the two of us go into the little room and shut the door so that the angels can talk as loud as they might want to without disturbing the customers browsing in literary classics on the other side of the wall.

Carolyn sits on one of the chairs, crosses her legs underneath her, and closes her eyes. Little shivers start running up and down her arms and spine, little jerks and starts, and she begins sighing and going "ooooh, ooooh, ooooh," holding her hands palms up, still smiling big and happy, while I am sitting opposite her in another chair trying to get comfortable. Then she starts talking.

I don't know if it is an angel talking. She says her name is Ruth. She has the blonde woman's voice but she doesn't use adverbs or adjectives very well. I figure it might be Ruth in the Bible and try to remember if Ruth was the daughter-in-law of Naomi or vice versa, although I do remember they both were women who had to support themselves gleaning in the fields of rich men, wasn't that the story? Then Ruth stops talking and the room is quiet. The blonde woman opens her eyes and looks at me. I am crying.

I think Ruth has just told me to quit my job. She has said that I should be writing my own stories instead of selling schlock for four dollars an hour. What's a brilliant woman such as yourself doing wasting away in a

Slumpful of paperbacks? She didn't exactly put it in so many words, but I got the message.

Carolyn hugs me on her way out the door and tells me that Jesus loves me, as do Ruth and the other angels. That evening I write my letter of resignation to John-the-Boss.

"Are you sure the angels told you to quit your job?" Chuck-my-husband asks me that, always the skeptic.

"Yes," I tell him. "*I am sure.*"

Chuck is afraid that I will stay at home, like women are sometimes prone to do, and live off of him, that I will ask him to pay my share of the rent, that I will steal dollar bills out of his pants in order to buy cereal and milk in the morning for my kids, that he will always have to pay for tickets to the movies when we go out, that I will get to stay in bed all day and write stories while he goes out and busts his ass working because the angels have given me permission to glean in the rich men's fields. He reminds me, in so many words, that he is not a rich man. He is lying in the middle of the foam pad on the floor we call a bed. He is looking out over his glasses alternately reading Adam Smith on how to make money and writing a poem on the back inside cover. I crouch down by him and put my hands on his beard and my nose on his nose.

"Honey," I tell him, "I know you are worried that I am going to ask you to start supporting me. But you shouldn't worry." I pat his beard. I look straight into his eyes.

(I might *borrow* a little money. Later on. In a few weeks after the rejection slips start flurrying in, after I have sent the stories out and they've come back in and I'm sitting at home living on quarters I find rearranging the clothes washer and dryer in the laundry room.)

He says he's not worried. He knows I'm not like other women. Like his ex-wife. Or like all of his friends' girlfriends. Or like the young girls in his freshman composition classes looking for some Walking Money to take them out on the town for the rest of their lives.

I kiss his nose. He kisses my mouth.

Fall is falling above our heads outside the bedroom window.

I walk out the door into flashing flowers, the sun isn't too hot anymore, the heat of it now fallen into the grass and flowers on the freeway access roads where I begin to walk skip hum sing poeticize across Austin to the squirrels and to myself without the weight of employment. Trees like embers, leaves flurrying sparks and wind coming in through the downtown buildings, and I'm strolling up and down Sixth Street picking weeds out of the parkways and chewing the stems of grass for natural sugar to rush in and out of my aerolic spaces, higher than fine Turkish hashish and lighter than mushroom spores from it being fall in Austin and me not having employment of any kind except my own work—which is being a poet, that is, singing, dancing, reciting, making up and telling stories, and generally enjoying life.

Now I wouldn't have believed that being a poet was really my work if the angel Ruth hadn't told me herself, but after the little blonde Carolyn went into that trance and Ruth was so firm with me about what a great poetic genius I was and how it was just a lowdown shame that I had to work for a living like everybody else, then I began to believe that being a poet was my calling.

So Brook-my-daughter comes home from school, and I've just got finished hiking about eight miles across town picking up acorns the squirrels left behind to take them home to see if I can cook them up—leach out the tannic acid like the Tonkawa women used to do and grind them up into acorn meal. I think I will try to make some acorn cookies or some acorn fudge—it seems like good work for a fall afternoon. But when I put my arm around Brook-my-daughter's shoulder, a lie comes out of my mouth. "You can tell your friends," I say, "when they ask you what your mother does for a living, that she is a Free-Lance Writer." I don't tell her poet. I don't tell her poet because poets don't make money. And people who don't make money don't get their rent paid. "I am cooking up these acorns like this," I continue to lie bald-facedly to this daughter, "because I am writing a book about food for psychic development, and this is my research." I show her the handful of acorns that have not yet begun to boil in a pan on the stove. The water is rapidly turning brown and there is a peculiar scorched odor that has begun to fill the kitchen.

I tell her this lie because I am telling myself this lie. I know that I've got to make this fall, these walks, these live oaks with their lightning branches and their little lightning babies bubbling in the pot on the back burner into work of some kind, even though I know when I'm lying to her and to Chuck and to myself and to some man in New York that I promise a manuscript on food for psychic development that THE ACORNS IN THE POT ARE ONLY POETRY SHEER POETRY POETRY FOR POETRY WALKING THROUGH AUSTIN AND PICKING UP ACORNS WILL NOT MAKE A DIME . . .

And pretty soon I don't have any money. But at first I don't worry about it too much. I mean after all Ruth the angel said that I didn't have to make money like ordinary people have to, so I figure that somehow this money will just be kind of magically generated. Money will fall from space. My needs will be taken care of. Consider the lilies of the field and so forth and so forth. So I tell Chuck that I'm writing all these free-lance articles for all of these magazines and that way I'm going to make some money. But I figure, since Ruth was so supportive, that the time has come here when I am a well enough established writer that I can write free-lance articles in the style that seems most comfortable to me. So when my friends ask me what I'm working on I say, "Well, I'm writing what *I* want to write about and I'm writing in the style that is *me*."

Now an interview or an essay or an article written in the form of a poem, coming out in long loops and chains of images, seems like a good idea to me. I would certainly read such a poem myself, and there is too much fall in the air anyway, and my head is like dandelion froth, and the words are coming in storms, like water after sudden rain in the creek beds I sometimes walk, and the ideas are tumbling around like the stones on the creek bottoms, so when I come home I scribble it down, I ramble on for pages in a red velvet book Chuck gave me to write in. And I write and drink tea and eat toast with honey and when it rains I spend some time walking in it.

No money comes.

Jack-my-roommate pays me some money for babysitting his baby.

Chuck pays me some money for typing a story for him.

I sell a file cabinet.

Still the wildflowers keep spraying orange flames and the poetry continues to come. One day I find myself reeling down the downtown sidewalks through the bustling secretaries and the executives on lunch breaks, and I have eaten a little bit of mushroom, and the mushroom in my blood is recalling the flight of mushroom spores in the wind to me flown for hundreds of miles and full of voices and animal noises and the talk of birds, and my arms and legs are loose and the poetry comes out of my mouth talking to the buildings the architects who built them the spirits that lurk in them the faces in their windows the corpses buried in their concrete the living dead pacing their hallways the grin of the skull on the dollar the stinking ink, and the poetry rushes and ricochets and I don't care if the people on the sidewalk stare peculiarly, I'm just one of the street folks of Austin myself, one of the growing number of unemployed, and I realize suddenly that I HAVE GOT TO GET A JOB! I HAVE GOT TO GET A JOB!

The roar of the poetry is coming through my blood like a living tornado and I am fumbling for a quarter in my bag, I am standing in the middle of the sidewalk and the poetry is howling but I dig around in the lint and peanut shells and pennies lining the bag's bottom until my fingers grab the right shape and I bring it out like a key like a treasure coin like *the way to my future,* and I hurl myself against the first newsstand I see and put the quarter in the slot and dig out a paper and open it up on the top of the stand to the classified ads.

And the wind of poetry dies down for a minute, and I see myself just for that minute outside of myself—a woman thrown like a leaf against the newsstand, struck with the sudden weightlessness of UNEMPLOY-MENT—that which was light becoming heavy again, that which seemed heavy now lighter from a distance, and so on and so on. And in that little calm moment a realization comes to me: that I can at least wait until I get home to read the want ads, that a woman as desperate as I look—clutching the newspaper and squinting at the fine print while the wind is beginning to whip the pages up and down and whip my skirts around my legs and my hair up into the air and reading ads aloud and muttering names and addresses and salary figures—does not belong out on the streets. She is a vagrant. *She is definitely not working for a living.*

But when I get home, it is the night of the winter solstice and there is a job to do. Instead of reading the newspaper, I light candles on the table. I roll up marijuana. I set out oranges. At midnight I begin to make some braids of whole wheat bread. There are some children in the house and they help me make it. We pound the dough and pull it from one of us to the other. We pat it and stroke it as well as knead it and pummel it. We cover it up and it rises higher than any bread that I have ever been connected with! "Listen, kids," I say. "We are going to stay up and eat this bread, and then we are going to watch the sun come up on the first day of winter."

And we do eat the bread when it's finished, about three o'clock A.M., and it is wonderful bread, it is the lightest most high-rising bread I have ever laid a tongue on and everyone agrees that it is true, the best bread for everyone. But after the bread we fall one after the other into our beds, so that no one is awake when the black sun of the first winter morning comes up, and by the time I wake up the earth has already turned itself inside out like a sock, and I walk into the winter day looking down into the darkling sky instead of up without even knowing it, without realizing yet the sudden change, except that the air has become an underground pool and the sun like a pale yellow fish gliding on its surface with its mouth open or an angel with blonde hair and filmy fins . . .

Tenderhead

HARRYETTE MULLEN

 Saturdays they went to the beauty shop to get their hair fixed. Something was wrong with their hair, so Miss Pearl had to fix it before they could be seen in public. Naps and kinks had to be smoothed, the way the body shop ironed those dents out of the car after Mama got hit by that drunk white lady on Commerce Street.

If it wasn't Miss Pearl, it was Mama at the kitchen range, attacking the rough hair with a hot comb kept for touch-ups at home. On Sunday, they had to dress up for the Lord—and so nobody would say Mama was getting slack. Children are a reflection of their parents, and church was full of eyes watching and measuring. Calculating who was rising or falling, who was sitting pretty or barely keeping up. They'd approve of Mimi's shiny, unscuffed patent leather shoes and spotless, unsagging white socks, and Latricia's broad-brim straw hat with pink grosgrain ribbon. They'd award Mama extra points for the girls' white gloves with tiny pearl-like buttons.

Jeanne was proud of her knack for making the kids look special on a tight budget, and she didn't want the overall effect ruined by hair going back. Between the twin demons of perspiration and precipitation, kinky hair straightened with a hot comb was prone to return to its former condition—but Sunday hair had to be smooth and glistening. It was that newly pressed look that showed they'd just been to the beauty shop—sacrificing Saturday cartoons to sit in a spinning chair that Miss Pearl never let them spin in anyway; flinching when hot comb and blue grease met and sizzled on their scalps; Miss Pearl warning Mimi, "Honey, sit still now, before you make my hand slip with this hot comb. Hold your ear down, sweetie pie, so I can get these edges."

Miss Pearl rented space in her shop to two other beauticians: Miss Ruthie, who sipped RC's all day, and Miss Clara, who was the youngest of the three and who preferred to be called a cosmetologist. Miss Clara avoided the words "nappy" and "kinky." She would say, "Darling, your hair has a lot of *texture*." She rarely mentioned a hot comb outright, but spoke of "thermal treatment." In her lexicon, straightened hair never "went back." It "reverted." And, of course, the harsh chemical process that burned the scalp while straightening the hair "permanently" (at least until the next touch-up) was called "relaxing," but Mimi thought the women getting the treatment looked anything but relaxed.

Mimi had noticed that barbershops had plate glass windows, so the barbers and their customers could keep an eye on the happenings out in the street. But beauty shop windows always had curtains drawn, so nobody outside could see the women and girls while the transformation was taking place. Sometimes a white salesman would come into the shop to do business with Miss Pearl. They would stare at his back as he passed, but avert their eyes if he seemed to look at them directly. Best to be under the dryer if a stranger, or even somebody's daddy or husband, came in. A woman caught with kinks exposed might try to disappear behind a copy of *Ebony* or *Sepia,* which made better screens than the smaller *Bronze Thrills* and *Tan Confessions*.

Mimi had made it through first grade without any visits to Miss Pearl's. Mama washed her hair at home, both of them kneeling at the bathtub, Mimi blinking suds out of her eyes. But Jeanne complained that shampooing and rinsing the thick hair twice, then carefully combing the tangles out from ends to roots (with Mimi kicking and yelling the whole time), and finally parting the hair into sections to make four sausage-like braids, was becoming a tiresome ritual.

Besides, as Grandma Clinton said, "She's too old, anyhow, to be running around nappy-headed. She needs to get her hair pressed, like the other girls her age." Mimi had heard that in a few more years she would be "maturing," and this was the reason she had to change her ways, be more ladylike, which, as far as she could tell, meant keeping her skirt down, staying out of trees, and carrying a cute little purse with nothing in it but a stick of spearmint gum and a hanky. And with all of that, the visits to Miss Pearl's were supposed to tame her down, like ten-year-old Latricia, who broke Miss Ruthie's heart with her silent weeping as the big plastic comb tugged at her tangles or the hot metal came uncomfortably close to her scalp.

Miss Pearl usually insisted that Jeanne and her daughters come in first thing on Saturday, before the heavy traffic of the day, so they could tackle those three heads of impossible hair in the first cool freshness of the morning. They all had heavy, coarse, fast-growing hair, each with her own unique pattern of waves, kinks, and plain old naps. Latricia's was just a little too kinkish and thick to be "water wave" hair. Mimi had a weird combination of tangled waves and bushy kinks. Jeanne, in contrast to her mostly wiry, strong, springy hair, had a conspicuous patch of soft baby curls at the back of her head, just above a stubborn "kitchen" of crisp, tight naps.

Each of the ladies would take a head, marveling, as they shampooed and combed out and hot-pressed, at the length and bushiness of the girls' and their mother's hair, and the fierceness of certain kinky patches, which, combined with the tenderheadedness that ran in the family, made the job a challenge. Miss Pearl was sure she had never seen such tough hair together with such tender heads.

Miss Pearl and her associates were all graduates of the Ideal School of Beauty, as Mimi knew, since she had personally inspected their diplomas. When she went around the shop, reading each one, Miss Ruthie joked that their school motto had been "I deal, you deal, we all deal with nappy heads." Their various certificates and licenses hung on the walls, along with glossy magazine pictures of women with glossy hair. Most of the women in the pictures were so light they looked like slightly exotic white women, but a few of them were dark to show that a black-skinned woman with naturally nappy hair could get the same stylish results from hot combs and chemicals. Waves and curls. Feathery bangs and pageboy flips. Hair hanging long and straight or teased into a bouffant.

Each of the ladies had her station, with an adjustable chair for her customers, a mirror, and a small gas heater for the hot comb and curling irons. On Mimi's first visit they had all let her look into their drawers full of combs, brushes, clippers, and hairpins. One wall was lined with plain wooden chairs for women and girls awaiting their turn. A fat vinyl chair with dryer attached figured prominently in a corner. The three ladies tried to stagger their customers so that no one had to wait too long with wet hair before getting to the dryer. They dreaded the occasional head of unruly hair that took half an hour to dry, throwing them off the established rhythm of their work. Yet they were fascinated by Jeanne's and her daughters' "semi-good" hair that managed to grow long and thick, even though it was undeniably nappy.

What a triumph for the beauty shop ladies when all three heads were shining with oil of bergamot and the wild, rough hair was finally pressed down and civilized! Now they were beautiful, with kinks and naps transformed into the sleek and gleaming locks of the magazine pictures. It was most satisfying because their hair was long. How many nappy heads had they transformed only to find the slick hair still woefully short, even after it had been stretched by the pressing. Most of their heads needed curls to give them any style at all. If Miss Pearl did Jeanne's hair, she would just curl the ends under a bit, then part it on the side and comb the hair over one eye. She'd show her the mirror with a grand flourish, saying, "Now tell me, sugarplum, if you don't look just like Veronica Lake!" Seeing them with their straight hair spread around their shoulders was a satisfying reward after all that work. It was the reason the ladies had decided not to charge extra for doing such headstrong hair.

Now, three years later, ten-year-old Mimi often went alone to Miss Pearl's, because Jeanne and Latricia had permanents, which meant more widely spaced appointments. Miss Clara had talked Jeanne into trying a permanent once, and she'd been coming back for touch-ups ever since. At least she only had to come in about once a month instead of every other week. When Latricia turned twelve she had begged to get her hair relaxed too. Jeanne had made her wait until she turned thirteen.

This Saturday Mimi was to be dropped off at Miss Pearl's while Mama took Latricia to buy a dress for her first junior high school dance. Jeanne parked the car at the curb, gave Mimi three dollars for Miss Pearl, and made sure her daughter was inside the shop before starting the engine. Out of the corner of her eye, she noticed two laughing men leaning against another parked car, passing a brown-bagged bottle back and forth between them. One of them seemed to be pointing at the wide, rolling hips of a woman striding barefoot down the sidewalk. Even from a distance, Jeanne knew it was Dot. Her feet must be tough as horse's hooves, and she was nappy as a jaybird. Jeanne, headed in the opposite direction, started the car again for the trip to the new shopping mall.

"Here's my little Tenderhead!" Miss Pearl would greet Mimi now when she arrived on Saturday afternoons. And later, when she was fidgeting under the hot comb, "Try and sit still now, Tenderhead. You just make it harder on both of us with all this wiggling." "Tenderhead" was one of the nicknames given her by the ladies in the shop, because she still squirmed and flinched under the hot iron and yelled when her kinks were being detangled. Sometimes they reproached her for her immaturity in this matter, holding her sister up as an example. Miss Ruthie would say, "Sweetheart, I know for a fact your sister Latricia's just as tenderheaded as you is, but she still could always hold a good head."

Her other nickname was Big Eyes, not only because of her large, dark eyes that were envied for their long, curly lashes, but also because she was curious about people and had never broken her child's habit of staring. It was regarded as a gross sign of disrespect for a child to stare at a grown person, particularly to lock eyes with an adult as she sometimes did. She'd received many a threat from Mama and Grandma Clinton because of that unnerving stare.

There was so much more to see and hear in Miss Pearl's shop when she was dropped off alone these Saturday afternoons with business in full swing. She could read the confession magazines her mama had dismissed as "trash for idle minds." She could listen to the lively gossip, which was plentiful when the shop was full of customers, and stare at the sheepish-looking white salesmen who dropped by with sample cases of beauty supplies. There was another white man with a strange tattoo on his arm of a big snake wrapped around a heart, who came to fill up the soft drink machine with bottles of RC Cola, 7-Up, and Nehi.

Black men hawking produce in battered pickup trucks made a stop at Miss Pearl's to sell fresh corn, snap beans, tomatoes, okra, and water-melon to the beauticians and their customers. Camp Fire Girls and Girl Scouts in neatly starched uniforms, with ribbons on their plaits, and their legs and elbows shined with petroleum jelly, knew they could sell their quota of candy and cookies at Miss Pearl's shop, and many a winning raffle ticket was purchased there. Occasionally someone would come in trying to sell stolen watches or other hot merchandise, but Miss Pearl could always spot a thief and send him packing. Around lunchtime, the ladies would call out to order and someone would arrive with aromatic brown sacks full of hot link sandwiches from Mason's Bar-B-Q, huge cheeseburgers from Big Daddy's, or fried chicken and potato salad plates from Carla's Place. Mimi would have gagged trying to eat around all that hair, but the ladies were unfazed. What did it matter that the oil on their hands was equal parts Crisco and hair grease?

Then there were the famous domino tournaments. The beauticians were too busy to play, but customers waiting for a turn competed with one another—not for money because Miss Pearl allowed no gambling in her shop (not counting the raffle tickets sold for a good cause), but the loser traditionally bought the winner a soda from the soft drink case. That strange woman, Dot, who sometimes came to sell fresh eggs and goat's milk, was said to enjoy a good domino game. Some of the custom-ers complained about her and thought Miss Pearl should keep her out of the shop, but except for known criminals, and a certain spectacularly ob-noxious Jehovah's Witness she had put out after the woman told the ladies they were all sinners condemned to hell, no one was barred from entering. So long as they abided by her rules against cursing, gambling, fighting, or bringing alcohol into the shop, Miss Pearl welcomed everybody into her place—even Dot.

"Ought to be a rule against stinking up the place, Miss Pearl," was Lula Mae's opinion. "I sure would rather listen to the worst cursing than have to smell that funk. Miss Pearl, she make your shop look bad and smell worse."

They said she made her coarse-looking dresses out of flour sacks, but occasionally she was seen in a homemade dress of cheap cotton fabric, always in a bright floral print. Children had composed a jump rope song about her:

> There you go, feet so bare,
> All over town with your nappy hair.
> Wearing a sack and living in a shack,
> If you ain't ugly, tar ain't black.
> Heard your name but I forgot—
> All I remember was it rhyme with snot.

On the last word, the jumper would pinch her nose as if in disgust and dance away from the swinging rope to give someone else a turn. Although they sang this rhyme daily in their play, none of them ever taunted her directly. They all had been taught with belts and paddles and backhand licks to show at least an outward respect toward adults. It was in fact a kind of tribute to her eccentricity that she had inspired a new lyric in their repertoire.

Dot lived alone in her small, unpainted wooden house. Her front yard was a leafy vegetable garden fenced with chicken wire. Along with several beady-eyed hens and one dandyish rooster, she kept a few sturdy goats in her backyard. "Yeah, she smell like a goat, too!" A dark, musky, country smell. The serious underarm and between-legs funk of a grown woman who never bothered with deodorant or perfume or feminine hygiene products. She was neither dainty nor delicate. She took up space. When she sat, her thighs spread. When she walked by, men joked behind her back, "Must be jelly, 'cause jam don't shake like that." If any of them had ever spent a night with her, he surely would have died before admitting it. Their jokes among themselves were intended to sound mock-sexual, since the usual half-joking, half-hopeful sexual banter—which was, after all, a precious part of their days and something to be savored—should not be wasted on a woman like her.

Her appearance was that of a character in a comic strip, buttons popping and seams strained. Flies buzzing around her head like electrons in a chemistry textbook. They lit on her thick arms and she slowly fanned them away, seeming hardly to notice that she had become fly furniture. Perhaps you have seen those full-page color photos in expensive coffee table picture books about Africa. Beautiful men, women, and children, whose faces have the dignity and formality of masks, faces perfectly composed while flies rest lightly on an eyelid or cheek, at the corner of a child's mouth. No one would call Dot beautiful, but she did attract flies.

As Mimi kicked a 4/4 beat against the leg of her hard wooden chair, reading Miss Pearl's stack of old *Jet* magazines, Lula Mae Bishop, enthroned in the shampoo chair awaiting the magic chemicals that would turn her thin black hair a rusty red, was holding forth, hard on Dot's case like white on rice.

"You *know* she don't wear no underwear, the way them titties be flopping when she walk, and the way her dress get caught in her crack 'cause she ain't got no draws on."

Mimi looked up from the bikini-clad model in the *Jet* centerfold, who'd been snapped as a soft breeze blew her long, straight hair across her full but not *too* full lips that curved in a seductive smile. Mimi had been examining the photograph to see if the model's belly button sank in or if it stuck out a little like hers did. The women were talking about the notorious Dot, who lived in the exciting neighborhood where Miss Pearl's was located (along with the Eight Ball Pool Hall, the Pink Flamingo Club, Shorty's Shoeshine Parlor, Carla's Place, Big Daddy's Drive-In, and other establishments with open doors leading to dark interiors she had often tried to peer into as their car passed on the street).

It was Jeanne's old neighborhood and she continued to drive to Miss Pearl's out of loyalty. Once, Miss Pearl had suggested that Jeanne buy goat's milk from Dot when Latricia was found to have an allergy to cow's milk. Jeanne had said, "No, Miss Pearl. I say live and let live, but I don't think I could feel peaceful with myself if I gave my child something from that woman's hands. She doesn't have clean enough habits to suit me."

Mimi remained curious about this woman who raised goats in the city, walked barefoot down paved streets, and never came into Miss Pearl's shop except to play dominoes or sell eggs and milk. Now she was hearing what people thought of Dot for all her strange behavior. Girlie Moore, wincing as the burning lye went to work on her nappy roots, fervently spoke her feelings on the subject: "She don't even bother to try and make herself decent. Just walks out on the street looking any old way. Don't try to fix herself up or nothing. This ain't the country either, but she walk down the middle of a paved city street like she on a dirt road out in the sticks."

"I mean, talk about *colored!* Do the woman ever go to the store and buy real clothes? I ain't never seen her wear nothing but them mammy-made sack dresses. My Lord, the woman's so country she don't *never* straighten her hair. It's a sin and a shame that a full-grown woman can walk around looking so bad all the time," Peaches Johnson complained, her head bent under the teeth of the hot comb, the odor of her singed hair mingling with the harsh alkaline fumes of Girlie's permanent and the sharp smell of Lula Mae's bleach. "Well, it's like they say, you can take folk out of the country, but . . ."

The talk stopped short as the screen door swung open and a heavy, dark, barefooted woman stepped into the shop. Mimi heard Girlie Moore's low whisper, "Speak of the devil." It was true. Dot's scalp had never felt the heat of a straightening comb or curling iron, nor the sting of a lye-based permanent. She had never been dyed, bleached, streaked, tipped, or frosted. Her hair was black and had always been black. It was nappy and had always been nappy. She didn't even braid her hair to make it grow long. Braids on a grown woman could look country too, but at least they were neat. She just let her hair go wild like the brambles in Brer Rabbit's briar patch. She kept it short and nappy, cutting it with the same scissors she used to cut the coarse fabrics of her simple dresses.

"Afternoon, everybody, how you ladies doing?" were Dot's first words. "Ain't nobody playing dominoes today?" The two women waiting to have their hair done looked away pointedly, searching for magazines they suddenly wanted to read. Neither of them cared to play with someone who had just been ranked so low by Lula Mae, Girlie, and Peaches.

Miss Pearl, after returning Dot's greeting, suggested, "Why don't you play with old Big Eyes here? It'll be a while before I get to her head."

"But I don't know how to play dominoes" was Mimi's quick response as she stared up at the substantial figure.

"That's all right, it ain't hard. I'll teach you. We'll play a few warm-up games 'til you got the rules down. Then we can play for a soda, if you can afford to spend a dime."

"I got a dime." Mimi dug into the pocket of her shorts and pulled out the three crumpled dollars her mother had given her, and a dime saved from her allowance. She held out the dime in her hand. "What about you, ma'am?" She was suspicious. The woman carried no purse and the dress she wore had no pockets that she could see—and obviously she didn't have a dime in her shoe. Her eyes scanned the woman from head to foot and then returned to stare at the uncouth hair. The smell of the woman's body was strong, but not offensive to her. Mimi thought she smelled like damp earth and salty sweat, with something else mixed in: a furtive smell that reminded her of whispers behind a closed door.

Dot laughed until her whole body jiggled. "Big Eyes sharp, ain't she? I can tell she gonna learn this game fast." She eased into a chair at the scarred wooden table with the dominoes on it and started turning them all face down. "Hey, come on, Big Eyes! Pull up your chair so we can get this game started." Mimi didn't budge as Dot began divvying up the dominoes. Finally, when half were in front of her and the other half pushed to the opposite side of the table, Dot cast an amused glance at the girl. "Oh yeah, that's right. You wanna be sure I got my dime." Then she reached down into the front of her dress and pulled from the cleavage of her huge breasts a knotted handkerchief, which she untied to show a few dollars folded into a square and a handful of change. "There, you see. So—you gonna play or not?" She tied the money back in the handkerchief, and returned it to its hiding place as Mimi pulled up her chair.

In no time at all Mimi was slapping the dominoes down hard, just like she'd been playing all her life. "Look at my girl," Miss Pearl chuckled. "She really getting into this game. I just hope she gonna be ready to stop when I have to get to work on that tender head of hers."

After two warm-up games, with Dot coaching her so she won each time, she wanted to play for the soda. Dot grinned and said, "You sure you ready now? 'Cause I'm really thirsty by this time."

Dot played to win, using strategy not only to get rid of her dominoes fast, but also to block potential moves that Mimi might make. This was the part of the game that took experience. Mimi had thought it was simply a matter of matching sets, like in math class. She was so stunned when the game was suddenly over and she still had lots of dominoes left that her eyes filled instantly with tears.

"Let me see now, what kind of soda I want. I can't make up my mind between a orange or a grape." Dot's voice sounded loud and cruel. Mimi felt she'd been taken advantage of, but Dot exhibited no shame. "What would you pick, Big Eyes? I'll let you buy me what you like, since it's your treat. Just go ahead and put your dime in the machine and bring me my nice cool drank, if you please."

Half-blind with the hot tears brimming in her eyes, Mimi went to the drink cooler, found the coin slot and heard her dime fall in. She watched her hand emerge with a Nehi grape. She had always loved drinking them and then looking in the mirror to see her purple tongue.

"Oh, and while you're there, would you mind opening it for me?"

Mimi handed her the cold, moist bottle. Dot's calloused palm felt rough against her fingers as the woman took the Nehi and set it down on the table. For the first time, Dot appeared to notice her distress. "My goodness, look at this. Has Dot hurt your little feelings?" She seemed genuinely concerned. "You look like you gonna bust out cryin' any minute now." Not the most sensitive remark, but Mimi held the tears in her eyes, not yet wiping them, as she waited for some sort of apology. Dot leaned back in her chair, as Mimi stared at her.

"I thought you was a big girl. Didn't know I was playing with a *baby*." With that Mimi was beside herself. The tears she couldn't hold back any longer scalded her eyes and cheeks. She was shaking with anger at the humiliating insult.

"Oh Lord, see I done made this baby cry. What I'm gonna do now?" Dot looked around at the women in the shop, who seemed determined to be silent witnesses to the whole transaction between her and the child. Despite the malevolent gleam in the woman's eye, no one intervened. All seemed preoccupied with their work, or the magazines they were reading.

"Baby, maybe it was wrong of me to beat you at the game and take your dime and leave you with nothing to drank. It might've been unkind of me to do that." Mimi wiped her tears with the back of her hand and sniffled, looking up hopefully. At last the woman seemed to recognize the injustice she had committed against a mere child. Now she would tell her she was sorry. Indeed, as if to make reparation, Dot was already reaching into the front of her dress again, as she continued speaking.

"Since you was nice enough to go ahead and treat me, I guess I might as well get you something to drank, especially if it'll make you feel better." So saying, she plopped out of her dress a melon-sized breast, which she cradled and bounced in her palms with a maliciously amused leer at the girl, whose eyes had widened with shock. "Yeah, here's what you need. A nice fat titty so the baby can git some titty milk." Mimi was lost. Her whole body crumpled as she hid her face in both hands, her breath coming in jagged sobs. "If you thirsty, here it is. I just hate to see a baby cry."

At last Miss Pearl broke in. "That's enough, Dot girl. You best go on home now. I got to do this child's head." She hurried Peaches Johnson out of her chair and beckoned to Mimi, who now wept silently.

When her mother returned to pick her up, instead of the usual plain braids Mimi had the big-girl curls she'd always been denied. "Don't worry, sugar," Miss Pearl assured Jeanne. "I didn't charge a thing for the curls. I just threw 'em in 'cause for the first time since she been getting her hair fixed, Mimi sat still in the chair and held a good head."

The Summer My Uncle Came Home from the War

SANDRA SCOFIELD

 The night before our trip, my grandmother comes to say good-bye. She comes straight from the mill in her work clothes; head to toe, she is dusted white with flour.

"You shouldn't be working tonight," she says to my mother. She darts a look down the hall. My father is singing in the bathroom. "You should be resting up."

My mother is dressed for her job—her most recent job—as a waitress in an Italian restaurant. She wears a scoop-neck red blouse and a very short black skirt over red panties, like an ice skater. Her legs, sticking out from red sateen, are very white. "Every little bit helps," she says lightly, without turning around. She is cooking an egg at the stove and her back is to my grandmother and me at the kitchen table. I've just learned to play solitaire, and in the silences I slap my cards down on the formica loudly, so they won't think I am paying attention.

"To think what you're spending on this trip—" my grandmother starts, and then trails off. She can't believe we are really going off with new terry cloth seat covers and fancy Texas outfits for my sister Faith and me (hats, boots, fringed jackets). Going off like we had money to spend, when my Aunt Opal's husband Thatch could get my father a job in West Texas, in the oil fields. I've heard this, in snatches, for months. My father could go out there and rent a room and get ahead. My mother and sister and I could go back to my grandmother's. I wish like crazy that we would; this isn't home. There isn't even grass in the yards, and silverfish leave tracks on the wall by my bed.

The day we moved here my grandmother said it was throwing away money to go live by a Pig Stand drive-in, in a housing project for mostly Mexicans. She has a perfectly good house with two bedrooms and cots and a couch that lets down. My father went in and out of her house that day, carrying boxes of our belongings to the car, brushing by her on the steps without ever looking at her or saying anything. She stood and watched, with her arms rigid at her sides, until my mother sent me and my sister out to sit in our old car. My father came out and said, "Well, that's it," and went straight to the car and got in. "It's my life," I heard my mother say, and then she came down to the car too. When she slammed the car door, it was like my grandmother got shot at. She ran down and jumped onto the running board of our Chevy, on my father's side, and grabbed his shoulder through the open window. "What have you got to be so proud about?" she yelled. "When have you had a better job than Thatch can get you? When have you ever been able to feed your kids?" My father started the car and backed up slowly, while my grandmother hung on, screaming. By then Faith was squalling and I was crying out to my grandmother, "Mommy! Mommy!" while my mother slapped at me to keep quiet, and my grandmother yelled, "They oughta have better!" and hit at my father while he pushed her hands away.

My mother eats her scrambled egg from a teacup, standing up. She could eat at the restaurant but tomato sauce makes her belch. She acts like she doesn't have any idea what my grandmother is talking about. My mother's been working since spring, taking codeine and aspirin when her head hurts, so we could save up and go. She didn't say anything, not even to me, until one Sunday at my great-grandparents' farm, at dinner. My grandmother had just read a letter from my Uncle Poke in Korea, and my Aunt Opal was singing softly and rocking her baby, and my mother said, ever so casual, that we were going to Ohio right away, to see the Widemars. Opal looked like she might cry; she was counting on taking Faith out to Big Spring for the rest of the summer. My grandmother said, "First I heard," in a weak little voice, to no one, really, and went out the back door, down toward the chicken house. I knew just how she felt. In a while she came back in to do dishes and play dominoes, the same as any other Sunday, like nothing was wrong.

"Charlie's got stuff to do with the car," my mother says, before my grandmother can ask why he's not working tonight and my mother is.

"You don't have any business working on your feet," my grand-mother says.

"*You* do it." My mother's chin goes up.

"I'm stronger. The work I've done would kill you. I spent a whole summer under a tree dipping water on you, the year you were two; I was afraid that fever would blind you or kill you or make you go crazy."

"I'm not an invalid." My mother reaches up with her thumb and turns it upside down to press on the top of her nose, between her eyes. This time last year she was in the hospital, "sick and tired," my grandmother told me. I never thought to ask my father. Sick is sick.

"You don't know what it was like, cooking for a railroad gang in the Depression after your papa died. Six dozen biscuits at a whack—"

Mother knows all this by heart. "Well, now you've got a union job," she says, looking right at my grandmother.

"What's so important about Ohio all of a sudden?"

"Come on, Mother. You remember what it was like when I lived up there. You weren't five months waiting to come and see us. Well, Charlie hasn't seen his own folks in four years. Last time they saw Faith, she was barely crawling."

"You gave me two days' notice and you were gone," my grandmother says with a quaver in her voice. I can see it riles my mother, but she turns back to put soup on the stove and crackers on the counter for our supper. At my grandmother's house we had mashed potatoes every night, and chops, and pickle relish.

My father comes down the hall in his green work pants, barefoot and bare-chested. He and my sister are the stocky ones. His arms are big and fleshy at the top and short in the forearm. He has a crew cut and a chin flat at the bottom, squaring his head. Beside him, my mother looks beautiful and wispy. She's so frail and feminine (instead of skinny and knotty like me). I have her copper hair, the way it was before the time she got sick and it went flat like a cooking pot and fell out in hunks from her head and all her eyebrows and lashes.

My father sits on the couch and douses his toes with cotton balls he has dipped in alcohol. With nobody talking, the noises in the room compete: my father's nail clippers, my mother bumping things around on the counter, my cards slapping the table. I jump up and throw my arms around my grandmother from behind. "If you want to bathe here, I'll scrub your back," I offer, and she reaches up and grabs my hands. I can tell she won't do it, because my father is in the house. My mother says, in a quick, loud voice, "I need to get to work double-quick, Charlie," and my father stands, making a noise as he does that comes from his belly and sounds stiff and gruff as dry grass. "You go get Faith," my mother snaps like it's not the first time she's said it. While I go next door to Immaculata's (where my sister plays most all day long), I know she says something to my grandmother she doesn't want me to hear. I don't think it's because I'm only nine. I think it's because she's afraid I'll take my grandmother's side.

When I come back with Faith, my parents are gone.

After we've had supper and my grandmother has done the dishes, she tells me to walk her to her car. My father is down in the bedroom listening to "People Are Funny."

"I got you some things for the trip," my grandmother says. These things turn out to be lemon drops and candy corn and coloring books with crayons. There are some postcards too, already addressed back to her. "There's something else," she says. Her eyes move around, like she can't focus in the dusk. She gets something out of the glove compartment, a little purse. "I brought some money," she says. "For emergencies. It's a trust. Do you know what that is?"

"Trust? Believing something?"

"With money it means something special. It means you hold onto it and don't be careless." I don't know anything to say. "If nothing goes wrong," she goes on, "you can just bring it back, and nobody needs to know about it." She looks very determined, the way she looks when she says she's doing what she has to, like taking her dog Tiny to be put to sleep, or paying bills other people ran up. It doesn't seem to bother her that I don't talk. She breathes noisily and says, "Your mother has planned this trip against the bone, as if things don't go wrong, when they always do." My grandmother has reason to believe this. A team of horses drove their broken hame right through her father's chest when she was twelve. My mother's father rolled off a railroad bridge in 1931, like a gumdrop off a table. (There are missing men all over the place. Dead or not, they take the blame, and make you wonder about men in general.) My grandmother puts the purse in my hand. "This way they won't have to call and ask. And I won't worry, because I'll know you have it."

"I'll be careful," I say. Suddenly it is thrilling. Only later, in bed, do I wonder what my mother would think if she knew I kept secrets with my grandmother and not with her.

"You have a good time," my grandmother says. The way it comes out, I don't think she means it. I can tell she doesn't think a good time is what is going to happen. It makes me wonder if a good time is what we're going for.

I don't understand all the things that go wrong with my mother and make her sick, but I know about her headaches. Sometimes one comes on her in the dark and I wake to hear her whimper. Sometimes it comes like a snake through grass. When she hurts, we can't shut doors or flush the toilet. I move like a cat. She lies on her bed with her head straight down in the pillows; I don't know how she breathes.

I know too that my mother has a wounded heart, because she has told me so, and for it she cries another way, sobbing and angry. She weeps for her brother Poke, who lied to join the army at sixteen. She weeps for things that might have happened and did not: a boy she loved in school who hung himself in a barn; the stardom she might have found in Hollywood; the nun she might have become if she had been Catholic early on. She weeps for the spy Ethel Rosenberg, though I've never understood quite why. The Sunday after the Rosenbergs were executed, my mother lay on my great-grandmother's bed at the farm, with a wet rag over her face, until dinner. She had written Mrs. Rosenberg a letter in the spring and had shown me the envelope before she sandwiched it between two bills so the postman wouldn't notice. I knew why she was sick that hot summer Sunday, and I wanted her to explain to me what spies did, to have to die. I stood close against the bed and asked her. She moaned and turned her face to the inside wall, toward a paper field of buttercups on cream, browned by age like something baking. Back in the kitchen I heard my grandmother say, "She'll have to snap out of it. It's not like they were kin." I knew she meant my mother. They look after her when she's around—her mother and sister—and talk about her when she isn't. Being sick costs money, I've heard them say; besides that, my mother makes them cry. She talks about life as lost opportunity; she says that God plays favorites. She says things might still work out for me. The difference in our ages is a gulf between us, and I am on the better side.

In an Arkansas park, we lie sprawled beneath a tree. All around us are the remains of our lunch. My mother lies with her head in my father's lap while he drinks beer from a cold brown bottle. I find a softball in the grass and roll it back and forth with Faith to make my mother happy. When I look back over my shoulder to see if she has noticed, I see my father bending to kiss her on the lips. She pulls away and sits up, fluffing her hair out and shaking it. She washed it in the morning before we left our room, and all day she lets the air in under. She used to have such thick hair.

At night I lie in bed and hear my mother say my name. I don't answer. "They're both asleep, the sweeties," she says. She and my father laugh and whisper. Bedclothes rustle. My mother sighs.

The next day we see a two-headed calf. My mother buys a newspaper and reads it out loud in the car. "Damn fools," she mutters. She shakes her head and says, "Hysteria! That's all it is." My father says, "Let up, Laura, this is vacation." When my mother turns to glare at him, I see her cheeks splotched pink, and tears brimming in her eyes.

The day before we get to Ohio, my first headache arrives as something grand, to make me weep and tremble in the car. My father hurries to find us a place to stop, though it is early in the day and he wanted to drive straight through. I crawl up on the bed and cry. My father takes Faith out somewhere, and my mother stays behind to lay wet rags across my forehead. After a while I don't care about anything, not even the pain. I have found its center, and from inside I understand that it is my own and not my mother's. My mother sees this, I guess. I think I see her smile when I hurt the most.

Because my father's parents live on a farm in Ohio, I think I know what to expect. I am used to summer Sundays at my great-grandparents' farm, where puffs of red dust line my nose, and I run barefoot until I've burned flat wet blisters, like lima beans, on the balls of my feet. The Widemar place is another country. Rolling hills fill the horizon, and houses are built with basements. Just inside my grandparents' house a staircase curves down to a banister with a beveled post; the steps are carpeted. Outside, rows of apple and nut trees stand in lines like soldiers behind the house, and to the side, a neighbor's field of barley is going from green to golden. My grandmother raises vegetables, but my grandfather, no farmer at all, is a railroad clerk in town. One afternoon he takes me on his little tractor, for a ride. Down a corridor in the trees we go, toward the place at the end where they seem to come together and then widen at your approach. I try to tell Grandfather how different his place is from the Oklahoma farm, with its wobbling vistas of yellow wheat and red dirt. He shakes his head and says nothing. He doesn't understand why a person would want that. He doesn't know what keeps his son in Texas, which he calls "the South."

More remarkable than the shape of the land and the tidiness of my grandparents' lives is the attitude, in this his mother's house, toward my father. Grandmother serves, and heaps my father's plates so full they ooze over the edge like mud from a road rut. She tucks her son's collar, frowning as she inspects it. She "remembers" some shirts she bought for his father that "turned out" too big. She gathers up his tee shirts and boils them in a stewpot with blueing. She never looks my mother in the eye.

I watch, and think of the days we eat boiled eggs and buttered bread at home. Sometimes everything we own is dirty before my mother drags it off to wash. My father never complains. Sometimes carpenter, sometimes cabdriver, he has abandoned the college classes my mother pushed him to attend, and on free days he sells Watkins vanilla door to door. Yet I have seen my mother come upon him in his chair and skitter her fingers across his collarbones and rest them in the flesh of his shoulders. I have heard her coo, the sound of a mother, or a wife.

My father finds chores to do, or goes with his father to town. Faith follows Grandmother around all day, and my mother and I are left to fill the days as best we can. I find piles of old magazines in the musty basement, and a daybed with a chenille spread. I take my mother down to show her. She chooses half a dozen magazines to take upstairs. "You okay?" she asks at the foot of the stairs, so lazily I wonder how she will climb them.

At supper my father and his father talk politics while my mother sits neutral and silent, toying with her food. Grandmother sits like something made of hardwood, her hair wound in braids that strain the flesh along her hairline. Grandfather thinks we should have blown North Korea to hell and back. "Damned Commies," he says. "They'll be over here next."

I look to see how my mother is reacting. I know this skirts topics on which she disagrees with everyone she knows. She raises her chin in a defiant pose; my father sees, and clears his throat. Suddenly it seems we are all looking at my mother. She bites her lip and refuses dessert. After that, she never speaks at meals. When my grandfather runs down, there is only the sound of forks on china, my father chewing, and sometimes Faith's silly chatter. Pale-haired and fat in the arms, my sister does no wrong here.

My mother and I walk in the apple grove, moving through the sticky heat like catfish in mud. She tells me about the letter. "I didn't want her to die thinking nobody cared," she says. "I could see her in prison, staring out from behind bars, locked up because of some foolishness of her husband's." She stops to run her fingers over a bit of bark, light as a spider. "Oh, Lucy," she says, "that's what loving does—it wraps you up in someone else's business." Her nose trembles like a rabbit's. She wipes it with the hem of her skirt.

My father's sister, Roseanne, lives in Washington, D.C., with her husband—a state trooper—and their three boys. We go to see them, traveling in my grandparents' nice big Buick. Faith rides in front with the men; I sit stiffly between the two women in the back, who never look at one another. When we stop at a spindly house with a sign that says ROOMS, my mother says she's too tired to eat, and I stay behind too, hungry as I am, to be with her. As soon as we are alone she says she isn't tired at all. "I couldn't eat another meal looking at their miserable stuffy faces," she says.

She moves to the stool in front of the dresser and begins brushing her hair. I see unhappiness creeping across her gaze, and I wonder how to cheer her up, but she stands up unprovoked and says brightly, "You sit down instead!" She purses her lips in disapproval as she draws the brush down through my hair. My grandmother gave me a permanent for the trip, and my hair frizzed. "I don't know why Mother did this," my mother says.

I miss my grandmother. "She wanted me to look my best."

"I'm sure she did, sugarplum," my mother soothes; her antennae are out and there are to be no conflicting loyalties for now. She parts my hair and plaits short braids. Pieces of broken hair escape and stick out, but it is off my neck and I like it.

"Let me do yours," I beg. I am gentle as I can be, seeing how thin my mother's hair is at the crown. In the mirror she watches my face, and I look at hers. Caught, we laugh. She takes the brush and scoots over, patting the stool to make a place for me. Side by side we study ourselves in the mirror. I see how much like her I am, and not like anyone else. Surely not like my father, who is thick in the neck and ears. I see the slightly exotic planes of my mother's cheeks, and my own—a half-Chickasaw Indian, somewhere on her father's side? I turn and put my arms up around my mother's neck. She croons something about sticking together. "I wanted them to see that he's all right," she sighs, pushing at me to get up. The trip has been a trial for her. I wish I knew what I could do to make it better. I want to be my mother's reason to keep at it, to believe in the future. How can life go on if you don't think it's worth living?

Once we lived in Ohio but I remember nothing of it. If my mother went away (and she has before) I might forget her too. Or she me. It comforts me to think about Mrs. Rosenberg. My mother wrote her. She would never lose touch with me.

I sit at a picnic table in my Aunt Roseanne's yard, drawing trees.

Uncle Matt (as I've been told to call him) is playing gin rummy with my mother. Their voices slap at one another like cards on the table.

"I'll have you now!"

"Ha!"

"You can't weasel out of it."

"You're no cardplayer, Laura, you're just having a run of luck. I'll win in the end."

"Mmmph," my mother says. Her face is a little sunburned and she is enjoying herself. She lays her last cards on the low glass table between her and Uncle Matt and crows triumphantly. "Look at that, big shot!" I am at an angle behind my mother, and I see Uncle Matt's face as he takes in her glee. It is the look of boys who have made baskets over the heads of taller boys; I don't understand why he should be happy too.

My mother wears a backless halter top she has made by twisting two big squares of cloth together at the neck and in the front. The material is a bright red-and-white check, and the red is picked up by her wide-legged, cuffed shorts. She sits with one shoulder higher than the other, leaning the other arm forward on her knee.

Uncle Matt is Italian and quite dark, with lots of hair on his chest, and on his shoulders too. It took me all the first day to get used to his hairiness. I couldn't stop staring at him, even though I thought he was ugly. He's sour and growly to everyone but my mother. I'm sure he doesn't even remember my name. When the hamburgers were done last night he jabbed a finger in the air and said, "You, come get one."

We have all piled into two cars to see the Smithsonian and the White House, the Lincoln Memorial, and a cemetery. Uncle Matt hasn't left the place. He stays outside all day drinking beer. He moves his lawn chair around to stay in the shade. When the sun sets he starts the barbecue.

"Be a good sport now," my mother says as Uncle Matt gathers the cards and lines them up with a sharp rap-rap-rap against the tabletop. "You pay up."

"I don't remember, Laura, that we set any stakes."

"Well, that's why I get to say what they are now. I won, didn't I?"

Uncle Matt smiles. "Try me," he says.

Mother laughs. "I in-sist; I deee-mand—" Her voice is thick and fakey-southern, not Texan at all. All my father's relatives think it's the same thing. "I com—mand you to give me a beer!" She laughs again. The beers are in a cooler an arm's reach away from my uncle.

Uncle Matt says, "I guess I don't have much choice." He leans over, cocking his chair to one side, and takes the beer out of the cooler. Very slowly, he reaches to the ground on the other side of his chair, looking at my mother all the while, and his hand comes down right on the opener. He holds the bottle just above his belly button and opens it. My mother leans back in *her* chair, tilting it, holding herself steady with her bare feet on the edge of the table. She has painted her toenails red to match her shorts. She hasn't been sick any of the three days we've been here.

Uncle Matt sets the bottle down on the edge of the table, near him.

"Oh, I can't reach that!" my mother warbles.

Uncle Matt puts his bare foot up on the table and slowly nudges the bottle across the table, a little past center, to my mother's side.

I think she ought to tell him straight out to hand her the beer. I think the way he has pushed it over isn't very nice. She bends down on both elbows on the table, her chin in her hands, and waits. Uncle Matt, looking about to laugh, gets up slow as sludge and comes around the table and picks up the beer. He picks it up by the top of the neck and dangles it in front of my mother's face. She reaches up and pulls the bottle down against her cheek, so cool I can almost feel it myself. Uncle Matt turns around, toward the back door, and when he does he sees me staring. I am scared to death in the two seconds it takes him to reach me. "Watch your mother while I go in the house," he says. "Don't let her stack the deck."

I watch him go inside. Aunt Roseanne is standing on the step with her arms crossed, leaning against the door. She steps aside neatly to let him in. Then she looks straight at me, her mouth all prissy. "Mind what he says," she tells me, and slams the screen door, going in.

On the steps of my aunt's moldy basement, I hear my mother's voice. "Don't be coy, Matt. Neither of us gives a damn about the others." Roseanne has sent Matt down to the basement for beer and pop. "See if there's a bottle of rosé," she called to him. My mother was standing near the back door. "I don't think he heard that," she said pleasantly. She followed Uncle Matt, and I followed her.

I can see her white throat, her flat breasts above and between the checked straps. My uncle runs his hand down the side of her throat and onto her breasts. She sucks air in, raspy and long, filling up with air like someone going to the bottom of a pool. I crouch on an upper step in the dark. I see his hand go around her, to her bottom, while the other slides down the front of her like butter on something hot. I run outside.

I sleep in a tiny room piled with books and boxes. In the night I get up to go to the bathroom, and almost scream when a door opens right in front of me and there is Uncle Matt beside me. He takes a step to block my way to the bathroom. Sleepy and confused, I stare up at him and wait. He grins and bends closer, as if to study something in my eye. Instead he reaches over and tucks a straggly hair behind my ear. His touch frightens me, though my sleeping parents are only a few steps away.

"Gonna look just like your sweet mama, ain't you?" he whispers.

"I gotta go," I squeak.

"You're just a little twig off her tree," he says. He puts his big hand on my shoulder.

I reach up with both hands and shove him as hard as I can. I feel his fingers dig into my shoulder and then slide away as I push past. In the bathroom I cry with my face in a towel and then go back to bed, past the closed doors, down the empty hall.

The next day is very hot and muggy, and my mother says after lunch that she will have to lie down. She says she feels worn out. "Me too," I say, though there are plans to go swimming at the park. "It hurts, behind my eye," I say, and Mother shoos the others off, even Uncle Matt, who looks like a bear in his swim trunks.

My mother and I lie on her bed with a fan blowing across us. I think about Uncle Matt, and wonder why my mother likes him. I know she won't anymore, once I tell her about last night. *He stood in front of me just to be mean,* I think. I'll tell her that.

Instead I say something else. "I saw you last night."

She isn't really listening, I think.

"In the basement."

She whips her head around and stares at me with hateful eyes. I have never seen that look before. Not at me.

We stare at one another for what seems a long while. She reaches out and strokes my hair, making my skin crawl. Her look has softened. "You're just a little little girl, sweet Lucy," she says in her dove's voice. She won't even admit I know what I know; she means to keep her secret.

I think of my grandmother's money in my bag.

And my uncle's hand hard on my shoulder.

I'm big enough, I want to say, for keeping secrets. But she won't believe me unless I tell my own. I hold onto them like a penny in each palm. I'll never tell.

The day we leave Ohio, it rains. With cooler weather, my father wants to drive longer. It is almost dark when my mother says we should stop to eat and find a room.

"Things went pretty well," my father says. My mother is studying the right side of the street while I study the left, looking for something clean and not expensive.

"Didn't it?" my father says. Mother hasn't talked all day.

"Yes. Fine," she says.

"My pa's getting older—"

"Look. Up there—"

My father pulls into a space in front of the café and shuts the motor off. My mother picks her purse up off the floor but before she can open her door my father catches her arm. "I just asked you a simple question," he says.

"I gave you a simple answer."

"You didn't mean it."

My mother wrenches free. "Your mother could have been kinder."

"She's the way she is. She doesn't mean to be unkind."

"It was godawful hot."

My father leans up against the steering wheel and speaks in a strained voice. "It worried me, seeing Roseanne like she is."

"Oh, Charlie," my mother sighs.

"That sonofabitch drinks too much."

"It was his vacation, Charlie."

"Rosanne told me he hit her before."

"Before what?"

"*Before*. Once. Don't pinch at what I'm saying, Laura."

"Roseanne might exaggerate."

"She's unhappy."

"Beds made, partners chosen—" My mother's voice fades.

"No man hits a woman. No real man."

"What *do* real men do, Charlie?" my mother asks wearily.

We all get out of the car. When Faith has run on ahead, I hear my father say, "Damn you, Laura, it can't all go your way."

My mother looks beautiful, despite her thin hair and sad eyes. "When has it ever?" she says.

Outside Oklahoma City, half a day from home, the car breaks down. We stand around on the side of the road while my father pokes at things under the hood. He motions us all to get back in. "We can get to town," he says. "With your fingers crossed."

We park on a street near a garage. Sweat trickles down my mother's face. My father's neck is a deep purple red.

"I guess I'll call Mother," my mother says.

"I've got some money," I say, barely above a whisper. Both of them turn to stare at me. "Mommy gave it to me before we left. It's in my suitcase." They look at one another and my chin trembles. "We can take the bus home," I tell them. "Daddy can come with the car when it's fixed."

I take the little purse out of my suitcase while they watch. I've counted it a dozen times.

"Figures," my father says. My mother goes down the block to check the bus schedules and fares. When she comes back, I dole the money out. "Okay, this is for tickets," I say, handing some of the money to my mother. "And five dollars for some lunch." That leaves sixty dollars. I count three tens into my father's open hand. "For a motel and food," I say.

"Lucy, I have to get the car fixed," he says, exasperated.

I see instantly that I have gone too far. My father's face is a dark red, streaked white around his nose and chin. My mother is speechless. I throw the rest of the money into the front seat and run from the car. I can see the Greyhound sign ahead. I run and run, my face burning with shame. For me or them, I don't know.

My grandmother has dried apricots from her yard while we are gone. They are in a jar on the table. Only she and I are awake. As we talk, I eat apricots. They are slimy inside and fuzzy outside, like an ear. I tell my grandmother about the funny way towns come one right after the other in the North. I tell her about Grandma Widemar's stingy meals.

"Poke will be home any day now," my grandmother says. She starts to cry. "He called me. For the first time in over two years, I heard my son's voice."

I am so sleepy. There are other things I want to tell my grandmother, if only I could stay awake. I know I won't tell her later. Already the trip is settling into one thing, with no parts.

"Whenever I think of this summer," my grandmother says, "I'll think of that."

"Of what?" My head is heavy as stone.

"Why, of Poke," she says, not altogether pleasantly. "I'll think how it was the summer he came home from the war."

I nod, hoping she will think I understand.

"You know, though," she adds softly. "In all this time, any day, months at a time, he might have been killed. And all this time, I always worried more about your mother. Since she was two and had a fever, there's never been a time I haven't worried she wouldn't be all right."

Mother's letter to Mrs. Rosenberg comes back unopened in October. By then I am ten. My father has gone to Ronan, way west of Big Spring, to work for the same oil company as my Uncle Thatch, and my sister and my mother and I live with my grandmother again. Just for a while, everybody says, until Charlie can rent a house.

I write a report at school, about oceans. What really impresses me is reading how it can be dangerous to swim in the ocean. You can be floating along in smooth water, like a lake, and just below your toes the current might be crossing, waiting to suck you down.

I start a diary. "We got a television," one entry reads.

"Mother is sick again," reads another. This time I understand her sickness better. She goes away in November, when she can't stop crying about the letter. One day I come home from school and she is gone. Aunt Opal comes and takes Faith home with her. She says I can go too, but we all know I won't leave my grandmother.

I write in my diary faithfully, but never very much at a time. I got to skip a grade, and the work is more fun. The nun who teaches piano has started lessons with me, even though we can't pay.

I don't use the diary to write down my feelings. I just try to write something down to stand for the day that's gone. I don't really care about remembering. Recording is enough. I like the look of my two or three lines at the end of the day. I like the way they look on the page.

The Apex Man

CAROLYN OSBORN

 They were a strange couple, even from a distance. She watched them coming toward her. The man was as thin as a stick. His skinny legs outlined by tight-fitting blue jeans had a convalescent appearance, and when the wind blew his shirt against his chest she saw that despite the fact that his shirt hung from relatively broad shoulders, the rest of his body was as emaciated as his legs. His head dominated. Long and broad at the same time, it was almost too big for the neck that supported it. The brow and jaw were both wide, and the chin so long it seemed as pointed as one of Picasso's triangular portraits. He had one arm around the shoulders of a girl who was his opposite in every way except height. They were both short people, but she was all bumps and curves and roundness, a bulging sausage of a girl stuffed into green pants and a sweater. Her dark hair was gathered into a fat bunch on top of her head while his, fair and straight, blew lankly around his ears. They talked and nodded, staring ahead into some sort of special lovers' unreality. Mrs. Drake watched them cross the street, and was so transfixed by their strangeness she didn't take advantage of the gap in traffic to maneuver her car across. She felt she must wait to see them safely on the other side for they seemed absolutely unaware of cars, the girl simply rolling along, a movable prop for the young man. Without her how could he make his way through the world? Maybe he had a job he was peculiarly fit to do. He could be a circus performer, an acrobat. Or perhaps he was the top man in one of those balancing acts, the apex of a pyramid of strong men holding others on their shoulders, and this smallest one was the last one, the one who stood on top.

When they were safely across the street Mrs. Drake drove on to the grocery store, where she chose strawberry ice cream, green vegetables, potatoes, a loaf of bread, a rump roast, some canned beans which were marked down three cents, and, in a rare moment of whimsy, plucked a can of tomato juice from the top of a pyramid.

When she got home with four sacks of groceries, a whole week's supply of food, she rested in the car a moment. Doing a week's grocery shopping was tiresome. She got tired of wheeling the basket up and down aisles, trying all the time to make decisions about what to have for supper, wondering what Richard would like . . . strange to be wondering again what a man would like for supper. It was eleven years, twelve in July, since she'd seen the last of Mr. Drake. Those first few years after his death she'd been a widow grieving and remembering. Time had taken care of that first harsh grief and her memories of her husband were—until Richard came home—usually of the beginning, happier years of their marriage. He'd died of injuries after a car wreck, an accident of his own making—driving while intoxicated, the policeman said. He didn't know Mr. Drake had been walking, running, sleeping, working while intoxicated for at least ten years. Thank God no one else was killed! He crashed into an empty parked car. When he was gone, Mrs. Drake drove more carefully than ever, reproached herself occasionally for the vague feeling of relief she felt, and slipped gradually from widowhood to spinsterhood. The insurance money was carefully invested and she turned the upper story of their home into an apartment. She lived in the apartment below, alone but comforted by the sounds of footsteps upstairs. They protected her from what she called, with an appropriate sniff, "old ladies' fears," terrors of noises in the night and strange knocks at the door.

She knew those terrors. Mr. Drake had left her in the house by herself late many a night. She'd sit up in bed quivering, listening to something that could be a tree limb brushing a screen—or someone stealthily creeping through the back door. And the strange knock? It was generally one of her husband's friends delivering him, bringing him home like a postman delivering a badly wrapped parcel, one with loose string and ripped paper. Mr. Drake's tie was always untied and his coat off or lost. But it could be the leering face she'd seen once, nose pressed against the upper glass panes of the door, mouth gaping in a demonic grin. She screamed. He ran. After seeing the face she slept with a meat hammer under her pillow and a broom propped against the side of the bed. "Whatcha going to do, sweep the devil away?" Mr. Drake used to ask. "It's a good weapon for a woman," Mrs. Drake replied staunchly, and kept it there. One morning she'd come in and found him brandishing it at one of his imaginary devils he said was standing in the corner.

When her husband died and the first tenants moved in she arranged a signal. The broom bumping against the ceiling, the floor of the upstairs bedroom, meant "Help!" Fortified in this way, she relaxed. Then her son, Richard, started getting divorced and came home—to stay it seemed.

Mrs. Drake sat in the car and wondered if she honked would Richard come down and carry the groceries in for her? He needed privacy, he said, so she'd let him have the upstairs apartment when the last renters were gone. She knew, after living with Mr. Drake, about the need for privacy. Richard saw her only at mealtimes. She hated to honk, to sit out at the curb making a lot of noise, demanding service. What if she did let him have the apartment rent free? What if she did support him for a while? He didn't have a summer job. He was her only child. He needed it, and she wasn't going to demand he repay her by running errands. She poked the strawberry ice cream carton cautiously with one finger. Getting soft. Might as well start taking things in. Richard might hear her and offer to come down and help. Mrs. Drake got out of her car with one sack and slammed the door. Her son didn't appear, however, until she was on the way in with the fourth sack. He looked sleepy. She'd heard him get in his car and drive off sometime in the night. Determined not to stay awake worrying, she made herself go back to sleep, but she woke up again when he came home around three, a familiar hour, Mr. Drake's favorite time for rolling home. "Rolling home, rolling home, by the light of the sil-ver-ry moo-oo-oon," he'd sing, when he was able to sing. She'd get up to let him in. For years after he was gone she'd find herself wide awake at 3:00 A.M. waiting for someone.

"Here, Mother, let me carry that for you."

He took the heavy sack from her with easy male insistence on doing a favor for a woman. She'd missed that. She used to think she wouldn't care if Mr. Drake came home drunk every night of the world as long as he didn't grumble about carrying things in and taking the garbage out.

"Where do you want this?"

"Over there." She pointed to the kitchen table already loaded with sacks. Richard shoved them all over to one corner and sat down.

"Mother, could I have some coffee and orange juice?"

"Yes, of course. Just a minute." She paused to gaze at the sacks. Which one was hiding the frozen orange juice?

"What are you digging around for?"

"The juice."

"I don't have to have orange juice."

"There isn't any other kind. I don't have anything else here— Oh!"

"What?"

"Here's some tomato juice. I forgot I bought it." She pulled the can out and began shaking it vigorously.

"Do you do that often, forget what you buy at the store?"

"All the time. It's the only fun of going shopping, the surprises you find when you get home."

"Impulse buying," Richard said. "You must buy a lot of things you don't need that way." He poured himself some coffee.

"Your father used to say the same thing." It slipped out before she thought, but it was so like Mr. Drake. He teased her about impulse buying every time she came home from the store.

"Did he? I didn't know he ever noticed things like groceries."

"He was a sharp man. How else could he have carried on his law practice?" Why couldn't she stop? She knew Richard didn't like for her to talk about his father. Somehow he always pressed her to it, though. They'd be talking about the simplest everyday things and there'd be Mr. Drake, drifting in like a ghost, demanding she defend him to his son.

"You miss him, don't you? You even miss all the noise, the singing and shouting and pounding!"

"It's been a lot quieter around here these last twelve years," she said amiably. "Here's your juice."

He started to take the glass from her, then flattened his palm against it. Juice sloshed out of the glass all over her hand.

"What's the matter? I thought you liked tomato."

"I do, but it's too acid."

"Richard, orange juice is acid too." She put the glass down and wiped her hand with a wet dishrag.

"I know. I forgot."

"If you've really got ulcers you shouldn't be drinking coffee either. At least I don't think it's supposed to be good for ulcers."

"You don't believe it's ulcers?" He blinked his eyes slowly at her.

"It's not like not believing in God, Richard."

"What in the name of heaven does God have to do with my ulcers?"

She giggled helplessly while he stared at her. "Nothing. I'm sorry. You ought to see a doctor."

"I saw one in Houston. He said it sounded like ulcers."

"Yes, I remember. You told me before. That doctor sounds like a quack to me. Did he give you any tests?"

"No."

"Did he say anything about tests?"

"He told me to come back for them, but—"

"But you didn't!"

He drew circles with one finger in a blob of spilled coffee. "I hate to take the damn tests. He was going to make me drink a lot of stuff and X-ray me."

"It's the only way they can find out about ulcers. Let me make an appointment for you with Dr. Schwartz."

"Oh, Mother!" he sighed.

"You need to find out about things like that. I'm going to call him today."

He drew some more circles in the spilled coffee.

"Richard, don't you want to know if you've actually got ulcers?"

"I'm— I don't want to be operated on."

"Who said anything about operating? You always think the worst possible things are going to happen. They cure ulcers all the time by giving people medicine and keeping them on bland diets. If you're afraid of surgery the best thing to do is see a doctor now before you have to have surgery. Sitting around worrying about it will only make—"

"All right!"

"Well sometimes I think you enjoy agonizing over things."

"You sound like Laura."

It wasn't the first time he'd mentioned his wife's name. When he first came home he'd said he didn't want to talk about the divorce so she hadn't asked him about it. She'd kept absolutely silent on the subject, but Richard was always on the verge of telling her everything.

"You didn't sleep well last night, did you?"

"Oh, did I wake you up?"

He answered her with such an air of fake innocence she wanted to shake him, to grab both his shoulders and shake him good. He wanted attention so badly.

"No, you didn't wake me. I thought you looked tired."

"I don't sleep well any night. I did at first when I came home, but I don't anymore. I try to read. Then I get in the car and drive around."

"Where?"

"Just around."

Dangerous, dangerous as could be, and that was what she wanted to tell him, that driving aimlessly around until three in the morning was dangerous. Look where driving around got your father! No, she wasn't going to tell him that. She was supposed to exclaim, to cry out, Don't, my son! You must take care of yourself. Let Mother take care of you, poor child, poor little boy. What a mean, nasty bitch your wife is to leave you alone, sleepless at night, alone in bed. Here's a teddy bear. You can go to sleep with old bear. Think about good things. Think about merry-go-rounds, birthday parties, ponies, puppy dogs. She could feel the small boy's head under her hand, the soft hair smoothed by her palm. She looked over at Richard's bald spot and wondered if she had made it. Had she worn away the hair rubbing his head? Poor Richard. He had finished his coffee and was absently stroking the top of his head, trying to cover the bald spot with a few thin hairs.

He'd gone without a haircut for some time now. He ought not to let himself go like that. Another week or so and his hair would be as long as the strange man's she'd seen early that morning. She thought of telling him about the little man who drifted along held up by the stout girl. She wanted to ask him if there was such a thing as an apex man in a circus balancing act. Again, she checked herself. Richard would not be interested in her speculations about peculiar-looking people. He could only be interested in questions about his own problems.

"Richard, if you get a divorce, when will it be final?"

"I'm not getting a divorce. It's Laura who says she wants one."

"Do you think she'll go through with it?"

"I don't know. How am I to know?"

"Haven't you talked to her?"

"Yes."

"Well?"

"I still don't know." Pushing his chair back, he got up and started out the door. She would have liked to ask him where he was going, but she was not going to ask him one more question that morning.

Mrs. Drake found a clean cup, poured herself some coffee, and sat down at the table surrounded by tin cans, vegetables, and the ice cream beginning to melt and run in pink streaks down the sides of the carton. Rising quickly, she grabbed it and stuck it in the freezer. Then she sat down again. The chiming clock in the living room rang eleven—morning almost gone. There were still groceries to put away and she should go upstairs to make Richard's bed at least. He'd told her not to bother. Sometimes she didn't. The stairs were steep, too steep for a woman sixty-two years old to be climbing every day. When she did go up she was appalled by Richard's filth. How could one rather small man make such a mess? She'd tried to teach him as a child to be neat, not fussy, but neat. Someday he'd have a wife who would appreciate neatness. That lesson, like some others, hadn't taken. He left dirty shirts on the floor, threw his pants over the backs of chairs without bothering to see if the creases were straight, dripped ashes all around an overflowing ashtray, let his ties slide off the rack in the closet, pulled the shades down crooked, and tied the curtains back in big knots when they got in the way. Tiresome . . . made her peevish to think about what she'd surely find up there. There was nothing in the least odd about Richard's messes. She wouldn't have minded finding all his dirty clothes under the bed, a collection of silk top hats on the dresser, or funny faces drawn on the windows. Mr. Drake had done that once after she'd seen the face at the door. All she'd find in Richard's room, though, was the listless sort of dirt made by a man who refused to take care of himself.

She hadn't seen any liquor up there yet and wouldn't open the bureau drawers, not because it was an invasion of privacy; she was afraid of seeing a whisky bottle rolling toward her out from under a heap of clean socks, afraid of seeing the vicious brown liquid rocking back and forth in its bottle.

She was certain he drank. When he was in high school he'd come home one night, or rather was delivered like his father by two staggering friends. The next day he sat around shamefaced and quiet until she told him, "It's all right. You've got to experiment sometime. I don't expect you not to drink. You don't have to take a pledge." Moderation was all she required. She knew she'd have to be moderate as well. She wouldn't gain a thing by pleading, crying, or losing her temper, much as she wanted to do all three.

"I should know better." He gave her a weak grin. "I don't want to turn out like Dad. You don't need another alcoholic in the family, do you, Mother?"

"No."

"You think I'm going to be like him, don't you? I mean . . . maybe it's inherited?"

"You are not going to be like your father."

"Why not?"

I won't let you. That's why. I won't allow it to happen. She stood glaring at him in determined silence, then said, "It's not inherited. That's only an excuse."

"Mother, have you ever taken a drink?"

"Yes."

"But you don't drink at all now. Did you ever, in college maybe?"

"No. I don't like the taste of it."

"I do," said Richard and ducked his head.

She left him studying his hands. If she hadn't walked out she would have screamed at him. Not words—she had no words in her mind. Only an unintelligible scream.

He probably drank too much at other times. She didn't know about them, didn't want to know. Mrs. Drake heaved herself up out of the chair, flicked her fingers over the tin cans like a pianist trying to decide which chord to hit, picked up two cans, and started to the pantry. When Richard was a little boy he'd played grocery store out there, shifting the cans on the shelves, selling them to imaginary people and to her while she cooked supper, a meal they ate alone together. Mr. Drake seldom got home for supper as it was his custom to go to the bar immediately after work. She and Richard ate together every night. He'd tell her what happened at nursery school, at grammar school, at high school; she'd correct his table manners and tell him the details of her day. She had to be careful not to let him become a mama's boy. She pushed him out to play with other children. He always came home. Then she'd get angry and tell him he had to stay outside.

"Go play. Play with the other children."

"I don't want to."

"Go anyway."

He'd go off for a little while, but he'd come back. "Mama, I hurt my knee." "I fell down." "Mama, I cut my finger."

It was only a stage, she consoled herself, only a stage all children went through. He loved Band-Aids. Didn't all kids? For a few weeks she refused to buy any more. Richard kept falling down.

"Scabbiest kid I ever saw," said Mr. Drake.

"He wouldn't be if you paid him some attention."

"What do you mean? I'm paying attention. I see him."

"The only thing you—" She was going to say the only thing he paid any real attention to was the level of bourbon left in a bottle, but, knowing the rage she could evoke, she cut herself off with a loud "Humph!" She'd had plenty of all that—the shouting, the rage, and she wasn't going to do it anymore. There was just so much of her, not enough to divide between fighting with her husband and being a mother to Richard at the same time. Richard needed so much. Not material things, those were managed; he needed affection. Richard was a glutton for love. She gave him all she had, holding back nothing though she was fearful all the time she'd smother him with it. She was more grateful than he for every friend he had. Then there were girls. They seemed to like him. She kept up with them all. Finally, when he went to college—he'd gone to SMU right there in Dallas instead of going away to school—there was Laura.

She was exactly the sort of girl Richard needed, stable, thoughtful, pretty though a bit plump. Mrs. Drake was a bit plump herself so she didn't hold that against anybody. After he married Laura, Richard, who'd always been small and thin, began taking on some weight. They had an apartment in town until they finished graduate school. Mrs. Drake didn't see them often, once every two weeks for Sunday dinner at their place or hers. For once in her life she luxuriated in the clichés of happiness: Richard and Laura were a perfect match, a mathematician married to a musician. Richard was untidy; Laura was a good housekeeper. He was a glutton for love; she was overflowing with affection. He had his special chair, his special dishes, his important research. Laura made him comfortable, fed him, and played the piano beautifully. If she was relegated to making background music, it was good music. She had her practice hours to herself and someday she would have her own pupils. Balance, Mrs. Drake thought, balance was everything. She gave herself up to giddy dreams of a perfect pair of grandchildren, but there were none. Children would come later, they assured her. Right then they had to get through school and find jobs. They'd done all that, including finding jobs in Houston, and now, after four years of apparently happy marriage, Laura wanted a divorce.

Mrs. Drake banged the door of a cupboard shut. She was through putting up the wretched groceries. While she was considering taking herself out to lunch as a kind of reward, the phone rang.

"Mrs. Drake, is Richard there?"

"No. Laura, it's so good to hear your voice. He's gone out somewhere. Could I have him call you?"

"No! I don't want to talk to him. He calls me all the time from up there, but he uses a pay phone at some bar. I only wanted to make sure he was staying with you. I thought he was."

"He calls you from a bar? Why? He could use the phone here anytime."

"Well, I guess— You know he drinks?"

"Yes, but I didn't know— How much does he drink?"

"Quite a bit. Sometimes I think he's trying to beat his father's record. Oh, how awful of me! I shouldn't have—"

"That's all right. We all know about Mr. Drake. Where are you calling from?"

"I'm in Houston."

"The connection is so clear, I couldn't tell. I was hoping you were in town. I'd like to see you. I'm so sorry about you and Richard. I thought perhaps this was just a separation."

"Did Richard tell you that?"

"No, not exactly." She paused and pulled at the kinked phone cord. It curled back up the minute she let it go. "He says he doesn't want to talk about it, but I think he really does. He acts like he doesn't know what's going to happen next."

"He ought to know by now. I've told him. He doesn't want anything to happen. He wants to let things drift on and on. He agreed not to contest the divorce, but he left without signing anything. A process server is supposed to bring him the papers today, this afternoon in fact. It's just a formality, but I wanted to be sure he was staying with you. The man's got to hand him the papers. I told him to check there first, then I thought I'd make sure." Her voice dwindled away.

In a desperate attempt to hold on to Laura, Mrs. Drake asked, "Did Richard ever say anything to you about his ulcers?"

"Yes, but he won't do anything about them. I made him go to the doctor once. I even went with him, but he wouldn't go back for the tests. You know how he is. And whatever he's got, drinking won't help. I know I shouldn't be saying this to you, but I thought you'd understand. I can't change him, and I've helped him all I can. Mrs. Drake, didn't you ever think about divorcing your husband?"

"Of course I thought about it, but there was Richard. We were different somehow."

"The difference is you're stronger than I am."

"Perhaps I'm weaker."

"I don't think so. You've never seemed that way to me."

There was so much kindness in Laura's young voice Mrs. Drake felt she was going to start crying. She pulled herself up straight against the wall. "I'm sorry, Laura."

"So am I. I loved Richard, but I can't back him up any longer, and I can't live with him the way he is."

They said good-bye. Mrs. Drake put the receiver back on the hook and sagged down in the nearest chair. An alcoholic father, an alcoholic son. Classic. But no, they were different. Mr. Drake was a robust drunkard. He howled and roared against a terrible world. "The depravity of man!" he'd shout in his blackest moments. "Cursed are the stars that led me to this course!" She didn't know where he'd gotten the line, but he'd made it his own. Being a criminal lawyer didn't help his outlook any. No matter how he struggled he was caught in paradox. "Law and order. We must have law and order!" Every table in the house suffered from his pounding, and sometimes he'd emphasize the words by pounding his knee. Then he'd be in court the following day defending some poor wretch against the strictness of law and order. That was his reverse side, his belief in the rights of everybody. He used to tell her about some of his clients. "If only he'd finished high school . . . if only she hadn't gotten pregnant . . . if only . . ." He found excuses for them all, but as the years wore on he ran out of excuses or quit believing in them. He could not, however, wear out his compassion, though he tried to protect himself with cynicism. "Some people are just sorry," he'd say. In his sorrow for them, he drank. At times he was happily drunk. Those were the nights he came home singing, "By the light of the sil-ver-ry moo-oo-oon," and she would get out of bed to lead him in. There were probably other, deeper reasons for his drinking, but she'd reached the limit of her understanding about Mr. Drake. She couldn't go on asking why, why, why forever. Some people were just sorry and some men just drank.

But Richard— Richard was not his father all over again. The one time she'd seen him drunk he was neither raging nor singing. He was quiet and ashamed . . . only a boy then. Now he was almost thirty years old and all she knew was he went to bars and called his wife because she was divorcing him. He had a good wife and a profession he seemed to like. What could be more orderly than the study of mathematics? What could be more removed from the daily paradoxes his father had tried to escape? Richard had a well-ordered existence. He taught his classes, went to his office, talked to students, graded papers, and did research on something or other. She imagined him standing in front of a board filled with geometric figures. He was neatly dressed in the sport coat and slacks she'd given him last Christmas. With a piece of chalk in one hand he was carefully retracing the outline of a triangle, chanting professorially a theorem ending in a logical conclusion. He was not standing before a judge pleading for the rights of some no-count who'd stabbed another fool in a knife fight. And he had an audience, too, plenty of attention, thirty-some-odd students in three different classes, ninety or more people hanging on to his every word. What was Richard trying to escape?

Did Laura seriously mean he was trying to beat his father's record? As if there were a record, as if anybody had ever marked an X on the barroom wall for every bottle of beer or bourbon Mr. Drake had consumed! She laughed at a momentary vision of X's winding around the room. Mr. Drake might have done it himself. He had the ability to make fun of his own weakness. Richard didn't.

If he was trying to compete with his father's drinking— Mrs. Drake shuddered. The idea raised gooseflesh on her bare arms. "Mr. Drake," she said aloud, and shuddered again. She'd talked to him a lot out loud at first. Then she'd let grief die and cured herself of her ghostly conversations. Here she was at it again after almost twelve years' silence. Richard's coming did bring his father back so.

"Mr. Drake," she said petulantly, "your son's on the booze."

She was sitting in the front room looking at the newspaper when the process server came. He was such an ordinary-looking man she thought at first he was an insurance salesman.

"Does Richard Drake live here?"

"Not here, upstairs." She crumpled the paper in her lap and sat still listening to Richard's bell ring, his steps coming downstairs, him and the man going upstairs together. She could hear the murmur of their voices, but not what they were saying. The process server came downstairs by himself. In a few minutes she heard Richard's footsteps descending slowly. His door slammed. Still clutching the paper, she went to the window and saw him drive away.

Should have told him what was coming, she thought. But what difference would it have made? He didn't want to know. He'd rather remain in limbo the rest of his life.

It was late when he returned and there were some other people with him. She heard them running upstairs singing loudly as they went. She didn't know the tune, but identified it as one of those cowboy songs about rambling and gambling and hopeless love—a strange song for a mathematics professor to be singing.

Mrs. Drake dozed off again to waken to the sound of something heavy falling down the stairs, voices shouting, car lights coming in her window. She jumped out of bed, put on a robe, and went to Richard's door. It was wide open and behind it was Richard sitting on the last step with his head on his knees. There was a trail of blood on the carpet of the stairs. A man's voice behind her said, "We got to take him to the hospital."

She smelled whiskey in the air all around her. "What happened?"

"We were trying to put him to bed. He wanted to go out again."

Richard raised his head. Blood trickled down his face.

Another voice said, "It's the top of his head that's cut. We got to get him to the hospital . . . 'mergency ward there."

She turned to see him leaning against the post by the steps.

"You'd better watch out or you'll fall!" she shrieked.

"Fell, Mama," Richard wailed. "I fell down the stairs and hurt my head."

She bent down to him and put one hand on his shoulder. "I know, Son. We're going to take you to the hospital and get it bandaged.

"Here!" She straightened up and called to the two strange men. "Help me carry him."

Class

BEVERLY LOWRY

I have followed Benjamin Fly all over this city. Without blinking an eye or ever complaining, from gymnasium to empty stage to vacant store, from armory warehouse to VFW meeting hall, to—once, once—a properly lighted studio with mirrors and prepared wood floors. It didn't last long: in two months we were out, evicted for a better-paying, more established group, moved to a second-floor storeroom with inconvenient support beams and a rolling floor that slanted toward corners.

Downstairs, a Vietnamese grocer and Kung Fu instructor share the ground-floor space. Beyond our feet we hear them, shouting in bursts. Eee-YAH through the floorboards.

Zelda was nearly thirty when she announced her intentions to Scott. She would become a dancer. A Pavlova, she said, no less. Imagine. She installed a barre and walled one room with mirrors; punished her body with hours of class. Scott waited. No doubt this would pass, in time. A Pavlova. Imagine.

I keep Zelda in mind.

Say this for Benjamin, he never gives up. Benjamin Fly always finds a place and in time for next week's class. And I go with him, my clothes in a bag, toes pointed in his direction, life and children in the background of my concern. Wherever he goes.

I am older than Zelda was. I am the same age as Nureyev and Jane Fonda.

Sometimes in my car I am driving along, perhaps ferrying children to some adventure or game, and pass one of the buildings we went to and am surprised all over again. There, I say to myself. Remember? I was there with Benjamin Fly. To have followed a man so many places. When I think of it and in my mind move myself from room to room like a game piece, it seems to be something I am telling myself I did but in truth probably did not. Probably some dream. Some wish. Did I? My kids say: you *wish*. But I know I did. I remember sweating. Like a Turk, as they say, until my armpits slid.

Joanne Woodward takes class every day. She too has her own mirrors and barre. More realistic than Zelda, however, she sponsors young companies instead of seeking auditions, gives fund-raising affairs, lends her name out to help their causes.

Me. Who's never read past prefaces in any how-to book. Me. So diligent and persevering.

But, oh, Benjamin. I believe I would follow him anywhere. Climb any stairs that led to him, open the darkest door he was behind, drive through the most sinister of streets to get to him, put before my family the meagerest of meals in order to be on time for his class. Benjamin does not tolerate lateness. Come five minutes late and you are turned away. The discipline of dance. We pursue a dream: joy itself, in space. Not to feel joy. To become it. Joy itself, transcribed into movement and muscle and the moment, in time and space aloft. It is everything. The perfect dream. What Benjamin asks for, we never question. We only try to do.

Class is a way of ordering time. It was Zelda's last-ditch attempt at staying sane. If she could only perform. If she could learn the drill and then do it. Without questions. Simply keep in step and in time. Three and four and . . .

I am such a feather sometimes. So weightless and graceful and free, in my soul. Benjamin. His huge broken feet, his blonde angel locks, his trim lean flanks. His blue eyes, fringed with thread-thin lashes of palest gold. It was never too much to ask, those cold floors on which I waited for him to begin, the hard thump I felt when, coming down from some elevation onto improper surfaces, there was no give. My knee complained, so did my arch. But it was never too much. I am a butterfly when I think of him. I pull up on one toe, up and out of gravity and hipbones, I lift ahead, and . . . I am a song in space. Becoming music.

I wish.

Tuck in, turn out, extend the spine, press the heels into the floor, lower the shoulders. Chin up, stomach tight, chest open, ribs back, not that far back, heels forward, the stomach, the stomach, three and four and NOW.

Fly.

He stands before us, our mirror. He wears jeans, is barefoot, flexes his arch. Student of Cunningham and Holm, of early Graham and a new dancer on the scene named Lewitsky, Benjamin wears no shoes, nor do we. We are disciples of the modern, pursuing not classic devotion to the perfect form, finding perfection here instead, in our own bodies and how they move through space and time, a dance centered around what the body literally is. Instead of maintaining stiff torsos, our rib cages shift, side to side, isolated, stretching up out of themselves, from the waist. Something he calls the overcurve: the ribs come up and out of themselves making circles, up and out and over, up and out and over, like breath itself. Benjamin does it, and we try to imitate him. His hands make circles as his chest does, to show us what he means. We are babies. We will try anything he tells us to.

He has not always been barefoot. He once performed in ballet shoes, in a famous company north of here. And he is not young as dance age goes. Maybe my age? He won't say. Older than Zelda.

His feet are a prize. Huge, they are as expressive as hands. They look able to grasp and thumb. Prehensile feet. Rodin feet, all effort and heart and sadness. They seem to have been broken, then pieced back together again. He wears the old-fashioned kind of undershirt, dyed a deep pink. It moves as he does. His hair is golden. From his scalp it flows out, down to his shoulders in a fan. He has a small golden moustache, a trim Van Dyck beard. His mouth is full and pliant. He knows what he is to us. He knows we adore him.

Take first, he says.

We begin. The studio, this second-floor storeroom, is cold. We wear sweaters over our leotards, tied cunningly above the waist, and either long socks with feet cut out or real dancer's leg-warmers, in the current add-on fashion, as seen in pictures of the brilliant new companies in New York, casual in appearance at all costs. Sweat pants in place of tights. Cover up on the streets: you never see us outside the studio walking about in leotards and tights, not us serious ones.

There is a picture of Zelda in her tutu, sitting on a trunk. Nothing about her looks like a dancer. There is no drama in her face, or in the curve of her calf. She looks ordinary, a woman. Just somebody. Wearing a costume.

We begin with stretches. Pulling rib cage out of waist. Lifting the stomach, trying to flatten it against the spine. Moving hips the other side of waists. Rounding shoulders up and around, come-on fashion. Pushing against the day's tightness, we loosen up, working arches, stretching hamstrings, calves, spines, isolating the neck, isolating shoulders, isolating torso. Pulling up out of ourselves, reaching beyond. We prepare for class.

We try to mirror Benjamin. He is all light and joy and selflessness, a picture of devotion. Everything we wish to become. Serious. Professional. Wish we would turn into. The real thing.

Sometimes at home I pass a mirror and if no one is looking, stop to assess a plié, a tendu, an attitude turn. Keep working the turnout, I hear Benjamin say. Lift the knee higher, feel it hurt in your lower back, press against your behind, higher, higher, *push*.

Sometimes in off moments, I stare out a window at a tree and imagine myself gliding—as Benjamin glides. I move with him, across the floor, effortlessly. Gravity is no problem. We are without weight. I hold an arabesque. I am like the figure on the prow of a ship.

Be Pavlova, she said. Imagine.

Rosa attends class too. Rosa is Benjamin's accompanist and wife. She plays piano when they manage to roll in an old blue upright of hers, and I understand she is a singer as well. She would also be a costume designer if Benjamin had a company. Everybody says Rosa is the brains of the two. Sometimes she takes class with us if there's no piano; other times she only sits in one of those low corners and plays records as Benjamin makes requests, or thumps out rhythms on a small Indian drum. Wrapped up in a coat if it's cold, she gives us these terrible looks. With her head tilted back in her way, she stares through her long lids and thick lashes at us. We must be crazy. Taking class in such a place on such hard, ungiving floors. Attempting stag leaps when many of us could be safe and warm at PTAs.

A few could not. Some are young and show promise. Young enough to be my daughters, they stand on the front line. By choice, I stay in the last row. They follow Benjamin too. Silly as fish, they giggle in his presence and flash him secret looks. A few of them are fat. Not fat like fat, but solid, a youthful kind of chunkiness. Benjamin keeps after them about their weight. They duck their heads and promise. I am not thin, but take care. These chunks outweigh me by twenty pounds.

And outleap me as well. I see the chunks go up, while I struggle and remain essentially earthbound. Elevation does not come late. You have to learn it early or your body refuses to lift. You can't even imagine it. You are solid, rooted to the ground.

When Leah came, everything changed.

We were in the second-floor storeroom working away when, one night, she showed up for class. From the first we knew she was special. From the first step she took.

Leah had danced with one of the brilliant new companies in New York. They are modern but wear shoes. Not ballet slippers but those funny jazz kind, like tiny men's lace-ups. The kind you see in storybook pictures, made by elves in the night.

Leah stole Benjamin's heart, as easily as a quick kiss on a cold night. She had such swift feet. They moved like tiny whips. She could stand in one place and go a hundred miles without moving from that spot. And all the time, on her face this look of dazzlement, that her feet were making such moves. As if her feet were separate, a phenomenon she could not account for, whizzing like knives. When we did improvisations, nobody could keep up with Leah or tell where she might be going next; those feet took her so far beyond the last possible boundaries the rest of us knew about, even the young leaping chunks.

She was tiny, with hair cut shorter than any man's, like the hairstyle of boys I grew up with, the crewcuts of that time. She was style, all style, a kind of Peter Pan urging us to fly. Benjamin began to adore her. Her feet and their dancing, her haircut and her zest, all energy and zip and let's go. And the way she had of trying the impossible; things even she knew she could not realistically do.

Was Leah the dream? I grew surly on the back row.

Scott made fun of Zelda's ballet madame and even flirted with her one night, to show Zelda that Madame was no purer an artist than he. Finally Zelda was offered a role. She turned it down.

Meantime Rosa played on, watching the tide change, Buddha-like, through her long sculpted lids. She had her ways. Sometimes in the middle of a combination we'd suddenly realize we were dancing to "Dixie," or "Hail to the Chief," or a church tune, complete with bass runs and high tremolos. These were distracting, but the rhythms were never wrong. Rosa's beat always went with Benjamin's combination; the tempo and style were exactly what the steps required. You could not get past Rosa. She did not have fast feet, but you could not get much past her.

One night, Leah fell. That was when we discovered how it truly was with Benjamin.

He had given us a tricky combination that started with an off-balance move. The feet slid sharply to the left, while the shoulders and torso counterbalanced in the other direction. It was the first move of the combination and you had to hit it instantly, on the . . . *and ONE*. Like a drunk on the edge of a curb, Benjamin said. It should look like you're falling. Like those clown divers who tilt so far forward they seem doomed to fall but never get wet. Like this. And Benjamin did it, extending himself it seemed beyond what he could safely hold on to.

You have to be chancy, he said.

Leah was in the first group to go across the floor. She always was. (The first group tends to be show-offy example-setters, teachers' pets and the best among us. I am never in it, but avoid going last like the plague. If I bring up the rear, ragtag, straggling, I dance worse. Then I have to face the others who, having had their turn, stand at the end of the room watching the poor stragglers-on. New students always make the mistake of going last. It took me a solid year to learn the trick: go in the middle. Even first is better than last.)

Leah slid her feet on cue, at the first beat, and moved them so quickly and so far to the left in such a chancy off-balance pose that she went farther than even she could handle. Her feet kept going; she could not catch herself; she fell.

Rosa stopped playing. Leah lay on the floor in a heap, curled up in a tickled, laughing ball. Benjamin went to her, laughing as well, and lovingly lifted her up. Hands on her lap, Rosa watched. When Benjamin looked back at us, we saw in his eyes how far it had gone and how it was between him and Leah. He adored her, he could not get over her, she was the real thing.

Leah had no head for theory. She tried to choreograph but her explanations were too abstract to understand. She danced. She was a dancer. Period. Joy in space. Her feet too fast for her mind to keep up with.

When James Jones finished the long haul of *From Here to Eternity,* he, Zelda-like, gave himself up to the dance. He too would be a dancer. Standing before mirrors, beyond words and pagination and revisions, he would find art in the moment. In time and space. Now. In the here and now. Not on some shelf collecting dust.

The next change was inevitable. One night after class, Benjamin made an announcement: he was going to give a concert. A Dance Gathering, he called it. It was time, he said, to announce himself, to advertise himself to the town as a serious artist. "I have certain things to show them," he said. The performance would be in the second-floor storeroom-studio, avant-garde style. It would have a spontaneous air, with light, humorous pieces thrown in, and a number of what he called Structured Improvisations.

"We will take certain problems," he explained, "such as negative space.

I will explain the problem to the audience. You will improvise in such a way that they will understand."

Down to rudiments and abstractions. A dance to dance itself.

He would form a company, he said. The Benjamin Fly Dancers.

I knew it. The real thing. And I will become Joanne Woodward, sending tax-deductible checks to the cause.

Benjamin would dance as well. With Leah, in an improvisational study, the topic of which would be kept secret.

I sold tickets, gave out brochures, helped write the program. I knew I should be excited but was not. I felt like a brick. I was a chunk.

They were sensational, the hit of the evening; Benjamin got contributions enough that night to rent a real studio. He danced with Leah as if she were glass. He gave the show to Leah. He did not adore the dance anymore. He adored Leah. He was a man. She was joy in space. She was his love, his life, his love, his life, his joy. He was shameless in his adoration of Leah.

At the end of their piece, they struck a pose: Leah off-balance in her funny, cocky way, with that look of bedazzlement in her eyes, Benjamin humble, not even taking advantage of the lights, not even raising his chin to what light we had, the way a performer should. He was support for her. The real thing. With feet as swift as tiny whips and no head for abstractions. Leah. Benjamin was shameless.

I left before the ceiling lights came back on. When the applause roared up I was on the stairs, heading out. I could hear it still as I passed the Kung Fu studio. I looked in. Inside, a young man was kicking the air with his feet. My car had a ticket on the windshield for being improperly parked.

This is how it ended. Zelda's teacher came to call. Zelda had been dancing well. Zelda might join the company soon. Zelda would perform. Scott was out. Zelda started acting funny. At first, Madame ignored the strange remarks and curious gestures. Then Zelda began insulting the woman, calling her names, criticizing her classes, telling her she was no purer an artist than Scott. Madame suffered Zelda's tantrum a while, then, seeing how it was, simply got up and left. And that was it for Zelda's last-ditch dancing career. No halfway measures for her. No perpetual student she. Her days grew chaotic. She could not tell day from night anymore. Her calves turned stringy and lax. Everything went.

Benjamin's classes are fuller now. Next month we are moving to the new studio. There, the entire front wall is mirrored, and the floor is cushioned, to give knees some relief and feet a pillow for weary arches to rest on.

Everything has changed. Rosa has found her Leah too.

We have a new percussionist, a scraggy, woolly fellow who, like Leah, suddenly appeared one day. Rosa plays the blue upright while the percussionist taps his bells and drums and castanets. They are a perfect team. He is all burly touching; she the cool intellect. We hear rumors that all four live together now, in a big two-story house. And nobody cares. Everybody is happy. The real thing.

The Benjamin Fly Dancers have received a grant. They are to perform downtown among skyscrapers, to demonstrate the links possible between commerce and art.

And I am on the last row, still struggling for elevation. Most of the chunks are gone, replaced by girls who have worked themselves down to a dense leanness, tiny but strong. With no chunks to gloat about, I am the fat one now. The new girls ignore me. I do not cramp their style. I could be invisible.

Benjamin describes in the air with his big, beautiful, articulate hands what kind of movement he wants.

"With joy," he says. "Lightness and uplift and joy."

Rosa and the percussionist play.

I no longer go across the floor. I do the floor work, pushing hard at my turnout, grinding muscle against muscle in contractions, flexing my foot until my shins ache. But when across-the-floor starts, I pack my gear and go.

I would like to quit. I don't know how. It orders my days. I keep Zelda in mind.

In dreams my feet are swift as Leah's. In every waking fantasy, staring at trees and buildings and stoplights I'm waiting at, I dance. I am weightless. I soar. I am life and love and the epitome of joy. Joy itself. In movement. In space. The perfect dream. I will not give it up.

The Idle Time

S. E. GILMAN

Deborah's father pointed out the signs to the two girls. First the gray granite one on the left bank of the river, cut in the shape of Texas. "See that? Texas State Line." The truck tires hummed over the honeycomb of steel. "Red River," he bellowed over the vibration. He pointed to a faded red billboard topped with a spiked sunburst on the other side of the bridge. "'Oklahoma Welcomes You!' Now you can say you've been outside of Texas." He laughed, showing irregular white teeth that gleamed even in the shadow of the cab.

Riding shotgun, Callie looked down at the water. Muddy clay, a wide ditch of slow ruddy water. Was this what the song was about? Remembering the Brown River Valley wouldn't make much of a song. But there was no valley either; prairie surrounded them for miles. Nothing was the way she expected it.

Her friend Deborah sat in the middle, frowning in stony silence. Angry, not like the year before. Until the Carrolls moved to Wichita Falls the girls had been inseparable. They imagined lives of adventure together—staking out Deb's apartment house with flashlights and cap pistols, stealing secret formulas, making daring escapes from the traps of counterspies. Deb looked just like Illya Kuryakin, Nordic blonde, wide-faced with eyes like a hawk's. Looked so much like him that Callie never got to play the Good Russian even though her own grandparents had come from Russia. Her own kind were too heavy and dark for Hollywood, so Deb made her play Napoleon Solo, though neither girl liked him. Maybe it was too late to play those games; Callie didn't mention it.

Mr. Carroll left Cummings TV to open his own shop in the Falls close to his wife's people. One whole year had separated Callie from Deborah. This was Callie's first trip to visit, the furthest she had ever been from home.

Mr. Carroll turned onto the access road, a strip of asphalt that ran parallel to the river. Callie stuck her head out the open window. "Look, a riverboat! A paddlewheel, too!"

"You want to go see?" said Mr. Carroll with a laugh.

"I seen it one million times already," said his daughter.

"But Callie hadn't. Hold on, girls, I'm making a huey."

They swung wide into the parking lot and Mr. Carroll left the truck running in neutral. The boat was a flat-bottomed barge painted to look like the *Mississippi Queen*. The gingerbread and fancy molding were only gray painted shadows against plain white wood. The paddlewheel was real enough. Its blades stuck at rest in the muddy silt until time came for the pilot to gun the motor, for the wheel to turn and hide the oily chop the engine made. A loading file of tourists, a moving clothesline of Bermuda shorts and Madras shirts, carried infants, ice chests, and Brownie cameras on board.

"Get a load of that," said Deborah, crossing her arms against her chest. "Going up and down a river that goes no place. Some fun. Think they're pretending?"

"Sure *looks* real." Callie stared at the dock. Young kids clambered ahead to get to the static paddlewheel or hugged the railing to lean over the turbid water. Adults watched their feet tread cautiously on the ribbed gangplank. TAKE A RIDE ON THE IDLE TIME read the sign at the ticket booth. NO GLASS CONTAINERS. NOT RESPONSIBLE FOR ARTICLES LOST OR STOLEN. PLEASE WATCH YOUR CHILDREN.

A soldier leaned against the booth. A green beret perched cocked on his head, and he wore a full-dress uniform even in the summer heat. A crowd of local boys surrounded him, tall and awkward as colts, talking to the soldier, drawing their fingers across his silver wings, the bright ribbon bars.

"Lookit that guy! He musta been places. Stop the truck, Pop, let's go talk to him."

"Debbie, show some manners. Young ladies don't go up and bother young men just 'cause they want to. He might not want to talk to you, did you think of that?"

"C'mon, Pop. Callie, open your door."

Mr. Carroll put the truck in low gear. "Those little boys hanging off of him like deerflies. That's no way for a girl to behave. Besides, Mama's got supper waiting for all of us." The Ford spun in an arc out of the bare tar lot, one jolt, then back on the access heading the direction they had come. "Callie, we're skipping the cruise, but you still get to go in a circle and get home by sundown."

"Callie and I got all the time in the world, right, Cal?"

"I want to see some mountains next. How about it, Mr. Carroll? Can you get us to New Mexico and then back for supper?"

"That would be something. Debbie's mama would be sore if we didn't take her with us, though. I don't think she's seen a mountain either."

Callie watched the plains peel by, past the flag decal on the windshield. The ride back took half the time it had to reach the river, and though Callie could feel the sun behind them, she wanted to turn around not to lose it, to follow it right into the Pacific.

The truck turned down their gravel street. Mr. Carroll hit the horn with his fist, five long, two short blasts. "Shave and a haircut, two bits!" he sang.

"Why'd you do that for?"

"I don't know, Callie. Just to do it, I guess."

"He always does that," said Deborah. "Let's Ma know we're coming."

"Whole neighborhood'll know."

"Whole neighborhood should know when it's suppertime. If they don't, I take it upon myself to tell 'em."

Deborah and Callie sat on the back porch after supper. Behind them they could hear Mrs. Carroll filling the sink for dishwater, steady plod from the faucet turning in on itself.

"You think I ought to offer to do the dishes?"

"Nah. She wouldn't let you do it, especially if you offered. Save your-self the trouble. She expects me to ask, but I learned not to. If I ever started I'd be trapped for sure." Deborah looked over her shoulder at the back door screen. Her mother was still soaping dishes. She looked around the side of the house and, satisfied, pulled a Viceroy out of her shirt pocket. "Want one?"

"Yeah, cool." They lit them off a kitchen match Deb struck smartly on the concrete foundation. "Hey, remember when I wrote the CIA?"

"What a nothing," said Deborah. "Bunch of pictures of guys at black-boards, sitting in some class. Women with those things on their heads— headphones, typing. Computers and stuff. It didn't look like fun at all."

"It said you had to graduate from college to join." Callie flicked her ash at a fat biting fly that dove between them. "You thought about what you're going to do when you get out of school? College?"

"School after school, are you kidding? Mama wants me to go, but Pop says we can't afford it. Says he can't get rich being the best TV repairman in Wichita Falls. Besides, going to school all your life is dumb. The other kids here quit early to go to work. They work on rigs or for the Santa Fe. I wouldn't mind getting a job on a rig, but Pop says no way they'd hire a girl to work on one. You going to college?"

"Plan to," said Callie. "I don't like where I'm going now, but they tell me college is different. I found out what I'd like to do."

"Like what?"

"Give tests. Personality tests. I saw them in a book about psychology I read. You draw the shape of a face and the one you're testing fills in the eyes and the mouth. That's supposed to tell you what they feel inside."

"Tests, Jesus. I hate tests, all tests. Besides, who wants to know what's inside somebody. Who wants to know?"

"I do. To find out what makes people tick."

"You don't have to be a shrink for that." Deborah made a jab at the fly with the burning end of her cigarette. "Take my mama and pop. Mama does the work around the house. Works all the time. If I stick around here I end up doing the work too. But she'll help me with anything. Now if I want money or permission to go someplace, I ask Pop. He's easy but he only listens to himself. You work both of 'em."

Callie blew out smoke, kicked at the dust. "Back there, at the bridge. How come you looked so mad?"

"Pop," Deborah said. "Every time someone comes up to visit, he takes 'em across the state line and drags me with him. Then he laughs, 'har-har,' and thinks it's funny. He makes me tired."

"I don't know. I got a kick out of it. I never been out of the state."

"Now you seen them both, Oklahoma and Texas. Boredom times two." Callie stubbed her Viceroy out on the porch. "Don't leave it there where she can see it, dummy. Put it in the trash barrel." Deb held her butt pinched between her thumb and index finger, and flicked it with the middle one into the big orange drum. "Like desk football. Like that."

"I like your dad," said Callie, practicing her flick. "I like both your parents. I wish I had them for my parents. They look like they like each other."

"Sure they like each other. They're married, aren't they?"

"I mean they probably share a room. My mom was always sleeping on the couch. Dad moved out this spring. I don't miss him so much, they were always fighting anyway, so at least it's quiet. Whenever we had meals together and Dad asked for the potatoes, Mom would say, 'Tell your father to get his own damn potatoes.' They made me sick, fighting like that. They fought even when they were quiet. I never even knew my grandpa. You even got a grandpa living here."

"You don't know how lucky you are, man. Two parents, grandpa too. They gang up on you. I get it coming and going. 'When are you going to grow up and act like a lady?' They're trying to get me to go out on dates."

"That's gross. I went out on a date last fall," said Callie. "Worst nothing experience of my life."

"Oh yeah? Who with?"

"Some creep. My mother is friends with his mother, so thank God nothing happened."

"You do anything?"

"Drove around Corpus on his fat lap. Pretended to like beer. Pretended it wasn't happening. He kept asking me to sit on his thing, him driving and me with my stomach pressed right up against the steering wheel. I'll never do it again if it kills me."

"I'd kill myself first. Come on, I got something to show you." Callie followed her to the garage. Deborah led her to an upright metal chest that stood in a corner, and opened it. "You know how to shoot one of these? It's real easy." Deb pulled out a .22 rifle. She held the stock under her arm, opened the chamber and looked inside. She blew invisible dust from the chamber. "Want to go hunting tomorrow? Out in back. Cowpaddies about a mile walk. At the watering holes."

Callie's mouth dropped open. "Shooting cows?"

"They'd shoot *us* for that, stupid. You ever heard of frogs' legs?"

Callie had heard people ate such things, but the people she thought did it ate them in fancy restaurants in places like New Orleans, the same people who ate snails. "You must have to shoot a thousand frogs to get the meat of a regular drumstick, don't you?"

"Not tree frogs, real frogs. These are the size of your head, girl. There's plenty of 'em at the cowponds. You game enough to do it?"

"Shoot a real rifle?"

"Real rifle, real frogs. Shoot it same as pretend. Grandpap grew up eating frogs' legs. He'll help us with them after."

"This I gotta see."

After laying out their ammunition, Callie and Deborah joined the grown-ups watching TV. The Carrolls owned the best set in Wichita Falls—color, big screen. The ten o'clock news was on. Soldiers in green lugged black plastic bags through the jungle slop, the sound of helicopter blades slicing through the soundtrack. Walter Cronkite was reading the body counts for the week. Soldier faces under spattered, netted helmets looked dazed into the camera. Some faces turned their heads away.

"What I don't understand," said Mr. Carroll, "is why they don't just bomb the hell out of the Viet Cong and get it over with?"

Mrs. Carroll sighed and turned a page of her magazine. "Nixon'll know how to fight a war. He's been saying all along that Congress has been doing nothing but tying his hands. And those hippies. They about killed poor LBJ. Times like this I thank the Lord for giving me a little girl, even if He did give me a tomboy."

Cronkite moved on; Roger Mudd reported from Cape Kennedy. There were pictures from the Apollo, pictures of the earth taken while circling the moon, sent all the way to Wichita Falls. Deborah crossed her bare feet on the coffee table. "I'll tell you both what. When I'm eighteen, I'm joining the army."

Mrs. Carroll looked up again, her voice angry but weary from practice. "Get those dirty feet off my table, young lady. You know better than that. And you're not joining the army and that's the end of that."

"Papa, I know how to handle a gun. Why can't I go fight for my country too?"

"Let's pray this war will be over with by the time you're old enough to fight for it." Mr. Carroll took off his bifocals and rubbed his eyes. "Debbie, someday you're going to thank your lucky stars when you realize how lucky you are, to be born a girl and be married and have a family of your own. That's the only thing important in this world."

"I'd rather do something really important with *my* life, not warming my butt like both of you." Deborah strode into the kitchen and came back with a Coke. "I'd go to Vietnam. I'd go in a minute."

"Don't you think it's wrong?" Callie had to say something in the seconds of silence that followed. Something polite.

"What's wrong, honey?" asked Mrs. Carroll on the couch behind her.

"All this fighting is wrong. People are being killed. I don't know why; nobody seems to know why."

"Of course fighting is wrong. And girls shouldn't talk back to their parents like that either." Mrs. Carroll glared at her daughter, who flopped down on the couch beside her. "That's wrong too."

"Of course it's wrong, Callie," said Mr. Carroll, turning down the volume when a commercial came on. "Everybody knows killing is wrong, it's in the Bible. But I went to war too. My friends died in that war and I saw them go. Sometimes a man can't control what happens around him. He has a job to do. You take what the Lord gives you as your duty. Many's the time you don't understand it. Debbie will understand too by and by."

Deborah snorted into her bottle of Coke. "Sure," she said. "Hey, city girl, we split at dawn. We better get some sleep before reveille." She grabbed Callie by the shoulder, pulling her toward their room.

That night, awake in the dark, Callie remembered the Kodiak patches, the yellow and red bars her father got in the army in the other war. Every year she could remember, her father pulled them out of the cigar box he kept them in, but he never talked about the war. She didn't know what he did there except spend long winters icebound in the Aleutians. In the summers he played baseball, wanted to play in the minor leagues when he came home but worked in the refinery instead. He was a changed man, her mother told her, when he returned. He rarely smiled and rarely talked except to curse goddamn-son-of-a-bitch at every one or thing that sapped his life—the Depression that robbed his childhood, the war that siphoned off his youth, the marriage that trapped him in constant fights with her mother. And that was the good war, when America pulled out of work camps and back into the factories. Terrible times her mother told her were the best days of her life. Saturday nights at the USO dance, her father a sergeant in his crisp uniform. Happiness that was a prelude to open warfare, man and wife.

In the morning Mrs. Carroll cooked them salt pork and eggs; Mr. Carroll hugged them both before leaving for work. While Mrs. Carroll collected the dishes and ran the water, the girls pushed the table against the kitchen wall, then headed to the garage for their gear.

Each girl carrying a rifle and a tall gunnysack, they walked half a mile out back of the house. They pushed through a stand of scrub oak and juniper and then, crawling out from under a barbed wire fence, came within sight of the first watering hole. Except for the horseflies and cicadas the prairie was still, the morning cool. The grasses were burned stiff and yellow like new camel hair brushes. The clay shone scarlet, exposed by the circle of brown water. The long walk stretched Callie's muscles and she breathed deep, her nostrils flared, open.

"Hold it like this." Deborah rested the thin rifle in easy balance in the palm of her left hand. "Bring it up straight and squeeze the trigger easy. Aim for the head."

Callie looked at the still, dark forms at rest in the mud, in and at the edges of the cowpond. "Once you start shooting you better keep on. Make it fast or the rest will scatter. I'll show you what I mean." Deborah shot first and the first was a hit. The frog sprung up in a circus leap, like some kind of acrobatic act, but it did not land on its feet. It careened over, shook with spasms. Another shot and another frog followed a different trajectory backwards into the shallow red water with a slapping sound. Another and another.

Callie aimed for the mass of them clustered in the center. She made a hit and after the first hit kept firing. She found the rhythm to it and it didn't matter if most got away, she relished each slap. Both girls fired and the slaps were interspersed with the repeating cracks of the rifles, the metallic spit of the shells. The broken ranks of frogs jerked toward the safety of the high tufts of grass, retreated in every direction.

Crouched over, Callie scooped up the cool bodies, frogskin soft and supple in her hands where the brown mud had already begun to cake from the rising heat. Deb's clean shots had found the head, the exploded hole no bigger than the size of a child's fingernail. Deborah's half of the kill lay motionless as they gathered them into the burlap bags. Callie found her victims shot in the back or chest. Her bad eyesight and uncertain aim had not allowed them an easy dying. They kicked when she picked them up. Their blood ran almost black, leaking in rivulets on her hands, smeared ochre. Those creases in the hands called the Lifeline, Line of the Head, Line of the Heart. Callie's red claws combed the mud. She stuffed their flesh into the sack without looking. The sack jumped, pushed out in random places until those places grew blotched and still.

"Jesus, ain't those things dead yet?" Deb pushed her blonde hair out of her eyes with a clean arm. "Come on. There's another pond on the other side of that fence yonder." She pointed to the yellow horizon. Callie walked back to the high grass for her rifle, the heavy sack bouncing against her calves.

It began again—the silent watch, the hunt, the command to open fire, the signal to stop, the mopping up. The process was repeated until both sacks were full. When they turned for home, Callie felt exhilarated, victorious. She learned to find the head and move on to the next clean kill. Even Deb told her she was getting good, better than any city girl. Her legs ached with a sweet burning and she was hungry. The killing was in her now. She liked it. She liked it.

Mrs. Carroll's father was waiting for them, smiling to them when he saw them come. The old man was waiting to show them how to skin frogs' legs. He took a Barlow knife out of his overalls pocket and the three of them sat out back on the concrete porch skinning, cutting off the legs at the hips, throwing the rest of each frog on the growing jumbled stack.

"It's real easy if you slit the back and belly first." Grandpa talked while he worked, a Bugler cigarette dangling between his lips. "Get it started before you take the hip. Comes off in one piece easy. Leave the feet for last."

"Just like biology class," Deborah grinned.

Mrs. Carroll appeared at the kitchen screen door, a greasy knife in her hand. "Just so you all know, we're having chicken tonight too, so you all will have a choice." Mrs. Carroll looked right at Callie, who kept on skinning, so Mrs. Carroll directed her attention to the expanding pile of amputees. "That's pure disgusting, Papa," she said, wiping the chicken knife on her checkered apron. "If you ask me they look too much like old Uncle Herman. He always took away my appetite."

"They acting about as lively now as Herman ever did, God rest that old pegleg."

Now that the bodies were inert, Callie looked some of them in the eyes. The eyes were fixed, open. They knew what hit them, what was happening, what was to come.

Dinner tasted good. Big legs and little lay on platters side by side, crisp and brown; garden beans, okra, fried toast. The girls helped out putting things away. Grandpa and Mr. Carroll sat in the living room, watching TV. The moon shot was on every channel—the Eagle had landed. Everyone gathered at the TV set, the volume on loud, crackling with white noise, the hazy transmission. The family saw the stepladder come out of the capsule, and Armstrong place one white boot on the first rung. They saw him bounce down, get flustered with the first footstep. "One small step for man . . ."

"How 'bout that, girls? We got ourselves the moon!" Grandpa clicked his tongue. "I seen it all now."

The astronauts planted a flag made to look like it was waving in wind that wasn't there. "You tell 'em," said Mr. Carroll. "Kilroy was here."

"Praise God," said Mrs. Carroll. For the better part of an hour, around a plate of fudge, five sets of eyes watched the two astronauts leap around, set up equipment, collect some rocks, play a mock round of golf. "Special ball," said Deborah's father. "Must have cost a hundred dollars."

"Whole thing cost a billion if it cost a dime," said Callie with a frown. "Bunch of rocks, that's all they'll get for it. What's so great about going to the moon?"

"Sweet Jesus, Callie, why do you have to be a prune about everything?"

"Deborah, you're taking the Lord's name."

"The Lord won't mind, Mama." She gave Callie a poke with her tennis shoe. "Why not go to the moon? See if it's made of green cheese for all you care! Look at 'em! Jumping higher than their heads. And the pictures! The whole earth nothing but a big blue ball rising above you. Nothing underneath you, nothing but space all around, nothing to catch you but space! Geez, I'd give *them* a million to get to go."

The transmission crackled and returned to earth, the black and white replaced by the head and shoulders of a man with a sandy pompadour reading the local nightly news. The blue prop wall behind him was comforting to Callie, something square and stable, not jumping anywhere.

Then the false blue square dissolved into the grainy film of a casket covered in silk being lowered out of the rear of an air force cargo plane. A lieutenant from the Falls was coming home. The pompadour said the soldier would be buried under the blast from twenty-one rifles. The newsman cleared his throat and shuffled his papers. "In Dallas, a brutal double murder was discovered tonight. Mrs. Leah Arvad and her daughter Jocelyn were found in their home stabbed with a kitchen knife . . ."

Mrs. Carroll stiffened in her seat. "Turn it off, Jerome." She put her hand out to touch the arm of Mr. Carroll's chair. The announcer continued, describing the murder suspect, the Arvads' boarder, recently released from the state hospital. Mrs. Carroll slapped Deborah on the seat of her pants. "You all don't have to hear this kind of stuff. Y'all go out to the kitchen and get a Coke. Take Callie with you."

"They'll fry him in Huntsville for sure when they catch him," said Deb, standing in the open arch of the kitchen door.

"Go on now. Get!"

The girls took their Cokes outside. The backyard bristled with the noise of a thousand crickets, soft white noise growing operatic with the heat.

"You think the cops'll get him?"

"Cops, hell, they've got Rangers crawling all over Dallas by now. They don't fool around." Deb craned her neck to see the few bright stars cool above the ring of hackberry and cottonwood at the edge of the yard. "I swear to you, if it was my family I'd be there to throw the switch, wouldn't you? I'd hunt him down and not come back until I saw him swinging six feet off the ground with my own two eyes."

"If it was your family, you'd have a knife in your back by now, didn't you hear?"

"But say I escaped. Boy, then I'd have a reason to do something. Like a blood feud. It would be my duty, see? I'd blow the son of a bitch away." Deborah kicked hard at a patch of clay. "Jesus, all I do around here is wait for something to happen. I don't think I can stand it anymore, I feel like I'm gonna bust wide open. Nothing in this place makes me feel like I'm alive, Callie. I want to feel something. I want to be somebody. All I feel is angry half the time and scared the rest. Mama just wants to protect me. She wants me to be like her, but if I do I may as well be dead. All Pap does is make stupid jokes. He won't talk to me about anything that matters. You got to feel something, don't you, Callie? Feel like something is really right, and that you've got a duty to do out there and never question if it's wrong or not?"

It was dark, and Callie did not look at Deb's face. She thought she could hear Deb's voice seize up like she was about to cry and was ashamed of it. Callie talked to the patch of red earth instead, dirt that only gave in under violence, that provided home for roots only when forced.

"I want some kind of reason," Callie said to her shoe. "I dream about being famous, maybe like Freud. But Mom wants me to learn typing so I can be a secretary. Dad didn't even want me to go to college. He said school's wasted on a girl, that I'd only drop out and get married anyway. I heard them fighting about it. But even though they want me to do what they want me to do, nobody really expects anything of me. I'm going to college just to get away from Mom, and prove Dad was wrong, but neither one of them wants to know what's really inside me. It's like the world don't want us. Even when you grow up— What happens if you grow up and nothing really changes?"

"I want a smoke. Come on. I don't want her to see us."

The two girls walked down the graded street, one streetlamp for a handful of frame houses. Here and there were pecan trees, yucca, thirsty mesquite. The same moon shined above them. The houses were dark inside—one yellow bulb closed in a kitchen, a blue TV in a living room. Silence between everything.

"This whole year has been strange," said Deborah. "I never used to fight with Mama and Pop before. But all they harp on is school and boys, and I can't see the use of either of them. You got to leave tomorrow?"

"On the bus. I miss the beach down there. I haven't been swimming yet this year."

"That's 'cause you read all those books. You're gonna miss a lot of livin'."

"So far what's to miss?"

They walked until the streetlight grew hazy in shadow.

"Did you mean what you said? About going into the army?"

Deborah took a long drag. "I don't know. Pop's got his job, Mama has hers. I just don't want either of 'em. But maybe something will happen. Anything can happen, Callie. Maybe I'll go into the air force, learn to fly."

They stopped in front of a white box of a house. It was sealed up tight. The windows reflected silver, a flag decal crooked and colorless in the corner of one of them. "See that house? The old lady who lives there wraps tinfoil all over her windows. You'd like talking to her—she's crazy. She told me once the Russians were sending ultraviolet rays into her house, trying to scramble her brain. Her brain's already scrambled. Then the next time I saw her she told me it was Martians. She had my pap disconnect her TV set and sell it 'cause the Russians and the Martians were sending her messages by TV."

A speeding car turned the corner, spitting gravel. Laughter spilled out of the anonymous heads inside, and an arm threw a beer bottle at somebody's driveway. The heads howled at the smash it made. Deb pulled Callie into the shadow of the crazy woman's house. "Sshh," Deb whispered. "Stay down. We'll wait." They froze in the dark of the house until the boys gunned the Chevy and peeled away, one taillight disappearing as suddenly as it had come.

"Jesus Christ, they could've killed somebody."

They walked in the blackness until Deborah turned to face the gulch that made the boundary of all the backyards, a creek when it ran in spring, dried by summer. She picked up a rock, a piece of smoky quartz that had cracked and lay in the gutter of the gravel road. She hefted it for weight softly a few times in her hand, then threw it as hard as she could into the jumble of limbs and weeds in the dark on the other side. "It's me, you bastards! Hoo-wee!"

Deborah found another rock and placed it in Callie's hand. "Now you."

This rock was worn smooth, cool to the touch, made ancient by some river that no longer ran, or maybe one that slept at rest deep again in the earth. Callie weighted the globe in her palm like Deborah had done. "Why?" she said.

"For Christ's sake, why. See what you've got in that arm of yours. See how far you can make it go."

Callie pulled back her shoulder and heaved it as hard as she could. The globe of rock flew straight and smooth. They saw it for an instant, suspended in the moonlight, then disappear from sight. Callie longed to hear something break, still she pitched it clear. They couldn't tell where it landed, but they heard it come down. It sounded final, satisfying. To register something in the interim of silence all around them. Just to do it and see how far it could go.

The Hawk

ELIZABETH DAVIS

 Anna's hair is a golden red, wavy. *Like your mother's,* my father told me. He sat at my table, the one I had salvaged from his barn and painted white the summer Jim and I were married, and watched Anna, in her diaper, careen barefooted across the kitchen floor. I was standing at the sink washing the breakfast dishes, setting scalded coffee cups to drain on a muslin tea towel. My father wore his seersucker pants with blue suspenders, a white open-collared shirt. He sucked on his pipe as if he were embarrassed.

Her hair, he said, is like your mother's.

His voice was husky; his face became the mask he assumes when he speaks about my mother. It's a deliberate blotting of all expression, an automatic erasure, more sorrowful to me than tears.

He had waited until Miss Lucy left the room before he spoke. I have always called my stepmother Miss Lucy, ever since she was my teacher at Sweet Gum school. She was out in the yard watering my tomatoes. Papa never mentions my mother in her presence.

And I have always been afraid to ask him about Mama. That's what I call her in my mind. "Mama." I feel shy about calling her that, presumptuous even. I fight myself for my right to say it. But I won't call her Alice. And "Mother" is too formal. It's not that I haven't asked him. When I was seventeen and going out with Jim I said, Papa, did my mother . . . did she like *dancing*? But the curtain of pain that falls over his face, his inner bracing, makes me timid, as if I'm at the edge of a taboo. And I have never asked him a fraction of what I want to know.

So you think Anna takes after my mother? I didn't say "Mama" out loud. And I waited, motionless, letting the hot water rush from the faucet. From outside my window I could hear the scritch of Jim's spade as he shoveled topsoil into the wheelbarrow.

Anna sat down on the floor and played with Papa's shoelaces. No, he said, stroking the back of her neck. I reckon not. She's too dadburned tiny, too delicate. Your mother was a tall, full-figured girl. He doesn't say "woman": Mama was just nineteen when she died. But there's something about her hair, he said.

Rachel, Miss Lucy yelled at me. I jumped. There she was, creaking open the screened door. Rachel, did you know . . . ? She halted for a moment, staring at Papa. A slow flush, as real and as obvious as an erection, crept up his neck, blotched his face. Rachel, she continued, eyes suddenly bright, did you know, dear, you've got cutworms in your tomatoes?

Mama. Alice. Her essence, tangible as the smell of roses, hovered in the kitchen between Papa and me. I turned off the water, wiped my hands on my apron. No ma'am, I said.

You'd best tend to them, honey. Before they spread. Then she was gone, the back door twanging behind her.

Papa stood without looking at me. He picked up Anna, awkwardly kissed her hair, and strode outside with her to Jim. I sat down in his place at the table and stared at the green linoleum, the spot where Anna had been playing. My heart was rushing and my cheeks too were hot against my palms. The room was hushed. Empty.

Anna's hair curls like my mother's and will be thick like hers. I have Mama's wedding picture on my dresser, the one they put in the Sweet Gum newspaper at her marriage. And then a year later at her death. My hair is auburn too, like my mother's, but it's straight and fine, no curl to it at all.

Miss Lucy has a green thumb, and when she comes to visit she enjoys tending my plants. She started my snapdragons and helped Jim and me plant day lilies in a row beside our fence. When Jim and I were newly-weds, I was ashamed of her attention to my plants, as if in her puttering she were declaring me negligent. But now I stand back and let her do it. Last time she was here she took my ailing ivy home with her to Sweet Gum and then, a couple of months later, returned with it healed, its variegated leaves standing tall and sprightly in their clay pot. She likes to fiddle with my plants, so I let her.

When Papa married her, Miss Lucy was an old maid, thirty-two years old, older even than he. She was my first teacher at Sweet Gum School. Taught me my letters and how to read. From the front of the classroom her voice sang out,

> The old oaken bucket, the ironbound bucket,
> The moss-covered bucket, that hung in the well.

Cheeks flushed, she stood before the blackboard directing our chiming voices with a piece of chalk in her hand—the same hand that adjusted her glasses on the bridge of her nose, and that offered me a clean hanky when I had a cold. After Papa started taking Miss Lucy out, I flinched when that hand smoothed back my hair on the playground.

Where was my mother's voice? I searched for it in the speech of neighbor women, my Sunday School teacher, the lady behind the counter at the dry goods store. In my bedroom, Mama's photograph sat on the top of my bureau; and she watched me with keen and gentle eyes. I told my mother good-night, deep into my pillow, after Papa had tucked me in; and, under the live oak tree, I set a place for her with my acorn-cup tea set.

I was seven when Papa and Miss Lucy married. The wedding was held at the Methodist Church, decorated with Christmas candles and smelling of pine boughs. I was never sure that afternoon, holding on to my nosegay, whether I was happy or not. And I suppose I feel that way still. Miss Lucy has always been good to me, and I'm grateful. Polite. But we have never become close.

Today was Anna's birthday. Her first. One pink candle on my silver loaf cake. Papa and Miss Lucy arrived on the train with gifts wrapped in butcher paper and tied with bright ribbon: a wooden wagon made by Papa and filled with smooth sanded blocks, and a pinafore Miss Lucy had embroidered. Anna squealed when we sang "Happy Birthday"; then, bewildered, she suddenly started to cry. I picked her up and lulled her as Jim's rich tenor soared above us all, grazing the kitchen's panes and crevices like sunlight. I cupped the back of her curls with my hand as I bent over the high chair to blow out the candle.

Later, while Jim carried Papa and Miss Lucy down to Union Station, I took Anna to the backyard to cool off in the washtub before her nap. I was relieved that everyone had gone. My head felt dry and stuffed, and my throat was tight. I ran a few inches of water in the washtub and set Anna inside. Then I removed my shoes and stockings, sat in a canvas sling chair, and stretched my legs out in front of me on the grass. My head was in the shade of the pecan tree, my skirt above my knees, legs bared to the sun.

My mother died in childbirth. She died giving birth to me. This is the refrain that circles within me like a hawk above a meadow on a still, burning day. When I was born, my mother died. Even now that I am a mother, the hawk is still there. It lurks deep inside, as constant and imperceptible as my heartbeat. Swooping, hovering, searching, it persists. Or perhaps the hawk is she. Perhaps she is my mother. Now, as I watched Anna splashing in the washtub, in the soft shade of the pecan tree, cicadas making a racket in the heat, even now, that hawk was circling.

Anna stood up in the washtub, slowly, gripping the galvanized tin with her fingers, concentrating. Her hair, wet at the back, was plastered to her neck. At the top of her head, her curls caught the sun, burned with light. She stomped her feet in the water, watched the ripples, then looked at me. A blue dragonfly darted above the washtub. I touched the tip of her nose with my finger. She sat back down.

My mind kept drifting back. Had, all day. Because of Anna's birthday, I suppose. To the fragments, the jagged pieces, of all that I have learned about my own birth. I was tiny when I was born, came too soon. No one expected me to survive. Papa and my grandparents had decided they would lay me in the coffin with my mother. Bare buck naked, I suppose, since all of my baby clothes would have engulfed me. Bundled in one of the flannel receiving blankets Mama had made for me during her confinement. Tucked into the crook of her rigid arm. Mother and child.

They didn't expect me to last the day. But someone, I don't know who, had the foresight to keep me warm. They swaddled me in blankets and put me in a shoe box. Then they heated bricks in the wood stove and surrounded my box with them, replacing them with other heated bricks as soon as they began to cool.

I survived the washing of Mama's body, the stripping of bloody bedclothes from her bed. While someone's hands sprinkled her with lavender, and dressed her in her pink Easter dress which would no longer fasten at the waist, someone else was heating bricks for me, the mewling, ugly girl-child who had caused such chaos.

A wet nurse was found. My Ellen. Ellen was born in slavery, and she died when I was six. She had recently given birth to her twelfth child, Lydia. It must have been Ellen who told me about the day I was born. I can remember her rocking me on the front porch of her little house, in a rocker with a cowhide seat. Where was Lydia? Perhaps napping on a pallet beside us. Honeysuckle climbed all over a trellis, shading us from a glaring sun. Bees, which normally terrified me, hovered nearby. But Ellen paid them no mind. I was exhausted, had spent myself crying. I don't remember why. My eyes were sticky and swollen, and I shuddered in Ellen's lap. We rocked, soft and easy. My head rested on her bosom as Ellen told me the story of my birth. Her voice, like the bees buzzing around us in the heat, was tinged with a hint of danger, a terror associated with my mother that I could not quite grasp.

I survived the laying out. The funeral. Bricks were heated night and day. The neighbors pitched in to help. I was a miracle baby, Ellen said. Thriving in the midst of grief.

Anna sang baby noises, absorbed herself with a leaf drifting in the water. When she touched it, it wrapped around her finger. Extricating herself required both hands. I looked up. The pecan tree's leaves floated against the sky. Their dance was slow, lethargic. The color green, kindled by the scorching August light, rippled in the air. My neck was wet with perspiration. It had been one year since I survived my pregnancy. Now that I had made it through, I let myself look back. Rested my head on my knees. Closed my eyes. Saw violet, emerald green, a black square. Funny. I felt like I might could cry.

Papa and Miss Lucy hated it that we left Sweet Gum. But Jim and I were ready, wanted to see for ourselves about Houston life. So we took off. I was eighteen, Jim twenty.

Jim and I settled in this little house in Woodland Heights and he found a job selling oil field supplies. He had a company car, a Model T, and every day he either went downtown or out to the oil fields—Goose Creek, Blue Ridge, Pierce Junction, or some others. He took me with him once to a spudding-in on the Navasota River. A pretty lady in yellow taffeta christened the test well, then the oil company served watermelon and cigars to the crowd. One Sunday we drove out to Baytown so Jim could show me the Goose Creek field, a forest of wooden derricks that went on and on like the Big Thicket. I had noticed the stinky oil smell from miles away. Jim and I got out of the car and he pointed out to me the various parts of the rigs, like pipe racks, hoists, and boilers. Occasionally we had to step over puddles of greenish oil. Goose Creek was ugly to me and bewildering, but Jim's face was flushed with excitement.

By jingo, he said, this place is a boomtown.

He said hello to the roughnecks, smiling, his cigar wet between his thumb and index finger, his other hand gentle on my elbow as we picked our way through the muddy ruts of the road.

I was learning to cook. Could fix bacon and eggs in the morning, with baking powder biscuits and Miss Lucy's peach preserves. For our first dinner I made chicken with sweet milk gravy, mustard greens, cornbread, and cucumbers and cream. Baking put me into a dither. My cakes would fall, run over, or be soggy. I would ice them before they had quite cooled and rip up the cake with my frosting knife. The layers would split apart, require toothpicks. If Jim came home in the midst of this, he would find me red-faced, flustered. I jumped at his touch.

Jim and I slept in the three-quarter spool bed that had been my mother's, handmade for her by my grandfather. Everything on it was a wedding present: the sheets from Sears and Roebuck, the embroidered pillow slips from my mother's hope chest, a patchwork quilt, the cream-colored crocheted bedspread with the letter *H* in the middle—for Hobson, Jim and Rachel Hobson.

One night, a couple of weeks after our marriage, I woke up to my own screams, found myself in the corner of the room, shuddering and crying. Jim jumped out of bed in his drawers and stood in the corner with me barefooted, his arms around me.

There now, he said. There now, Rachel.

Jim had turned over in his sleep and had flung his hand across my face. Next thing I knew I was across the room hollering. He held me tight for a long while, kissing my hair until I was calm. Then we walked back to our bed.

Anna began to whimper in the washtub, rubbing her eyes with her fists. I picked her up and wrapped her in a towel. Inside, the house was dark and claustrophobic. I diapered Anna, then nursed her in the noisy rocking chair until she was heavy with sleep. I laid her beside the back window where a faint breeze fluttered the curtains above her crib, and went outside again, beneath the pecan tree, within hearing distance.

When we were first married Jim was after me all the time, like a puppy. I tried to be playful, tickling Jim's ear with my tongue, giggling as we undressed. But soon, for some reason, a cold hush came over my body. And I moved far away from Jim in my mind. Noticed a cobweb in the ceiling corner. I would need to wrap a dust rag around the broom and knock that thing down. I began planning what I'd do afterward. I'd take a hot bath then fix dinner. Then it was over. I held Jim with clay arms, stroked his hair with my fingertips. Put a smile on my face when he at last lifted his head.

It's not that I wasn't passionate. Just that once we married, my passion vanished.

There was a time, when Jim and I were engaged, sitting on the front porch swing— We had been kissing, could hear Papa's snores from the front bedroom. Jim pulled me onto his lap. I could feel his maleness hard beneath me. And something inside, my womb I suppose, started turning over and over. I didn't let on to Jim, I just pressed closer, pushing my breasts against his shirt. Turning and turning. Jim was gasping. I kept myself quiet. Swirling, melting.

Rachel!

We heard Miss Lucy's voice from the darkness inside the house. I could picture her. In her nightgown, hair undone, falling gray to her shoulders.

Rachel, are you still out there? It's late, dear. You'd best come in.

One morning after Jim had left early for Blue Ridge, when we had been married a couple of months, I went outside and sat under the pecan tree, my sanctuary. It was October and the pecans were still on the tree, their green jackets turning brown. I leaned against the rough bark, closed my eyes, sank deep into myself, and had a conversation with my mother. Mama came to me in her pink Easter dress and we sat together on a rock in the middle of a rolling stream. We let our feet dangle in the water, chunked pebbles into the froth. The sun sparkled down on us. This is how it is, I told her. She held my hand and listened.

Well, she said. Suppose, God forbid, you do die. Just like me. You get yourself pregnant and die in childbirth. Don't you want to have all the pleasure you can have now, child, while you are still alive on this earth?

I pondered this, holding Mama's hand, playing with her fingers. Then, down the street, someone started up their car. It sputtered. They cranked it up again, and Mama was gone.

I considered what my mother had said, but couldn't get her out of my mind. She was so young when she died. My age. If she were able to come back to life right this minute, she and I could sit in the kitchen, drink hot coffee, and talk. We could catch the Studewood streetcar and go shopping together at Foley's. The two of us would be friends.

Like Mama, I conceived right away, after Jim and I had been married about four months. I began to feel drowsy in the afternoons, took naps. Then began waking up in the mornings nauseous. Is this how it was with you, Mama? I thought. I knelt on the bathroom's cold linoleum floor, heaved into the commode as I had every day for a week, then stood up, cupped water from the spigot with my hand and rinsed my mouth. Could not yet bear to brush my teeth.

I imagined my mother at the same stage of pregnancy, gagging quietly into a chamber pot each morning before breakfast, wiping her lips with a hand towel. Then she would dress herself and go outside. She'd feed the chickens, gather yard eggs in her apron, and stand for a moment in the brisk winter air, her shawl around her shoulders, and listen—to the various roosters echoing each other throughout Sweet Gum, to my father humming inside as he shaved, to a train whistle over at the depot. Then she would climb the back porch steps, scrape open the door, and ease the eggs from her apron into a bowl. To settle her stomach she'd nibble on last night's cornbread as she stoked the oven for breakfast.

Anna was born on a Friday. Miss Lucy was here, had been with us all week. Waiting. Jim called Dr. Nelson that morning when my pains became regular. But he didn't arrive until mid-afternoon. By then I was biting my wrist with each contraction, as if I could cut the whorls of agony with my teeth. The pain on my wrist I could control; the other was a tide carrying me far, far away, beyond my bedroom and the people in it. *Go away,* I thought I told Jim, as he was rubbing my back; but he continued rubbing, so perhaps I hadn't said it at all. Then I bit my wrist again, and left it there wet and substantial against my teeth until the next crescendo. I lay sweating in my nightgown, on a clean sheet, towels layered beneath me. On the kitchen table, brought close to the bed, were two basins of water, cutting instruments, and strips of white sheeting boiled sterile that morning by Miss Lucy. My pains were coming fast now. *Mama,* I panted. *Mama. I want my mother to come take care of me,* I said to myself, but not out loud. I bit on my wrist, my talisman, until I tasted blood. The room was sweltering. My nightgown stuck to me. I feel sick, I said. Then I retched. It's coming now, Dr. Nelson said. *Mama,* I screamed. *I want Mama.*

Someone put chloroform to my nose, and held the cloth there. Suffocating, I wanted to jerk my head away, but they held firm. I gasped through my mouth. A tingling burn coursed through my nostrils, transforming my sinuses into a black flaming cave. Then I was still.

Later, much later, I heard the baby. Miss Lucy was holding it, wiping its face with a cloth. There was Jim, his face swaying, enlarged like a balloon. I wafted away again. When I awoke, someone was slipping the sheet from beneath me. On the table was a tangle of bloody towels. Hemorrhage, Dr. Nelson said. He packed my womb with strips of sterile sheeting.

There was Mama standing beside the bed. She wore a thin white nightgown spattered with blood. Her hair was long, in disarray. She whispered something I couldn't hear. Her eyes were black as olives, expressionless. *Mama,* I said. *Here I am.* I tried to hold out my arms. She began tilting. My mother. She was floating now, at an odd angle. Her auburn hair swirled before her eyes as if whipped by a gale. I reached for her. Someone was slapping my hand. Miss Lucy. *Rachel, Rachel. For God's sake,* she said. I opened my eyes. Her face was fierce. Her hair had come loose from her bun. She rubbed my hand back and forth between her palms. Jim was stroking my face, weeping. Far away the baby was crying. Dr. Nelson loomed in his shirtsleeves at the foot of the bed. The room rocked in the heat like a buoy. But I was cold, shivering. Miss Lucy pulled the sheet around my shoulders. The cries became louder. I turned my head toward the sound. *The baby,* Miss Lucy said. *Bring her the baby.* Jim obeyed. And there was Anna. I reached for her as best I could. She was placed in the hollow of my arm. Squawling, savage in her rage, her little hands beat at the stifling air. There, I whispered. There now. *I'm here, my darling. I'm right here.*

I heard Jim's automobile chug into the driveway, and I jumped up from the grass quickly so that I could warn him before he went inside and woke Anna. I smelled his cigar even before I opened the gate and saw him. He had climbed out of the Model T and was wiping the windshield with an old rag he keeps under the seat. He clamped his cigar between his teeth and had pushed his straw hat back on his head. He had not yet seen me and I took my time observing him, pretending for a moment that he was a stranger. He is a short man, barely as tall as I, and has thick, dark hair, a tanned face from being on the road so much, and brown, almost black eyes. He was humming "I'm Always Chasing Rainbows." His sleeves were rolled up, his shirt wet at the back. I could see through to the ribbed cotton of his undershirt.

Jim, I said softly.

He turned around and smiled, his eyes crinkling. He walked over to me and held me close. Thank God they're gone, he said. I've been wanting to do this all day. He kissed me, maneuvering me backward, as if we were dancing, to the kitchen door.

How was your trip? I asked.

My trip, he laughed out loud. I put my fingers to his lips. The baby, I said.

You mean the baby's asleep? Good Lord in Heaven, he said, steering me to our bedroom.

The trip was downright funny, he said, if it hadn't been so sad. You know Papa and Miss Lucy. They're at each other all the time. Your papa was telling me this story about their preacher, Brother Willard. And Miss Lucy was correcting him at every single turn. Now, Edward, she would say, that is just *not so.* Your daddy finally tightened his lips, ignored her as if she were a dadgum ninny, and kept on talking. Then Miss Lucy got quiet and huffy. She stared straight ahead at the windshield, a sour-pickle look on her face all the way to the depot. I tell you, Rache, I couldn't get them on the train fast enough. Now then, he said, where were we? He caressed my neck then began to remove his shirt. It's too hot for this god-damn *apparel* anyway, he said, pulling me to him.

I played with his earlobe and brushed his hair back from his forehead. Jim, darlin', I said.

Why did I become frantic at the height of Jim's passion, slap at him as if he were a swarm of bees?

Leave me be, I shoved him away. My voice was harsh. Guttural. Tears ran hot down my cheeks. I was shaking all over, edging away from him on the bed until my feet hit the floor. I yanked at the rumpled top sheet. Wrapped it around me like a cloak and left Jim lying on his back, rigid, on the far side of the bed.

I hurried to the bathroom. Ran hot water in the tub. Washed myself with a new bar of Ivory. Cried all the while. Put my head on my knees.

I knew I had wounded him.

I leaned my head against the back of the tub and closed my eyes.

Jim knocked at the door.

I said, Come in.

He sat on the edge of the tub. I put my arm around his waist and leaned my head against him. Crying.

How do you *abide* me? I said.

We were still for a long time. I couldn't see his face. Then Jim reached into the bath water for the washrag and started soaping my back. The washcloth was hot against my shoulders. The water trickled down my spine like tears.

Cheers, Everybody!

CAROLYN WEATHERS

 The Orchid Bar was a dingy rathole, a shoe box painted black, with sagging wood floors and a forest of signs, like "Credit? Forget it!" It thumped with life in an eerie area of locked warehouses and abandoned storefronts where life had left, as though an alien spaceship had beamed everyone else up during the night. The Orchid, scene of stories both lurid and hilarious, was called the Hollywood and Vine of San Antonio because if someone sat there long enough—one weekend—every gay person in San Antonio would be seen walking through its swinging doors.

Next door to the bar was the empty Orchid Café, where Lila lurked. Lila Tankersly, half-owner of the Orchid, eighty-year-old Georgia belle, could cut people so severely with words, they were not aware of the extent of the damage until moments later, when the numbness wore off. By then, she would be dripping honeysuckle at them. From time to time, Lila would imagine herself wronged by the bar customers, slam the café door, stamp along the covered wooden walkway to the bar, sock open the swinging doors and demand to see everyone's I.D., even though she had seen them all before.

On this particular Friday night, she had only minutes before barged through on an I.D. hunt and was now back in the café, cooking hamburgers. Ray Davis, the other owner, squeezed his way around the room popping one-liners to pop the tension left by Lila. Ray looked like Arnold Stang with muscles and was reported to be a tart. No one reported it more than Ray. Nan Grinder leaned over the table, invited everyone over for martinis.

Jane Baker, sitting at the table, was thrilled, but then everything about the Orchid thrilled her. No rathole to her, the Orchid was an enchanted room, the first gay bar her sister, Diane, and Diane's lover, Maria Garcia, had taken her to when she arrived in the colorful, picturesque city of San Antonio from West Texas two weeks earlier. Diane and Maria had pointed out Lila and Ray, and she had met Nan Grinder too. They had told her how poor Nan carried martinis with her in a thermos, like W. C. Fields, because she was a walking ulcer who lived in dread of the day she might be found out for a queer, disgraced and fired without benefits from her twenty years in federal civil service. Nan's paranoia required that she never had just one woman at her house. It was always two or more, or martini parties. Even when Nan Grinder was in bed with a lover, she had a friend posted on the porch, or a crowd getting stone drunk in her living room on the pitchers of martinis she had prepared.

When Nan came over, Jane had been listening to Louis Potter and Garnet, at the table next to her, congratulating themselves on their personal heterosexual disguises, Louis priding himself on the intricacy of his deception, Garnet on the blunt effectiveness of hers. Six-foot, flame-haired Garnet, her knuckles knotted from cracking them and from cracking annoying people's jaws with them, said all Nan or anyone had to do, when people asked how come they were so old and still not married, was say like she did that when that pickup skidded off the road and plunged five hundred feet to the bottom of the canyon ten years ago, it took with it the only man she could ever truly love. Handsome, apple-cheeked Louis Potter had created the fabulous Susan Deering, right down to the Chanel No. 5 which he gave her last Christmas, and which she always wore. To his colleagues at the office, to straight people everywhere, Louis hand-fed nuggets about his and Susan's fabulous love. Louis was so self-assured, so imaginative and articulate, that people ate these stories from his hand like free candy. Only the people of the gay bar circuit knew that fabulous Susan Deering was based on fabulous Carlos Vega, who sat drumming his fingers on Jane's table with the same speed that Jane, sitting next to him, swung her foot in doubletime. Whenever Carlos and Jane played skittle ball, he got so engrossed, he forgot to drink his beer, something Jane never forgot to do.

Sylvia Herrera sat down next to Jane, and Jane's heart hopped. She lit Jane's cigarette, her slave bracelet slid down her graceful wrist. Her knee touched Jane's, it burned through the cloth of Jane's jeans. Jane struggled to think of something clever to say but couldn't even think of something dumb. Still thinking, she reached for her beer too fast and knocked it over. As though directed by the hand of God, it spilled directly into Sylvia

Herrera's lap. Nimble Ray pitched Jane a towel, and she could not sop the beer up fast enough from Sylvia's drenched lap, while Sylvia smiled her gorgeous smile, not like she was laughing at Jane or gauging what she could get from her but because she meant it. *Hey, no problem,* she said, which Jane knew to be gracious, for she had seen Sylvia grimace when the cold beer hit her new blue Bermudas. Rita Bright, watching the two of them, said nothing, just hitched her upturned collar, smoothed her platinum blonde duck's tail with both palms and acted cool. "Cool" meant she made herself have slow reactions, like waiting till her car careened down the street out of control, through the red light and into a parked car before allowing herself to say: *Um, low brakes.*

Rita Bright made Jane's heart hop too, and so did Teresa Simon, sitting across from her, so composed, such fine small talk, such allure pulsating from such a summer halter.

Winnie Butts, the bartender, shouted hamburger orders through the wall window to the café. Next to the wall window, Bee sat back on her barstool and smoked cheroots, rolling them around her beringed fingers. Her enormous Great Dane, Seabiscuit, circled the room, sitting in people's laps by sitting her hindquarters in them and standing her front paws on the floor. From this position, Seabiscuit gazed contentedly around the room, certain she was a lap dog. She would probably have been horrified to learn that she was squashing the chosen one's guts into his or her backbone. The hamburgers were ready. A powder-dry hand with scarlet nails reached a hamburger plate through the wall window and hurled it down the bar. *God help you, Winnie,* said Bee, *if you ever didn't catch it.*

As Jane watched, Diane took her hamburger plate from Winnie, managing a sickly smile at one of Winnie's shallow jokes, while Winnie guffawed at herself and slapped her thigh with her bar cloth. In white shorts and tennis shoes Diane looked almost like a camp counselor lined up for chow, except that her beer belly spoke of nights in the bars for two years, since she got kicked out of Texas Woman's University for being gay and came to San Antonio to work in nuclear medicine on the rebound from her thwarted B.A. Maria Garcia took a hamburger plate from Diane and set it aside for later. No mixing of activities for Maria. When Maria drank, she drank; when she was through drinking, she ate. Whether she played, worked or worried, she kept activities separated like food on an army plate.

Jane took everything in. The Orchid Bar was packed. Everyone knew most everyone, and she was still learning. She remembered the first time Diane and Maria had brought her here, just two days after she came to

San Antonio, which was two days after her twenty-first birthday. They promised a celebration like she'd never had at home. They came in the afternoon, and Jane cherished that light pouring in from the open door and across the floor, saying to her: *You, Jane Baker, are in a bar, and you are legal. You can see by the light it's only afternoon, and you still have the whole night.*

The jukebox played the Twist, the Everly Brothers, and Clarence Henry's "I Don't Know Why I Love You But I Do." Jane raised her longneck Lone Star and said: *Cheers, everybody!* As though they had planned it, everyone in the Orchid Bar raised their beers and said: *Cheers, Jane!* Always prone to surges of emotion, she could have swooned.

Late that night, after the Orchid, after martinis at Nan's and dancing the Twist in Nan's living room with those who made her heart hop, and making dates with them, and after fainting in the bathroom from too many martinis, Jane sat looking out the window of Diane and Maria's apartment on Brahan Boulevard, long after they had gone to bed. The smell of jasmine floated in through the open window, with that of grease on the grill and loud music from Prince's hamburger drive-in stand below, on whose roof was a giant papier-maché hamburger whose toothy onions appeared to cannibalize its own protruding pickles.

All night long, cars came and went at Prince's. All night long, life like a jukebox, just the kind Jane wanted.

Opening one eye to the blue light of early morning, Jane saw Maria stumbling into doorjambs, spilling coffee on the run, and she marveled that someone so hungover could get so promptly to work, so crisply dressed. Maria Garcia, virtuous pilgrim, was a good soldier, who would say, as she retched her way out the door: *I had my fun, now I have my work.* She saw Jane watching from the daybed and waved in her direction. Jane, still under the sheets, wiggled her fingers back, and saw Maria straighten her shoulders and lurch toward the door—where she careened into Diane's new hanging fishbowls. She flayed at the ropes and cussed in Spanish. The fishbowls pitched and sloshed. Furious, she judo-chopped the smallest of the fishbowls, and it slopped out most of its contents on her, except for the fish, who flopped wildly in what was left of the water. Maria glared at them. *Quit your bitchin',* she said. *Be glad you can breathe.* Jumping up from the daybed, Jane steered Maria out the door. Soppy but resolute, Maria ran down the stairs, calling back: *Gracias, Miss Scarlett.*

Jane turned back to the living room to see the apparition of her sister standing by the daybed with her white radiation technician's uniform hiked up, scotch-taping her nylons to her thighs. Diane saw Jane's wide-open mouth with nothing coming out of it and explained, as Jane shrieked with laughter, that her garter belt had worn out and she'd be goddamned if she'd spend any more of her hard-earned money on another one of those mousetraps. *I'll show you,* she said. She fished in the trash, pulled out a wad of shredded white fabric held together here and there with safety pins. Jane shrieked again and said: *Wait till Maria sees.* Oh, Diane said, *she'll think it's frugal.*

They bent with laughter down the stairs and into the creamy light of morning. Jane laughed so hard. Life was like that—a little loose, a little unplanned, parties all over, every Sunday morning a crowd at Diane and Maria's for hashbrowns, bacon and Bloody Marys.

She was hired that day at Joske's of Texas, a department store so huge it wrapped around a Catholic church like a dog around a bone. This job was to be in the accounting department, so Jane had misgivings, since she still counted on her fingers. But—after two months of reading classifieds, marking bus schedules, after walking in circles at bus stops to keep mosquitoes off because even at seven in the morning it was so hot and sticky they were already out, after riding countless buses to job interviews that went nowhere—to get any job was elating. She ran into the hospital and to the radiation wing, where Diane worked. Rounding a corner, she bounded into a woman who held a towel over her mouth. She was in her thirties, classy, in an ivory dress. Instinctively, Jane smiled wide and said: *Hi!* The woman's eyes widened and stared with a horror and despair so chilling, Jane's breath stopped. For both their sakes, she ran. In the staff room, over coffee, Diane told her the woman had cancer of the tongue, her tongue was huge and hideous, and she would die of it. Diane slammed her cup down on the formica table. Coffee spilled across the table and dripped down the chrome leg to the floor. *I hate my job,* she said. *I hate it, I hate it.*

Jane hated it for her, hated that the woman had to have the horror in her eyes and hated that she had seen it and could do nothing about it, she and the woman staring at each other below the random ax. She told herself to appreciate her own smiles, her pearly teeth, her reasons for smiling, before the ax fell on her too.

The Joske's job only lasted four hours. The boss trained Jane, pointing to bookkeeping records as she talked. Jane nodded and said: *Uh-huh. Now then, Jane,* the boss said, *tell me what each of these columns of figures signifies.* Jane said: *Uh, well, this is for balance, this is for credits, and this is for dee-bits.* With shock waves barely concealed in her eyes, the boss said: *Debits, Miss Baker.*

Hell, Jane explained that night to Diane and Maria, *when lunch came, I walked out and never walked back. Without a word?* asked Maria. *I was too embarrassed,* Jane said. *Besides, what was I to do—point to the books of figures and say, Here be dragons?*

Well, hey, let's have a little school, said Maria, already clasping her hands in front of her. *Yes,* said Diane, pointing her finger at Jane's nose. *Tell me: if a carrot is more orange than an orange, has the carrot or the orange been misnamed? It would appear,* Jane said, *that the word* orange *has appropriated the definition which more properly belongs to the word* carrot. *Hmm, excellent,* said Diane.

But not math, said Maria. *Here, answer this. Pretend my hands are flash cards. How much is fifteen times a thousand?*

I don't know.

Nine times six?

I don't know. Fifty-something.

Ten percent of seventy-five?

Are you kidding?

Well then, how much wood would a woodchuck chuck if a woodchuck could chuck wood?

That remark, they all agreed, concluded school. They decided to have *après*-school cocktails, meaning beer, in the kitchen. Low afternoon sunlight filtered in through the window and banana trees outside, casting dusky light and frond shadows on the cool Spanish tiles. Jane watched Diane and Maria cutting up the peppers they had bought that afternoon at the downtown open market. Hot pepper juice ran down their hands and paring knives and glistened on their fingers until the skin peeled. When they finished, they poured the fiery hot sauce into Mason jars, and it rolled in swiftly, thickly, where it waited like lava to burn their mouths through eggs and menudo. Diane and Maria named it Three Sot Hot Sauce in honor of the three of them, giving Jane credit for nothing, she thought, her with her sissy fingers folded round a beer can.

Sylvia Herrera had a screened-in porch. On steamy, sticky nights mosquitoes buzzed outside. Flowery vines pushed dark shapes against the screen and perfumed the porch, where they lay, sweating on her sheets. Sylvia Herrera was smooth as cream. In Jane's arms, Sylvia's body baked. Her touch on Jane's thighs made them steam. Sylvia stretched open her legs. Jane's fingers peeled apart the layers of Sylvia's swollen lips, like a mango, to the seed. After Sylvia's transported face, after her orgasm and woman's moans, then Jane's. Back and forth they went, from being lover to lovee, juicy and swollen as the red berries that nudged against the screen. They stickied up the sultry nights, those tropic nights, wallowing, throbbing, teeth bared and eyes rolling.

Teresa Simon and Jane met for lunch on riverboats plying the San Antonio river, where it cut through the heart of the city. Jane danced down stone steps from street level to Teresa, who waved to her from the flag-stones by the green river. To the music of Mexican guitars they ate, their knees touching under small tables, sparks flying from their eyes and thighs. Teresa ate heartily, but Jane never ate enough, too dazzled by Teresa and the setting, by love of booze, cigarettes and Dexedrine, too tyrannized by fear of fat.

Rita Bright wore sunglasses inside and lived with her grandmother but stayed all over town with other people, with no plans for the next day. She took Jane to dark old houses with closet doors open and clothes hanging out, smelling like mothballs, with hi-fis playing hot jazz at top decibel, where they hung out and partied with drag queens, beats, pimps, prostitutes Jane learned were lesbian too and unidentified characters from San Antonio's underworld. Their cadaverous kingpin said Jane was the best thing since Prohibition, so fresh-faced and candid. He said: *Rita, she's the best girl you ever had.* Rita hitched her collar, acted cool and said: *Yeah, she's gonna stay that way, too.*

Diane and Maria said to stay away from Rita Bright, said Teresa Simon was okay, said: *Sylvia Herrera's the tops, sweet and wholesome, just like you—good for you.*

Jane, she just loved everybody.

Jane and Louis Potter dined on peas and baked chicken, they made eyes and sighs, they charmed, chatted and cha-cha'd. They were at his office party being Louis Potter and fabulous Susan Deering together. Ha-ha, so suave, so chic. How they torched each other on the dance floor, how they made bright chitchat at the table, not neglecting to cast each other knowing looks, more knowing than anyone imagined, double agents they. So pert, so smoldering. Such a clean-cut young couple, with a hint of naughtiness, *un soupçon de boudoir,* as someone said. Louis was so gallant, Susan so alluring. Louis's boss clapped him on the shoulder, man to man, and said he was a lucky fellow. The boss's wife thought Louis quite a catch and Susan Deering such a darling, who wore her Chanel No. 5 with such tasteful discretion.

How successful they were, how restless. How they left before the party was over, hurried, laughing, to his car and sped to a gay bar as fast as they could, for a fix. Louis told Jane where he kept a flask of Scotch. She poured drinks into tiny pewter cups. Louis drank and said: *The boss told me we were the sexiest couple there. I had to bite my tongue not to say, The sexiest couple is a couple of queers. God, what disaster if I had.*

What would it be like, Jane asked, *if we didn't have to hide or pretend anymore to be each other's dates at office parties?* Louis and Jane fell silent, trying to imagine the impossible. Outside the car windows, tantalizing city lights offered adventures of the possible, like the burn of Scotch in Jane's throat.

Fernando's Hideaway was blooming with tropical flowers. Carlos Vega was there, waiting, Teresa Simon, Garnet. Louis and Jane joined them and they took beers to the patio, where, under paper lanterns, they sat on a low stone wall overlooking the river, which reflected back up to them the lights from the bars and restaurants that lined it along the Paseo del Río, River Walk, in the magnolia-scented night. Teresa took Jane's pills away, but Jane found somebody to sell her more.

Early in the morning, headed home from Fernando's and from Teresa, Jane could no longer ignore her hunger and walked down the shaded residential street to busy Broadway and a tiny Toddle House coffee shop. Her high heels clicked on the wet pavement, echoing in the still night. A cool mist bathed her face. She was wired and wined. The Toddle House had room for only a counter, and the counter sat only eight. Electric with good will and one-liners and without much trying to, Jane got the other diners and the short order cook laughing at her Joske's story and begging her to tell it to each new night owl who came in during those deep hours.

Now what was it you said again?

Let her have some coffee first.

Here's a donut too.

Just coffee, thanks.

Now what was it you said to the boss?

*Dee-*bits*, I said* dee-*bits.*

They doubled in laughter, pounded the counter with their fists. She laughed with them, and paused at the door before leaving, surveying her fellow ships in the night. *If you think I say 'em bad, you ought to see how I do 'em,* she said. What affinity, what fun. Life was still a jukebox, but up the street, where dark foliage stood in jumbled silhouette against the graying sky, and smelled sweet and rain-washed, Jane heard cryptic messages brushing the night every time the foliage rustled.

Diane and Maria's balcony seemed far up and the tree slender. How could she have forgotten her keys? She set her Toddle House cheeseburger on the ground by the tree, slipped off her high heels, dropped them by the cheeseburger, pulled her tight black dress up around her waist, held her purse in her mouth and shinnied up the tree. Tiptoeing through Diane and Maria's bedroom, where they were asleep, Jane changed to tennis shoes and Levis in her room, then tiptoed back to the window, climbed down the tree, stuck the high heels into her waistband, held the cheeseburger in her mouth and shinnied up the tree again. Finally, she tiptoed to her room and ate.

The next morning, Diane and Maria slipped on pieces of lettuce and tomato on the bedroom floor. Diane flew into Jane's room, with her left nylon taped on and the other one collapsing around her right ankle, demanded to know where the vegetable garden had come from. Jane told her, and Diane shook the Scotch tape dispenser at her and asked: *Why didn't you open the door from the inside once you were in?* Jane said: *I really didn't think of it till now.* Diane said: *Maybe you should start thinking more, teen queen.*

The next day, Maria got off duty and went straight to the WAC Shack, that fabled beer bar on Fort Sam for WACs only. From there, she came home and grimly cleaned her way through the living room, washing sticky spots off the coffee table as though she were washing up sin, sweeping up dust clouds with the broom. Diane and Jane hunched on the couch, trying to act like they didn't notice, knowing that was what Maria wanted. Even when she attacked the Venetian blinds behind them, wielding the broom only inches from their heads, they fixed their eyes on each other and stiffly pretended to discuss the Bay of Pigs.

More than anything, Maria had wanted the Good Conduct Medal. She wanted it because she was a good soldier, who, though she had been assigned to army typing pools from day one after boot camp, poured into her duties her patriotism and earnestness. Only Diane and Jane knew how she coveted that medal. Maria played it down for fear other people would laugh if they suspected. Jane knew how that was—Diane trying to act unbreakable but never able to stop her tender heart from wrenching at the misfortunes of others, Jane herself with her love of courtesy, her burning after abstract virtues even after learning these were laughable.

Maria had lost her Good Conduct Medal two nights earlier, when Winnie Butts took out Stacey, a new recruit, got her drunk, brought her back to Fort Sam, parked her red convertible in the WAC barracks parking lot and started making out with her. Stacey was so drunk she hardly knew whether she was in the parking lot or the Orchid. Maria was due to report in as Officer of the Watch, but when she saw what was happening in Winnie's car, she tried to get Stacey out and into the barracks. Winnie just sat there, smiling dumbly, rubbing her hands over Stacey, not understanding or caring, just wanting her treats. Maria was late for duty, and that one bad mark, she was told, would prevent her from getting the Good Conduct Medal she was to have been awarded the following week. The recruit, Stacey, was confined to isolation, where she awaited dishonorable discharge for moral turpitude. Sergeants Rusty and Scaggs, fixtures at Nan Grinder's martini parties, had turned her in as a homosexual.

Maria rattled the blinds with the broom. Diane stopped pretending, said she could wring the army's neck, murder Rusty and Scaggs, said she wanted to do something but there was never anything to do. She went to the kitchen and brought back three beers; that was all there was to do.

Three carloads went in a caravan from Sylvia Herrera's barbecue to Stein's Bar, ten miles outside San Antonio on the Fredericksburg Highway, winding up and down the Hill Country, where live oak forests, indistinguishable in the night, exuded smells of earth and river water. The car radio blared, *Here we go looby–loo! Here we go looby–li! Here we go looby–loo, on a Saturday night!* Sylvia told Jane to stop sitting in her lap like a broomstick, lean back and relax, and Jane said: *Sylvia, I can't. I have your jeans on, remember?* Nan Grinder had had the shakes since she heard about Stacey, and she had dropped a plate of ribs in Jane's lap at the barbecue, so Sylvia had taken Jane inside to her bedroom and pushed and shoved her into a pair of her own skin-tight Levi's. Jane asked how come Sylvia could slide in and out of them so easy and she couldn't. Sylvia said: *You're skinny, but look at your hipbones, so wide apart, just made for having babies. Oh, swell,* Jane said. *Why didn't God give them to somebody who'd use them?* From the corner, Nan muttered that maybe she should have used hers.

Two miles off the highway, at the end of a dirt road, set in a tangle of live oak and thickets, was Stein's Bar, known as the Cave. It was owned by two crusty buckets, Imogene and Edna, ages seventy-one and -two, lovers thirty years, who paid the vice squad and Texas Liquor Control Board plenty to leave them alone, because the law knew the Cave was the only place in town where queers danced together. If they could catch them at it, they could catch a big night's haul—arrest a hundred or so of them for being themselves and thereby acting illegally.

In the barroom up front, Imogene and Edna sat playing endless pinochle and watching for police outside, infringements of the rules inside.

No getting too loud or going two to the restroom. No getting quar-relsome or too drunk to stand up. Break these rules and be quickly eighty-sixed or, worse, exiled from the Cave for two weeks. Winnie Butts sat with Imogene and Edna at their table. She smiled and waved at Jane's party. Some of them mumbled hello. Maria nodded curtly. A shadow flickered across Winnie's eyes, and Jane imagined a brontosaurus, barely aware of its own existence, much less anything else's, realizing for a mo-ment that it had not been a good thing to step on and crush its own egg, then forgetting and going on grazing. Winnie shrugged and turned back to the pinochle game.

The back room, the dancing room, was crowded. Couples jostled on the dance floor, extra tables were crammed in at the long tables that lined it. There was too much tension in the room, something out of whack. A wan Carlos Vega came over and said: *Like the discharge isn't enough. Louis was arrested for soliciting two nights ago, on the River Walk.* So, Jane thought, on the night of his office party, while she was leaving them laughing at the Toddle House.

With time, booze and the jukebox, the mood shifted up. Except for Nan Grinder, who chain-smoked at the end of a table and would not dance. Sylvia had to sneak into the restroom every time Jane had to go, so she could help her work those Levi's up and down. Word went around that they were going down on each other in the restroom. Garnet slid into a chair next to Jane and hissed: *What do y'all mean going two to the bathroom—do you two sluts want to get the Cave closed down?*

At that moment, Imogene appeared at the door. The bandanna she had had around her neck was sticking out of her shirt pocket. This was The Sign. Police coming. All eighty scrambled to rearrange themselves heterosexually, lesbians on gay men's laps, whispering sweet nothings. On the dance floor, gay men and lesbians uncoupled from their partners and, without missing a beat, twirled into male-female twosomes gliding across the floor, doing the bossa nova when the police appeared at the door. The old game was on. The four policemen picked their way around the room, glaring and staring, seeking the lipstick mark on a woman's cheek, a man's fingertips touching another's under the table or, worse, by accident on top of it; seeking women in drag among these happy couples playing the heterosexual charade. Except for Nan Grinder, who pushed her chair away from the table and cast pitiful glances to the police, screaming with her eyes: *I am a stranger here. I wandered in off the highway and found myself among homosexuals. After you leave, I'll leave too.*

Maria was drunk and sullen. She swallowed her drinks head back and squinted at the police. The flashing Wurlitzer whirred from the bossa nova record to another one. Maria sang along with it, belting it out: *Hit the road, Jack, and don't you come back no more, no more, no more, no more! Hit the road, Jack, and don't you come back no more!* Ray Davis, in whose lap she sat, swallowed hard as the police turned to glare and the sergeant stalked toward them. The happy Wurlitzer flashed its rainbow colors. Maria's favorite lines were coming up again, and she opened her mouth, about to sing them at the sergeant, when Ray took her chin in his hand and said: *Give a guy a break, honeybun. I've said ten times I'm sorry.* He kissed her. Maria instantly understood, looked Ray in the eyes, said: *How could I stay mad at you, mightyman?* They embraced. The sergeant's lip quivered. He and his partners stalked out but said they would be back.

Nan ran to the restroom and came back green. Garnet said Nan threw up blood. Carlos said the cops made him feel like he was sucking a dirty dishrag. Diane blew out her breath, saluted Maria and Ray with her Pearl beer bottle. Rita Bright sidled up to the jukebox, stood with her weight on one hip, like the coolest thing you could do, man, was move like Mae West and drop those quarters in like you were feeding bonbons to your sugar mama. The jukebox played Dionne Warwick's "Don't Make Me Over." All eighty rearranged themselves naturally, homosexually. Jane lifted her Lone Star and said: *Cheers, everybody!* Everyone lifted their drinks and called out: *Cheers, Jane!*

After the bars closed, and Diane and Maria got home, Maria ran up and down Claremont Street, yelling she was going to kill those fuckheads, those Judas army sergeants, turning Stacey in just to make their own queer asses look straight. It took Diane, Sylvia and Jane to chase her down and keep her in the house until she finally passed out. She stayed in bed all day the next day. Every now and then, they would hear the Sunday paper rustle or the toilet flush, and that was all they heard from Maria.

In the evening Garnet called, mad as hell at Nan. She said she had driven Nan home from the Cave, then Nan had refused to let her come in. From behind her locked door, Nan had vowed that neither Garnet nor any lesbian nor any gay man would ever set foot inside her house again. *Hellfire*, said Garnet; *if she'd just say what I do about her fiancé being killed in a car wreck, she'd be okay.*

Nan not only kept her vow not to let them in, she receded into her house to the point she never came out. For the first couple of weeks, she left to go to work and get groceries. After that, she paid someone to get her groceries. Then she stopped going to work. One afternoon some of the women went over to empty the trash that was piled up and reeking on her back porch. Garnet pushed a note under the door. She had drawn little valentines around it. The closest Jane ever saw Garnet come to crying was when she heard Nan rip the note up, then push the pieces back under the door. Nan said: *Get the hell out of here.* She ran back and forth through the house. Her old friends stopped trying to visit. Every now and then they could see the living room curtain open a little, then drop, and they knew it was Nan. One day, Diane said: *Here's the latest. Garnet told Nan's employers that Nan went crazy because it was the tenth anniversary of her fiancé's death in the flaming wreckage. She really did say 'flaming wreckage.' Nan's employers said, 'That's funny. Nan always told us she was in love with a divorced man who was Catholic and would not remarry.' So Garnet thought a minute and said, 'No kidding? Well, that little sneak.'*

The self-entombed Nan Grinder became a legend and was spoken of as though she were dead, while the stories grew up around her, while the jukebox kept playing at the Orchid Bar and Ray Davis kept popping one-liners and dumb Winnie Butts kept thinking she was charming. The dramas and comedies kept grinding on, at the Orchid, at the Cave, where even petty domestic squabbles got their only public recognition. So they were played for all they were worth, at the tables and on the dance floor—couples quarreling, couples making up—playing to their friends who watched from the edge of their seats at the tables. Jane partied harder, harder, driven to party, driven to keep moving. She had a job as a file clerk, her own apartment and a fifty-name list of people who liked to party. The days and nights blurred past, one night, one party, one crowd the same as any other, the jukebox jangling. King William Street, tropical flowers and banana trees, expanses of green St. Augustine grass and mid-Victorian mansions going to seed. On this street on some morning, after some party somewhere, going to some place for breakfast with some people, getting a little lost in San Antonio, suspended above the grid of it. There was something vague in the hot, scented air, some dissatisfaction rising. Piggy banks were not big enough to make the roots Maria wanted; Diane was changing job plans and hobbies almost daily, looking, not finding, and now saying she wanted to move to California. Jane wondered why she wanted to do a thing like that.

Bee's garage apartment really was one. The cement floor was painted green, the cement walls red. She said she was haggling with the city to get her alley named Bee Lane. Her guests sat on apple crates and drank a new wine called Thunderbird out of Mel-Mac cups and Mason jars, and they watched Carlos paint a gorgeous bird of paradise along one of the walls. Seabiscuit, the Great Dane lap dog, slept at their feet, only because they sat too low for her to get in their laps. Bee pulled weeds growing up through the woodwork, picked caterpillars and threw them out the door into the alley and said, when Teresa Simon asked what she was doing: *Cleaning house.*

Rita Bright cooked paregoric in a teaspoon. Teresa took a slow drag off her Players, blew smoke in Rita's face and said: *It was shitty of you to tell your sweet grandmother that this sweet Jane was taking you to hear the 'Messiah,' but you had to have paregoric first, you had the runs so bad.* Carlos kept painting but said: *Rita, you dirty dog.* Jane hung her head, remembering how Rita's grandmother's face had lit up, and she'd asked Jane where it was being performed, and Jane had mumbled something or other into her shirt collar. She resolved to find a "Messiah" being sung somewhere in Bexar County and drag Rita to it.

Rita shook out the length of rubber tubing and said: *Go check your answering service, Teresa. Your johns have probably been calling all day.* Teresa turned to Jane, took a drag and blew the smoke away from Jane's face. *I mean what I said earlier, Jane,* she said. *I want you to come to my place and let me cook for you, and we can talk about books and music, which so many people in our milieu have no interest in.* Teresa slipped her smooth hand inside Jane's blouse and said: *You take too many pills, sweetie. Your heart's beating like a machine gun.* Ray Davis turned to Rita and said: *This baby's so naive, she really believes Teresa is only checking her heart.* Teresa drew her hand out and said: *Oh, for chrissakes. Don't let them bug you, Jane. Oh, they don't,* Jane said. But they did.

Say, what's that book over there with the naked lady on it? Why, Bee, how risqué, said Ray. Bee threw a last fat caterpillar out the door and brought the paperback over. *That's my book,* she said proudly. *I found it in a regular bookstore. It's about us, about homosexual women.* Teresa took the book, scanned it, made a face like it stunk and handed it to Jane. *'The Lesbian in Society,'* she read. *'A problem that must be faced. Detailed histories of the third sex. Copyright 1962.' Yeah, see?* said Bee. *It just came out, like 'The Children's Hour.' A bunch of us from the Orchid went to see it seven times. There we were, right there on the screen and in the lobby, right there with heterosexual people who could see that we were real people too, just like them. I was so proud.* Bee poured more Thunderbird for all, said: *At the end, when Shirley MacLaine hangs herself, I just knew all the straight people were so sorry.*

Jane winced and so did Teresa. Oh God, pathetic. Ray watched Rita cook paregoric. *Wouldn't it be something,* Jane asked, *if there were gay bookstores? You mean bookstores with only gay books in them?* asked Ray. *Yeah,* she said; *that said nice things.* Ray slapped his forehead: *She wants the world. Well, you never know,* said Teresa. *Yeah,* said Carlos. *When I was a little kid in the forties, I used to say to my mother, Wouldn't it be nice if the radio had a little screen in it so we could see as well as hear it? And she said, Beautiful idea, but it'll never happen.* He added a new color to the bird of paradise and said: *Louis got me on the costume crew in the Fiesta farce.* He said: *I've got some ideas. You'll see.*

Rita Bright blew on the steaming paregoric in the spoon and said: *Okay, Miss Try-Anything-Twice.* Teresa said: *Don't, Jane.* But Jane let Rita tie off her arm with the rubber tubing and shoot paregoric, tincture of opium, into her vein. Even Rita let down her cool and gasped *Oh, shit,* when the blood ran out of Jane's face, just as Teresa caught her, and Jane threw up on Teresa's white capris before she fainted.

Jane and Louis Potter stood on the ledge of the Olmos Dam in Olmos Park in the heart of San Antonio. In the wall of the dam was an opening which led to a tunnel. Workers reached this opening with special equipment. She and Louis reached it by inching along a three-inch-wide ledge that only had room for the heels of their shoes, by inching along with their backs and arms flattened against the wall. When they inched past a certain point and if the floodgates were open, there was nothing but fast, angry water boiling fifteen feet straight down, below their overhanging feet. If they slipped, they would surely fall in the water. If they fell in the water, they would probably drown. But if they moved slowly and if they kept flattened against the wall and if they resisted the urge to run or look down, they would probably make it to the opening in the dam wall, grab hold of the iron grate and swing into the opening to explore the inky, dripping tunnel to the end grate under some street somewhere in the park, where a faint light from a distant streetlamp shone dimly on the bars, where, in the pitch black tunnel, creatures they could not see skittered past their shoes, cobwebs surprised their faces.

Jane was always reckless, and Louis had been getting more reckless every day, ever since his arrest for soliciting, Nan's self-entombment and Stacey's discharge. He said what good was careful; it was stupid, stupid. This was their third time to come to the tunnel. This time Louis had brought a reluctant friend, a man Jane did not know. She stood at the opening and heard sucking sounds back in the tunnel. Suddenly afraid, she wanted to be back on the embankment, safe with Sylvia, who would not go through the tunnel, who asked Jane why she pushed her luck, asked her why she insisted on wasting her brains. Sylvia really wanted to know; Jane really wanted her to stop asking. To be safe on the embankment, Jane had to traverse the ledge one more time. She heard water roaring below her as she inched her way back, her shirt scraping along the rough concrete of the dam wall. She knew if she made it this time, she would not make it the next. She knew she was mortal and would someday die, and that experience of dying would be as real to her as this of standing on this ledge, listening to rushing water and to the sweet-smelling trees rustling in the night.

Patty, the new face from Baton Rouge, lay on Jane's floor by her apple-crate bookcase. Her hands artfully moved from fingering the straw on Jane's Chianti bottle to fingering Jane's nipples. Patty was toothsome and appealing, but Jane, remembering her new resolve, broke away from her and looked out the window for a Sign From Above but saw the same bougainvillea hanging over the same old street. Turning to face Patty, Jane announced that she had decided to change her ways and wait for the right woman. Patty's eyes opened wide. She burst out laughing. *Oh, noble youth,* she said.

How confusing it all was. Jane laughed with Patty, wiping tears that came from crying.

It was Fiesta San Antonio, that weeklong April blast, the Mardi Gras of San Antonio, inaugurated by the Battle of Flowers Parade and followed later in the week by the lantern-lit River Parade at night, with floats built on riverboats. Gay men waited on Fernando's patio to shout *Seafood, seafood!* to the embarrassed sailors riding on the U.S. Navy float, while the sailors looked the other way and tried to pretend it was not happening, forgetting what some of them had yelled and would continue to yell to women on the streets, while the embarrassed women tried to pretend it was not happening. The last parade of Fiesta was the torch-lit Flambeau, reiteration of the Battle of Flowers Parade but at night, where once again the lofty, intricate floats of the Duchesses glided down Broadway—perfume and gossamer, burnished gold and shifting lights, and torches flaming: the Duchess of the Court of the Orchids of Dawn, the Duchess of the Court of the Black Velvet Midnights, the Duchess of the Court of the Scented Gardens of Reverie, the Duchess of the Court of the Luminous Phantoms and, preceded by heralds, the Queen of the Fiesta, the Duchess of the Court of the Hovering Butterflies. Ah, poetry and fantasy!

Each night of Fiesta, revelers crowded the narrow, bougainvillea-studded streets of La Villita, serenaded by mariachis and by the oompahpah band of the German Beer Garden. Each night in La Villita, at the Arneson River Theatre, was a traditional parody of the Fiesta. Revelers squeezed together on the stone benches, packing the amphitheater. Across the lantern-lit San Antonio river, a stately woman wearing a crimson ambassadorial sash across her chest read the Presentation of the Courts and Duchesses from a scroll excessively weighted with hanging seals and ribbons. To howling cheers and laughter, the Duchesses descended stone steps down the amphitheater's center aisle and crossed a footbridge across the river to the stage.

A herald appeared, dressed in oversized livery, and blew a trumpeting call on his kazoo. The woman read and presented the unpublicized underside of all those bloody flowers: the Duchess of the Court of the Wheezing Phantoms, wrapped in mosquito netting and sneezing on command, dropping a trail of wadded Kleenex from hands painted to look covered with hives. Next, all barnacles and clothes that made her look like a capsized Little Toot: the Duchess of the Court of the Sinking Riverboats. Next, the Duchess of the Court of the Drinkers Till Dawn, a great frowsy, blowsy woman, whose dingy bra strap kept falling from her sleeveless, wrinkled, mustard-splotched ball gown, dragging behind her a six-foot train of clattering beer cans and empty fifths.

And then, the Duchess of the Court of the Hovering Vice Squad. Only those in the know knew that this was Carlos's work, and that this was Sylvia Herrera descending the steps in black leotards, knee-high black boots, policeman's cap and scarlet cape, carrying in one hand oversize handcuffs and in the other a cigar box marked "Bribes, please." Fitted over her lovely breasts were plastic cones that emitted the sounds of ear-splitting police sirens, and flashing red lights that swept across the amphitheater and the faces of the audience. Jane held her throat, her heart hopped so high.

Now to the stage came five heralds, five kazoos to trumpet in the Queen of Revelers, the Duchess of the Scented Guardians of Culture and Morals. Only those in the know knew that the Queen was not really a woman but Louis Potter in drag, swathed head to toe in ratty fake furs on which were pinned Limburger boxes and vials of dimestore perfume. He pressed his palms together in an attitude of prayer. Over his face was a stylized mask of a sweet little lamb, on the back of his head a jarring mask of the same lamb, slathering with depravity.

Next day, a crowd was gathered at Diane and Maria's enjoying hash-browns, bacon, eggs, Bloody Marys and Three Sot Hot Sauce, and having ennui. Fiesta was over. It was mid-morning and already eighty-two, the sticky heat pressing down so heavy it carried in it the hush of anticipation, the way the air gets profoundly still before a thunderstorm begins to stir in the leaves. How could they move in this heat, and what could they do besides watch birds hop across the dusty terra cotta birdbath? Garnet said they could knock them off with pebbles and give themselves points. *Nan used to,* she said; *only she used rocks. Come home from work and right away, after mixing up martinis, go out to her back porch and chonk rocks at the little birds. Busted their little heads, too. Never winced, never smiled, never nothing. Just grim, grim, grim.*

No one spoke for a time, just looked at one another and down at the ground. Jane felt there was surely something hanging in the oppressive air. It did not seem to be rain, but no one was sure. It had to break soon. They still did not know what to do. Jane suggested the Cave for *après*-Fiesta fiesta. Sure, okay, everyone said, all right.

They went in two cars. The parking lot was already getting full. They were in time to get beers and walk around in the thicket before it got dark, before Jane and the rest of them went inside to drink at the long tables, feed the flashing Wurlitzer and everybody sing at the top of their lungs to certain songs, like "When You Get What You Want, You Don't Want It Anymore."

Standing By

ANNETTE SANFORD

I arrive at the appointed hour, turning off Waterworks Avenue onto Fountain at five minutes to five on an autumn afternoon, a date that has been circled in red ink on my calendar for a month.

On the front porch of the corner house, a white one built in 1921, my mother sits waiting for me, a magazine open in her lap, her attention trained on the spotty traffic. When she picks out my car nosing toward her driveway, she comes down off the porch, hailing me with a wave. But her smile is not the one I am used to. Obviously she is already imagining the feel of her new teeth, practicing the ways she must accommodate herself to the inevitable.

We greet each other with enthusiasm. She is my mother, but she is a favorite friend as well. Her cologne is lemony, her arms are smooth and hairless, always the object of my envy.

"So tomorrow is the big day," I say, giving her a hug.

"D-day." She laughs more shrilly than is her custom. "*D* for dentures."

I am happy to be home. I was born in this house on Fountain Street. Actually, the house faces Waterworks, but since there are two entrances, my mother chose to turn the side door into the front door, enabling her to use Fountain on her stationery. "Waterworks," she explained when I was growing up, might have given an unfavorable impression to her friends.

In April of this year my mother turned eighty. I have come home to be with her while she has the last of her teeth pulled. Or drawn, as she says.

"Nothing but snaggles," she has finally confessed, giving in at last to the admonishments of Dr. Fitzpatrick, who has hounded her for years to have them out.

The problem has been that my mother is still beautiful. Her skin and white hair complement each other superbly. Humor brightens her eyes. Her chin is amazingly firm, her expression joyous. Only these last four teeth, disloyal at a time when loyalty means everything, threaten to deny her cherished hope that her looks will last as long as her life.

"Are you worried?" I ask, meaning is she still afraid.

She knows what I mean—and of what. "A little." She smiles wryly. "Who wants to end up like Shirley Temple?"

Shirley Temple the doll. Mine. In the spring when I was home last, we came across Shirley while cleaning out a trunk. Dampness had pocked her plaster complexion. Her hair was a sight. But her pearly celluloid teeth were perfect—indestructibly gruesome in that old child's face.

"You won't look any different from the way you look now," I say staunchly. "Dr. Fitzpatrick will see to that."

We all have our roles in this drama of extraction. I am the Sustainer. Dr. Fitzpatrick is the Executor. Mother is the Courageous Victim. For weeks we have been readying ourselves. On the home front Dr. Fitzpatrick took impressions and issued encouraging bulletins. Mother organized for the siege, and two hundred miles away I trotted from stove to freezer, filling the latter with meals enough to last my husband and two sons a month.

In Mother's kitchen I mix a drink. Mother pours a glass of wine and repeats for me what she told the check-out girl at her supermarket. "You won't be seeing me for a while. Dental work," she said to the girl. I am not told what the girl said to her.

Dr. Fitzpatrick's plan is to pop the dentures into place the moment the snaggles are out—an inhuman procedure, in my view, and one I have argued against from the start.

I make a last pitch. "Wouldn't it be safer to let the gums heal first?"

"Nan." My mother is justifiably annoyed. "It's all arranged."

I realize the question, coming at this time from the lips of the Sustainer, is inappropriate, but I am panicked suddenly. All at once the event is upon us. "On your raw *gums!*" I shudder. "Won't it hurt terribly?"

"Of course it will."

"Then don't allow it! Tell him you want to wait until they heal." I am ashamed to be switching horses in the middle of the stream—at the opposite bank almost—but I blurt out like a child, "You don't have to do everything he says."

"Dr. Fitzpatrick is an excellent dentist. The gums shrink if you wait." Then the clincher. "I won't look like myself."

What can I say to that? We finish our drinks and speak of other things, but into every topic my mother injects an "if" clause. *If* she looks like anything in time for Thanksgiving. *If* it seems worthwhile to buy a new fall dress.

At six we go out for supper, my mother's final public appearance until she adjusts to whatever defacements the new teeth impose. I order a Mexican plate. Wistfully she abstains.

"Onions, Nan," she whispers when the waitress has gone. "I couldn't subject poor Dr. Fitzpatrick to that."

The evening wears on, and she marks off the hours like pencil strokes against a cell wall.

"Tomorrow night I won't feel up to doing this," she says when we go for a walk around the block.

Over a bedtime beer she says solemnly, "None of this tomorrow if I'm drugged."

I sleep fitfully in my old room. My mother is used to living alone and groans aloud with no thought of the alarm she stirs up in my breast. At some awful hour she has a nightmare, but I let her escape by herself from whoever is choking her, fearing that to wake her might be worse.

At six the next morning, four and a half hours before her appointment, I hear her bustling around in the kitchen. When I come out, I find her brisk and cheerful. This is not a day she expects to enjoy, but at least her plans are properly unfolding.

For breakfast she serves bacon and eggs, toast, jelly she has made herself, and orange juice, freshly squeezed.

"Eat up," she advises. "It may be a long morning."

During my wakeful hours I have wondered about the incidence of cardiac arrest in elderly patients. Has Dr. F. checked her clotting time? What if her jawbone shatters?

While I push my eggs around, she ticks off the lunch menu: boiled chicken, string beans, tossed salad with oil-and-vinegar dressing, peach pie.

"If I'm able to take a little nourishment by then," she says, "you can heat me a bowl of potato soup."

She has prepared everything in advance. The dishes wait in the refrigerator under hoods of beaded plastic wrap. There is also baked ham, boiled rhubarb, and a corn casserole. The cupboard is stocked with invalid's fare: oatmeal, crackers and powdered milk to soak them in.

After breakfast Mother goes out in her duster to sweep the pecan borers' droppings off the front porch. She waters her fern and trims the ivy that is looping over the banister into her pot of sansevieria. I tell her I am walking to the store to buy a paper.

"Watch out for fast cars when you cross the highway."

In a few weeks I will be forty-seven years old. Unless before then I am struck down by a fast car.

At nine, when I am reading the paper, Mother comes back out on the porch to stand in front of my chair.

"I hope I don't bleed a lot."

"I'm sure you won't, Mother."

"I bled all afternoon when he yanked out the bottom ones."

She gives me a minute to think about this. "Myrtle Studer fainted when she had hers pulled," she says. "I may faint."

I get up and give her a kiss. "You won't faint." But I wonder what will happen if *I* do.

When she goes back in the house to dress, I move into the living room to wait. Her hair is already arranged. She had it done yesterday at the beauty parlor because that poor man (Dr. F.) will have plenty to do without having to look at a messy head of hair. In deference to Dr. Fitzpatrick's sensitivities, she has also purchased a packet of breath fresheners and polished her brown shoes.

At ten she appears with a leather purse hooked over her arm. She has bathed and smells of powder and her lemony cologne. She is wearing a dress I like, pale green with delicate violet stripes running like ribbon down to the hem, and a silver cutwork pin in the shape of a thistle.

"Lead me to the slaughter," she says.

A block from Dr. Fitzpatrick's office she remembers the breath fresheners on the nightstand in her bedroom.

Dr. Fitzpatrick is in his mid-fifties, tall, stooped, with an endearing air of indecisiveness.

Rubbing his palms together he says, "I've been waiting for this day for fifteen years."

Apparently he has cleared his calendar in celebration. No one else is around. Not even a nurse.

"Alma," he says, "would you like to get in my chair?"

"No," my mother says.

"Come on anyway." He takes her arm. "But leave your purse with your daughter. That's what you brought her along for."

Mother hands over her bag and they vanish through the door at the rear of the room. In a moment Dr. Fitzpatrick is back, fiddling with the thermostat above a jardiniere of ailing philodendron.

"Cool?" he says to me.

"Comfortable," I answer.

He studies the yellow leaves at his feet until a blast from the air vent sends him out of the room again.

I flip through a magazine. From the office there comes a familiar grinding sound. An instrument wheezes. My mother and Dr. Fitzpatrick laugh.

I hear my mother say, "I missed you at church last Sunday."

"I was fishing," Dr. Fitzpatrick says.

Across the street I can see the courthouse square. A broad sidewalk surrounds the old stone building. My friends and I skated there after school. The roar of our steel skate wheels skimming over the concrete must have driven the courthouse clerks crazy.

The grinding noise goes on, mixed with unintelligible murmurs. Staring at the courthouse again, I am reminded that skating was the cause of my broken wrist in the sixth grade. One rainy Saturday afternoon I sailed off the porch on Fountain Street and onto the sidewalk in a one-point landing. My aunt Nora took me to the hospital. Everyone else was off in another town, watching my brothers perform in a marching contest. My mother brought a fishbowl home with her. For a reason I can't recall, we never bought a fish for it.

Fitzpatrick reappears, hands clasped together at the back of his white coat. He rocks on his heels. "Give her a pain pill every four hours. Or use your common sense. Be sure she eats. Orange juice, ice cream. If they don't eat, the blood sugar drops. The pain pills won't work."

"Are you through?" I ask.

"Through? We've barely started."

Another forty-five minutes creeps by. Then suddenly they emerge, Dr. Fitzpatrick with his arm hooked in Mother's. She is jubilant, almost dancing.

"Look!" she cries, baring her new teeth.

"They're already in," I say weakly.

"In—and they fit!"

Dr. F. gives her shoulder a pat. "Don't forget, Alma. They have to come out for ten minutes every two hours. Come back in the morning."

Mother disengages herself and grins into the mirror. "They're beautiful," she croons. "The least little bit crooked, just like my old ones."

"It's the anesthetic," Dr. Fitzpatrick says to me. "Like two martinis. Make her lie down."

At home Mother takes off her brown shoes. She takes off the thistle pin and the dress with the violet stripes and her girdle.

"I wanted to kiss him," she confides. "But I thought he might faint."

"How do you feel?"

"Happy. Very happy. I'd like to sing."

"Go ahead."

"I'd like to sing 'When Jesus Washed My Sins Away.'"

"You'd better lie down."

She sits down on the edge of the bed. "I'm bleeding."

"You're supposed to. You've had your teeth pulled."

"Drawn," she says. "Go in the back bathroom and get that little gray pot from behind the commode. Put some water in it, for when I have to spit."

I do as I am told, wondering where the pot has been all these years, remembering its icy rim on my bare buttocks when six of us lived in this house with only one bathroom.

I set it down on a newspaper at the side of her bed and lay a towel across her pillow. She stretches out.

"I'm so happy." She sighs.

"Everything turned out fine. I was proud of you."

"I acted like a ninny . . . all my worrying. But how could I know I'd look this presentable?" Beaverlike, she lifts her lip again for me to admire Dr. Fitzpatrick's handiwork. "Thanks for standing by me, Nan."

"My pleasure."

"Pull down the shades," she instructs drowsily. "Go heat up your chicken. At two you can bring me some soup."

I eat the feast she has prepared for me, sitting at the kitchen table, as tired as if I had wrestled in the dentist's chair myself. I look in on Mother. She is sound asleep.

I stand over her for a minute, considering how fragile the illusion of her beauty is. In repose, her eyes sink back into the hollow of their sockets, flesh sags away from her jaws. In the shaded light her skin appears sallow; her lips form a thin line that barely emits a flutter of breath.

While I wait for her to wake up, I walk through the rooms of the house, inspecting their quiet, testing myself against the silence, practicing.

Hitchhikers May Be Escaping Inmates

PAT CARR

Hitchhikers May Be Escaping Inmates.

That's the first highway sign she sees as she crosses the county line. She grimaces, hears in her head Cody's caution, "Remember not to stop to help anyone. You can't afford to be a Good Samaritan any longer," as she calculates the nightfall and scowls from the highway glare to the horizon. All roseate vestiges are fading from the sunset, leaving the sky a pallid green wash, and the jagged mountains ahead are flattening, blackening against the emptiness. With two more hours of driving, she'll never make it to El Paso before night descends completely. And she's already groggy.

She shakes her head, tries to concentrate on the evenly spaced bars of yellow highway paint.

Then a sudden scarlet light flashes, a startling dot of blinking red that immediately alerts her lulled senses.

The light is inside the car, a ruby square in the dashboard flashing on and off. The needle of the temperature gauge has swung into the wedge marked *hot,* and as she stares down at it, the needle zooms into *danger.*

She swerves the car onto the snowy shoulder, brakes to a skidding stop. In the beam of the headlights she can see white smoke curling from the hood.

Her forehead thuds with the panicked certainty that the motor is on fire. She flings open the car doors, grabs for the tiny hands of the muffled children. "Benny, Arty, get up, come out on the road with me."

She drags them out and leaves them propped unsteadily against each other as she runs back and jerks up the hood.

Steam is billowing from the radiator cap.

"Damn!"

The two little boys are midget shadows beyond the light.

"It's all right, sweethearts. Get back in before you catch pneumonia."

Why didn't she remember to check the radiator water? Now she's miles from nowhere on an empty highway in the dead of winter. "Damnation." But she says it quietly as she ushers the children back into the car, turns off the lights.

Darkness crashes over the motionless car, and one iced star is brilliantly centered above the mountain. Without the heater, the car cools and the windshield begins to fog.

Should she walk on ahead, or perhaps back, to locate one of those emergency phones on a telephone pole? But Arty's little legs can't walk far, and she'll have to carry him or leave him in the car with Benny. Who knows how far one of those phones might be? And how far can she get in the cold? The drifts outside the car already have a solid ice crust. If she goes, possibly they'll all freeze before she can find help.

"Will anything get us?" Benny asks softly from the back seat, his little mouth very near her neck.

"Of course not. I'm here. And I've got my machete." She says it heartily, feels for the machete, and places its leather sheath firmly on the other bucket seat.

The machete, a joke present from Cody for some witticism she can no longer recall, is dull, slightly rusted, and even Benny is aware that the heavy blade, with its etched *Hecho en Mexico,* is unbalanced and virtually useless.

"Oh," his child voice says anyway.

"Now you get back under the blanket," she adds with the same heartiness, and she hears him dutifully burrow into the cover again.

How long does it take for people to freeze? She eases back against the headrest and fastens the remaining buttons of her ski jacket. There's no moon in the blue black sky, the dashboard clock hasn't worked in years, and she has no idea what time it is. She only knows that the temperature is dropping steadily and that the car, settled against the snowy embankment, is growing constantly colder.

Yet surely someone will be along soon. No highway, even in the dead of winter, stays deserted all night. She puts her icy hands inside her sleeves, closes the cuffs against each other, and stares into the night mountains.

Hitchhikers May Be Escaping Inmates. Escaping from what? Prison? An insane asylum? She'd never consider stopping to help some man with his stalled car, never consider picking up a hitchhiker.

But now she's the one who's stalled, who's alone at the side of the road.

She holds herself rigid while the car chills another three or four degrees. She closes her eyes for a moment, opens them again.

And she sees the tiny lights of a car approaching from the opposite direction.

She pulls her hands from their makeshift muff, clicks on the hazard switch. The regular mechanical distress signal begins to tick loudly inside the icy car.

The two lights seem stationary yellow dots very far away. What if the car doesn't stop?

But of course it will.

And the nylon lining of her jacket suddenly sticks damply to the back of her neck. What if the approaching car contains some of those escaping prisoners? Or a gang of hopped-up addicts or liquored teenagers?

Her hands reach toward the hazard switch, but it is as if her fingertips have already numbed with the cold. If she turns off the blinker, the other car will probably pass her by in the darkness. But if this oncoming car is the only other on the deserted highway, how much time do the three of them have in the frigid metal before they lose the last of their body heat? And if this car is that of a kindly elderly couple, and the next car, if there is one, is driven by the escaping marauders . . . ? The headlights are larger.

She shivers, her frozen hand extended toward, but not touching, the hazard switch. What should she do?

And then the other car is directly opposite, speeding past. She watches it in the rearview mirror as the two glinting red taillights retreat. It wasn't going to stop. It obviously holds that elderly couple who are terrified of being robbed and beaten by a juvenile gang pretending to be in trouble.

She lets her breath out slowly. Her tongue is dry to the point of cracking. Disappointment constricts her lungs like a metal band, and she knows she might begin to sob at any moment.

The reflections of the fierce red specks in the blackness abruptly merge and vanish. A narrow shaft of light sweeps across the highway, and the headlights she was watching through the windshield swing into her rearview mirror. The car has turned around to help her after all.

But even as she watches the lights, her relief evaporates, becomes mingled with accelerated qualms. The edging tears cling precariously near the top of her throat. The driver may not be the benevolent husband with a wife, but some man who has debated and has decided that the stranded car is that of a helpless woman. Did her lone figure show up in the blinking light? Does the man know she is a woman alone with two small children?

She hasn't prepared what she should do before the headlights have pulled up to her trunk, and someone is walking, kicking graveled snow toward her car door.

A face leans down to the window. A cap is pulled forward, obscuring the eyes; a beard over the lower half of the face effectively masks it from identification as it becomes alternately scarlet, black, alternately looming, retreating, in the nightmare blinking of the distress signal.

"Having trouble?"

The voice is rough and phlegmed as if it hasn't been recently used. She rolls the glass down an inch.

"My . . ." She swallows. "My radiator's empty. I think it may have cracked." She tries once more to distinguish the eyes.

"I live up there a ways. You can use the phone." He jerks his head to indicate. "If you drive slow it probably won't hurt." There is no inflection to the voice.

And the red/black face disappears from the window, the boots retreating quick and sharp over the iced shoulder before she can suggest that he phone for her while she stays with the car.

She wants to call after him, tell him she'll wait where she is, but as the freezing air rushes in the narrow opening of the window, she knows they can't stay. She has no choice but to follow him. She rolls the window up quickly as the lights glare again in her mirror, back away, and swing around her. The car pulls up beside her, and another bearded, disguised face in an identical cap looks out from the passenger side. "We'll go slow."

The car eases by. There are two of them.

The taillights coincide once more as the car turns again. She can't remain where she is. She turns the key, but the hum of the motor is obscured by the blood rushing into her forehead with aching force. The machete lies on the seat beside her, the sheath orange in the dash light. Fright has drained her strength, liquified her elbows, and she struggles against the steering wheel. Her foot on the accelerator jumps with a muscle spasm as she finally circles and begins to trail the car.

Ice coats the pavement, and she glances at the needle climbing again into the *hot* triangle.

But before the red needle enters the *danger* zone, the car in front veers down a road off the highway. She eases into the tire tracks in the snow behind it, her hands frozen to the wheel, down the narrow road, before she realizes that there isn't a road under the snow tracks, but merely an embankment sloping down from the highway.

The two men aren't taking her to a house with a telephone, but are leading her away from the highway, into a secluded snow valley, away from any possible reach of help, out into the frozen land where no road, no house, even exists.

She thought her anxiety level was as high as it could go, but as the fear explodes in her head again she knows that her terror has merely been on a plateau, that it can quicken, expand.

There's no way she can brake, get the car in reverse on the slope, and she tries to see into the snowy darkness at the side of the car. But before she has quite reached the level snow tracks, she sees in the lights of the leading car a building and then another, pale rectangles of siding that spring from and then recede into the blackness.

They are taking her to a house with an honest telephone.

She takes a shuddering breath, willing her pulse to calm, her pounding forehead to ease. She wants to wake up Benny, shout to him that it is going to be all right.

But her own headlights flash on one of the buildings as the other car passes it. It's an ancient gas station whose windows have been boarded up.

Her cold wet palms lose touch with the steering wheel, and she clutches its glacial plastic without feeling. Her tires lurch on the stones of the abandoned station lot just as the car ahead stops and its taillights suddenly black out.

She is so close behind them that before her frozen hand can release the wheel and shift gears, before she can gun the car backwards, both men have sprung into the night and are coming toward her with astonishing speed. In her headlights they are both heavier and bulkier than their faces suggested. They've reached her door together, grizzled, more terrifying than they were on the highway.

"The phone's in back," the driver says in his alarming, toneless voice.

The other man bends down, peers in the back seat. "I'll stay here with the kids."

She stares mutely out at them in the darkness. She knows that's the way pairs of rapists work. One keeps watch, guarding anyone else who might interfere, even though Benny is only a little boy, while the other goes first. Afterwards they'll change places. They've pushed back their caps and their shadowed eyes seem to be glinting in the dim headlight illumination as they stand waiting for her to get out. They're both large and powerful, and she won't be able to fight off even one of them.

The machete lies useless beside her. To reveal her terror will only goad them on, will only frighten the children, possibly traumatize them. She can't refuse to open the door, force them to drag her out with the little boys witnessing; she can't pick up the machete that they can wrench from her feeble arms and turn on her and perhaps the children. She can't even allow herself to hesitate too long before she follows the man into the darkened house, pretending she believes it contains a telephone.

Her paralyzed fingers turn off the lights, and the darkness this time is almost soothing, a shield to the acts that she must submit to, but that even she might not have to witness too closely. Whatever happens in the blackness might thus be easier to forget. She reaches over, lifts the lock, and opens the car door to the frosted air that is no colder than her hand. "You two stay here," she says, trying to keep her voice from wavering. "I'll be right back," she adds to prevent their suspecting what is about to happen.

She climbs onto the snow crust, which her heels crack through with ease. With the same ease that the powerful men could crush her bones, her skull if they chose to.

She follows the man numbly toward the farthest building. She doesn't glance back as she wills her mind to divorce itself from her body, to exist outside her limbs where sensations and memory can be suspended. But her mind is remembering, planning, with furious speed. She remembers that sometimes if a rapist can be made to see his victim as a person, he may be diverted from his purpose. If she starts talking about Cody and the boys, babbling about her life, about every homely thing that comes into her head, perhaps the man will recognize her as a woman, as a wife he himself might have had, as a mother, and perhaps he'll be stayed, and she can drive away unhurt.

"In here," he says.

Tall plants that may be massive abandoned weeds tower beside her, sift snow over her in the darkness. She stumbles at the threshold as she steps through a doorway down into an airless room blacker than the night.

The interior is hot, cloyed with ancient closed smells as if it hasn't been opened for months, possibly years, and the rancid closeness takes her breath away, halts her racing thoughts. Coming directly in from the clean snowy night, she feels as if she might suffocate, might fall insensible to the floor, cheated of a last chance to talk her way out of danger. The man is very near her, and his heavy wool clothes give off the odor of stale smoke.

At that moment, she glances beyond the hall partition, sees at the end of another dark room the pale blue-white square of a television screen, the shadowed figure of a woman in an easy chair beside it.

"Well, it's about time," the woman's voice says. "Did you and Jay get any deer?"

"Naw. Just saw half a dozen does the whole three days." He is shrugging off his jacket. "This lady here's got a busted radiator. She needs to use the phone."

Whooping Cranes

ELIZABETH McBRIDE

It was early in August when I saw Laurence in the library. He was dressed in an old cotton shirt with one initial embroidered on the pocket, narrow slacks, handmade shoes, the whole drawn together by an ancient but still elegant silk tie. He is bald, of course, but I love the intellectual look of a bald man. And I love his hands, the long fingers neatly manicured, the skin and flesh so transparent they seem to have been poured like wax over the deep blue veins. His foolish smile I do worry about. When a man is over eighty, one wonders if he is senile, especially when he's a genius and we have accorded him the right to view the universe in an eccentric way.

We settled side by side in the periodical reading room, I on his right so he could hear me more clearly.

"I have been thinking," Laurence began, looking over the room with little darting glances, for all the world like a bird about to peck at its feed. "You are at a dangerous age. I can't get involved with a woman your age, and in such a state." He lifted my hand. "I know you're looking around— something every woman does when she's thirty. But it would be awful for me." He shook his head. "I'm an old man, Alice. I would become dependent on you."

I laughed, a nervous laugh that had always gotten me into trouble. "No, darling, you mustn't laugh," he said. "I have my fantasies, but at least I know they aren't real." He leaned over and sniffed my neck. "You smell like spring." His lips twitched. "May I touch you?"

I didn't answer but he touched me anyway, smoothing my skin lightly where the collarbone meets the shoulder. I was uncomfortable. I knew he'd been talking loudly and when I looked around I saw two young men at the next table sneaking glances over the top of *Paris Match*. But as Laurence's fingers moved over my skin, my mood changed. When he ran his hand down the inside of my arm from elbow to wrist I forgot everything.

"I'm not thirty, Laurence, thank you for the compliment. I'm thirty-seven."

He examined my face. "That's different. That's different indeed," he said.

I couldn't imagine how seven years could make such a difference, but I was beginning to realize that I could be entranced by this man. He might be eighty years old, but if sex is a skill, he must have sixty years of experience.

"You're very responsive," Laurence breathed. "Does this bother you?"

"No," I whispered. "I like it."

Laurence began to describe my life, to analyze. "You're in a crisis," he said, "which is taking place precisely because your life is so satisfying."

When he said this it seemed possible—that a woman could search for something because she had everything she really needed. But I knew I didn't have everything. It might have been malaise, the cliché of a marriage gone dull. Blake was kind, but he had almost stopped talking to me, and lately, it seemed, he had even stopped listening.

"Your search is self-indulgent, Alice," he said. "You'll have to be careful. Someone could hurt you. Someone probably has."

I ignored the question in Laurence's voice. He laid his hands on the table and stared into the distance, far beyond the library walls. "It's wonderful to be young," he said, a sad weight in his voice.

I put my hand on his arm. "When you look at me, Laurence, I feel young."

When he looked back, his eyes were sharp, as if the lens he was looking through had suddenly changed focus.

"You mustn't waste yourself on me," he said.

"What does it mean to waste yourself?" I asked.

"You should forget me," he said, pulling reluctance into a full circle. "Do you want to forget me?"

I felt my body relax, the last strings of tension go limp. "No," I said, looking into the clear bright blue of his eyes. "No, Laurence, I can't forget you."

I had known Laurence casually for a year, but I didn't know him well. We met at a lecture, and then in the Eagle Supermarket on Kirby a week later. It was raining and Laurence was dressed in a raincoat and checked wool pants, with a funny shrunken hat on his head. I was wearing old boots, a long challis skirt, and one of Blake's jackets. Blocking the aisle with our scantily filled carts, we examined each other. Laurence asked me what I'd thought of the lecture; I said that I was impressed. He smirked.

"Then why did you go?" I asked, knowing the answer. He's never taught at Rice but he loves to attend functions there because everyone knows him. He taught at Yale and moved to Houston to be close to his son.

"What do you do?" he asked. I explained that I designed and made quilts, that I worked at home, that I was often alone. A few more encounters—the newsstand in the village, the all-night grocery store everyone calls Freaky Foods—and the relationship progressed from mere recognition to a warm acquaintanceship.

Meanwhile we began to correspond. I sent him an article about the golden eagles—he loves birds. He mailed me the draft of a paper. For your comments, he said. I wasn't fooled. He was reminding me he was a major figure in twentieth-century physics.

"My dear child," the letter began. It was peculiar how formal and sexy Laurence could be at the same time. "You should read Dante in the original." I groaned. "I taught myself Italian to do so. I also taught myself Hebrew. The Old Testament is entirely different, much more somber, not as lyrical as the King James." I could almost hear him, the emphasis, the formal cadence. "The English is wonderful, so erotic in places." The letter went on, but his lessons were always in shorthand. "Read Spengler. He understands." Understands what? I wondered.

One afternoon I almost collided with him in the American Lit stacks. He held up a copy of Stevens's *Collected Poems*. "Have you read this?" he asked.

"Of course."

"What does your husband read?"

"Mathematics and science mostly."

"Do you read what he reads?"

"I'm not a scientist, Laurence. He edits a medical journal. I sew for a living."

"I thought you were an artist," he said.

"I read an article if Blake asks me to."

Laurence sighed. "When I was young, everyone understood the connections between things—Heisenberg knew he was the Picasso of physics." I waited. "Mathematics and poetry spring from the same well of human knowledge," he said.

"But what does that mean, Laurence?"

He was already turning away. I hated it when he wouldn't complete his thoughts, when he talked down, when he evaded my questions. I called him the next day, but he wouldn't elaborate.

"I'm afraid," he said. "When my wife died, I thought I would never touch a woman again."

"Afraid of what?"

"My dear, I'm afraid of explaining myself to you."

"Laurence, you never tell me a thing. It's not fair. I'm as clear as a crystal to you and you deliberately make yourself opaque. You hide, full of your secrets."

"Yes," he admitted. "My self-consciousness is excruciating."

I was angry. "Even I can identify with that," I said. "You compare your inside with my outside and you think when I appear calm there's no turmoil."

I worked steadily into September, completing a new set of appliqué designs. I almost gave up on Laurence, though Blake reported several times answering the phone in the study and hearing only a click. Blake was working at home now. We were expecting George and Tanya, friends from Mexico. It was a good time for a visit. I was between commissions, tired of reading, a little depressed. It upset me that Blake hadn't noticed; I thought there should be more understanding between us.

George and Tanya drove in about noon. After we carried the luggage in, I sent George and Blake to Jamail's for steaks. While they were gone, I made a salad and chatted with Tanya. I have always envied Tanya. Even with her blonde hair cut as short as a boy's, she looks utterly female. She wears cool Mexican fabrics, dyed in muted colors. Her arms were covered with silver bracelets which clinked together every time she raised her glass. I started slicing the pepper.

"I want to see something garish," she said. "Typically Houston."

"You saw it on the way in," I said. "Flashy architecture, crummy expensive town houses."

"Yeah," she said. "I could even stand to walk through the Galleria."

"I love the Galleria," I said. "It's got everything no one needs."

"That's what I want," Tanya said. "Something I don't need."

"I want to take George with me to a lecture—a famous physicist is talking at Rice."

"What's his name?" she asked.

When I told her she got that intense feline expression she always gets when she's trying to look smart. "I've heard of him. George will probably want to go. I don't want to take him with me to Aileen's. He hates Aileen. But what about Blake?"

I hadn't thought about Blake. "He likes to stay at home," I said. I looked at Tanya. "Laurence seems to be courting me."

"Courting you?" She was visibly shocked. "He must be over ninety."

"Eighty-one." I scraped the pepper to one side of the cutting board and took a tomato out of the refrigerator. "Besides, he's fascinating. He seems to know what I'm thinking."

"I'll bet," she said. "What does Blake think?"

"I'm not sure he knows—he doesn't always listen."

"Especially when you tell him things when he's working. I know you, Alice. My God, can't you find someone your own age? I wonder what he can do in bed."

I lined the carrots up in a neat row on the cutting board. "According to the newspaper," I said, "it's possible to have a normal sex life into your eighties. All you have to do is be healthy."

"Don't you have to keep in practice? Otherwise it atrophies."

"Atrophies?"

"You know what I mean, Alice."

"I haven't asked him," I said.

Tanya looked out the window at the morning glory. "You've always liked old men."

I told her I liked them because they know things. "Laurence says my worst fault is trying to find out what people know. He says most people are selfish with knowledge."

"Well, Alice, if you get him into bed, talking is probably all he'll be able to do there."

Tanya sat quietly while I assembled the salad and wrapped the bowl in plastic wrap. When the phone rang, I answered it with my back to her. I could tell from the breathy silence that it was Laurence.

"Darling," he said finally. "Have you read about the whooping cranes?"

"Blake mentioned them just the other day. They're dying out."

"Have you seen them?" he asked.

"I saw them last year at Aransas. Blake says they don't have any right to exist, he says they should have vanished with the Ice Age."

"You don't care, Alice."

"Laurence, I really do. Everyone cares about the whooping cranes. I'm glad you called, but I can't talk. I'm bringing a friend to your lecture. I'll see you there."

George and I left my car at the Rice student lot and walked through the azalea garden and under the oak trees to the quadrangle. It was a time in Houston I love—when the heat is strong enough in the day for swimming, perseveres gently into the evening, and disperses at night. George and I had been friends before I met Blake; in fact, he introduced me to Blake. He has a talent for keeping the sexual tension between us below the surface. He had grown a moustache and I couldn't keep my eyes from moving over his face. When he wasn't talking, he was whistling a tune he had whistled for years, a melodic phrase from an opera whose name I never remember.

In a room warm with smooth inlays of wood and brilliant lighting, Laurence was waiting. It was a festive occasion—the anniversary of Einstein's birth—and all the intellectuals and pseudo-intellectuals had turned out. Sometimes it's hard to tell the difference. Finally Laurence spoke. His crisp voice wavered at times but it never stopped. He stood with dignity, his eyes burning. George whispered that the content of the lecture was questionable, but I didn't hear a word. I never once took my eyes off Laurence's face.

At the reception I was too dazzled to approach him. I could see his eyes exploring every inch of my body. I knew he thought my broad Slavic face was too wholesome, and tonight I had compensated. I wore an Indian silk dress slit down between my breasts, with the ties hanging.

"He's watching you," George said, handing me a glass of sherry. "I heard a physicist telling a joke about him. He still publishes, but it's a scandal. He's lived too long."

Laurence was moving toward us, his frail body almost hopping from one appreciative matron to another. "How lovely you look," he said to me, ignoring George.

I smiled. "I thought you were wonderful, Laurence. I'd like to introduce you to a friend, George Weidman."

"How delightful." Laurence murmured a few words, obviously insincere, and moved on. Just as we were leaving, he approached a woman about fifty years old, slightly plump, very attractive, with a fine olive complexion and black hair fastened carelessly at the back of her neck. Laurence placed his hand at a neutral position right at her waist, then let it slip to an intimate point on her hip.

Before we said good-night, George and I sat for a while in the living room. "What do you want to know?" I asked.

"I want to know what you plan to do with him."

"I don't know. Sometimes I think there's nothing I could deny him. You can see he's used to getting his way."

George agreed. "He's very determined."

"But what about that woman?" I asked.

"Don't be silly, Alice. He wants you."

"Is that so hard for you to understand?" I asked.

George stood up. He kissed me, a mere brush on the cheek. "It's late," he said. He turned and walked stiffly and formally out of the living room and down the hall.

I almost called out to him. Instead, I walked to the mirror and looked in the glass. "He's right," I thought, brushing a wisp of hair out of my eyes. "It's late."

The next day, I called Laurence. I thought he would be elated, but he was complaining. I assured him that although I couldn't understand his work, I knew how important it was. "No, Alice," he said. "What you don't understand is how important it *isn't*." I was shocked. Of course, compared to Einstein, Planck, or Von Neumann, Laurence was second-rate, and for a man like that, second-rate was not enough.

"Laurence, even Einstein could have felt like a failure if he'd wanted to."

"Yes," he said. "He never finished his theory."

He lapsed into a painful silence. It wasn't hard to understand; I wasn't satisfied either. I had wanted to go to college, to have a nice home, to have work which interested me, and I had all that. But it wasn't enough.

"It's never enough, Laurence," I said. "Nothing is. People are too perverse."

My words were no comfort, but his voice did come alive when he asked to see me. "Come to my apartment," he urged. I hesitated. "Come to my office, then."

"All right. I'll come on Friday. Eleven."

I started looking through my clothes at nine, knowing that Laurence understood the calculations involved when a woman dresses to meet a man. It was still warm, still summer. Finally I chose a red-flowered sundress which seemed demure for the amount of flesh it exposed. I was excited, but there was more to my excitement than meeting Laurence. Crossing the lawn between the parking lot and the library, I was crossing a grassy expanse I had loved for years. Under the crepe myrtle at the end of the chapel, I had dawdled through hot, passionate afternoons with a boy who left for Canada instead of Vietnam. At the side of the physics building I had knelt in the whispering gallery, two semicircular brick walls on either side of a doorway. I had argued politics here and contended with clever boys who knew the Aristotelian case for premarital sex, the Kantian case, the Kierkegaardian case. I was used to being excited when I came to this place.

Laurence's office was in the physics building. Because of his reputation, the department provided the space. In return, he made himself available for consultation. I tapped on the door. Fluttering awkwardly, Laurence invited me in. He pointed out the personal objects he thought might interest me. His wife had been dead for eleven years, he said. Her eyes gazed coolly out of an old wooden frame. Clean and innocent look-ing, her face was surrounded by gathered organza. Her eyes were wide and her brows thick and straight across. With that old-fashioned dress and her hair on top of her head, she might have been photographed just before the first war. Beside her their son was framed in silver, as prim and arrogant as any man who wants to eclipse his famous father. The two grandsons, healthy in plaid sunsuits and skillfully cropped hair, played in a garden. On the windowsill to my right there were dozens of books, hundreds more on the floor. I opened one.

"These are library books, Laurence."

"Yes, they keep asking me to return them."

"You've had this one over a year. Someone might need these."

"*I* need them. I'm working on something."

Outside the narrow window, the view opened out on the lawn. In the old days, wisteria grew near the benches, and a huge oak tree shadowed the walk. Now there was only grass. Laurence continued to flutter. His jacket was hung on the door and he was wearing a short-sleeved shirt. I sat down. I could imagine that woman buying him dozens of shirts, enough to last him a lifetime. When Laurence caught me staring, he put down his book and edged around the side of the desk. He asked me to stand and I obeyed. He held me by the arms, above the elbows, smiling slyly, remarking that I could lose a few pounds, perhaps five. Imagine, I thought, a man his age complaining about my firm, Botticellian flesh. He kissed me, a quick little kiss, and then another, his tongue darting voy-ages between my lips. I moved my hands over his back, pressing my body against his, rubbing the back of his neck as he sniffed my ear, crooning to me in his crisp, ragged voice.

"How can you smell so young?" he asked.

When I was with Laurence, time was of little concern to me. "I am young," I said.

"I dream about you," he whispered, his hand moving inside my dress.

"What do you dream?" I asked, barely breathing. He slipped the straps of my dress down and lowered the bodice. He moved one hand slowly up my leg as he put his face to my breast and touched his tongue to the nipple.

Suddenly there was a sound at the door and Laurence jumped back, like a clown popping out of a box. "There's someone at the door," he hissed.

"I know," I moaned, barely composing myself before the door opened.

"A goddamn graduate student," I thought—and I was right. A bearded young man stuck his head through the open door and asked an incomprehensible question. I was aching for Laurence to boot him out but instead he answered the question, moving only too easily from one role to another. When the student finally left, Laurence seemed distracted, lifting books, opening drawers, examining pictures as intently as if he had never seen them before. My body was strung tight as a wire and Laurence knew it. But he didn't touch me.

Finally, Laurence faced me, sadly, glancing several times at the door as if he wished he could be rescued. He pulled his chair around the desk and sat leaning forward, his shoulders hunched and the palms of his hands on his thin knees. His arms were narrow, the wrists and elbows too large for the rest of his body. He looked small then, with none of the bulk the sheer energy of his body could give him.

"There are things I don't talk about." His eyes were hooded, his voice textured with strain. "You are almost in love with me, but not quite." I looked down at my hands, lying still and clenched in my lap. "You are cautious," he said. "I like that. When I dream, I am tempted to tell you I love you, tempted to call you and say, 'I love you, Marguerite.'"

"My name is Alice."

"Alice. I have to tell you, Alice," he said, his voice so low it seemed he could hardly speak, "there is something I cannot give you. I cannot give you sex."

He was so intense, I could feel his emotions, almost see them, swirling together like the marbled endpapers in an old book. I remembered our first meeting, when he was so eager to speak to me I flattered myself that his interest was intellectual. I allowed myself to fall a little in love, because he was old, because I thought I'd be safe. I had always been afraid of men, who can make themselves part of your body and leave, as easily as I might leave half an apple uneaten on my plate. What I'd loved about Blake might simply be that he'd stayed. But every word Laurence had spoken had drawn me closer. If I'd been afraid at first of making love, I was afraid now that he couldn't.

I stood up and put my hand on his cheek. "It doesn't matter, Laurence, truly it doesn't," I said. "Besides, if I were you, I wouldn't be so sure."

Blake and I went to Denver. It was a good trip—the weather was pleasant, we were comfortable together, and I saw some wonderful quilts. But I missed Laurence. As soon as I got back, I called him. "I'm back," I announced.

"You've been back for days," he said.

"Laurence, you've got your dates mixed."

"It doesn't matter," he said. "I've been working."

When I told him I wanted to see him, he insisted I come to his apartment, where we wouldn't be disturbed.

"What about that woman, Laurence, the one I saw you with? Does she drop in?"

"That's nothing, Alice. I've never touched her."

"I'll have to think about it," I said.

A few nights later, the weather changed and I felt restless. When the rain stopped, I invited Blake out for a drink. He had spread magazines all over the dining room table. When he shook his head, I left. I drove to the Exxon station and called Laurence.

"This is Alice."

"My dear, you haven't forgotten me."

"Don't be ridiculous, Laurence. May I come over?"

There was a long silence, broken by small sucking noises. "Laurence, what are you eating?"

"A dried apricot. I suck on them for strength."

"Do you want me?"

"Yes," he said. "In thirty minutes."

I didn't want to go home so I drove to Chaucer's. It wasn't out of the way—Laurence lived in an old brick building behind the Plaza Hotel. I ordered one drink and drank it quickly.

Laurence was waiting for me in front of the house. I had never seen him so casually dressed—in a pair of polyester slacks and a terribly dreary knit shirt with a collar that spread limply. He put his arm around my waist and walked me inside. The apartment was the second surprise. I had imagined something more masculine, hodgepodge, perhaps, or something spare, certainly not such a cheap and pathetic attempt at chic. An especially dull brown silk hung at the windows, a nondescript print covered the chairs. And in the bathroom everything was blue—the walls, the floor, the shower curtains, even the soap. But I could see it suited Laurence, a terribly somber man. He had light to read and he had his books, stacked everywhere, on shelves, over the dingy rug, the silly French Provincial tables, even in the one comfortable chair.

I was anxious, and when I spoke, Laurence told me my voice was harsh. He put his arms around me only to have me pull away, then turn to embrace him, then pull away again. He reproached me, saying I laughed at inappropriate times.

"I'm nervous, Laurence."

"Is this the first time?" he asked.

"The first time for what?"

He looked into my eyes. "It's none of my business, of course. Come sit with me on the couch."

I sat beside him and he held me by the shoulders, turning my body until it was almost horizontal across his lap. He fumbled awkwardly with my clothes. "I want to smell you," he said.

I took off my blouse. I felt ridiculous lying half-dressed across the lap of a fully dressed man, but when he began to touch me, my body warmed. He sniffed my neck and breasts, teasing me with his tongue until I could feel the heat pooling between my legs.

I asked Laurence to kiss me, but he didn't. "You pay too much attention to kissing. Smelling is better." Instead, he turned my skirt up and rubbed his fingers lightly on my thighs. I was almost naked, my blouse lying across the back of the couch, my skirt bunched around my waist, the ribbon I'd worn lying curled alone on the floor. I shivered and Laurence took me into the bedroom.

The room he slept in was small, and full of light from the streetlamp outside. I removed the rest of my clothes, and with his eyes on my body, Laurence removed his. I had never imagined that he could look so young, such an old man, his chest smooth, his body thin, the hair a soft sandy color threaded with gray. The only part of him that really looked old was the part that showed when he was dressed. But even then I was anxious, until he unbraided my hair.

Laurence lay on his back on the narrow bed as I bent over him, my hair brushing his skin. I kissed the hooded eyes which could look so sad, the smooth chin, the cheeks, the small mouth. I curled my body around him and touched him, combing the hair with my fingertips. At first he seemed to respond. He would open his eyes to touch my breasts, to stroke my thighs, to run his fingers tentatively between my legs. But all too soon he would stop, and fall back on the pillow. I was sure he was happy. His mouth was spread in a smile. But as I caressed him, trying everything I thought might arouse him, he only grew less and less aware of me. Laurence had always hinted that he thought of me as Marguerite, or Beatrice, and himself as Dante, or Goethe, or Faust. Now, although I could barely catch his whispers, I thought I knew where his mind had gone. I was desperate. I did not want to give up. But no matter what I did, no matter where my hands lingered, my fingers, my tongue, his body remained quiescent. Finally, I sat up and looked at his face.

In the light from the street, I could see on Laurence's face and neck the signs of age. Like the whooping crane, he had lived past his time.

Laurence had given all he could and I guess for the rest of his life he would only dream, only receive.

He was right; I was hurt, while he lay happy, that foolish smile playing across his face. Like a bird, he had vanished—into another world. I knew it wasn't that Laurence couldn't make love to me that divided us now. It was fantasy. I had expected a man like Laurence to know enough to appreciate me. In fact, it was worse. I had thought he would know enough to be grateful.

Sabor a Mí/*Savor Me*

ADELA ALONSO

 All day I think about fucking. I see you in your tight black pants, your pointed boots and your mariachi tie and can't help but undress you till you twitch and sway, your mauve penis stiff with song. The more exciting because no one else knows. I undress you again. This time I hold you from behind, caress the hair of your armpits, kiss your back. No one notices. They go on playing the violin, the vihuela, unaware you no longer play your trumpet. I play your trumpet.

Modest, you claim you can't dance. I know it's moonshine. I can see it in your brown-sugar eyes. Gracefully you borrow my footsteps, dance in my shoes. Our hips move in hurried undulation, like the arms of a locomotive. I know you can dance—you're my echo. We dance merengues, cumbias, danzones, huarachas, boleros, salsa, chachachá, we outdance everyone at the party except Juan, who has offered you a ride home. My husband away on business again. Good Juan waits and waits like a patient grandfather and is deaf to our locomotive pulse. We dance and your warm body asks for mine. Juan watches, waits. You play the best drunken actor and we convince Juan that you must stay, that I don't mind, that I will take you home early the next day, that it really is no trouble at all.

No trouble at all. Your hands, soft tobacco, brush my fingertips. Your hard conga-ass like chocolate, hairy kiwi, buttered slice of bread. Your mouth stale from beer and wine, our kiss is a cabaret.

You like it soft, in the dark. We undress despacito, pianissimo. Y me hablas en español. It's been so long since I've heard palabras de amor in my own language. Cosas lindas, gentle words. The sweetness of my mother and father in your tongue. Your tongue on my nipples. I am la morena más guapa y tú eres mi Pedro Infante, you come with your horse, singing to me mouthfuls of voice, spoonfuls of falsettos. I gracefully tilt my head, and wrap my rebozo a little tighter. La güera más morena. Bésame, bésame mucho.

Love words are made from scratch, from any flour, from any language, and still are molded into bread. Odd that after many lovers you are the first Mexican, myself a Mexican. I bake bolillos and conchas again. I coo to you.

You ask what color son tus pelitos acá, son rubios? I show you my cunt in broad daylight, it is really not blonde as you thought, it is rather brown, so ordinary. You say: "You're not shy, are you? Other girls would be hiding under the covers." Yes, hiding like you hide, like you pull the sheet over us again and again when all I want is to see your mahogany body, your jet black down. Soy la más morena, la más guapa, envuelta en mi rebozo. Y tú mi Pedro Infante.

Halfway through sleep my mother visits me and whispers ugly words. Puta, me dice. Sinvergüenza, sucia, cabrona, ya no vales nada. Words I long ago buried in my boneyard. I fight her words but sleep pulls me under and I am forced to listen. With all my effort I open my eyes only to find my husband's beautiful smile looking at me from his picture frame. I cover his eyes with my purple tee shirt, like a saint covered for cuaresma, dive back and find your body, spicy, sticky.

It's all right duerme, duerme negrito they are only ghosts que tu mama está en el campo, negrito their eyes are closed duerme, duerme moreno, que tu mama está en el campo, negrito close yours.

Enedina Pascasio

ROCKY GÁMEZ

 All she wanted out of life was a radio, but her husband, don Bartolo, had always refused to buy it for her or to let her buy it out of the money she earned from washing and ironing for the americanas on the other side of the track.

She kept her earnings, coins and dollar bills, in a mayonnaise jar hidden from the burly giant, but he had a keen nose for money and no matter where she hid it, he always found it and pocketed it. At the cantina where he used to have his weekly binges, don Bartolo would empty the jar on the counter and sit there and drink beer, one bottle after the other until the mound of coins and bills had disappeared. Then he would stagger home through the alley and beat Enedina for hiding her money from him.

Enedina was a big, dark woman. Some people said that she was dimwitted because she had no other ambition in life than to listen to music, but my mama used to say that she was merely humble. And that was why Mama always lent her our radio whenever don Bartolo was away, fishing in the river. He never worked for anyone because there was not a boss who could stand his fearsome temper.

Every man in the barrio was afraid of don Bartolo, and so was his wife. That was why she never said anything whenever he found her mayonnaise jar and appropriated it. All she did was come over to our house and sit on the porch and cry, long dolorous sobs that would break my mother's heart.

There was hardly a bone in her body that had not been broken by him. She was not a beautiful woman, but her coarse features had been made worse from all the beatings.

One afternoon she came into the yard with her nose splayed and bleeding. She sat on the edge of our porch like a scolded child, sniffling and tracing little circles on her apron with her fat fingers.

I scrambled up the mesquite tree. I knew Mama would tell me to go away and play somewhere else if she saw me in the yard. She never wanted me to listen to Enedina's tales of woe. She only allowed me to stay when the woman was not troubled. That was when Mama would play the radio that was always tuned to the station in Reynosa, and I would watch Enedina dance to the mambos that were the dancing rage at the time. She was very good at it. She may have been big and fat, but she could dance like a bird when the music was lively.

When Mama came onto the porch, Enedina was wiping the blood from her nose with a piece of rag, but this time she didn't cry or carry on as before. Today she was actually laughing, throwing her head back, so I could see from my perch all the white teeth in her mouth. Her belly shook. "And he looked and looked and looked, Maria, all over the house but he couldn't find the jar."

"Where was it, Enedina?" Mama asked, a smile actually forming at the corners of her ever rigid mouth.

"Between my legs, doña, right where I knew he would never look."

Mama clapped her hands. She had always liked Enedina, ever since she and her husband had moved next door to us. Mama didn't like *him* at all. In fact, she was so obsessed with a hatred for don Bartolo that at times when he was beating Enedina out in the yard, Mama would call him nasty names through the kitchen window. He never said anything to her, though, probably because of my father.

"If I buy the radio tomorrow from the Jew, could I keep it in your house for safekeeping?"

Mama said she could. No faltaba más! And so Enedina hollered for her daughter Trinidad to bring the mayonnaise jar to her. Tomorrow when the Jewish vendor came to the barrio, she would come next door and claim her newly saved treasure.

She was so happy that afternoon, she couldn't stop doing her mambo all over our yard. Even Mama, in all of her rigid tautness, was keeping rhythm with her foot on the porch floor. Enedina knew that she was going to be beaten when don Bartolo came from the cantina, but figured she might as well celebrate her small victory anyway. She was so happy she could taste the music coming out of her soon-to-be-purchased radio.

Enedina was dancing to Pérez Prado's "Patricia" when a thin, cadaverous-looking man came running into our yard. He stood at the side of the porch, panting, and waited until she had stopped swaying and dipping before he spoke.

"Lady, I hate to tell you this," he said to her, "but your husband, don Bartolo, just fell off a barstool, deader than a rock."

Mama crossed herself and yelled for me to go and get my father, who was busy working in the garage, sawing boards for some shelves he was going to put up in the kitchen.

Enedina wailed at the top of her lungs and threw herself on the ground. The wails carried through the air. People from as far away as the big highway rushed to see what was happening. Many women accompanied her to her house, including Mama with a bottle of alcohol in case Enedina fainted in grief.

Soon a blue-eyed policeman came and repeated the bad news. What should they do with the body? Enedina wailed that they had no money for the services of a funeral home and so, later that evening, they brought the body to Enedina's house and that night she held a wake for him, with only Trinidad and Mama and me to sit up with her all night. Even in death, don Bartolo continued to be an object of scorn.

The next morning, Papa decided not to build the shelves in the kitchen. Instead he would use the boards to build the man a casket. It was crude and humble, he said, but at least don Bartolo would not be buried like a pauper.

Enedina and her daughter Trinidad disappeared for a few hours. Mama didn't know what to do with the mayonnaise jar filled with coins. She said to me: "I bet poor Enedina is going to lose her savings to that sonofabitch again. Someone has to pay for the grave." She made annoyed noises with her teeth and muttered something about life being so unfair to some people.

When Enedina and her daughter returned, Mama took the jar over to her house, but the bereaved woman said that she wouldn't need it, City Hall was going to pay for the grave. Mama sighed with relief but set the jar on Enedina's kitchen table anyway. Now that she was widowed, Enedina would surely need the money for food.

We were walking home from the cemetery, having left don Bartolo in his final resting place, when Enedina saw the Jew's black car lumbering down the street. Tearing herself from the group of black-clad women who were flanking her during her sorrow, she ran after the car, hollering for him to stop. The mourning women, including Mama, stopped in their tracks and stared at each other. What on earth had gotten into Enedina?

We walked and walked until we came to the cross street. The black car had already gone down the street and stopped at the next block, where a mob of women surrounded it to look at the wares the Jew was selling that week. And there, standing in the middle of the street, was Enedina Pascasio, cradling an oblong wooden box in her arms as though it were her newborn child. It was the radio she had always wanted. Her round brown face was beaming, red and shiny, her white teeth gleaming between her thick purple lips.

"It came with the battery," she said, bubbling with joy. She turned a knob and before the shocked women could say, "Ave Maria," music flowed through the air and Enedina began to dip and sway in the middle of the street.

Mama covered her face with the black veil she had worn and hurried across the dusty street into our yard. She was sure that the shock of don Bartolo's death had driven Enedina out of her mind. The poor man's body was still warm in its grave, and here the shameless dimwit was sashaying all over the street. She might as well keep on dancing all the way to the cemetery and dance some more on the grave.

What was this world coming to, anyway?

As soon as Papa came home from the cemetery, Mama ordered him to raise the fence between the two houses. She would never again speak to Enedina Pascasio. A person who did not respect those who had discovered the mystery of death, who found it an excuse to rejoice and dance around like that, did not deserve anyone's friendship, least of all her own. And thank God for Enedina's new radio, she sure as hell would never lend her ours again.

Enedina made several attempts to come and visit Mama, but the door would never be opened to her. She'd stand there on the porch, wringing her hands, waiting for Mama to come out, but she never did. Finally she gave up and never tried again. No one ever visited Enedina anymore. She became the pariah of the neighborhood, and I never understood why, or why those who had hated don Bartolo in life were now hurrying to put flowers on his grave on the Day of the Dead. All the poor dimwit wanted out of life was a radio, what was so sinful about that?

"You just shut your mouth, child, and don't ask questions. There are some things that must remain sacred."

"Such as what?"

Mama shook her head slowly and went tsk, tsk, tsk with her teeth.

But every time I heard Enedina's radio blaring over the fence, I couldn't help grinning to myself. I don't think she cared one way or the other. After all, she was a dimwit, so they said.

The Ladies' Room

SUNNY NASH

Slivers of early morning summer sun crept through cracks in the bathroom ceiling. Flowers of light bloomed on the unpainted, splintering walls and on the back of the door where Dorsey's faded douche bag hung limply.

Beside the door, a washbowl that once was white rested unevenly against the wall. A small dish holding oddly shaped pieces of soap rested over a hole where the washbowl's waterspout used to be. Just above the washbowl a row of nails, in perfect symmetry, held five frayed washrags of various colors. Above them hung a cracked mirror.

I sat on the toilet watching a ray of light play at the edges of the crack in the mirror. I couldn't see myself in that or any other mirror in the house. They were all too high. It never occurred to anyone I lived with, or even to me at the time, that a five-year-old child needed to see what she looked like. My grandmother brushed my hair. I was too young for makeup. And I had no choice in the fit of my clothes.

I didn't need a mirror even to brush my teeth. I just dusted a little baking soda in my palm, dipped my toothbrush into it and brushed. I rinsed my mouth with water from a green garden hose that ran from a yard faucet through a knothole in the bathroom wall. Coiled by the door like a sleeping snake, the hose brought in water for brushing, flushing and washing. A single light bulb with a pull string swung from a hole above the rust-stained toilet bowl that leaned crippled in the corner.

The wood there was always damp. Careful not to touch it, I sat with my small feet drawn up around the toilet. The floor was just bare planks of wood, not even nailed down. What held them in place? I used to wonder. Could it have been my grandmother's frequent sweeping and washing? Or perhaps the glue was her belief that our floor would not collapse.

I curled my toes and stroked the cool sides of the white porcelain and saw the ground staring back at me through openings in the rotting floor. From time to time, animal eyes stared back at me, sometimes thin stray cats, but mostly dogs. The latest to take up residence under the bathroom floor was a mangy, hungry-looking cur. A few days ago, I had begun watching the dog but it did not notice me.

A girl dog, I thought, when the puppies came, tiny balls of wet fur rolling from their mother's body. Relieved when finally the last one arrived, she had whimpered upon each arrival. The puppies lay, making no sounds at all. When they were not interested in nursing, she gave up and went to sleep.

Later, she got up and staggered out. When she returned, I assumed that she had found no food. Her puppies were not dead when she began eating them one each day. I was very disappointed in her until I asked my grandmother why the dog ate her babies. Something must have been wrong with them, my grandmother said. The dog knew the puppies would not live.

I watched the dog devour her last puppy. Now, for the first time, she seemed to sense my invasion of her most private moments. I felt embarrassed for having watched her. With the tiny body of her offspring still dangling from her mouth, she began to chew up the rest of her baby. She swallowed. I swallowed too. She rose and trotted from the bloody birthplace. She had done what she had to do.

The ground watched us daily in every room and especially where the lean-to back porch met the house. The back porch was a common area behind Dorsey's and our sides of the duplex. The kitchen doors from both households looked onto the porch like sad eyes.

To Dorsey, the decaying porch was cherished space. The screens had long ago begun to rot away. Birds and insects raised healthy families there. Although Dorsey did not own the duplex that we shared with her and her old man, Ray, she had occupied it for several years before we arrived. Her claim on that porch was permanent.

The rules were clear. Staring down at me and speaking to my grandmother, she said, "Da back porch is off limits. Das where Ray sleep all da time when it ain't rainin' and cold and sometime when it is."

My grandmother didn't like Dorsey's superior attitude, but without a choice other than fighting the woman, she was forced to accept it. My grandmother was left to take care of me while my mother took my brother to a doctor in another town. My brother's illness had forced us to leave the farm near Iola and move closer to civilization. Dorsey and the duplex on Candy Hill were as close as we had gotten so far.

An afterthought, the bathroom was built into the corner of the back porch nearest our side of the duplex. A new city code had forced landlords in Bryan to abandon outhouses and build bathrooms inside the homes.

"Dat baffroom be new. It off limits to Ray," Dorsey said. "He can use it, but he cain't keep none o' his thangs in dere. And he know it, too. All o' his stuff is out here on the porch. Dat room over dere," Dorsey said with more emphasis, "it bees the ladies' room."

"What about me?" I asked.

"You one o' da ladies too," she said impatiently. "It yo' job too to he'p keep dat room clean."

I felt proud that Dorsey considered me one of the ladies. But she warned my grandmother that Ray would regard me as a bothersome little kid. My grandmother was to keep me away from Ray and off the back porch, and she would keep him out of the ladies' room.

Walking back into her side of the house, Dorsey added, "Dat man so nasty I ought not 'low him to use da dern thang atall. But he gots to go somewhere." Her kitchen door slammed behind her.

One morning in January, a few months after we had moved into Dorsey's haven, I got out of bed to go to the ladies' room. I put on socks, slippers and overcoat and padded through the kitchen. The door was night-latched, bolted and chained, so I pulled a rickety wooden chair from the table, climbed up and undid the locks. I got off the chair and opened the door.

The air was frigid. I blew hot breath into my hands and rubbed them together as I stepped out onto the back porch. The sun was creeping gradually over the shabby roofs of Candy Hill. Its rays blazed through the puffs of white smoke that breathed from the metal chimneys of our neighbors' wood-burning heaters and stoves. My hands ached from the cold but my heart warmed as new light shimmered its way into day. At the moment of the sun's full ascent over my world, there was nothing more I could desire.

Contented, I went toward the ladies' room past a mountain of quilts piled on a cot in a corner of the porch. I thought I saw the quilts moving up and down. That couldn't be Ray, I thought. It was too cold even for him to be sleeping out here.

The pile moved all right. I stopped, tiptoed closer and lifted a corner. I was curious. Because of Dorsey's rules, I had never been close enough to Ray to really see what he looked like. Ray stirred, and a snort loud enough to disturb the graves in the cemetery a few blocks away escaped the covers. I yelped and jumped back.

I was relieved when Ray didn't wake up. His beer breath stank, and I knew he would be out cold for most of the day. It was a Sunday, and every Saturday night he and Dorsey drank at Tony's Beer Palace with soldiers from the army base. Afterwards they came home fighting. My mother's framed magazine and calendar pictures would explode off the wall when Dorsey threw Ray across the room. Finally, they would grow tired, do whatever Dorsey and Ray did on Saturdays late at night and sleep most of the next day.

Sitting on the toilet, I let my eyes wander to the back of the ladies' room door, wondering if what Dorsey and Ray did late at night had anything to do with the faded rubber bag hanging there.

Besides rent and cheap food, every cent Dorsey made cleaning houses and every dime Ray earned cooking at the academy went on beer. They owned nothing: not a car, not an inch of land, not a stick of furniture, not even a dog.

Remembering how Ray's face had looked when I glimpsed it that cold January morning a few months ago, I thought that as far as I was concerned, they didn't need a dog. To me, Ray had looked like a sleeping bulldog snoring under all those covers. Flapping folds of skin framed his face. I had shuddered seeing the suction of his big hairy nostrils pull at the blanket fuzz and the frayed edges of the cotton-filled quilts. But other than the mere sight of him, he always seemed harmless.

I doubted what Dorsey said about Ray, anyway. She used him to support her need to complain and whine about this and that and everything and then again nothing at all. She hated coffee, even the smell of it. She hated noise of any kind, even the sound of me singing a nursery rhyme. Most of all, Dorsey hated rain because she had to walk to work in it and because the house leaked.

I loved the heavy sheets of water blowing under the uneven edges of the front porch roof, the smell of dampening earth and the spray in my face. I sat rejoicing, my heart pounding with excitement while Dorsey, my mother and my grandmother strategically placed all the buckets, pots and pans we owned to catch what the house could not keep out. If Ray was at work or away from home, I would sneak out to the back porch and settle into a corner where I hummed along with the melodies the droplets played as they fell into all the different containers.

I reached for the *McCall's* that I had hidden in the corner behind the toilet. Several pages at one edge were wet, and I shook the water away and dried the cover with my shirt. My mother didn't buy magazines. She bought real books when she had real money. Magazines came from the house of the woman she cleaned for. I turned the pages slowly to where I hoped Betsy McCall would be waiting unharmed.

Retrieving my rusting scissors from the corner, I clipped out Betsy and her wardrobe for the month. I pressed the tabs over her shoulders to check the fit of her clothes. Then I searched through the magazine for pictures of beautiful rooms for Betsy's home—bedrooms, baths, play-rooms. A room with a television or telephone was worth much more to me than a room without. The house where I lived had neither.

I clipped frayed paper in the ladies' room until my fingers were raw. I flushed the toilet to make them think I was really using it. I had to be careful not to stay in my retreat too long. Once, after I had flushed too often, I opened the door to find my grandmother waiting on the other side with a bottle of Pepto-Bismol and a spoon.

I turned the page and came upon a picture of plump fried chicken drumsticks. Morning light stretched across the page. The color of the chicken in the ad was the color of my legs reflecting the golden sunlight.

My mother's legs were golden brown too, but they had a fine layer of black hair. My grandmother's legs had the same golden color, but no hair.

One day my grandmother was washing collard greens in a metal dish-pan on a makeshift counter in our makeshift kitchen. She moved smoothly to the wood-burning stove and stirred a pot. I was at her elbow trying to see. I sniffed the glorious aroma of her vanilla custard.

"I'll scoop some out for you," she said.

"Don't want to eat it. Just want to smell it," I snapped.

"You are the craziest little thing I have ever seen," she said, laying the spoon on the counter.

I was not offended. As many times as she'd said it, I knew she didn't mean it.

Without looking up, she reached down for the fire poker, opened the stove door and stirred the smoldering embers, her elbow accidentally poking my eye at the same time.

"Move back," she yelled. "You are too close."

Then I *was* offended. That was my space. She was the one out of place with her skinny elbow in my face. And she blamed *me* for being too close!

Smelling her Ivory-soap freshness and staring at her clean, neatly pressed, threadbare dress, crisp white apron and impeccably brushed strands of graying hair, I tried to think of something mean to say. I looked at her run-down shoes and cotton-stockinged legs.

"I sure hope I don't have no old slick legs like yours when I grow up," I said. "I want hair on my legs like Mama."

My grandmother made a strange little noise that sounded like a chuckle. But she couldn't fool me. I knew she couldn't be laughing at my meanness.

Back to washing her greens, she said, "You five years old. Ain't suppose to have no hair on your legs, just on your head. When you twenty-five, hair be all over, even in them places where you don't want it. When you forty-five, all that hair in all them places will start to turn white. When you sixty-five, some of that hair in most of them places will start to fall out."

Shrill laughter shrieked through our back door from the porch. Surprised, my grandmother and I turned to see Dorsey slapping her knees and sort of dancing around out there. Never having seen anyone carry on that way, I was startled and hid behind my grandmother's skirttail for protection.

"What's wrong with her?" I asked, trembling.

My grandmother looked down at me with pity. Reluctantly, she placed her hand on my head and stroked my hair. She didn't speak for a while, just looked at me. Her hand was warm on my head. I looked up at her and for a moment did not recognize her as the woman I had known and learned to tolerate those first few years of my life.

Dorsey was still carrying on with laughter and repeating parts of my grandmother's account of getting old.

"She's laughing, child," my grandmother said softly.

"Oh."

I was grateful that Dorsey hadn't gone crazy after all. But no one around me had ever laughed and danced around like that, not my mother and certainly not my grandmother. I could count on one hand the times that I had ever heard real, out loud laughter. And I couldn't recall any thought I had ever had or any scene I had ever witnessed that was funny enough to laugh out loud about.

My grandmother and I stared enviously at Dorsey. She was embarrassed when she saw us watching her. Laughter subsiding, she composed herself, wiping her teary eyes with the backs of her hands. By the expression creeping over her face, it was clear she had mistaken our jealousy for ridicule. Offended, she settled back into her superior attitude.

"Ain't cha'll never seed nobody laugh?" she snapped. Mumbling, she went back to her side of the house. "Damnedest bunch of sour apples I ever been roun' in my life. Act like they ain't never seed nobody laugh."

Her kitchen door slammed shut.

Looking up from the magazine, I could see, through cracks in the bathroom ceiling, small white puffs sailing rapidly through blue. Swaying from side to side to watch, I almost fell off the toilet. I blinked to control my dizziness. Steadying, I peed and reached for the roll of paper. We didn't have real toilet paper often. Ray brought it from the private military school where he worked. Rubbing the soft, white roll against my cheek, I closed my eyes. When I started to pull some off, it fell and rolled across the worn, wooden floor.

I hopped off the seat to get it. I reached for the paper but my hand froze. My stare was glued to the opening in the bathroom floor. The raging eyes of a mad dog peered through. This was not the gentle bitch I'd met the other day. I moved my hand. The dog snapped. I screamed. He snarled through the hole, bumping his head on the other side of the rotten floor.

Certain he would come through, I grabbed the paper, climbed up on the toilet and wiped my bottom. I was straightening my clothes and keeping an eye on the snarling dog when my foot slipped. Grabbing at thin air, I fell screaming into the toilet. His head broke through a rotten board. A sharp, jagged splinter separated from the board and pierced one of his bulging eyes. Blood spewed. Oblivious to its pain, the mad dog continued to snap.

There was a commotion at the door. The metal latch broke as Ray lunged in, the sun blazing around his massive body. The dog's head seemed to turn in circles, its pierced eye oozing out and running down its face. Ray stopped short of a scream when he entered and the dog snapped at him. Something heavy in Ray's hands raised and lowered again and again on the dog's head. He grunted with each forceful blow until the animal was way beyond quiet. The sight of the dog's bloody, battered head horrified me. I heaved on the floor, thinking Dorsey would blame me, I'd have to clean it up. How could they make such a mess? It was the ladies' room.

The Undertow of Friends

SHELBY HEARON

 My friends and I can talk for hours, we women who came of age together. We are attentive to the same details, each caring to the same extent. We don't tire of one another's lives. We cover everyone: mothers, sons, lovers, in-laws. No one who is not us cares about these people in the same proportion or to the same degree. Some, who love a particular family member, care for that one; while others, friends or former spouses, care for none.

George has his own friends too; they go back to the start, and I am no part of them. I can hear their stories but I cannot weigh them fairly. Some strike me as too odd, too pointless, some too harsh to be treated in a joking way.

I often worry that we, Jean and George, a recent couple without a past in common, will never keep afloat. You read about custody fights and ex-spouses as a strain on a relationship, but no one talks about the undertow of friends.

When I was small, I lived in the little town of Katy, Texas, named for the railroad that runs like a river from the piney woods to the coast.

Every afternoon I would cross two dirt side streets, scramble up a clay bank, and walk under a stand of dark pines to my best friend's house to play with her brother's dog. I was allowed to go alone because in small towns young girls could go where they liked, under the unspoken watch of neighbors.

Most afternoons she, Sally, would come back home with me because she liked to eat at our house and because my daddy would stop what he was doing and give her some little treat to take home: a cornshuck doll, a tiny rabbit carved from soap, an armload of heavy amethyst hydrangeas.

I was jealous of her until I got the message that my daddy was doing it because he knew her folks and that Sally only hung around my daddy because she didn't have one of her own who was any account.

Grown, both living in the state capital, we still call each other often and see each other when we can, when I'm not busy with my classes and Sally's not weighed down with the strain of being cheery about her ten-year affair with a married legislator and the burden of two aging Labrador retrievers.

George does not understand my attachment to her and arranges to be gone when she comes by.

He grew up in West Texas, and his pals are the good old boys who amble from side to side when they walk, as if they just dismounted from a horse.

His best friend, Archer, went through undergraduate days with him, got his final degree with him at Rice, also suffered the end of a painful early marriage, and has been a colleague of his in the math department at Texas for a dozen years.

George thinks Archer is a sketch and never tires of his friend's imitations of himself: "'This is your life, Archer Clovis.' . . . 'Why, hello, Dad, I haven't seen you since you stole the sheriff's car and sold it back to him.'" He and Archer have a routine in which they found Clovis University, the Harvard of the Southwest, the pearl in the oyster of the Gulf, staffed only by themselves. And George delights in all its variations.

This year Archer has been on sabbatical in Madison, Wisconsin, also a capital—university town laid out on a river. George gave him a farewell dinner complete with a horseshoe of real red roses and a speech that ended: "Henceforth you will go into the world and pass for normal. Strangers will mistake you for a mechanical engineer. Nubile graduate students will offer themselves."

Archer calls George every week, or George calls him. He sent us a frozen squirrel, fourth-class mail, in a package marked RABID: HANDLE WITH CARE. In return, George invented a fat Swedish girlfriend for Archer, who has none, to keep him warm against the cold, and sent them both long underwear.

Crowded by these antics from the past in our rented blue-walled rooms, I tell George, "We need a place of our own."

"What's wrong with this house?"

"I mean a place which knows us only in the present, Jean and George."

After the third time that Sally calls while we are making love beneath the dainty underbellies of the doves who peck at our skylight, George agrees. The next day he announces, "I found us a café."

It is called the Library Annex, and we make ourselves at home at once, going there almost every afternoon at the end of classes to have a pint of sun-brewed tea and a roasted-pork sandwich with homemade mayonnaise and banana peppers on hot fresh bread. We sit on the same side of the back corner booth, close together, enjoying the ambience and speaking only to strangers.

The place gets its name from the fact that the owner (a man named Howie, who wears a workshirt and apron and ties his hair back with a rubber band) wanted to open a bookstore but was afraid of failure, and so instead opened a restaurant next to a branch library, imagining a horde of thirsty readers with their arms full of thick summertime novels wanting a place to sit and wipe their buttery fingers and turn their enthralling pages.

It is a lovely space with booths along the wall, big wooden children's tables in the center, blue willow crockery, and blue-and-white-striped awnings on the inside. When the awnings are at half-mast against the glaring sun, the light draws a line on the blue-and-white vinyl floor, making the room seem at once open and closed. Voices carry; the slightest gesture on the part of anyone causes you to look up and smile. It is both a public and a private place, off the beaten path in a residential area, and we promise that we will share it with no one.

Then Archer calls to say he is to have his back operated on. He has been in pain for weeks, he relates. Then on his way to class today his left foot refused to function. "It flopped like a fish. Just imagine," he tells George, "in the old days you had to live with it. Dragged around like a lame dog. The doctor says they used to call it lumbago and send you home. Now he says I'll be back on the courts in two weeks, never mind that I haven't played in years." George relays that his friend's voice has grown edgy and brittle, even when he tries to joke.

"He ought to have somebody with him," he tells me. "I should go up."

"Maybe he'd rather you waited until he felt good again?"

"No, when you want someone is when things are bad."

George broods. He tells me again about the time Archer, at age nine, won the state Soap Box Derby and got a medal before a crowd of seventy-five thousand in Memorial Stadium—and his family missed it all, lost in the east parking lot. About how Archer's sons from his early marriage have a new daddy who possesses a Cessna, a Porsche, and ski-slope expertise.

"He shouldn't be alone." Fretting, he bundles off a cut-and-paste booklet replete with bosoms and legs, for reading in Clovis General.

That afternoon we linger longer than usual in the Annex, appreciating the shift of scene in the air when people enter: the way voices die down, gestures stop, eyes blink, and then—reassured that we are all safe in the lovely blue-and-white room with its slanted light—the commotion begins again.

Today while we are preparing classes (which for me means returning to the richness of the Middle Ages that seem such a marvel coming from tiny, uneventful Katy, Texas), Archer calls to say the deed is done.

"How do you feel?" George asks.

"Euphoric," Archer swears, although George reports that his voice has a new breakable quality even as he does an imitation of his old self. "The nurses mistake me for a mechanical engineer. The one named Olga is teaching me to say, 'Take off your clothes,' in Swedish. One week from today I'll be playing at Wimbledon. 'This is your life, Archer Clovis, medical miracle.'"

"I ought to come up," George says.

"No way. My old man is here. He's decided to help me sue the university and the shuttle-bus company and the last girl I was with."

George is hurt. Off the phone he opens a Lone Star. He is depressed by the idea that Archer would invent a family to keep him from coming up. "His old man's been dead for ten years at least," he tells me.

"Do you want to see a movie later?"

"We'll see." He gathers his things together. "Maybe I should go anyway?"

"He has his pride."

As we get ready to leave, George decides he isn't up to the Annex this afternoon, that we will go tomorrow, that he may work in his office until suppertime.

"I'll see what Sally is up to," I tell him.

When I meet her by the fountain, she looks the same—bright red turtleneck, sunglasses and lipstick matching, boots, her mane of hair flying—but I can see the cracks in her the way you can see the veins in an old person's temple.

"He changed his mind about renting us an apartment," she says into the bustle of forty thousand students going by. "Said it was too risky, at least for now, when he has reelection to think about."

I grab her arm and tell her to come with me, that I have someplace special to show her, guaranteed to cheer her up.

As we walk to the Annex, she tells me that her old hounds are getting too feeble to keep, incontinent, forgetful; that she's thinking of letting them go to her brother's ranch.

We walk in the door, breaking the sunlight, and sit at a table in the center, which I have never done before. As we order our Mason jars of iced tea and the roasted pork on homemade bread, I look up and see George—having a beer in our usual booth, listening to a story that Howie, in his workshirt and apron, is relating.

"So we come home, see, and we've been up at the lake, and we're water-logged and baked out, and the phone is ringing. I pick it up, and this strange man demands, 'Where is my daughter?'

"'Who is your daughter?' I ask him. It turns out that my son Mike met her at a party and went off with her, and she never came home. Her parents were ready to call the police when Mike phoned her father and said: 'I'm out on my dad's boat, sir, and the cotter pin is out. We're stranded on Lake Travis, but he's bringing one to me.'"

"Beautiful," George says, laughing. "Truly. You don't even own a boat, right?"

"Never have. But that's not the clincher." Howie leans down. "I say, 'Let me get back to you, sir, after I contact my son on the ship-to-shore radio.'"

"Perfect." George lifts his mug.

"So then I drive over to Mike's room and bang on the door and I tell them about the father's call, and they break up laughing. She is in this shirt of his, there are about two dozen longnecks on the shag rug. They haven't been outside for twenty-four hours." Howie delivers the kill: "Get this, George. I look at her and say, 'If you don't mind my asking, honey, how old are you?'"

"And?"

"Twenty-five. Twenty-five and not home all night." Howie heads for the kitchen, slapping his forehead.

I raise my tea glass slightly, and George meets my eyes.

I don't get Howie's tale at all. Do not understand why it is funny that his son lied to the girl's father, or why it is amusing that the father wanted to know where his daughter was, even at twenty-five. I am a woman, and, cut by Archer's life (What if we don't need each other the way we thought?), George has gone back to the safety of men.

I concentrate on getting the appearance of the room exactly, the knives and forks, the smell of hot bread, the blue willow plates, the chilled tea glasses with their wedges of lemon, the motion of crumbs brushed from the smooth polished tabletops. The filtered afternoon grade-school light which draws its line across the waxed Annex floor: girls on one side, boys on the other.

George nods his head toward Sally, and I nod back, acknowledging that in our hour of need, we all return to where we came from.

My best friend, unaware of what is past her shoulder, has brightened up over the unexpected treat of the new place. She takes a giant bite of her sandwich and, fortified, decides that she will get a new pair of puppies, playful young dogs. That maybe she will even tell the legislator to go back to his wife when the session is over. "Do you think your daddy would take me back?" she asks, laughing at our old joke.

The Purchase of Order

GAIL GALLOWAY ADAMS

 Lou Maxey is hanging over the top of the seat, her behind a likely target. She's slipped her pink plastic shoes half off and they dangle like loose skin. There are rustling sounds from the back.

"What in the hell are you doing?" Marlon asks, pushing in the cigarette lighter, which he has to lean around her in order to do.

"I'm looking for that package of Cheese Nuggets I packed in here. I'm hungry."

"We just had breakfast less than an hour ago," he says around his light-up. "You had the Trencherman. You couldn't be hungry."

She looks back over her shoulder, tries to lift her foot up and sideways to jog his knee; it's impossible, so she bumps his shoulder with her rear. "How do you know? You're not me. And I'm hungry."

Lou is one of those little women who never look any older than about sixteen until you're close up. Her hair is crisp and close and dark and her eyes are the brown of spaniels'. She's had five kids, four in the first six years of marriage, and then a decade's wait before her baby Jason, now in the navy on a ship anchored off Greece. Lou likes to think of her baby in the Mediterranean, near the place and the myth he was named for, and how apt the name she chose. Although there are lots of Jasons now, there weren't many then, and her boy, with his curly golden hair, thick and spongy as sheep wool on his arms and chest, was like a fleecy thing. "It looks like Santa's beard's on his legs," a little cousin said once at the beach.

You could never imagine your own children making love, Lou thought.

She could never imagine anyone making love, but she could picture a dark Grecian girl with red ribbons in her hair cradling against Jason's chest. Marlon's body hair was different. It was rusty and tufty with a strange patch on the left chest. He had smooth upper arms that were furred like pelts from elbow to wrist. Everything about the man amazed her, and they'd been married almost thirty years.

Last night at the motel while she watched *The Sting* on TV, Marlon, feet crossed precisely one on top of the other in a wedge, read the local paper, which he always did wherever they stopped. "Guess who this sounds like," he said, reading a letter to the editor from a man who complained about the sewer lines, the garbage pick-up, and the planting of iris bulbs in front of City Hall. "'And in conclusion . . . ,'" Marlon pulled the sentence out. "'City Council should get going or get out.'"

Lou, who'd only half-listened from the second tirade on, said, "That's your mama all over, Marlon."

He smiled, shook the paper back into creases, and settled in to reading the classifieds while she got up, one eye on the TV show, and wandered over to the window, which was oddly high, partly blocked by an air-conditioning unit.

"'Two-bedroom house for $195,'" Marlon read. "That's not bad." She mmmed that she heard, but mainly she was looking for something, anything previous guests might have left behind. Once, she'd found a bookmark, navy leather stamped with gold designs, tucked into the Gideon. Another time a little girl's hairbow, fashioned into a rose with a frill of plastic lace. Lou collected such things as souvenirs. She liked to own matchbooks that she found under beds in which she and many others had slept.

Marlon had finished reading, was watching the movie with a bemused expression.

"What part's that?" She bent over him and without a word he flipped her over on her back and splatted his mouth against her stomach. She pushed at his head, saying, "Don't, no, stop, don't you dare," and then Marlon went from splatting to pink belly, and while she giggled and shoved him away, shouting for Robert Redford to save her, she was excited by the sound of his hands patting her stomach, moving fast up and down her flesh.

This summer's trip is following a pattern set ten years ago. The Maxeys hop into their van aiming to just go. That first day when Marlon drove it home, Lou walked around and around it, thinking it was as big as a bus. Marlon scraped off the manufacturer's name, KING OF THE ROAD, saying, "That makes me sick. I'll choose my own name." Then he left the space bare, tacky with a residue of stickiness that collects insects and dust. A decade later KI and RD still show like lines in the wax of a magic slate.

This summer, like all before, they'll travel anywhere and everywhere they want, not a plan in their heads, except to follow their own feelings. "What will be, will be" is the Maxeys' motto on these trips, but truth to tell, Lou does worry and marks the maps and schedules the stops so they can visit with all their kids and grandchildren. After Labor Day, when families leave the road to see to purchases of new notebooks and under-wear, they turn back too, clean up their van, and park it to the side of the bungalow near Austin where they've decided to spend the rest of their lives.

Lou calls her friends, goes to the YWCA for her Jane Fonda exercise class, and twice weekly puts on her crinolines and she and Marlon go to the Square Dance Club. "No ties, not even string ones" was the deal be-fore he'd go. She loves the way he looks standing across from her in the square, wearing his plaid blue shirt with pearl buttons, open at the collar, jeans turned up in a pale roll, and boots, cut-under heels marking up the gym floor. When the caller does his do-si-do, Marlon moves his nose sideways, lets his eyelids droop in a criminal manner, and swings circle-box-circle until she's his, caught at the waist. Even when these evenings make her ache and soak her feet, see them peel in a pan of Epsom salts, she loves it. She feels exactly as she did when she first met Marlon, then married him, against everybody's will.

Early in their marriage, when he'd lost his job, the one he quit high school for, a restlessness set in in him. She'd be at work, a half-day job her daddy got her at a plate glass company doing bills, and in the after-noons stuffing burgers into bags, when she'd look up to catch Marlon whisking out of sight. Sometimes, later in the day, he'd come to get a roast beef that had got cold. "Can't stick around," he'd say. "Got to see a man."

Sometimes he'd borrow a dollar, or pat her on the belly where the baby now was. They didn't talk much about the baby; somehow she knew it made Marlon too sad. Only at night in bed in the trailer, when the neighbors slammed their glass-louvered doors so hard the foundation shook, Lou'd scoot up against him, feeling the swell of their baby be-tween, and she knew how Marlon felt. "Wasn't supposed to be this way," he whispered, turning to embrace her. The baby's bulk pushed him to the wall as she felt the corners of her mouth tingling at the touch of his lips.

Near when the baby was due Lou began to worry about what would happen, how they'd work things out. She'd catch herself sitting at her desk at Mitchell's Glass having stapled the same bill twice. She found it harder and harder to force a smile for customers. The smell of onion and grease at her afternoon job seemed never to leave her. She was constantly figuring out schedules, adding sums in her head even as she sprinkled grated cheese on the taco special.

"I've got a job," Marlon told her when he popped up at the Burger 52 one day right after lunch and was persuaded to sit down and have a cherry Coke and onion rings. Everyone liked Marlon. He was even-tempered, told good stories, and he worked hard: it's just that there had to be work to do.

"Where is this job?" asked the other hop, whose boyfriend had got the boot a few weeks before Marlon. "In Alaska?"

Marlon looked up, winked, held an onion like a ring over his finger and said, "Yes." Everyone laughed but Lou; she knew Marlon never kidded about change. He ate that ring, finished his Coke, and, pointing his finger at her like a gun, said, "Later."

That's how they ended up in a van with a three-week-old baby girl and some household goods, driving to this promised land where Marlon worked construction and Lou watched babies, her own among them, and all they made went for food and rent. The sunsets hung red for hours, it seemed, teasing them with the thought of dark, and Marlon wasn't happy. Evenings he'd sit in front of the television after the baby was in bed and hold his knees, shoving the heel of his hand like gunning a car, fast, faster, staring straight ahead and clenching his jaws.

One night when he came home Lou was nursing the baby, both curled up in a corner of the couch. He sat down on the coffee table facing her, clasping his hands like being good at school; then he leaned his chin against his steepled thumbs.

"Do you want me to rub your neck?" she asked.

He raised his head and his eyes looked swimmy, even though he was smiling. "I've got another job, babe. On the coast, doing something. Don't know what, but I'll guarantee you it'll be dirty and dangerous." He tapped Lou's chin with his fist, gently pulled the baby's hair. Lou was pregnant again, bigger this time, with things going strange. Her ankles swelled straight to her knees, turning white and crackly like old china plates. Marlon would pop her toes at night, rub warmth into her feet with his hands, which were small for a man's.

They never stopped making love, even when it seemed that everything they did or didn't do led to babies. Their second was born in Louisiana, then another boy in Tampa, then a baby girl born on their way from Arizona to Alabama, and Lou's chief memory of those years is of trying to keep her babies clean, keep them up off floors where who-knew-what had gone on. They lived on a live-in ship, in a one-room kitchenette on the third floor of a beach hotel, and once—she doesn't like to think of it—in the back part of a converted van. Some rainy days during that bad time she would gather her children around to sleep huddled like puppies. They saw a lot of places, and Marlon's excitement about them kept her going.

"Living in a place is not the same as visiting it," he'd said, "because while you get to know the towns better, you know them less." Lou thought that was true. Places were like relatives: somehow the longer you knew one, the less you valued it. Moving off and then coming back for visits let you see all the sweetnesses. She'd picked up Marlon's rhythm by this time and wondered as she wrapped her cups in the Sunday comics, readying for another move, if she could ever go back to one place. She'd met a woman who'd shopped at the same Piggly Wiggly all her life, and Lou marveled at that.

Sometimes the places where they had lived blended into each other, all seeming a dream that held these constants: a laundromat, a convenience store, and a drive-in on the edge of town where she and Marlon would get out to sit on a blanket spread in front of the grille while the children slept on in the back seat, the speakers turned low for their ears. Then sometimes Lou would be struck with a recall of a place so vivid that she thought, If I went back there now, I could find my way around. Sometimes at night, when she couldn't sleep, she played a game with herself. She picked a town they'd lived in and drove around in it in her head. When Marlon heard her muttering, "Turn left for the Dixie Pig," he'd sleepily ask, "Where are you?"

Getting used to change is easy for her now, but it wasn't always. She's happy to think she can adjust, move from place to place, seek out the stores, the banks, and the schools. She liked to get the family settled in and clear a place on the refrigerator for the kids' schoolwork while Marlon went off to all the different jobs that he had.

Whenever she went back to the town Marlon came from she saw the same people walking down the same streets. They'd die in the same frame houses they lived in, she thought. Then she wanted to get in the car and go, drive away with Marlon and the kids to somewhere they'd never lived before.

Each year when they start their trip they have a purpose. It is one that has never been taken out and examined, one that is rarely discussed except in memories that come up—a purpose neither of them really knows how to explain. What moves these summers for the Maxeys is a search that has shaped their lives for the last decade: they are looking for a family they once knew, without whose presence everything in life has been more pale, a family they've continued to think about and talk about. Lamont and Jean Dillon and their kids—when they met them twenty-two years ago in Arkansas, it was one of those meetings between two families where everything hits right and it is forever and always. But in this case, the Maxeys don't know how, it fell away through not keeping in touch, both of them moving on too many times.

When Lou wants to make an event memorable, she ransacks her brain for recollections of the Dillons, especially Lamont in his boneless height. "How he keeps his pants up is a mystery, and I'm married to the man," Jean said, rolling her eyes, always in a laugh putting her left hand up to cover where a tooth was gone, another gone gray. Lamont's back seam fell flat between his thighs.

At various times over the years when Lou has helped her children learn to cut meat, do a chain stitch in crochet, or print between the lines, she's seen Lamont's hands as they shaped a little figure with his knife. Concentrating as solemnly as the child who stood waiting to see what would emerge from between the wood and the blade, he'd roll the scrap of pine in his fingers and seem surprised himself to see it become a donkey or a tiny dancing man. He'd lift up his head and his thick eyebrows, under which his eyes, so light a blue they were almost white, were innocent, and smile a fool's smile, the corners of his mouth pulling up into his cheeks.

"Now lookee here," he'd murmur, balancing the figure in the well of his outstretched hand. "Let me take my payment." The knife blade quickly cut the thinnest lock from the edge of the child's hair; the blade tip near their ears made the older ones shiver, the little ones giggle. "This here's magic hair," he'd say. "Have to add it to my pile."

"If he'd ever get money for those carvings we'd have a dozen pillows stuffed with duck fuzz down, if we wanted them," Jean would complain, then light a Tareyton, pulling in smoke, the cigarette moving from the center of her lip like a dowser's rod in the strength of her inhale. When she wanted to be funny she'd cross her eyes before blowing out the match.

That day in the laundromat Lou couldn't have known that Jean would be any other than the kind of friend you usually make there who helps you fold. Even though Marlon was good with the kids, Lou always took her brood with her; too many things can happen in a trailer court on an off-day when men, in work or out, are drinking beer and fixing cars. One guy with a saucer scar on his shoulder scared the kids by popping out his top three teeth and clanking them up and down. At the laundromat Lou would sit her four down, give them Chocolate Soldiers and Nabs, and buy each of them a comic book. Later, during Dry, Marlon would come to help fold. Sometimes he'd wrap himself like an Arab in a sheet, dancing a mummy's dance, and make everybody in the long linoleumed room laugh.

That's how they first met, Jean with her pile of threadbare towels and striped Handi-Wipes she used for washrags—that's what she called them instead of washcloths—and all her kids, who made Lou's crazy. But she was such a good-natured lanky girl, so quick to smile at Marlon's silliness, so willing to let the children be lively in their romping around with peanut-shell earrings clamped to their lobes, that Lou liked her right away.

Lou was folding diapers when all of a sudden this woman with hair yanked straight back and features looking forward began to help. "These sure are white," she said. "Why don't you use disposables?"

"Can't afford to," Lou answered, wanting to laugh and not knowing why, but knowing right then that this friendship, based from the beginning on knowing everything bad about each other's underwear, would last.

"Where y'all staying?" she'd questioned Lou, having said she was Jean Dillon and with a wave of a hand, diaper flapping like a sailor's flag, pointed out her husband Lamont, who was loading a commercial machine with a jumble of goods from towels to blue jeans. Marlon was outside walking all the kids in formation on the parking lot, yelling made-up orders: "Walk on tippy-toes. Now stick out your tongues." The children collapsed on hot tar in giggling heaps.

"My bunch," Jean said, shooing them off, the other hand shaking out a Tareyton. "Maisie, Jasper, Gordon, Ceil, and Autumn Ann. Where'd you say?" she asked again.

Lou had no choice but to tell her. "We're out at Doakes." She didn't like to be there. It was a rough place. Too many people slept in during the day, and they weren't on the night shifts either.

"Not so good for kids." Jean tongued her cigarette to the side of her mouth, squinted her eyes, and began to fold. "No place to let them run their spirits out."

"I try to get over to the park each day," Lou said.

"Come live by us," Jean offered. "Looks funny from the street—Clark's Courts—but inside it's just the place for kids. I manage there. It's not free, but no more than you're paying at Doakes."

Lou didn't know what to say, looked up at Jean, her lank brown hair wreathed with smoke, her bright blue eyes eager and hopeful. "I'll have to talk to my husband," she said, and right then Marlon burst through the door crying, "Save me! Save me! Please!" holding the plate glass shut against the force of all the sweaty screeching children, pushing and laughing and shoving and shouting out the different sweet treats they wanted. "Stay still!" He mashed a frog face on the glass. "Sit down like sombrero men with your knees drawed up and each and every one of you will get a Fudgsicle." Then he came and stood by Lou and asked, "Who's taking over my diaper duty?"

Jean laughed, then hailed Lamont, who'd been resting, back against the porthole of the big machine, head down, dreaming. "Lamont, come meet these people. I'm getting them to come and live by us."

When Lamont Dillon looked up and smiled, Lou's heart fled out of her and she, who'd never given love to any man but Marlon, knew she loved him; not in the way of Marlon, nor that of her brother who'd died in the war, and for whom she cried for years, waking sometimes in the night, face wet with tears from a dream that he was showing her how to hit a pitch, sock the tetherball and knock it back to him. No, somehow it was as though Lamont Dillon was her, or as if, had she been a man, she'd have been exactly like him. He sauntered toward them, tall, skinny with thick black hair and an eerie half-breed Indian look of dark skin and blue eyes, all of him moving bonelessly and gracefully as he slid his shower shoes along. Lou looked over at Marlon, standing even with Jean's height: both of them looked like lean alley cats, rusty and triangular, emitting energy as they stood. She felt a burning, as if had they joined hands in a ring they'd explode into flames.

"You're at the turpentine camp?" Lamont drawled. His voice was rumbling, deep, almost phony in its bass level.

Marlon was jazzed up; he was joking already as he answered yes.

They moved into Clark's Courts and Lou began to watch Jean Dillon closely for clues on how she lived; usually she let her kids go as wild as her house and the yard. Her kitchen was the kind where a brush filled with hair sits right next to a stick of melted butter; Lou always washed her own cups there. Once when Lou'd spilled a can of corn, Jean said, "Here, let me help you," then proceeded to kick the kernels under the shelf's overhang. She was always saying her kids were up to no good, even as she passed their school pictures around, and they loved her the same way, interrupting as she read her *True Romance*. "What do you want, you dirty bum?" With a long arm she'd grab a boy and kiss him as he squirmed, protested, "Mama, no." They asked for Nutty Buddy money or a dime for the picture show. Jean always gave it.

They couldn't scare her either. "See here—spiders," said Ceil, a bony-chested ten-year-old with harlequin glasses that were pearl-tipped. "Bet you'd be afraid to touch them," she challenged Jean, who pulled her face all to the center and said, "Oh yeah?" then mounted them on her fingers and displayed them like rings. "Here, kids, Popsicles," she'd shout, or "Root beer floats, everyone." Her children had cavities and scabbed elbows and greasy hair and grayed knees and were totally secure in their parents' love.

Autumn Ann was a foster baby who'd been given them by a cousin to keep for a weekend, then left for a lifetime. Jean lugged her three-year-old weight around, fat diaper perched on a hip, Autumn sagging back like a Siamese twin joined at the waist. "Autumn Ann's like an extra pair of hands, aren't you, honey?" she said, and the little girl reached out for the bananas that were collecting flies in the fruit bowl. That year they'd taken in a little boy named Traveling Apple, born and raised in a veggie commune; he'd turned orange from being fed too many carrots. "Look at this sweet Seville," Jean said, kissing his apricot face.

"He's got a suntan all right," Lamont said and cradled the baby on his chest, the man's neck showing red in a V, the rest of his torso wiry with each muscle as defined as a drawing under his skivvy shirt. "Sleep, little fellow, sleep," he crooned in that deep voice that hummed the air.

One night they danced out on the cracked concrete patio of the courts. Jean tucked her hands into Lamont's back pockets and he wrapped both arms around her shoulders and all the children came running up to hang from their waists and trouble them; they looked like a whirligig that spins, ribbons floating in a circle. Wedged between was Autumn Ann, fat face pressed against their thighs, baby foot on each of their insteps, making them stiff-legged as they box-stepped to "In the Still of the Night." "Sho do, sha debe do," Lamont sang, and Lou, holding her littlest on her lap, legs dangling into the pool, felt the baby's feet kick splashes on her shins. She felt like crying as she watched them dance to Lamont's music. All the kids were giggling, Lou and Marlon's trying to get in. They insinuated their arms into the circling couple, dragging their feet, acting like flour sacks instead of kids. Lamont and Jean pretended not to notice, kept their eyes closed and looked extra gooey as they staggered this hoopskirt of children around. Marlon sat down beside Lou, put his arm around her, and rubbed the baby's foot. "Why is it," he said, "life makes people so good and treats them so bad?" Lou buried her head in his neck, smelling chlorine on him, loving him as she felt the baby squirm and wiggle to get free.

So on this trip, like all the others since they began their quest, Lou and Marlon followed the fairs and flea markets and asked in each town where it was that people might raise goats or lots of kids, and always got a laugh. They'd gone to each town in a Louisiana parish Lamont once mentioned he lived in, asking if anyone knew them, knew a fine mechanic, a wood-carver named Dillon, and got no answer but no.

On the third week out they decided to lift their spirits by looking for barbecue. Here on the edge of a Louisiana town they saw a place that was exactly what you looked for when you were hungry for good barbecue: a wood shack, discolored by smoke and redolence rising out of the wood, the sky perfumed with the odor of wood chips and vinegar and crisp roasting, and in the yard off to the side, a lean-to with tables and little children climbing on them.

"Let's stop here," Marlon said, pulling in. When they got out, Lou looked down the slight hill and saw a small frame house with a square dirt yard. A woman about her age in a faded blue housedress and slippers down at the back, a coffee-colored woman with fried hair tucked under at the ends, was sweeping down the yard. On the porch sat a tin watering can and at the side a rake.

"I want a chipped pork," Lou said. Then, "I'm going down there." As she half slid down the slope she could see the other woman looking at her. "I'm Lou Maxey, and excuse me, do. It's only I saw this dirt yard and I simply could not go past it, don't you know?" Lou was talking fast to cover up her nervousness and embarrassment, but she knew she couldn't go back. The woman was husky but her face was kind, with a long, full mouth. "I haven't seen a dirt yard in I don't know how long."

"I'm Lacey," the woman said, nodding toward Lou. Her voice was warm.

"Would you? I mean, this is probably going to sound crazy to you—but would you let me rake a little bit with you? I had a friend once . . ." She found herself unable to stop. "Jean Dillon—her granny in Greensboro, North Carolina, had to have a dirt yard or go crazy."

The woman listened. A smile crimpled her cheeks; she held out the broom, walked back to get the rake.

"It's the oddest thing. Here we are—we're looking for them—the Dillons, trying to figure out where in the world they went to. And I saw this yard. How do folks lose track of things?" Lou's scratching the earth now; it is mostly weeded out and very dry. Lacey sprinkles it to keep the dust down and even, to try and set the pattern.

"Are you putting the arches here?" Lou asks, then feels compelled to explain, "One time—one time we lived together when we were young in this old crummy motel with kitchenettes and cabins," the woman nods, "with all our kids. You notice now how no one has lots of kids anymore? I had four and that was nothing to my grandma. My fifth was too far apart—like an only baby."

"I had six," says Lacey. "Six and one boy killed in the war, four girls."

"Any of them around here?"

"My youngest girl—up there. She runs the barbecue. A good girl. A fine husband. Three grandkids."

"That's nice," Lou says. "So nice to have the kids near. This time I'm telling you about—the time we made us a dirt yard. We made it from scratch. That sounds funny, doesn't it?"

"It does. It does. Usually you just clears them away."

The two women are moving shoulder to shoulder now, walking backward. Lou sweeps the dirt clear and then Lacey pulls in the design, slightly wavy lines that curve around the cement stepping-stones.

One late August day Lou and Jean sat in plastic strap chairs, fannies hitting the ground, watching the kids run dirty circles around the motel compound. Clark's Courts was marked by a line of soot-covered plaster ducks advancing on a three-legged concrete deer; his left antler was a single metal spike. Rocks, painted alternately blue and white, rimmed the swimming pool, which was choked with leaves and olive algae etched on its sides and circular stairs.

"What you need, Lou, to calm your nerves," Jean said, "is a dirt yard." Lou had had a crying jag that morning as a result of the heat and the baby pressing on her spine and peepee sheets and a three-year-old who bit. "My granny in Greensboro once told me she'd have gone crazy if she hadn't had her dirt yard to rake. Kids love them too." Then she yelled, "Hey kids!" They stopped their wild running to stand sweating as dirt puffed over their feet, then turned to face Jean in a band—Lou's in sunsuits and clean pinafores and roman sandals, Jean's in torn shorts and aprons tied like capes. One wore a nylon bridesmaid's hat.

"I've got a game!" Jean called. They leaped into the air, all in a bunch, mud daubers rising to cluster near the two women. Lou's timid son, tagging at the rear of the group, rested his hand on her bare shoulder. Ceil and Maisie pushed up to the front, Ceil's eyeglass frames balanced on the end of her nose, Maisie's braids fuzzy and coming undone. Autumn Ann clambered up into Jean's lap.

"Get down. It's too hot. And listen to this." Autumn Ann curled closer. Jean huddled them and Lou saw how Gordon and Jasper bent over just like Lamont, as though they had no bones but were willows being arched. "We're going to make us a dirt yard—no more mowing the lawn for us." And all those little children, some not over two years old, never having heard the words "dirt yard" before, knew exactly what she meant. You could see it in their shiny eyes as they looked around the compound to size up the destruction that could be wrought. Autumn Ann picked up a handful of pebbles and licked them. Lou was getting tickled and the baby inside her kicked out—hard. "Ouch!"

"What, Mama? Mama, what?" all of hers shrilled, even as their hands ached to pull up clumps of grass.

"Nothing," Lou laughed. "I guess we better start pulling."

"From here . . ." Jean stood up, unfolding her long arm like a measuring rod. "From here to that deer's broke foot, I want down to the dirt by suppertime. Now run get some things to dig with," she said.

"Can we use combs?" Gordon asked.

"Why not?" she shrugged. "Combs, spoons, sticks, anything that'll dig'll do. We need to lay this lawn bare, get it back down to the basics. Now go on and get."

Now, on this day twenty-two years later, as Lou sweats next to Lacey, using a borrowed broom, waiting for her turn at the rake, she tries to tell the story and why, whenever she is feeling low, she'll bring up that afternoon.

"There we were," she says, gesturing with the broom, bringing it down to make half-circles in the dust. "Jean in Lamont's skivvy shirt knotted at the shoulders, cut-offs, and her stringy hair plastered to her head—it must have been 95 degrees—and me, p.g. with a summer top and shorts with that hole cut in the middle for space, feeling air cool against my belly and the sweat running right across my navel, both of us hunkering in the grass, pulling weeds and clover and everything that grew. All those kids—Jean's five, my four, who knows how many others and where they came from, and everybody with a spoon, a stick, a pointed thing. Autumn Ann used the prong of her barrette to scratch the dirt back."

And every one of them, she can't explain, with a purpose, as they unearthed old bottle caps, rusty nails, cigarette butts, a pile of treasure put to one side for when the digging was done. Lou can still see clearly her son squatting, both hands dug deep into the grass, tugging at a clump, straining back on his heels to lift it by its tufted roots, pulling hard to break the sod away; can see him fall back, clod against stomach to cry out in triumph just as a grasshopper leaped free, the movement of its wings no more than the shimmer of heat.

"We did it too," she says to Lacey. "We did. By six o'clock that evening, before Marlon and Lamont got home, we had a perfect circle of dirt, so sweet smelling. Too thick to really rake, but the children went and stuck the edges with forks as if it was a big patty pie."

"Lord, Lord." Lacey shakes her head and smiles. She's stopped raking in order to hear this story and she leans on the end of her rake, using it like a cane. How can Lou tell her of the great grass hummock to the side of the yard that got thrown and sat and climbed upon? Jasper mounted to the top of it, put a dirt clod on his head, shouted, "Lookee here! See my false hair?" then blew back dribbles of dirt that peppered his cheeks. All felt the taste of mud melting in their mouths, gritting their teeth, and the thickness of soil caking under their fingernails. As the day deepened into night the sky paled and shadowed the trees while the streetlights outside the Courts sneaked light over the wall. Then the children lay down in that cool damp dirt to push roly-poly bugs around and swim their arms and legs in those dark elements.

"Later," Lou says, "I later lost the baby I carried then, but I've never lost a second of that day." She can still feel life turning inside her as she dug her fingers knuckle-deep into the earth.

Lacey reaches out her hand and lays it on Lou's arm, and as Lou slows her sweeping, her tears spatter the dirt. "Thank you," she says. "Thank you for letting me help you with this yard." Then Lou is confused. She is standing on the edge of the intricate design and she doesn't want to spoil it. Lacey takes her arm and leads her up to the porch and over to the side. "Right here," she motions. There are three steps down to the grass. Lou sees the clothes flapping on the line and up on the hill sees Marlon leaning against a car talking to a man who must be Lacey's son-in-law. Children and a dog circle the car in a running game. Lou realizes she is still holding the broom in her hand and turns back. "Here."

"Wait," the woman says, going quickly through her belled-out screen door; it slams behind. Lou stares at the smooth dirt yard, so different from the one she remembers—this one dry and designed but still powerful enough to move her. The screen door opens again; Lacey is at the steps. "Here." She holds out a navel orange—deep russet and glowing. Lou can already taste the sweet tang of its flesh. They smile at each other, each old enough to remember when an orange was a gift you hoped for, hoped to get tucked into the toe of a stocking, or icy cold from lying on a block of ice when you were sick, sweet pulp sipped over ice chips. The color of carrots, or persimmons, of the baby Lamont cradled on his chest.

"Here's for your traveling," Lacey says and puts the orange into Lou's hand.

"Thank you. Thank you again." Lou, holding the orange tight to her chest, climbs the hill.

Sometimes on these trips, when she's tired, Lou despairs and wonders aloud to Marlon if they will ever find the Dillons. If maybe they should quit, break down and take out ads before it's too late. Maybe Jean and

Lamont are dead. He always pats her on the hip, leans close to kiss between the point where her shoulder meets her neck, and says, "You know
we'll find them. Now, don't give up. But we'll take out an ad if you want
to. Hell, let's buy a banner. Buy a blimp. I can afford it."

She is cheered holding him and being held by him, her face mashed
sideways against his shirt buttons, an errant wire of hair pushing from his
neck-V. She feels his heart thrumming through her hands as she fits her
palms around his shoulder blades. "I love you, honey," she mouths
against his buttons. He murmurs back, rocking her in a silent dance.

Two days later Lou can still feel the broom in her hands, the scritch of
the dirt, the powder of it as it moved away in patterns, and how it puffed
up when Lacey sprinkled it. She fancies that if she holds her right hand
cupped over her nose she can still smell the yard, smell again the end of
the broomstick stuck into stiff straw, the wood split with paint flecks filling the creases in her hands. She's happy to recall that Lacey leaned on
her rake, tucking the end under her breast to stand like a tripod and listen, shake her head, and smile at Lou's telling. The orange she gave her is
in the cooler case at this very minute.

When she'd joined Marlon at the hill, looking back to wave, grinning
until she thought her face would split, Lou felt mixed up. Once in the
van, she turned to Marlon. He was looking straight ahead, left leg bent at
the knee and propped up on the seat in a way that was dangerous and
drove her crazy. She didn't even know how to begin to tell him what
she'd done, and said, or why. She wanted him to already know it.

"That reminded me of Mama," he said, shifting his position, making
the van speed up, slow down.

I could kill you, she thought. She was nothing like that. Marlon's
mother was not a thing like that. Never was.

"Reminded me too of the time y'all dug that whole yard up," he added.
Then, alarmed, "Lou, what's the matter? Lou? Why are you bawling?"

She could only shake her head. Then she lowered her face into her
hands and cried while Marlon kept changing the stations, swiveling the
dial to find some music to comfort her.

That night in bed at the Promo Motel, where everything was harvest
gold or green shag and scarred with cigarettes, she tried to tell him
what had happened to her in Lacey's yard. He held her, patting, saying,
"Hmmm," or "Yeah," or "Oh, honey," gentle interruptions. "It'll be all
right, sweetheart." Then he stroked her thigh in a way she always remembered. She moved to him, marveling at the wonder of knowing Marlon
all these years, and so long ago, that other Marlon who'd first pulled her

away from her safe home and life. She almost thought she could feel that young Marlon, so skinny, so eager, so crazy to get up and go, as he moved in her now.

A few mornings later they are driving along when Lou is alerted by the blue van ahead of them. "Catch up with them," she says. "Hurry, Marlon. That's exactly like the kind of thing they'd drive. Look at all the stickers on it."

The van is plastered with *Knotts Berry Farm* and *Save the Whales* and *Luray Caverns* and *Disneyworld* and the whole back window is covered twice, once with drawn-down green shades that filter light, then with stickers of mountain ranges and other natural wonders in this hemisphere. *Wash me! Quick!* is fingered out in the bumper dust.

Marlon, revved up by Lou's excitement, guns the motor, catches up to cruise side by side with the van. It is muraled on the side with great tongues of flame pointing to the headlights, a map of the United States with stars in every state and a tribute to the Baltimore Orioles. All the side windows are shaded in green too, and the rushing sunlight makes it seem to be traveling underwater.

"That mother's going fast," Marlon says, lowering and twisting his head to see the van off which Lou is reading signs.

"*White Sands Proving Grounds*? They never would go there, would they?"

"Hell, I don't know," Marlon says. "People change."

Lou looks at him. "This seems too new a van for them."

"Look at us, dammit," he says. "We've got a Saab at home. You think Lamont and Jean ever expected to see us in anything but an old Pontiac?" He speeds up even with the driver as Lou pokes her head up and out. The front window of the van is copper glazed with a reflective sheen.

"Speed up some more, Marlon, so I can get the angle." Then she sees, as though through fire, a young man, bearded and bespectacled, singing at the top of his lungs. Marlon pulls ahead, blinkers right, and pulls in front.

"Not them?"

"No." Lou falls back in the seat and adjusts her seat belt. "But it looks like the kind of van they'd be driving." Marlon is looking out the rearview mirror at the van; its great coppery windshield glints, shooting silvery lights off its convexity.

"That guy was singing with his head thrown back—singing at the top of his lungs—just like you do," Lou says, and she puts her hand on Marlon's knee.

He breaks into a tuneless but buoyant "Home, home on the range" as Lou says, "I'm gonna wave anyway. I bet there's little kids in there." She scrambles up and over to the back, undoing her seat belt and standing bent-kneed in the back seat, leans until her upper body is wedged into the back window. She begins to wag her head and wave back and forth, looking like one of those bobbing backview beagles that are so popular. In the rushing of the light made by the two vehicles, Lou's face looks back at her from the other van's copper windshield. In this strange trick of light for a moment it seems that she is sitting beside the young singing driver. She sees herself bronze, smiling, waving back at herself.

"Hold on, honey, I'm pulling out," Marlon says as he steps on the gas and moves them away.

A Good-looking Woman

JOYCE MEIER

 I don't mean that I never thought of having an affair. Fantasizing is normal. Then too, knowing someone, even casually, like Ellie Gunderson, I have been exposed to that kind of thing. There was a time when I envied Ellie. She is a good-looking woman . . . one of the chosen few. People have told me we look alike. We do, except her arrangement always seemed to work better.

Every year Robert, Ellie's ex, gives her a two-week trip to the Golden Door spa in California. It was in the settlement. Ellie takes part in the whole program. I have seen her incision scars and it's amazing what a good plastic surgeon can accomplish with a little nip and tuck in the proper places. She wears large Panama straws with bright scarves to keep her hair color from turning brassy (oxidizing, she says) and the wide brims protect the stitches around her eyes, too.

Frank, my husband, saw Ellie at the Tom Thumb in the Village one day early last spring. He was picking up some dill for me so I could finish pickling the cucumbers from my spring garden. She was wearing big, rose-tinted glasses, Frank told me. They covered most of her face, he said, and he wondered what she was saving it all for.

When Frank came back with the dill that day, I was sitting out on the porch in the wicker rocker squeaking to the same spring song as the squirrels and enjoying the redbuds flowering along the side of the house. When those redbuds and the jonquils open up, so do my veins. The sap starts running faster. The redbuds were dressed to kill in their pink and white buds and looked so young and fresh against the dried-out March season. It made me ache just to see them showing off like that.

Frank put the dill on the kitchen table along with the receipt and sauntered out the screen door to the backyard. I waited for the door to slam. That man cannot close a door softly.

"I'm going down to the end of the lot to check the crepe myrtles," he called back. "Want to make sure the freeze didn't get them."

I wanted to know more about Ellie so I hollered to him, "Come out on the porch when you've finished. You can smell spring and summer all at once today." Those darn crepe myrtles, they worry Frank to death. They'll bloom all right. Overnight they'll change. Burst out in their organdy all at once and steal the whole show.

Frank came back up later and sat with me on the porch. He smiled at me. The sun was hitting his bad shoulder just right and he could smell the brisket I had cooking in the kitchen coming through the white curtains at the window over the sink. He was comfortable.

"Saw Ellie Gunderson at the grocery while I was picking up your dill," he reminded me. (As if I needed reminding.)

I waited while he groped for his pipe in his shirt pocket. Wasn't there and he patted his front pockets, both of them. Leaned forward and patted the back ones. Didn't say a word. Looked out across the yard. Got up. Checked the sprinkler. Walked back. Sat down again. Still no word. Started patting his pockets same way as before.

"Well, Frank Jennings," I said, trying to keep too much interest out of my voice, "don't just sit there, tell me how she looks." And I leaned across to his chair and put my hand on the arm of it to prevent him jumping up again.

Frank gave me a long look. He was thinking about Ellie, I could tell. He leaned back, folded his hands across his chest and said, "It's hard to tell, sugar," and he looked at me real seriously before he went on. "'Bout the only thing I could see of her was her navel." Then he laughed. Slapped his knee and laughed. Frank has a way of laughing at things he doesn't understand.

Ellie must have had on her green silk shirt that ties above the waist. That woman really knows how to dress. I've often wished I had her way with style. Frank always wants me in sweaters and skirts or my little beige linen.

"Did you talk to each other?" I asked.

"Said 'hi.' She was racing through the store," he answered.

I could just see those long legs of hers on spike heels, of course, and the wide-brimmed hat with the green silk scarf floating through the Tom Thumb. Must have been a sight for sore eyes.

Frank stopped laughing. Finally, looked at me. Said, "She did throw over her shoulder, though, for you not to forget Spring Market next week. She said she'd told you to come pick out some clothes and use her discount. Told me to tell you not to forget."

As if I would.

I met Ellie's latest lover that week. She had just come back from California, from her annual sojourn to the Golden Door out there. She was doing some modeling at Market for Mr. Ray's of Dallas and I had taken her up on her discount offer. I spend every extra dollar on my flowers and plants around the yard, or else I'm sending a box off to Marilee, our daughter in Fredericksburg who teaches at a school for deaf children. So the discount Ellie offered sounded like a good idea.

Frank said, "Why not make a day of it? Why don't we have lunch at that new little restaurant by the Apparel Mart?" So that's just what we did. Frank was so happy to get me out of the house for a day. He always acts like he wants me to be a regular "out and about" girl. Like some of our friends whose wives play a little golf at the club and then relax at the 19th Hole with martinis all afternoon. Guess it would make him feel good to have me lounge all day. Men are funny.

The day for our trip to Spring Market, Frank was ready before I was. I had to sew a button on my beige linen dress. I had forgotten it fell off from Marilee hugging me so hard when we went to visit her at Easter. I had saved the button there on the mirrored tray Frank gave me last Christmas. So while he was stacking the clothes boxes that I wanted to mail to Marilee into the car, I was slipping into my pumps (thank goodness for tan legs) and brushing my short hair extra hard. After I fit gold loops into my ears, I was ready. Frank pinched me and said I looked younger than tomorrow.

I was excited about seeing Ellie at Market. I hadn't seen her since her trip to California, and I knew she would have some fascinating tale to tell. One time, she and her roommate at the Golden Door had gone over to Lake Tahoe and gambled at one of the casinos. Ellie made it sound so thrilling that I forgot all about the time Frank and I had been there. It had been hot. Hot and crowded and I told Frank I could hardly wait to get back to Dallas where I could breathe. But Ellie always seems to be at the right places at the right times.

It was dark as a cellar closet when we walked into the Clothesline Restaurant that day. Lattice-covered candles flickered on white tablecloths and a young lady with blonde hair and a black velvet bodice led us through the semi-darkness and soft conversation to a booth against the wall. While I scooted to the middle of the upholstered seat, Frank ordered a vodka tonic for himself and a frozen daiquiri for me. (I am not much for rum, but I love the word "daiquiri.") Our drinks came and we sipped them and ordered lunch from huge menus. We were talking about the addition we planned to make on our farmhouse near Austin and wondering if it would be finished before the mare foaled, when suddenly I just forgot Frank was sitting across from me. For there, coming toward us, was Ellie. Ellie and a very handsome young man. Cherries Jubilee was being prepared at the table next to ours and at the same time the copper pan went "whoosh," there they were. As if they'd emerged from the alcohol vapors. Ellie was smiling at us, her teeth apple white. Head tilted way to the side. One hand played with some beads at her throat, the other clutched the young man's coat sleeve. She tugged him toward our table.

I saw them first because I was facing that way. Frank followed my gaze, saw them and stood up. Ellie introduced the young man as Mr. Ray and then she swooped down and picked up my daiquiri. (All Ellie's movements are exaggerated.) She held my drink to her bright lips, threw back her head and raved, "How *divine*." Mr. Ray just looked at the stickpin in his Christian Dior pindot scarf and told Frank to please sit down.

"Oh, darlings, the food is divine. Do enjoy," Ellie cooed.

"We didn't expect to see you until later at the Market," I reminded her, all the time appreciating the fine cut of Mr. Ray's sport coat. "How nice that we did, though," I said. I felt Mr. Ray looking at me and before I realized it, I was asking them to join us. "Can you join us for lunch?" I chirped, and suddenly I wanted them to say yes. Yes, of course.

But Ellie answered, "Sorry, loves, just finished. It was delightful."

The waiter came with our lunch and Ellie and Mr. Ray started to leave. Ellie replaced my cocktail glass on the table like it was a bird she had caught. She looked at me. "Don't forget your clothes shopping. Mega bargains, darling." She flicked her tongue across her lips and fluttered beside the fashionable young man for a minute, then they left. Several people turned to watch them make their way through the tables. Frank and I stared after them. Ellie is a good-looking woman.

At the front desk, the young thing in the black bodice handed them a small tray. I saw Ellie sign the check before the heavy quilted doors of the restaurant opened and a streak of sunlight, like an explosion, shone through the darkened room and a hollow "Bye, darlings" floated back to us over the china and silver.

Frank and I went on to the Apparel Mart, as planned, for the shopping spree. We parted company by the guard at the front gate because Frank said he wanted to mosey around the building and maybe find someone who could tell him how they installed the huge wire baskets of greenery that hang from the ceiling five floors down. I went on up to the third floor.

Mr. Ray's of Dallas is just one large room, actually. There is a showroom window on the front that faces the hallway and traffic, and the girls who work for Mr. Ray change the mannequins every time you turn around. The main business, though, is done in the large room with the swatch books and style numbers that Mr. Ray keeps on his desk, which is in the middle of the room. When I came in, he saw me and came right over. He smiled and I offered him my hand. He covered my hand with his own and said it was nice that I came by and to please let him help if he could. His hand was warm.

I told him that I was mainly looking for something for my daughter, Marilee, and that I just might sure enough need some of his expertise. I gave him Marilee's coloring and explained her build—pretty much like mine, sample size. He could not believe I had a daughter teaching school. You look like a schoolgirl yourself, he told me. We were interrupted several times with the buyers asking questions about the styles, when would they be available, et cetera, but we did manage to find several things for Marilee. Mr. Ray was most helpful. His eyes are soft blue and when you ask him a question, he has this way of looking straight at you with those blue eyes as if you are the only person for miles around. He really concentrates on you and when he answers, you know that that *is* the right color, or the right combination or the right length. There is no doubt in your mind that he is right.

The women who work Market are all so attractive. Most of them live in North Dallas and their husbands are in oil or investments, or both, and they work Market because there they are for all the newest clothes, the latest styles, and also it is a great place for catching up on who is seeing whom. It's all very exciting. I was truly amazed when I found out that Emily Forsythe was having an affair with Robert Gunderson. Why, she'd been married to Bobby John Forsythe for fifteen years and they have two beautiful children. She was Marilee's room mother in the eighth grade.

Mr. Ray and I got along fine right from the start. He seemed to realize that I knew what I was looking for and what I wanted without my ever having been up close to how it all worked before. As I checked fabrics, I could feel Mr. Ray with his eye on me. I knew he was studying me but I wasn't embarrassed. After all the sewing I'd done for Marilee, I was in familiar territory. I knew materials. It reminded me how I had felt twenty years before when I had a date with a good dancer for the prom . . . confident. That is how I had felt. It was like playing a game, a game I enjoyed. While I was holding different colors up to me and looking into the floor-length mirror that hangs on the back side of the entry door, I caught his eye several times. One of the salesgirls came up to him with a question as he sat, knees crossed, on the edge of his desk. I could see the two of them in the mirror. She was wearing one of the new garments, the tags dangling from her wrist, when she sidled up to Mr. Ray. "I can't find the price for this chemise, Mr. Ray," she whined as she hipped her way up to him close enough to touch. She came still nearer and Mr. Ray stood up quickly, eyes over her head; didn't look at her at all, just sort of paddled her away with one hand and moved around her and closer to the mirror where I was standing. He watched me the whole time. He knew then that I knew he was watching me. His face, reflected above mine in the mirror, grinned into the glass—into my face. The creases at his eyes danced. His chin came up. "I like your style," he said to me and it was like I was moving into a good dancer's arms at the edge of a dance floor . . . a big band playing and a ballroom all around and saxophone rhythms blending together the colors of the evening. Time was gone before I knew it.

I got so involved with all the hustle and bustle up there on the third floor that I almost forgot about poor Frank waiting for me at the front gate. But there he was just where he said he would be, by the gate, standing there running some soil through his fingers from the large potted ficus in the lobby. Checking the dampness, he said. Wanted to see how watered they keep them.

On the way home all I could talk about was the afternoon at the Apparel Mart. Frank said he bet Marilee would be excited about her new clothes. "You going to call her tonight?" he asked. He was all scrunched down in his seat, concentrating on the downtown traffic, trying to find the best part of his bifocals to see through.

"I will if I'm not too tired. An afternoon like this just wears me out," I answered. Guess I had spent all my energy oohing and ahing over all the pretty clothes at Mr. Ray's, because just then all I wanted to do was just not talk. I wanted to think about the past couple of hours and all the new styles and things I had seen.

But Frank went on. "Yep, I bet Marilee will sure be excited," he said. He was looking straight ahead and waiting for me to ask about the hanging baskets at the Mart and had he found out what he wanted to know. If he had taken time to look at me he would have seen that my eyes were closed and he knows when my eyes are closed that means I don't want any more conversation. He'd want to talk about Marilee, the farmhouse, his flowers, his vegetables, anyway. All the things he always wants to talk about. He looks away when I start talking about anything romantic. Never does have time for what makes the world go round.

At Market they all just dote on Mr. Ray. It's yes, Mr. Ray, this, and no, Mr. Ray, that, so you can imagine my surprise at the reaction when three days later that same week I happened to be in the neighborhood and decided on the spur of the moment to see what was going on over at the Apparel Mart and then found myself on the third floor almost in front of Mr. Ray's of Dallas and decided, just like that, to pop my head (fresh from La Coiffure) in the door. I waved and smiled when Mr. Ray looked up. "Just wanted to say hi," I cupped a whisper loud enough so he could hear me. "Marilee's mama, 'member?" I hoped he remembered how surprised he had been three days ago when I had said yes, I had a daughter twenty-two. I decided the other day when I met him that he couldn't be a day over forty. There were just those few gray hairs beginning at the temples which only make a man like that more attractive.

Mr. Ray pushed back his chair and came around from his desk and his eyes never left my face. I can still see those sensitive blue eyes of his above the pale yellow scarf at his neck, his hands extended . . . both hands stretched out in front of him . . . as he moved over the thick carpet and seemed to float toward me.

He took my right hand with his, his other arm slipped across my shoulders and became a kind of little hug. He smiled down into my face. "How *marvelous*," he said. "Louise, isn't it? Louise Jennings."

We were standing very close to each other and I could smell the Ralph Lauren (of course I didn't know it was Ralph Lauren then, but I do now) aftershave on his skin. All of our men friends and the men Frank works with just plain shake my hand when we see each other, most of the time talking to Frank about something as they do. There is nothing *personal* about it. But Mr. Ray is sophisticated. He understands women. I was surprised when he hugged me like that, but I didn't move away. "I just thought I'd come by and say hi," I said.

He led me to the chair by his desk and sat me down like I was one of the big specialty store buyers. Then he moved around to his side of the desk, sat down, and leaned across the mahogany, his hands folded in front of him. His face was earnest. "Did your daughter like those fantastic things we got for her?" he asked me.

"She called last night," I told him. "And that is one reason I'm here. Everything was so perfect for her, I thought you might help me with some accessories, too." That last just came popping out of my mouth like I had planned what I was going to say. It was just such a natural thing to ask what with Mr. Ray being so style conscious and kind and wanting to please people so.

He poked a button by his desk, a light came on, and he leaned into the button. "Cathy," he said, "cancel my hair appointment at Mr. Peter's. I'll be gone for a while." Then he turned back to me. "I'm all yours," he said. He checked his watch and I could see his tanned wrist against the white cuff of his shirt. The heavy gold watch glinted with a charm of its own. Charm seemed to fill the whole room, the whole afternoon. He smiled and stood up ready to go. "Let's try Market Boutique first. Then we'll have time for a spot of lunch and if we haven't found what we want by then, we can go next door to Durrie's, where they have magnificent costume jewelry." By this time we were out the door and on our way.

Shopping is no problem when you are with someone like Mr. Ray. He knows immediately what is right, puts colors together you would never dream of doing and makes it all fun besides. Our arms were filled with packages when we stopped at the Clothesline for lunch (twice in one week for me and I felt like one of the regulars when we walked in). We sat in one of those cozy upholstered booths and Mr. Ray ordered me a daiquiri (he remembered!) and we talked and talked and talked. Or rather I listened to Mr. Ray tell me about his line and how he got started with his unique combination of facile suede and knit. Mr. Ray is an unusual man. Except for some tiny bit of help from his mother and a sister when he first introduced his designs, he has managed his whole career strictly on his own. I watched him while he ordered lunch for us and I must say he can read a woman's mind; the shrimp salad on avocado was just the right thing. Frank always lets me decide for myself, even when I have no idea what I want. In fact, usually I end up ordering for both of us. It was nice to be so well taken care of. The Clothesline was cool and comfortable that day and I just let myself sink down into those luxurious cushions and be a part of the whole excitement of the market district. Mr. Ray pointed out several well-known buyers and designers.

When the waiter brought our check, I insisted on paying the tab because after all, Mr. Ray was doing me a big favor in helping me with Marilee's wardrobe. We finished and he held my elbow and guided me out through the lunchtime crowd. Several people stopped him to say hello, all fashionably dressed and smart looking, and one especially attractive brunette—tall, long legs—threw her arms around him and I almost lost sight of his head in the tangle of gold earrings and hair as she pressed him to her bosom. Mr. Ray is not very tall. He looks like a dancer; a ballroom dancer. There is a boyishness about him, but the gray hair at his temples reminds you that he is a man of distinction.

Outside, the air was clear and bright and I felt happy to be alive on such a nice day. We were walking toward the Apparel Mart still chatting about our purchases when suddenly Mr. Ray asked me if I had ever done any modeling.

"Well, no, actually I haven't," I answered.

"You have the figure for it. You're small, but I could use a woman like you in the new line. Care to try? I think we would get along famously."

My hand was tucked inside his elbow at the time (I barely reach his shoulder) and we were crossing the street. When he suggested I do some modeling for him, I stopped dead still. Could not move—right there in the middle of the afternoon traffic. I looked up at him. Still could not say a word. Opened my mouth, but nothing came out.

Mr. Ray threw back his head and laughed, oblivious too to the cars congesting around us. "Why are you so surprised? You're a good-looking woman," he said.

"I never expected anything like this to happen to me," I told him.

"I know, Louise—Lou, may I call you Lou?—it's part of your charm. But whether you know it or not, *you*"—his eyes caught mine—"are a beige-linen beauty!" And he laughed again, young, incredible laughter.

Well, before the week was over I was down there in Plastic Land with the rest of North Dallas (have been all summer now) showing merchandise, taking orders, and modeling Mr. Ray's new line. You get kind of caught up with it after a while. Seems like I hardly ever have time for a trip to see Marilee in Fredericksburg anymore. It's not only the great fabrics (the fall line is fantastic with paisleys and brocades) but some materials must have bold jewelry—ornate stones and lots of gold plating (dipped in brass, usually)—and so there you go, it takes time to put the whole look together if you want it to be successful. Frank asked me the other day wasn't I going to put up the chili sauce this year. The tomatoes are spoiling on the kitchen counter, I know, but there is just *so* much time. In the evenings I am too tired for that kind of thing. I told Frank that taking care of this house, working Market, and seeing that he is comfortable, doesn't leave me much time for myself. But I manage. (*We* manage. Ray and I manage to have our moments.)

I have hardly had a meal at home all summer. In fact, Frank and I have barely seen each other, and now a whole summer is almost over again. I heard just the other day from Sharon, the checker at Tom Thumb, that Ellie (she called her Mrs. Gunderson) has moved to Los Angeles. Guess Ellie is more the California type. She sure does keep on the move, anyway.

Yes, summer is almost gone. Yesterday I had an hour before I had to be at Market and Frank and I were relaxed and enjoying an unusually quiet afternoon on the porch, Frank sipping an iced tea and feeling contented. "I do believe those crepe myrtles down there," and he motioned with his head to the back of the yard, "are the prettiest things I have ever seen," he said. "They blossomed after all, didn't they? Guess they just like to keep me on my toes," and he laughed at his own words.

It was almost four o'clock, the hottest part of the day, but the crepe myrtles looked fresh and lovely. "Yes, dear," I answered as I stole a quick glance at my watch, "your trees finally flowered." I leaned back in the chair and smiled pleasantly at Frank. "Our garden has never looked more beautiful."

Infections

KAREN GERHARDT BRITTON

 Under the rotting quilt, the letter lay damp with the moisture from Granny Robbins's hand. Her broken nails scored the edges of the envelope. Her fingertips touched the stamp, over and over, making sure it would not come off.

I don't want Owen to take the disease, she thought. He's my son. I don't want him to get infected, but he's got to come, him and that new wife of his. They've got to come and get me.

In the long summer afternoon the thick feather mattress was hot. It smelled of old urine. Sometimes Laura kept her in her room too long. Sometimes the flies swarmed around the bucket in the corner and she wouldn't use it. Sometimes . . . she smiled at the water spots on the ceiling . . . sometimes she wouldn't use it on purpose.

She lay still, breathing in time to the stroking of her fingers on the letter, listening to grasshoppers shriek in the cornfields across the dirt road. She smelled onions cooking. Laura was fixing supper awful early tonight. Had Laura guessed what she was up to and changed mealtimes to trick her?

No, Granny decided, if Laura had known about the letter, she'd have grabbed it away. She didn't know what had made Laura so mean. Laura was her daughter and was supposed to take care of her.

Granny stroked the letter. Her mouth watered a little. She was hungry. She wanted some cooked onions, just a few, stirred into hot-water cornbread. Laura had told her that hot-water cornbread wasn't good for her. Granny got oatmeal or cream of wheat or mashed potatoes every meal.

She didn't complain.

She didn't cry.

She didn't dare.

Now she lay listening to the grasshoppers and smelling the onions and thinking about how far it was to the mailbox.

"Owen has to come," she said to herself. "He's my son, the youngest, my baby. He'll come and get me. He doesn't fault me the way Laura does."

Sweat soaked her hair and neck. The long sleeves of the thin flannel gown lay in sodden puddles on the sheet. She slid the letter under the pillow so the address wouldn't be smudged off.

As she waited for nightfall, she stared at the rows of fading cornflowers on the wall. In the strong afternoon light, straight from the west, Granny saw the paper bubble and heard the tiny sound it made as it loosened itself from the wall, but she didn't grieve for it. Owen would come and get her. She would be glad to die in a nice clean room, with or without wallpaper. A nice clean room that faced east. A nice clean room without water stains on the ceiling and old scarred furniture and a bucket for a toilet.

She closed her eyes and rested, dreaming of that room.

When she awoke, Laura was standing at the foot of the bed, the broken crockery bowl in her hand. She gave Granny a sharp look as if surprised to find her alive.

"Sit up, Mama," she said. "I've got your oatmeal."

"Did you put me some apples in it this time?"

"No. Apples are too high right now. Wait'll fall. Then I'll buy you all the apples you want."

I won't be here, Granny thought. Owen will come and get me.

She sat up on the side of the bed. The sun was sliding into distant fields, its rays broken by stalks of corn. Through the rusty window screen she saw golden tassels shining above the dirt road that led from the creek below the house to the mailbox at the highway.

She turned toward the pillow to make sure the letter was there, but Laura was watching her. She rearranged herself on the bed so Laura wouldn't think she was hiding something.

"Now you clean up your oatmeal," Laura said as she thrust the bowl at her. "You don't eat enough to keep a bird alive."

"Bring me something fit to eat."

"You're sick, Mama. You can't eat regular food."

"I can eat anything I want to."

"That's not what the doctor said."

Granny took the bowl and stared down into it.

"Now, Mama, Henry and me's going to have a bite to eat and then I'll come back and visit with you."

"Don't bother yourself," Granny said. "I'm going to sleep early."

"Well, suit yourself."

Laura said that every night.

Relieved, Granny watched her daughter leave and heard the door close with a snap. She didn't want the oatmeal. She wanted onions and hot-water cornbread.

But she had to get to the mailbox.

She ate the oatmeal to give herself strength.

When she finished, she set the bowl on the floor. She moved around the room exercising, making sure she had the energy to get to the mail-box. She would have put on a fresh gown, but Laura had given her clothes to the tenants' wives. "They're just rags anyhow," Laura had said. But Granny knew it was to punish her.

Twilight was creeping up the road from the creek bottom when Laura came for the bowl. "Now if you need anything, Mama, you just holler. Me and Henry's going to be in the living room. He's got a brand-new box of dominoes. We'll be right here if you want anything."

"I want you to empty out my bucket."

Laura glanced toward the corner as if she could see the bucket hidden behind the chifforobe. She turned up her nose and frowned. "I'll get Henry to take it out in the morning." She scurried out the door.

A fly came from nowhere, buzzing as it circled the bucket.

Granny shooed it away and made herself use the bucket. From the cor-ner where she squatted, she could see the trees above the creek where Laura's baby had stepped on that rusty fish hook. Granny didn't go there anymore, but she thought about that creek a lot. "If I just had my strength," she said to herself, "I could go fishing for perch like I used to."

When she was through with the bucket, she found an old washcloth and cleaned her face and hands with water from a cracked pitcher. I don't want Owen to see me looking this bad, she thought.

She lifted the pillow to make sure the letter was still there. It was, but she touched it anyway to renew the covenant. Once she got the letter to the box, it would be safe. Tomorrow the Rural Free Delivery man would come along in his Ford truck and collect the mail. In a few days Owen would come and collect her.

She paced the bare floor, filling her weak lungs with all the air they would hold, practicing, until nightfall. She heard Laura and Henry argu-ing about their dominoes. She tucked the letter into the frayed sleeve of her gown, bending the envelope a little so it wouldn't make any noise.

She went to the door. With Laura busy arguing with Henry, Granny could slip into the long, dark hallway and out the front door. She was barefoot. She didn't weigh enough to creak the floorboards. As long as Laura didn't see or hear her leave, she would never stop her, never check the box, never take out the letter.

She reached for the doorknob, then caught herself. Laura always told her not to touch the knob. She would pass on her disease to others that way.

Granny placed her thin wrists on the knob and tried to turn it without using her fingers. The brass was slick. She couldn't hold onto it.

But she had to mail the letter.

Taking the hem of her gown, she gathered the skirt up to her bare thighs and wrapped the loose end of it around the knob. She turned with all her strength, but the knob wouldn't budge. She dropped the gown and gripped the knob with both hands. It rattled. But it wouldn't turn.

Laura had locked her in.

Granny's heart thudded against the tumor in her chest.

The only other way out was through the window.

She knelt at the sill and pushed on the frame, praying that it would open but not fall and crash and bring Laura running. She prayed that it hadn't rusted shut. She prayed and she pushed. The window squeaked once and opened. Granny held on to it with both hands, not caring if she infected the window. It opened a little more.

She gathered up her gown again and after taking a deep, painful breath, backed out of the window. Her feet touched the grass, then solid earth. The screen bounced off the back of her head and brought tears to her eyes, but she grabbed the frame and shut the window carefully, knowing she would have to get back in that way.

She made herself breathe evenly. She listened for Laura's voice or Henry's footsteps.

All she heard were tree frogs near the creek and crickets under the house. From the fields came the odor of skunk. Somewhere in the distance a dog was barking.

Like a cat trailing a mouse in the barn, she stole across the weed-infested yard to the cool dust of the road. She looked up at the Big Dipper and the Milky Way and she saw a shooting star. Lightning bugs flitted around her head as if to guide her. A cow mooed from the farm across the highway. The grass was sweet with dusty dew. Maybe, she thought, I'll just stay out all night.

Too soon she reached the highway. The mailbox was mounted on a post beside the gate. She didn't try to open the gate. Henry had latched it with a wreath of wire. By standing on tiptoe she could touch the door of the mailbox.

As she slipped the envelope inside and shut the little door, she prayed, Oh, God, don't let Owen get infected from my letter.

She stood at the gate a long time, smiling to herself, thinking about how Owen would hug her and brag on her cleverness. And how he would be so angry at Laura that he would curse. And how he would buy her a new gown, one with short sleeves, and maybe a new dress, one she'd be proud to die in.

If she had a new dress, she could go visit a neighbor.

They must think I'm awful rude, she thought, not to come calling anymore. Maybe Owen will take me to visit his friends. He's a schoolteacher. He must have a lot of friends.

Or if Owen was afraid she would infect his friends, he might bring them to see her. They wouldn't have to touch anything of hers, just stand inside the door and say, Hello, nice to meet you, Mrs. Robbins. She would sit up straight in a chair and smooth her new dress and say, Hello, nice to meet you, too. And when she died, they would tell Owen how sorry they were for him but how glad they were to have met his mother. Maybe they'd send huge bouquets of little white daisies, she thought.

Not yet tired, she turned and started along the road to the creek.

A cat shrieked.

The front door slammed open.

"Mama?" Laura sounded a lot like the cat. "Mama, where are you?"

Granny didn't answer. She was remembering Laura's baby's funeral and the hundreds of daisies bowing their little heads over the casket.

"Mama!" Laura grabbed her left arm.

Granny sucked in her breath.

"You're not supposed to be out of your room!" Laura shouted into her face. "What are you doing out here?"

"I just wanted to go for a little walk."

"Well, you just walk back into the house. And don't you ever sneak out like that again!"

Granny felt tears of pain burning her eyes, but she didn't cry out. The last time she'd cried out, Laura had taken all her clothes away and given them to the tenants' wives. Granny bit her tongue and kept silent.

Laura dragged her into the house. She opened the door to the room, pushed her inside, and locked the door again. "Now you stay in there, you hear?"

Granny stood alone in the darkness. Laura's the only one who touches me, Granny thought. I wonder how come she doesn't get infected.

Or has she already got it?

If Laura's already infected, then I can't pass it on to Owen!

Exhausted, she went to the bed and lay down. She stared at the blackness where the ceiling should have been and felt the cool night air seeping into the room. She tossed back the quilt and smiled to herself, proud that she'd been strong enough to get to the mailbox and back. She was strong enough to wait for Owen, too.

Suddenly, a yellow light bobbed just outside the window, casting eerie shadows onto the wallpaper. She saw a head silhouetted against the screen, then a body. She heard metal scraping wood. Frightened, she called out, "Who's there?"

"It's just me, Mama," Laura answered.

Something slammed into the warped framing around the window.

"What are you doing?" Granny cried out.

"I'm nailing this window shut. I can't lay awake at night worrying about you wandering off to the highway or down to the creek. You might get hurt, and I don't want anybody saying I was as neglectful with you as you were with my baby."

"I was catching some perch for supper. I didn't see that old hook." Pain clutched at Granny's heart and squeezed against the tumor. She could hardly breathe. "Are you making a prisoner of me, Laura?"

"Don't be silly, Mama." She hammered and hammered.

Granny wanted to vomit in her panic, but now she didn't have the strength to go to the bucket.

She remembered the letter.

Laura can hammer all she wants, Granny thought. It won't make any difference. In a few days, Owen will come and get me. I can wait that long. Just a few more days. Owen will come.

He's my son.

He has to.

Luz

MARY GRAY HUGHES

I ran errands in my neighborhood. From the time I was two days past four years old and could decode the red and green of streetlights at the corner, I maneuvered on my own through the concrete world of blocks that stretched ahead of me in all directions, seemingly without end. With age and experience I learned the limits of my larger territory: blacks ten blocks to the west; the bayou's edge bounding the far east; rich white street-empty apartments to the north; and pure commerce to the south. By the time I learned the boundaries, I had discovered that a boy alone is welcome to his neighbors. They would send me on errands, and they would pay me. I found there was good money in it.

An old man in our building, a huge man, over six feet, maybe six feet six, sent me to get his lady friend. Luz was her name. He would send me for her at early evening or late afternoon, when his wife was out. He had a badly crippled leg clamped in a full metal brace, and he could not get around easily even in his own rooms. There was no phone in his apartment, and I could see he was not able to get out by himself to telephone Luz, but he never wanted me to, either. He wanted messages sent. I don't know why. Perhaps her messy room, the edges of which I came to know, also had no phone and no one in her building would take calls for her. And maybe the beauty parlor where I went for her in the afternoons did not want her getting personal calls when she should be working. Whatever, my old crippled man would call to me from his landing as I passed and give me three or four coins and tell me to go to her. He always sent the same message.

"Tell her the freezer's melted," he would say.

Luz would laugh no matter how many times she had heard it. She was always in a good humor, but when she laughed she would show her sharp, snapping teeth. She too would give me a coin or two and in the winter, for good measure, she would pull my cap down over my ears and massage with her strong skilled beauty operator's fingers the deliciously relaxing back of my neck.

Luz was half-Mexican and had the thick black molasseslike hair she could layer in whorls, or drape flat across her head, or pile high as a sand castle with a rose stabbed in it.

"I know what her name means in our language," I told the old man in our building one evening when he wanted me to go for her. "It means light."

But I never once asked him to pay me for not telling his wife, though when I took messages to Luz I did look everywhere, in the grocery store, at the bus stops, for a glimpse of what I knew to be his wife's old blue dress or that brown coat she wore even past when it was needed. I never saw her then.

I tracked Luz often after I took her messages, and she did go on those days to my old man in my own building. And times when I was doing nothing better I ran ahead of her and was on my own landing two floors above and watching when she came. Old crip would be there waiting for her with the door wide open and himself doused in lotion to cover his old sick-man smell. I did not know what she saw in my old ailing man with his brace, but I knew, even before I was ten, that if he paid her it was not the same as his paying me, for she did not go to him only for money.

She went for laughter, I decided. For I could hear them chuckling and giggling and hooting when the door shut opaque and solid behind them. She went for laughter. When I saw her on the sidewalk afterward, for sometimes I would hang around and wait until she came out, her caramel skin would be blushed with humor and her lips relaxed from smiling and her eyes coal black and popping like the round polished not yet burning coals in the Japanese restaurant on the corner.

The summer I turned ten I learned to know Luz better, for I was hired, illegally at my age, by her beauty parlor's owner to sweep the floor of the limp, cut curls and polish shelves of vivid colored bottles and, as ever, to run errands—this time to get coffee and sandwiches. I kept my old errand business on the side to have that money too. I did very well, for the neighborhood, so low in telephones, was infested with messages. Some were legal, some not, and I trotted through the litter and the people of the summer streets carrying names or numbers that for the sender had the aura of riches, carrying payments of bills and promises of money, and carrying sandwiches, Cokes, and coffee for the customers and staff in the beauty parlor.

The regular customers I soon learned and what they usually ordered, and I learned the customers who were steadies for Luz. One of them I corrected.

"Her name's not said that way," I insisted. "It's like 'loose' in 'loose change.' 'Luz.'"

Because I no longer came home after school my old crippled buddy could not call out to me when I passed his landing. So from the beauty parlor Luz would send me to my building. There I was to stay on the landing below the old boy's door and whistle a tune loudly enough for him to hear. If his wife was out, he would open the door and give me the message about his freezer.

Luz amused herself by changing the tune. Sometimes she had me whistle "The Star-Spangled Banner," sometimes a Christmas carol, sometimes a Mexican bullfight song she would try, between combing out customers, to teach me by pretending she was playing the harsh Mexican trumpet.

She laughed at each different tune she suggested, as if she were pulling a joke that was even better than changing the way she fixed her black, glossy, treaclelike hair. Luz was always good-natured. But details and routines of the beauty parlor business would bore her and her eyes would rise to the street, to life going by her out there. Then she would send me to my building to whistle her latest tune and perhaps, perhaps the old man would open his door and give me the right report on his freezer's state of being, and also give me one or two coins to put deep down in my pocket.

I would run back to Luz in the beauty parlor, and if the message was right she would greet it with delight in shining, effervescent eyes. She would finish with her customer and as soon as she could rearrange her appointments clip clop on her bright polished heels down the dirty street to our building. I liked to watch her walking. She had slim, shapely legs despite her solid body. Unlike the other operators, she had no varicose veins, and she never wore pants. I do not know if she followed a Latin custom, or vanity, but she wore only skirts and black or white blouses to exaggerate, I believed, her black, snapping eyes. When I could think of a reason to get away from the beauty parlor, I would follow her all the way to our building.

Our entrance was more elaborate than any other in the block. There were figures of animals and decorative whorls that were like Luz's hair except they were in worn white concrete. The figures entertained Luz and invariably on her way in she ran a finger over one bird's nose and poked its eye. She had a practical cruelty about animals. I never saw her pet a dog and often heard her rage against people feeding pigeons; the only attention I ever saw her give any beast was to poke the concrete eye of the bird in our entrance, mutter a Spanish word at it, and laugh.

Yet she was kind to me. When she sent me with a message she always paid me, and often gave me parts of her lunch. I took these and ate them. Then I did not have to spend any money buying my lunch.

It was inevitable that the day came when the old man was ill, but still it was a shock to me. I had not thought about anything inevitable. I whistled and whistled Luz's Spanish dancer's tune (part of her people's real national anthem, she told me) on the landing, but the old boy's door never opened until, to my surprise, a white-haired old lady came out. She was old crip's wife, Mrs. Schnelling. I recognized her face though mostly I had seen only her back, shoving in our building door when her arms were loaded with flat boxes of envelopes she and the old boy stuffed to make a living.

She squiggled a finger and uncomfortably I moved closer to her. She told me in a whisper that old braced-leg was bad sick. And she was scared. I was to hurry up medicine from the drugstore, for he had told her, she said to me, when he heard all that racket I was making, that I often helped with his medicine. So I was to do just what I always did, he had told her to say.

Clearly she thought I usually acted out of brotherly love and the relationship was based on my generosity, fondness, pure good will, and kindness. For even though I waited, she made no move to give me money.

A little sour, for I did not see how I was going to be paid by her, I forgot the part about the medicine. I had never in my life brought him medicine. Instead I set out to do what I knew the old boy meant for me to do. I ran down the stairs and out of our entrance and, as I always did, skipped the last worn stone steps not to add my weight to what had been done already. I ran straight to the beauty parlor. I got Luz aside and told her the news.

To my ten-year-old astonishment, tears as easily as laughter broke from her eyes and spattered down her face. I was overwhelmed. I had been going to explain to her, I had already decided on it, that no one had paid me yet because I knew Luz would. But it did not seem right to ask her while she went on weeping right there in the beauty parlor for anyone to see, weeping for the cripple-legged old man who was her companion in locked-in laughter.

What had they done, I wondered as she cried, that had made her love this laughing so much? The old man's apartment must have been just like my family's two floors above it. There was nothing that great about ours with its tight square rooms which looked out across a clogged air space at a brick building, just as the old man's must.

Luz wiped her face, smearing her eye stuff and tossing the blackened towel in the laundry bin. She begged another operator to fit in two customers and then, on her trim legs, Luz trotted out onto the street and toward our building.

"I forgot to tell the delicatessen no tomatoes," I shouted at the owner working in the rear. He never knew what I was talking about, only that I kept his customers filled with food and drinks and the floor swept clean. He nodded and I followed to catch up with Luz. It was easy for me to do as my sight was not masked in tears, but every half-block she had to stop and wipe hers away while people walking on the street bumped into her. She turned into the entrance of our building, this time without pecking the bird's worn nose.

As in all the buildings on the block the staircase looped back and forth against one wall and the hallways and apartments clung to the opposite side. The stairs were narrow with steep steps, but Luz ran up as if her high heels were runner's sneakers.

I was in a quandary. I dared not follow so close I got myself caught, yet I had to be there when that door opened. I was weasel thin that summer. By squeezing my body into the narrow space around which the stairway made its turn at every landing I believed I could sneak my head level with the Schnellings' floor without being noticed. I balanced myself on the handrail that sloped below their landing and slid my fingers around the spokes sunk in the floor above. I gently lifted my head up in the slot between the banisters. There before me, visible through the spokes, were Luz's red and highly polished heels.

Now, at the door, Luz was hesitating for the first time; not to wipe her tears, but unsure of what to do. She may never have come here before when the door was shut. All the times I had watched, old crippled-leg had been standing there, braced and lotioned, announcing their time had come and that he had heard her feather step floating its way to him. He would be grinning away as he said it, his face pale as uncooked bacon. Life inside had bleached him, yet he was always smiling for her. What they had to laugh at I could never think.

Luz shifted back and forth on her high heels. I raised my head higher, level with her ankles, so I could really see.

With the ringing sure sound she made clapping the cut ends of hair out of a brush rapped against the washbasin, Luz knocked on the door in a series of taps. I was startled enough to slip down, then raised myself up to see.

The door opened the chained few inches, and old Mrs. Schnelling looked out. Even from my angle, peering, I could see how frightened she looked.

"You're not the doctor from the welfare clinic," Mrs. Schnelling said first thing. "I know them. Why hasn't one come? I called twice my husband's so bad. I went upstairs two times to call."

Upstairs? From *my* apartment? My home? Home, I'd learned when I was four years old, is where you run to when you crap in your pants. But my mother was usually out, working, or if at home was cleaning house, and she was never friendly with the neighbors. Mrs. Schnelling must have gone to another floor, or another apartment. Not my home.

"I am the social worker," I heard Luz lie. And in her white beauty parlor operator's coat it seemed possible. To Mrs. Schnelling anything may have seemed possible in our neighborhood. She shut the door, took off the chain, and opened the door wide.

"I didn't send for a social worker," she said.

"I have come because there is needing," Luz said. Her English was heavily accented. "All these blocks is my areas," she said, with the sublime air of confidence with which she would shear a thick length of hair with one twist of her wrist and a prolonged steady swishing of her cutting scissors. "All these blocks I am inspector," she finished. Very positive.

I jiggled on the banister. Was she going to bluff and bully her way inside into the old man's sickroom? And if she did, if they went inside, how was I going to see? I could never get around to the fire escape in time, and anyway I already knew it did not work.

From the inside of the apartment came the old boy's voice.

"Is that the doctor?" he called. He sounded terrible.

"No," Luz said instantly, lifting her voice and tossing it like a javelin into their home. "Just your own neighborhood's excellent and esteemed social worker who hearing you had a not well feeling made the appearance. Yes?"

There was a period of silence which could have been filled by either woman but was not. Then, unexpectedly for them both, the old boy, all six foot plus and brace, appeared beside his wife. He was wearing a bright blue terry cloth robe wrapped loosely around his body, and his gray chest was a strangely virgin field peeping out behind it. From my weasel's perch I could see he was red-eyed and unsteady, and that his face was blurred by his unshaven beard. That's a man only a wife has to love, I thought, and I turned and gazed up to see what my beauty parlor operator was going to do.

Luz had let her head tip to the side, as if overcome by the weight of her magnificent dark hair piled in a double soft-ice-cream cone spiral.

"I could bring you the juices," she said to him.

"I asked the boy to do that," Mrs. Schnelling said. It was a lie. She had not. "How did you get your brace on by yourself?" she said, scolding, to terry cloth robe. "You shouldn't be out of your bed."

The old boy was clinging hard to the doorway beside her. If they took a notion and closed that door, I thought, they were going to crush his fingertips.

"I give the help for the medicines. Or for the othercoming procedures," Luz said. Those last long words, I knew, were proud new acquisitions.

"I suppose you got that job because you speak Mexican," Mrs. Schnelling said.

For it was amazing how official that beauty operator jacket made Luz seem. But that was not helping old crip. He was trembling in the doorway and grasping the frame with his finger edges.

"When I need you," he said, and his voice sounded like a record being scratched, "I'll send the boy with a message. I'll be able to do that soon. Soon."

His unshaven, uncombed head vibrated not unlike the hand massager in the beauty parlor, but in his case from some inner lack of power.

"I can do nothings now?" Luz asked him.

"I suppose your Mexican is better than your English," Mrs. Schnelling said.

Old crip did not answer. He was concentrating on holding to that doorway. Luz, with an elegant shrug, was about to turn and I was lowering my head so I could drop to the landing below, when the old boy gave a juicy grunt and lurched forward. He would have fallen but Luz, with a beauty parlor operator's speed (two seconds and a rinse is a ruin, she had taught me), was holding him up.

Mrs. Schnelling came under his arm and tried to lever him back up to the doorway while closing his flapping robe around him, but the brace and its clumsiness and the old boy's size made it impossible. He had nothing above him now he could reach for, if he had been able, to help raise himself upright. Luz's elegant legs were beginning to go under with his weight, and I let myself slide down to the floor beneath and raced back up the stairs. I burst in between the two women and like a tugboat began pushing our giant upright; and I chattered all the time about how

I had just happened to get home, which was natural enough as I did live right there, upstairs, so near.

"Thank you, thank you," Mrs. Schnelling said, but Luz cast me one long look, black and unwinding as a screwdriver's action. She knew how come I was there.

Having stopped old crip from falling, we found that the problem with his brace was turning him around. He was helpless, sweating and groaning. Mrs. Schnelling kept saying she and I could manage, she and I could do it alone. But old crip had a death grip on Luz's neck, so the four of us jammed and juggled and then popped through the doorway into their apartment and we lowered, slowly, the old boy's long body to the floor.

Mrs. Schnelling began to tug at his robe to get it over the gray matted hair on his chest.

"He should not have come to the door," Mrs. Schnelling said. She tried to free the robe which was crumpled under him. "He should have stayed in bed. Give some help, now you are here," she said to Luz.

But Luz's head was clutched to the old man's half-bared shoulder, and he held on to her so tightly she could do nothing.

"Is that what my taxes do?" Mrs. Schnelling asked. "Can't you help? It's a disgrace," she said, all the while pulling at her husband's robe to cover him with it.

"Here, Luz," I said, "I'll help you." I tried to lift the old man's arm but he whimpered aloud and clung to her.

"No, no," Luz said to me. "Let's him go." And then, "Now watch me. I took the yoga. Watch what I doing."

She was so pleased I thought she meant to untangle his octopus grasp, but instead she swung her bottom around sideways and flexed her neck and arm and shoulder so she was half-sitting, half-bending; she was like a lily, with her head and its dome of black hair with the bright, plastic rose still pressed tight to his shoulder. She had a satisfied smile on her face after her exertions.

Mrs. Schnelling was busy trying to slide the blue terry cloth robe between the old boy's shoulder and Luz's face. Luz, as willingly as she followed her customers' suggestions on their hairstyles, tried to raise her head enough to provide the needed space.

"He has much force," Luz said in a conversational way. But Mrs. Schnelling was occupied elsewhere.

The old boy was whispering to her. I was close enough so I could hear him. He wanted a handkerchief, he whispered. He wanted her to help him straighten the teeth in his head and to wipe his mouth clean. Old Mrs. Schnelling got up and came back with a cloth and wiped his lips for him with it. Then she let him use her fingers to shove his upper plate in and press it up and tight into place while he held fast to Luz with his more deft right hand.

"You," Mrs. Schnelling said to Luz, "you do nothing at all. You are a disgrace."

The old boy had his face ready and he turned it to Luz, and when he did the corners of his mouth climbed up like roses on the trellis of the wrinkles in his face.

I was ten then, and I knew everything there was to know about sex. But when I saw the corners of his mouth climb up I wished I had four eyes and two heads to watch them both constantly so every single thing that was going on between them I could see.

Old crip began gasping and gurgling, making sounds like a fluttering refrigerator. And his chest started going hugely up and down, and up up up, reaching for something.

"Oh why don't they come?" Mrs. Schnelling cried. "I told them twice they need to come instantly." And she stood there alone beside him, watching his chest.

"Ah ah ah," the old boy was gasping to Luz, "tell . . . tell . . ." he said to her. And with her face held close to his, Luz began to tell.

"Oh they are so funny, the women," Luz said. "The foolish vain women," and the old boy's breathing eased in its gasping. "Never are there so much vanities," Luz said, forgetting she was supposed to be a social worker and not a beauty parlor operator in that white coat.

I watched and watched old Mrs. Schnelling to see what she would do when she noticed, but she was lost in gauging the breathing in her husband's body.

"Always trying to win the mens," Luz was saying. "They do everything to win the mens." How he smiled, how pleased he was when she said that. "They make the hair orange or purple if the hair comes by itself white. They do whatsoever to please the mens. And the creams, oh for the face they use so much bottles of creams you can't believe."

Luz halted in telling because the old boy's chest had begun mounting and falling and the struggling refrigerator sound had started from him again. Luz looked around for Mrs. Schnelling, but Mrs. Schnelling had rushed into the other room. The old boy gave Luz a pull, a nudge— meaning, get on with the story.

"Yes, yes," Luz said, "there is no ending the vanities. There is the woman today who coats with powder ten times thick, like this," and Luz patted her cheek and then the cheek nearest to old crip, as a woman might making herself up before a mirror, and old wrinkle-jaws pulled his lips wide in his amusement. "Oh to get the mens they use much vanities," Luz said.

He was enthralled, enthralled, and yet even so he was beginning to shiver all over his long body, and his brace made a slender vibrating noise against the floor and his chest reached up and up a mountain.

Mrs. Schnelling came hurrying back into the room with an old gray blanket she was shaking clear of moth crystals, and she tumbled it across him and began to wrap it around his quivering body, bundling him up tight as a mummy.

Even I, who had never seen anything bad sick but animals, knew the old boy must be dying, and that nothing was going to change that, not even the blanket with glittering bits of moth crystals.

"Why don't the doctors come?" Mrs. Schnelling pleaded as she wrapped his legs, folding the blanket double over them. "God let a doctor come," she said. She knelt to bundle the upper part of the old man's body and kneeling there, covering him, said, "Let the real help I called for come."

"Mrs.," Luz said to her, "please. Don't wrap him two times up. It has no need. He is not cold that way."

The old boy's arm no longer clasped Luz's neck tight and though he still held to her, she could straighten herself.

"Sit instead, Mrs.," Luz said to Mrs. Schnelling. "Sit there beside," meaning beside old crip. "Take a cushion to yourself to sit comfortable so you can give comfort for him."

The old boy was giving Luz tugs with his arm, which was limper now, which held her even more loosely. But he wanted her to get on with her story.

"So like always my Tuesday-morning-at-ten come," Luz began again. "And this time she want a teenager's hairstyle, to make her beautiful. Can you believe? Out of our twenties is this style, out of Egypt before, with the hair curled down on the cheeks in baby circles so," and Luz traced with her expert fingers on his wrinkles where the curls were meant to go, and the old boy was enchanted, I could see it, yet even so his chest pumped and climbed up its mountain and he gurgled in air.

Mrs. Schnelling had got herself down on a cushion by old crip's other side, but his gasping got harsher as his chest rose, and she plugged her hands against her mouth.

"No, Mrs., please. No," Luz said to her, in the exact tone she used to the littler girls when they cried for the locks they could see in the mirror they were going to lose. "No, Mrs. Take his hand in yours two, please, and rub in the way you are both using all the years, and with force, so he will know is you doing it."

"Yes," Mrs. Schnelling said, "yes," and she unwound old crip's hand from its mummy wrappings.

She shoved back his terry cloth robe and laid his bared and long old arm across her lap and stroked the length of it. The old boy's head trembled toward her and he turned up his hand at the hinge of his wrist and took the edge of her sleeve in his cumbersome fingers. How with those fingers he had folded papers and stuffed envelopes, unless she had done it all, I don't know. But he began to roll and massage the edge of her sleeve between his fingers and the palm of his hand.

His head wobbled back toward Luz and she took up her story.

"I tell you also about that Keyes woman. Oh, she is foolish. So foolish you can't believe." The old man's face was setting itself to smile. "For much months this foolish woman she is keeping all her curls, no matters the colors. She is keeping them, she say, for the fall of hair she will make, a twist you see, to braid and put in a net for wearing. But the colors, I say to her, you dye you hair all differing colors."

The old man's chest was lumbering on its climb with the air gurgling harshly in and Luz began to hurry her story.

"So you know what this foolish woman say to me? You can't believe," Luz said, and she began to sway as she told her story, rocking his body along with her. Old Mrs. Schnelling smoothed her husband's arm and with her head bent close to his hand watched his fingers slowly working the material of her sleeve. "This woman say," Luz went on, "she will dye all the curls one color. Black, the exact color mine is. She will braid them to wear exact the way I display mine. Can you believe?"

Old crip seemed to want to laugh at it too, he seemed starting to laugh, but the laugh was a hawk in his throat, and Luz rocked on taking him with her and rushing her story to its end, saying, "To wear it like I do? Why? And she say, oh, can you believe? she say then she will look just like me," and the old boy's arm was sliding down her back, his arm let her free, but she went on rocking his body, telling, "Such a foolishness. I know she is exact sixty years old, this vain woman, and I say why does she want it her hair like mine? And she say she want because, she tell me, I am beautiful. Can you believe? Beautiful."

Luz began to giggle at her own story, to rock his long still body and giggle but her eyes were weeping, were glossy and glimmering and weeping. And I thought if that's how her tears make her eyes look while laughing, if that's what her tears can do then, she should patent them now, I thought. She could make her fortune.

The Sweetheart Is In

S. L. WISENBERG

What the Boys Were Like

They were all over Ceci Rubin's house, swarming like bees around her sister Ellen. Though her sister was not the kind of flower you might think; even though Ellen was Sweetheart of the Senesch boys' group, she was a Nice Girl. She needed to be met two-thirds of the way in order to flirt. Had to be coached. Did not bat her eyes with frequency or naturalness. Did not laugh with the requisite ease; it was always a nervous giggle, an internal clattering of the throat muscles.

But this is about Ceci. And the boys. The boys did not swarm to the playroom, lean over the pool table, twist the handles controlling the little men on the Foosball game, in order to see Ceci Rubin. She was another accoutrement of the house, like the playroom itself. For them, finding a perky extra girl in the home of their Sweetheart was like any other pleasant surprise—like finding someone has a wonderful dog so friendly and shaggy it bridges all conversations, or a mother who listens to problems and sings bawdy songs (only an example; no mother like that existed in Houston in 1970, in that neighborhood at least), or a father who gives advice about something useful—not as personal as sex but, for instance, about car insurance, or avoiding the draft. Ceci's father was in the bubble bath business, and handed out samples to all the boys each time they came over. He'd shake their hands first.

The boys fascinated Ceci. They leaned and lounged like cats, and were just as mysterious to her and to Ellen, who had always had as pets beagles and sea monkeys, nothing in between. The boys would sprawl on the love seats (everything had a name; there was not simply furniture in that house but buffets, davenports, credenzas, and islands), talk one moment about the rubbers in their wallets, the next about ways to avoid the draft—both suggesting realms that were equally strange to Ceci. Ricky Bogen was seventeen and a half and was already thinking of joining the Coast Guard. He'd called the office once for brochures. Dan Cook knew a guy who'd drunk ten cups of coffee in two days, swallowing five tablets of No Doz with each, and been so jittery and nervous and produced such contaminated piss that they got him out of the recruitment center fast, almost calling an ambulance, and speaking of piss, Sam Frederickson's older brother had bought some from a diabetic hanging out in front of the center. Rob Chazin was thinking of the seminary, even at this early date, and Joe Amos was reading everything from Maimonides to St. Augustine (even though Peter Griswold said Augustine was irrelevant to Jews) in order to fill out conscientious objector forms. He'd already had an appointment with his rabbi. Who'd Been in Korea, so that didn't help much.

Ceci, listening as she looked for some string in the drawers of the nearby built-in buffet, didn't quite understand this Being in Korea, thought maybe it was a metaphor, as she'd learned in English, maybe for venereal disease? She tested it on her tongue, and in a few minutes, said to Sam: Korea like in the Korean War? Yeah, Babe, he'd said, and that Babe was enough to give her tingles up until the time she brushed her teeth and fell asleep.

How the Boys Sounded

The boys were noisy in their machines, no matter what the machine was. Even if it was a bicycle. They scraped the kickstands against the cement of the driveway, scraped it up to the front door (bikes, even European ten-speeds, were not allowed indoors on the highly polished and buffed ter-razzo). And cars—! They zoomed in doing something with the exhaust or the muffler, Ceci wasn't sure what it was called, to make their presence known. Then the honks. Each boys' group had a certain honk pattern which the members pounded out while passing by the home of a member or a Sweetheart. The one for Senesch was Come-out-come-out-you-son-of-a-bitch, but for the sake of appearances and parents, it was Come-out-come-out-wherever-you-are. The cars were crucial. In Ellen's scrapbook was a photograph of an unidentified odometer showing 1803.00 miles, which was the Senesch chapter number. Ceci was unsure how the chapters were assigned these numbers; this whole boys' club business, she was apt to say, is beyond me. Ceci had elements of an old lady to her. She stopped just short of being fussy. She was serious and studious and fancied herself deep but laughed often, mostly to herself. But since the boys had been coming around, she was beginning to laugh more in public. With the boys, she didn't have to play dumb, which she'd been doing since fourth grade. The boys of Senesch really wanted to know what she thought. They saw her as some artifact, encouraged her to be devil's advocate, praised her when she asked: If I killed my sister—or you—while you were standing right here, it would be wrong, so how could any war be justified? Someone left behind a copy of St. Augustine's just-war theory, and she read it in one night. Sam mentioned Thomas Merton, and she went to the Meyer branch library to check out his books.

They encouraged her, called her St. Cecilia, and Joe sang the Simon and Garfunkel song to her: *Cecilia, you're breakin' my heart, you're shaking my confidence daily*—. Other times he would call her Dorothy Parker and require a pun before they could have a normal conversation.

I am truly changed, Ceci would think to herself. I am no longer shy. But Ellen still called her The Pain. When Ellen wanted Ceci to leave the room, she would say, Ceci, go breathe.

What This Breathing Business Was

It began when Ceci was born and she was taken right away into a special room called I See You— This is how she had heard the story, ever since she was a little girl.

She was in ICU for two days, deprived of mother's milk and mother's love though the nurses were quite attentive and one even sang songs to her. Christmas songs, it turned out, but the family was not that particular, no worry about imprinting. Just as long as she was kept company by another warm human voice, they said. They prided themselves on their rationality. Though Ceci's parents kept kosher and went to shul whenever they knew the family of the bar or bat mitzvah. They were modern Jews, followed the mitzvot that made sense. Though there was behind everything—so faint you could barely feel it—a strong belief in God the primitive goat-bearded deity of the Old Testament. He hovered. He took note of their Sh'mas they said every night before going to sleep.

As she grew older, Ceci's lungs cleared, but they never really cleared up. She would breathe fine then it would start up—never an attack, she hated that word, but more like an advancing case of the flu. So she couldn't run very hard or jump rope, because that would bring on the wheezing. In her childhood, as she said, she stayed inside, read, painted at the easel in her room. Mixed colors again and again, watched them swirl in the blue enamel pot of water. Like cream disappearing into coffee, changing it to cream and coffee. Coffee with cream.

When Ceci was eleven, two years before Ellen was made Sweetheart, she'd had pneumonia so bad she'd had to spend four days in the hospital. She came home with a breathing machine the size of an old-fashioned radio. She filled it with distilled water and liquid bronchodilators morning and night, breathing in the mist for twenty minutes, as she said, at a stretch. It made what she'd just heard called white noise. Drowned everything out.

With hand-held sprays and pills and the machine, though, everything was A-OK, under control. Next semester, said her doctor, she could take gym for the first time in two years. Partly she dreaded this because she'd never properly learned the games the teachers expected her to know: softball, volleyball, and badminton. She'd never quite got the hang of team lines.

In the meantime, no one could tell anything was wrong. Couldn't (usually) hear her wheezing. Under control. Like anybody else.

What Ceci Did with the Boys

Once one of them stayed even after Ceci told him at the door that Ellen wasn't in. They played a round of pool and he won handily. He taught her wrist action in Foosball. He told her about his application for Harvard, the grueling half-day of SAT testing, told her that he thought he might become a conscientious objector. Oh I know about that, she said; CO. She'd read about Quakers being COs in World War I. Nowadays you had to get a draft board to approve it. She knew some people Up North had poured their blood over the draft board file folders. But not in Houston.

The boy's name was Jerry Schwartz. His brother was at Stanford, living in a co-ed dormitory and being part of The Movement. Ceci imagined him there among palm trees, studying, shouting, learning about Europe.

When Jerry left that afternoon, he said, Fair Lady, I doff my hat to you (though he wasn't wearing one), and shook her hand, lingering over it so long she thought he was about to take it to his lips. But he didn't.

What the Parents Thought of This Sweetheart Business

They were proud but befuddled. They'd always said it was important for their girls to have friends in the Jewish community. But they were not quite used to these long, loud boys. The Rubins didn't have norms for boys. Their directives boiled down to geography. The boys couldn't smoke in the house. The backyard was OK, as long as they put out the butts in the ashtrays of their own cars. They weren't supposed to step one foot into Ellen's bedroom. Though they did troop there sometimes, in a group. It was there that Ellen kept the large brown-spotted stuffed salamander that the boys of Senesch had special-ordered for her. There was another salamander, made of plywood, which stood in the windowsill in the den and faced the circle driveway. It stood on its tail and wore a sly grin. On its stomach were the words *The Sweetheart Is*. Screwed into its joined front paws was a hook which held a cardboard square. On one side the square said *In*; and on the other, *Out*.

Ellen always forgot to change it. Ceci thought of making it say *In* all the time so the boys would come to her. Hadn't she read in *Little Women* that Mozart or Shakespeare had tried for one sister, and gotten the other one? There was also Jacob in the Bible, wasn't there? She remembered something about a wedding, and Jacob (or Isaac?) hadn't been allowed to lift up the heavy veil and see who was under there until after the rabbi had already pronounced the words. And then it was too late.

How Ellen Was Crowned and Chosen

It was at the Sweetheart Dance. It was a surprise but Ceci and her parents had been alerted and stood there in the back, sneakily, hiding in shadow. The name was announced and Ellen fainted. Ceci, hardy in all parts of her body except the lungs, envied Ellen her ability to faint at crucial moments, a coda to underscore the specialness of events. After the dance, Ellen and the boys and their dates went to the IHOP (Ceci heard later) and ordered breakfast to go, drove to Galveston, and ate soggy pancakes on the beach. Someone brought a bedspread to sit on.

At dinner the next Friday night, Ceci's grandmother said she did not like this at all. For twenty years she'd been a guest in that house for the Sabbath meal. She could not imagine anyone finding the sunrise something to go to, like a movie or symphony. She told Ceci's mother: A waste, a waste it sounds to me. Ceci's mother worried but found it impolite to worry in front of other people, and her mother-in-law was still other people. Of course the thing that no one said but everyone thought about was the impropriety of boys and girls of a certain age traveling unsupervised to another town, another county, the untamed ocean overnight. The overnight part. That's what they're doing now, Ceci's father said mildly. He was modern and trusted the mores of the age and therefore individuals because he could not conceive of them violating the norms. After all, this wasn't Chicago or New York and these boys and girls Ellen was friendly with were honors students, not hippies or zippies or whatever. Ceci's mother didn't trust anything but convention. And not even that. But she was afraid to say so.

What Ceci Knew

In writing, in cold hard facts in Ellen's diary, Ceci had read that Ellen's best friend Naomi had swum naked with not one but three boys. The diary was kept locked, but easily opened, in an oversized photo album on a bookshelf. Ceci wondered if like the character in the book *1984* Ellen kept a hair or something equally minute between the pages to determine whether the diary had been tampered with. But it was Ceci's firm belief that Ellen secretly wanted her to read it—even if only for the challenge of catching Ceci give herself away by releasing a bit of information in conversation that could have been obtained from the diary alone.

Ellen was rather reserved in what she revealed about herself in the diary—as taciturn as she was in person. Once Ceci had asked her if she'd ever French kissed, and Ellen, embarrassed, an edge of incredulity to her voice, responded: Yeess! She would not elucidate.

This sex business was something Ceci didn't think about concretely, except figured it was something like New York City—big and confusing and exciting. The mystery at hand was smaller and closer—periods. There were tantalizing light blue boxes under the sink in her parents' bathroom and pink ones in the bathroom she shared with Ellen. Ceci had not yet begun. She waited for it, mistaking stomach cramps for those kind. She would see Ellen's sanitary belt hanging on the towel rack, and twice in the school bathroom she had unwrapped the cotton and blood jelly rolls in the steel basket attached to the wall and smelled the rust-iron personal foreign blood.

At night, Ceci had her own more than dimly related secret habit. She rocked quietly in bed, thumb against that ridge of flesh, until she felt a turnaround unwinding feeling. She'd been doing this for years and thought it was something little girls did, something like holding on to your baby blanket too long. Next time, she'd think, I'll stop.

What Ceci Worried About

She was afraid that she wouldn't do the exciting things life owed her. Afraid a boy wouldn't love her and kiss her. Afraid she'd be too tall all her life. Afraid she wouldn't be famous. Afraid her feet would never stop growing. Afraid she'd be ugly forever. (She didn't believe her mother when she called her beautiful.) She was confident she'd get into a good college Up North. She did well on standardized tests. She hadn't told Jerry Schwartz that, he with his reports of grueling APs and SATs.

She was afraid her best friend Sheryl Lefkowitz didn't really like her as much as she liked another girl, Annie Kaplan, who went to another junior high. She was afraid of being abandoned. She feared and anticipated returning to gym classes. She imagined that her return would mark an opening in her life—she would pick up everything she had missed and forge unbreakable bonds. Because surely it was in the locker room that these alliances were formed: the invitations to walk home after school, to go shopping for shoes and purses at Palais Royal, to go get haircuts, to look up *Everything You Always Wanted to Know About Sex* at the Meyer library, to spend the night.

She felt both older and younger than her friends. Sheryl Lefkowitz, for example, was already ahead of Ceci in some departments. She had let a boy feel her breasts. She told Ceci about a girl giving what was called a hand job. Ceci wondered how these girls knew what to do. She would have no idea. She'd heard that once you started they wouldn't let you stop until the sperm came out of there and some of them made you drink it.

How Ceci Was with the Boys after a While

Ceci began to feel adopted by them. They took her bowling and one night got her drunk on André Cold Duck at Joe Felts's house (his parents gone) and she sang songs with them, making up the words. Ellen got mad. Ceci didn't care. The boys were very careful with her. They did not, for example, have her sit on anybody's lap, the way they had girls their own age do. They made a joke: Sit on my lap and we'll see what comes up. She didn't get it, but knew it was not something her mother would want her to laugh at. Just like jokes they made about the pool table balls.

She helped Jerry Schwartz make up the creative services for Senesch Sabbath Morning with Herzl girls' group. They chose works, as Jerry called them, by Eugene O'Neill and Leonard Cohen and the Beatles. This excited Ceci. She had not known that Jews could pray by reciting *Blackbird singing in the dead of night*. He showed her a poem by W. H. Auden: *But poetry makes nothing happen*. He explained to her that people have to do things in the world. He talked about the Chicago Seven; all she'd remembered about it was a TV screen full of hippies with long dark hair making peace signs. He explained the difference between hippies and Yippies. (No such thing as zippies, he said.) He told her about his underground paper at St. Mark's, a private school in River Oaks. His family lived just outside River Oaks, near Rice University. He told her how Jews couldn't even live in River Oaks unless they were very very rich. He brought her a copy of his paper with reports about Vietnam and protest and editorials with cusswords. The typing was poor and so was the reproduction. He told her she could keep a copy. The mimeographing ink came off on her hands.

How Ellen Felt about All These Developments

She was mad. Said the same thing she said when she was seven and Ceci was three: Maa, tell Ceci to play with her own friends.

How Ceci Entertained Another Boy

Tom Hessler rang the bell even though the brown-spotted plywood salamander in the window said *Out,* and he and Ceci made Tollhouse mint brownies even though her mother had told her not to do any baking because she needed the kitchen at five. Her mother was mad but only for a few minutes. Tom took half of the batch home (that had always been the house rule—share with the guest baker), wrapped in foil, pecans sprinkled on top.

Late that night he fed it into his girlfriend's mouth, lightly flicking the dark crumbs from the corners of her lips. The girlfriend said, Mmmm, mmm, my favorite, chocolate! And he said, Oh you, you're mi señorita favorita.

Tom didn't tell this part to Ceci when he played Foosball with her a week later. All he said was that his girlfriend would only eat one brownie because of her *dy*-et. Ellen was standing next to him as he was saying this, and he turned to put his arm around her lazily. For some reason he was thinking of Bogart at this moment and turned to Ceci and said, Game's over, get lost, kid. The next time Ceci saw him he put his arm around her that same way. She tried to bite his hand and was embarrassed at how desperate it seemed, not at all playful.

How Ellen the Nice Girl Got to Be Sweetheart in the First Place

Ellen was not a tart. When she was just a civilian, back in tenth grade, she'd had one good friend who was a boy; he'd moved to town from Dallas the end of the semester, and she'd been nice to him because she was nice to everyone, especially new boys in her homeroom. He was popular and persuasive with other males. He joined Senesch that summer. The other boys in Senesch wanted to elect one of two girls who were Class A Number One flirts, supreme gigglers and hairtossers. Ellen was the dark horse, the spoiler, the one who upset the established power-mongers. She won the election. She was pretty so it didn't matter. She was like a sleeper movie. By the time people have seen it, they feel bad that but for a quirk, they might have missed it. And so they feel doubly grateful.

What Ellen's Manner Was

She would say, Hello, how are you, making a reference, as the girl-gets-boy guidebooks suggest, to something the boy had mentioned the day before. She began to read the sports pages, to talk about the Astros' chances on the pennant. The boys were nonplussed. They'd never heard of girls who knew about sports. They'd say, like indignant fathers, Now what do we have here? Secretly they were pleased. They congratulated themselves on their choice. They began to say, Hay as in horses, we sure know how to pick 'em.

Ellen was the supreme democrat. No one boy got more attention than the other. She regulated her inflections. She became all things to everyone. A queen. Dabbing the foreheads of the dying teeming poor camped at her gates. Unwashed. Each time she descended she became more and more aloof. And therefore more and more disinterested. Which is not the same as *un*interested. And thus more and more fair.

What Ellen Did to Herself

She took hair from the top of her head and rolled it around two empty orange juice cans, wrapped the rest with oversized bobby pins and over-sized clips, and sat under the dryer for two hours (so adept at this, folded this into her life, that she could hold telephone conversations while under the hood with other girls similarly encumbered). She shaved her armpit hair, her leg hair, plucked her eyebrows, curled her lashes, applied a silver or blue silver or gold Yardley face mask once a week, and used all manner of potions and astringents and henna hair lighteners and straighteners at various intervals.

Ceci tried to emulate, hoping for her underarm and leg hairs to darken and lengthen so she could rid herself of them. She bought her own Clearasil tube (cherishing that pasty smell), awaiting pimples, was elated when Ellen showed her the hiding place of blackheads: the crease between lip and chin.

What Ceci Learned from Ellen and Others

The Surfer Stomp. That she was supposed to be afraid of boys. That you didn't go to second base until the fourth or fifth date at the earliest. That you were always supposed to say No at least twice to new ventures of the flesh. That no one wore tampons.

Also: Don't call boys (her mother said), boys don't like to be chased. Study their interests. Plan your makeup color scheme to coincide with and complement your clothing scheme, which means planning ahead on the little charts provided by the teen magazines.

What Happened When Mr. and Mrs. Rubin Went Away for a Marketing Convention

The boys were like an occupying army. They ate Granny Smith apples from the drawer in the refrigerator and picked tangelos from the backyard and poured themselves mixed drinks. They tracked in mud and seemed to have no homes of their own. They were dark and alive and loud.

Sam Frederick and Joe Amos left behind on the antique davenport a tape cassette from their legendary Sam and Joe I Won't Go Show. Ellen left with them to go to a meeting. As they were shutting the door, Joe said, Don't wait up for her. They all three laughed. Ceci made herself a tuna melt, loaded the dishwasher. Her homework was finished. She had no one to call. Her hair wasn't dirty enough to wash. She took her parents' old copy of *The Group* (She can read anything she wants, her father would say. If she doesn't understand it, it won't hurt her.) and leafed through it while she breathed on her machine. She wanted to be with people. She wanted talking.

Don't wait up for her, Joe had said. Ceci took the boys' tape and re-wound it to the beginning and brought it to the bathroom. She turned on the bath water.

Sam and Joe were singing the anti-war song they'd made up: *Ain't no use to wonder why, I think I'm gonna die—and it's 5–6–7, open up them pearly gates—*. Then they trailed off to advertise an upcoming interview with the Ass-tit Jewish-American Indian princess who showed off her wares for the poor boys in boot camp in Butt Butte, Wyoming. The field of Ceci's mind was an expanse of far-reaching cities and villages, but she had not thought of that. Ass-tit, Butt Butte, had not been in her vocabulary. Though she had had those kinds of images while she was in her bed, rubbing with her thumb. Or in the tub.

She ran more warm water over a handful of Barnston's bubble powder and imagined the Ass-tit Princess, greeted by the cheering invading army of Salamanders, boys touching her nut-brown breasts shed of their loin-cloth just for them, large nut-brown maiden, the eye of her tit warmed in someone's eyeless hand. Someone's brown cheek and lips, and she was the princess and the hand and the hands.

Ellen had never mentioned to Ceci any nut-brown maidens or princesses or do-it-yourself thumb projects of her own. Ellen wouldn't, Ceci thought. She was the Sweetheart and she was four years older. Besides, she hadn't mentioned it in her diary. The juiciest thing Ceci had read in Ellen's diary was about Ellen's friend Naomi.

Ceci thought of Naomi, naked, water streaming over her shoulders and swishing her pubic hair. Like seaweed. Mermaids. She wondered if Ellen did that too. That overnight in Galveston with the boys and pancakes—

(Always the baby, the one it doesn't matter if she's wearing her robe and two orange juice cans on her head, she's the baby, the one who doesn't count, the one too young to go out with. You, Ceci, go and get the door and tell them I'm almost ready, Ellen would say. Entertain them. But not too much. Make them laugh *once*.)

Ceci in her tub filled with bubble bath from her father's factory imagined a dance hall hostess knocking and not noticing Ceci, and lying on top of her, still not feeling her, then a man coming in the door and soaping the lady on top of Ceci. Ceci would stay so so quiet because she finally would learn something, here was her chance. She began to hum. Quick—she thought she heard Ellen unlock the back door and Ceci reached over and stopped the tape (thinking: Thomas Merton was electrocuted in his bathtub) and jumped out to turn on the radio real loud, KPRC, news and talk.

What Ceci Knew about the War

That it was wrong. The government was wrong but mostly only the Jews and Northerners and Catholics and students in California knew it. Jerry's underground paper was against it from the word Go, and it also editorialized about, as he called it, concerns of its constituency. It editorialized against the uniforms they had to wear in his private school. One day he organized almost everyone not to wear their ties. They won. Now every Friday they could leave the ties at home. It was a great victory. But he said he felt uneasy about it. The principal had given in too easily.

How the News Came to Ceci's Class

There was some sort of murmuring, the sort of buzz that precedes a big announcement. The history teacher, Mrs. Simpson, was late to class. She said there would not be a quiz but to prepare for a discussion on the League of Nations. Then she left. While she was gone Joel Arner and Jimmy Buxbaum covered the entire two boards with ticktacktoe graphs. Mrs. Simpson returned and said, All right, class. There will be a pop quiz. Then she whispered and looked furtive. She told them: Four students in Ohio were killed in a protest against the war. They were wild, she said. They burned down a building.

Did they have weapons? asked Joey.

I think so, she said. Yes definitely. They attacked officers of the National Guard.

Ceci wondered if that was what Ricky Bogen was going to join. She imagined him lying dead. But those weren't the ones that died. The ones that died were college students. Up North.

She imagined herself a college girl, lots of dates, boys carrying her books, boys running fingers through her hair, which had somehow changed to blonde and straight (you could accomplish great transformations in college), laughing, maybe a little lipstick, long lashbuilding mascara with those little hairs in the wand, blue eyeshadow, laughing and talking about philosophy. My philosophy of life, the college Ceci would be saying, is helping people. Get to know everyone. She would be walking on a campus green, by old-fashioned Old English buildings. And then the boy on her right, call him for the sake of argument Barry or Jerry, would be shot. Blood on his lumberjack shirt. Jerry Schwartz, blood on his salamander tee shirt, coming out of the paw.

The report I heard in the teachers' lounge, said Mrs. Simpson, is there were two boys and two girls.

A college girl, Ceci thought, putting her hand to her heart, and could almost feel the wet blood trickling. She wondered if she would have her period by then. Of course of course. By then it would be old hat. She thought of the *X*s she would make on a wall calendar. But for nothing. Blood all over the nut-brown maiden, down her seaweed hairs. She, Ceci, fallen on the grass in front of three-story stone college buildings that looked like Steak and Ales.

It wasn't my fault, she said to herself. It wasn't the students' fault, she said in a whisper. They didn't do anything wrong, she said loudly and evenly, loud as a boy.

Then she ducked her head and wrote her name, shakily, and Pop Quiz #5 on the looseleaf sheet.

What Happened at Home

The phone was ringing. Right off the hook, Ceci thought to herself. Jerry Schwartz said, Hello, did you hear? She said, This is Ceci, this is me, not Ellen. He said, I know. Did you hear? Did you hear?

Yes, she said, yes, the college students. Ellen's not here.

He said, I have the car. I can come by—

Out of some instinct, some sense of propriety, she said, I'll meet you at the JCC.

She knew it took ten minutes to walk there. It would take him at least that long to drive. Walk slowly and carry a big stick, she thought. Walk slowly and your lungs will be friends with you forever. No flare-ups.

How They Were at the JCC and in the Car

He was on the steps waiting. Eyes kind of red. You need Murine, she thought. Once at Bruce Gottschalk's house, Bill Somebody had splashed Murine up and down his face, turned off the lights, and shined a black light on his face. The Murine tracks were purple. Everyone said, Psy-cho-del-ic.

At the JCC Jerry said, I'll take you to my house.

Some alarm started to go off in a far reach of her mind but Ceci had not been properly trained. No boys in her bedroom. But could she be in a boy's living room?

Maybe the front steps.

The car radio was full of music and bulletins, and *Open up the pearly gates*— That's Sam and Joe's song, Ceci said, except I don't think the words are the same, exactly. How did that get on the radio? Jerry laughed, not turning to her. That's Country Joe McDonald. He sang that at Woodstock. You thought those two clowns wrote it? They couldn't write their way out of a paper bag. They couldn't even get the lyrics down in that stupid tape they made.

She absorbed this.

How They Were at His House

The TV was on, and the radio, on KILT, old music—"Dead Man's Curve." It was dark, the glow of the TV on a braided or brocaded couch. Kleenex in a wad. Tennis shoes in a corner. Newspapers awry. I wanted to tell you this, he said. He sat her down on the sofa. His finger brushed past her ear. She felt it, felt it more right afterwards. One two three four seconds later. Still. Two four six eight. Why don't we defoliate. Like a shadow touch. Look at this, she thought. He's angry about the students at Kent State but there are tears in his eyes. She was afraid he was going to sob. He took an envelope from his back pocket. He was wearing jeans. Must have changed from his school clothes, she thought. She'd never seen him in his St. Mark's High School private uniform. She saw some dark material bunched in a corner. Maybe the uniform. Ceci wondered if this was one of the days they wore ties. Every day but one. Which? Friday? He was saying something about a moratorium. Sounded like natatorium. Auditorium. Black armbands, he said. The TV was saying, Allison said she wanted peace; she said this to her mother on the phone yesterday. Tears on faces. Weeping. Gasps. Tear gas, said a man.

She wondered what the burn of tear gas was like. Pneumonia was a cold, rattly feeling. Did tear gas burn your bronchial tubes forever, down to the alveoli, something no machine could fix, would it give you emphysema? She took a deep breath to remind herself that she was in good shape. I'm in good shape, she said to herself. My lungs are my friends. She listened to her breath, she felt the little bruise of pain at the end of each long breath, as always.

Look, he said, unfolding a letter from the envelope. Harvard wrote me and said, Fuck off.

For a moment she believed him and wondered at this disregard. Didn't they expect parents to read it? He unfolded the letter and read: Dear Mr. Schwartz, Unfortunately we cannot accept you for admission into Harvard. We had many qualified candidates and we regret that we could not accept all of them. Our waiting list is full also, but we wish you success and achievement in your academic life and in the world beyond.

There's nothing I can do, he said. Nothing. He was down now, head on her shoulder like a baby, like a puppy. She touched his hair. She had never touched a boy's hair. Her father's hair was thinning, wet with Vitalis. This was poodle hair, like her own. She massaged his head, and with her other hand rubbed her own scalp, to feel what it felt like.

A kind of tickle. More exciting when it's two.

But not the kind of tickle that made her feel like laughing.

Then he was rocking his body against hers. My ribs, she thought. His ribs. Tackling. I'm a football player. My lungs are strong and fine. Maybe I will outgrow this asthma business after all. He held her in a bear hug. She had danced the bear hug three times at two different dances at the JCC and at Westwood Country Club. She pressed her lips against his face. Her mouth. Little scratchiness: he shaves! She wondered if he'd been crying, inched out her tongue. Salt.

He tongued her ear.

She tongued his. More like dirt than wax.

He cupped her chin.

Sweet nut-brown Indian maiden.

She clamped her thighs. For no reason. And again. Again. She could feel his fingers all up and down her back almost like a massage. Or how she'd imagined a massage.

She clamped her thighs.

He moved his hands back to her face, made circles on her cheeks with his hands.

She rocked and rocked, the nut-brown Indian maiden. He was a puppy and so was she. Boys weren't like cats at all. I am not thinking, she was thinking. This is what it is like not to be thinking. Though if she was thinking this, she must be . . .

Puppy hair puppy tail, knobs, elbows, salt. The boys didn't want to go, Allison said, the people were telling the microphone on TV. The boys didn't want to go. Poor poor thing, she was thinking. Poor thing, poor little puppyface, poor boy but so old he can drive, *2–4–6–8, don't give a damn, next stop*—

My poor poor little beagle, she thought. Ceci, he whispered, Ceci honey, he whispered.

Ceci honey, she thought. I'm a honey. I'm Ceci honey. God please, she was praying rocking crying too, please God don't let him call me sweetheart . . .

Old Enough

MARY K. FLATTEN

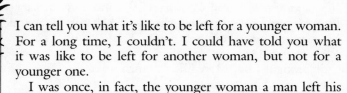I can tell you what it's like to be left for a younger woman. For a long time, I couldn't. I could have told you what it was like to be left for another woman, but not for a younger one.

I was once, in fact, the younger woman a man left his wife for. Now you can argue (as I did at the time) that no one actually leaves one person for another. Something is already amiss between the original couple or no one would be looking for a reason, a person, to leave. You can make a case of that, but it's a crock. The fact is, he was living with his wife in some sort of peace, they had been married long enough to have three children too young to go to school, he met me, he fell in love with me, he left his wife and three children to take up with me, and I thought the whole thing was incredibly romantic. It was the beginning of summer and I thought our love was destiny. I felt pretty smug about it all (although, of course, it was a shame about the kids), until a few months later when he told me, "It's not enough anymore." That was the end of summer, and I had learned a thing or two about destiny.

I remember the scene perfectly. He had come to my apartment, just a niche in a warren of niches carved in a solid old brick house that had once been home to a single family. Pecan trees darkened the narrow backyard and shaded the screened-in sleeping porch on the second floor; oleanders and altheas, unpruned and rangy, lifted their blossoms almost as high. Colored beads curtained the windows, an Indian spread covered my bed. Incense worthy of a papal High Mass wafted around me as I sat on the floor, listening for answers blowing in the wind.

He stood in front of me in this student-of-the-sixties Austin apartment and said, "It's not enough anymore." He began to explain at great length exactly what he meant, but I didn't hear a word of it. I was looking into his face thinking, "I'll be anything you want, I'll do anything you say. But once in a while let me know the warmth of your mouth, and once in a while let me feel the weight of your body on mine." Those were my exact thoughts—really—and I knew as I thought them that never since history began had such achingly beautiful sentiments filled a woman's heart. But at the time I wasn't even old enough to vote or buy beer, so I've learned to forgive myself.

So wrapped up was I in the purity of my sentiments that I did not immediately notice when he quit talking. I looked up to see his soft brown eyes upon me, expecting a reply, and I thought, "All that I am I have given to you. How can you say it's not enough?" I didn't say that, though. What I said was "Do you think that was fair? Was it fair of you to come to me with your ten years more and your broken marriage behind you and tell me there's such a thing as love?" He didn't answer. He only said once again, as though to repeat it were to make me understand, "I'm sorry, but it's not enough anymore." Then he turned and walked out the door.

Devastated, uncomprehending, I listened to his footsteps going through the kitchen, across the screened-in sleeping porch, and down the back steps. I listened as everything I cared about, everything that made life bearable, began walking down those steps, and I knew I had to stop him. I could not let him go. I was willing to plead, I was willing to beg, I was willing to kneel at his feet, but I had to do it before he turned the corner and walked out of my life forever.

My footsteps followed his through the kitchen, across the screened-in sleeping porch, and stopped at the top of the back steps. I saw him walking away from me—the black curly hair that had lain on my breast, his darling neck where my breath had lingered. I had wrapped my body and my life around him, and I stood at the top of the steps and prayed for words that would bring him back, words that would stop his flight, words that would carry him to my embrace.

If only I could find the right words, he would stop and turn. Our eyes would meet and I would run to him and he would enfold me in his arms. "Oh, my love," he would say as his lips brushed my hair. "What a fool I almost was." I would cry in my happiness and he would cry in his happiness and we would cry in each other's happiness. I would wrap my body and my life around him and there would never again be discord between us. But I had to have just the right words.

Inspiration hardly less than divine seized me. "Shane!" I called after him. "Shane! Come back!" He didn't stop. He didn't even turn around. He never could take a joke. But I thought it was hysterical. I sat down on the top step and laughed until I cried.

I figured it was all my fault. I had been too intense. (I was clearly off the track there. He had not, after all, said, "It's too much." I would tell you what he did say, but it has slipped my mind for the moment.) Yes, I had been intense, but only because I had found true love, which at the time I thought was the same as everlasting love. I loved him so much I had written him a poem which I left on my pillow one morning when I went to class before he woke up. Here is the poem, in its entirety:

> Man beside me that I love—
> Sleeping now—
> When you wake up,
> Will you remember
> Me?

Believe it or not, I spent quite a bit of time on that poem. Not so much on writing it, but on whether or not to capitalize the first letter of every line, whether or not to start all the lines flush left, whether or not to make the first line all one word. Twenty years later I am well aware that this poem might have initiated the beginning of the end. The man had his faults, but he was a professor of English.

Or it could have been the retainer imitation. I had begun to speak with my tongue adhered to the top of my mouth in imitation of a friend who had gotten a retainer. It drove my beloved crazy. He asked me repeatedly to stop, and I really tried to, but I had spent so much time perfecting the technique that I spoke that way without realizing it. He got tired of being addressed as "Schweechhearch." He had no appreciation for the skill involved. He thought it was stupid. He never actually said, that day when he left, "It's the retainer imitation," so I can't know for sure, but I had to entertain it as a possibility. It certainly made a lot more sense than the ridiculously ambiguous "It's not enough anymore," or any other feeble excuse I could think of, such as maybe he had quit liking me.

"Well," I thought, "I guess he's going off to be alone and be introspective, to find out about himself, where he's coming from, where he's going." I thought he was going off to get his head together, as we said back then. He probably needed to do that, I reasoned, after several years of marriage and a relationship which, although brief, had been one of the world's great romances.

One thing he had definitely not said was "There's someone else."

Which is why I was so surprised, the very next day, to see him walking across campus with his arm around a girl who was neither myself nor his ex-wife, but someone whose peasant blouse fluttered with the rise and fall of her large, unfettered breasts and whose full and naturally blonde hair grazed her sun-bronzed thighs just below the ragged edge of her cut-offs. White trash if I'd ever seen it.

So being the woman another woman was left for was followed closely by being left for another woman, and if it wasn't the greatest time I've ever had I did learn a few things from the experience. I learned that saying, "Oh, my darling," during sex is not the same as looking into your loved one's soul. See, I thought it was, and the fact that it is not was such a revelation to me that I have never since said, "Oh, my darling," during sex. It's not that I don't talk. Sure I talk. I say, "Oh, my God, that's fantastic," or "No, no, no, you're doing it all wrong," but never again have I said, "Oh, my darling."

I also learned never to ask, "What are you thinking about?" This lesson was taught to me one sultry summer afternoon as we lay together in the tangled after-throes of passion. "What are you thinking about?" I asked as, with one finger, I traced the circles of his curls. "My wife," he answered. That was the last time I ever asked that question, and I'm always amazed when someone asks it of me. "How can you ask that?" I want to say. "Don't you know someone might tell you the truth someday?"

But the most important thing I learned was to be the one who leaves first. It's a lot easier to be the one walking out the door than it is to be the one standing at the top of the steps yelling, "Shane!" I tell you true. So I learned to be wary, to watch for the signs, to make an early exit. This can be a little self-defeating at times, breaking up with someone just when you start to like him, but you can't afford to let sentiment creep into your life and cloud your thinking.

Yes, I learned my lessons. I kept them in mind as the years passed. And the years did pass. Then one day it happened, just like in the movies. I fell in love again. It was one of the world's great romances. The word "forever" reentered my vocabulary. I became a believer. Friend, I was born again.

But destiny had a few more lessons to teach me, and several years after I moved in (to the day, to the very day), I moved out. I gave him three months to come around. At the end of three months he had not come around. He was probably bluffing, but I couldn't live without him. I called him. I saw him. He told me he had started seeing someone else. I almost threw up.

A week later he called and asked to see me. He picked me up from work and we strolled along the Colorado River, joggers and bicyclists and dogs chasing Frisbees passing us on either side. I used to take friends there and point out the landmarks: "We were sitting on this bench when he told me he wanted to try again"; "Under that tree he said, 'After I saw you the other day, spending time with her just didn't make any sense.'" It's a lovely walk, especially if you go in early spring as he and I did. With the fruit trees flowering pink, rose, and red, and wisteria purpling the gazebos, I said yes, I'd love to try again.

I had him back. I had him back. My long, lean Texan. The sun made a crown of his curly gray hair and his eyes had never shone so blue in the burnished skin of his Cherokee ancestry. I kissed the backs of both his hands, his artist's hands that cooked all my meals, serenaded me on the ukulele, and carried me up to bed. I was very happy, not only because I was in love, but also because vindication carries its own rapture.

"Hah!" I thought. "She couldn't compete. She couldn't undo in three months what we spent years building. Hah!" I thought, and prepared to live happily ever after. But he didn't quit seeing her, which is why I call that path along the Colorado River where you can always find joggers and bicyclists and dogs chasing Frisbees "The Heartbreak Trail."

For some reason he had told me where she worked. I guess he thought it was important that I know. I called the people I knew who worked at the same place and said to them, "I don't want to know anything about her. I don't even want to hear the sound of her name." I had hardly hung up the phone before this girl had no secrets from me. My friends (my *friends,* can you imagine?) couldn't wait to tell me everything about her. I knew where she was born, where she was living. I knew where she went to church! I'm only surprised no one told me her sign.

"She's not as attractive as you," they said. ("Oh, thanks. I got thrown over for a dog.") "He gave her a ring for her birthday," they said. ("Is that so? He never gave me a ring for my birthday." Mind you, he gave me many lovely things, among them a heart on a chain which I took off the day I left and never put back on although I used to clutch it in my hand as I cried myself to sleep each night, and isn't that the most achingly beautiful thing you've ever heard? But the point here is that he gave her a ring and he never gave me one. If he had given her tropical fish I would have remembered he never gave me tropical fish and I would have felt injured about that.)

I handled it all pretty well until they told me her age. I won't tell you her exact age, but I'll give you a hint: it's a number that starts with a one. To say I went to pieces suggests I took it a lot more bravely than I did. To say I lost my composure sets something of a standard for understatement.

In fact, I cried for six months. I don't mean I cried off and on for six months. I mean I cried every day for the next six months. I woke up crying. I cried while I dressed for work. I cried while I drove to work. I cried at the copy machine. I sat in my car and cried during my lunch hour. I cried myself to sleep each night. I woke up in the middle of the night crying. And as I cried, I called his name.

Whenever I started to feel a little better, when, for instance, I had gone a couple of hours without crying, I would see them drive by in his car. Them. Him and her. You know who I mean. He had a convertible, the top of which he almost never put up, so there was no mistaking who they were. They were the happy couple in the convertible. There was no mistaking me, either. I was the solitary figure watching through eyes swollen to slits as they drove past, spitting their exhaust fumes in my face.

But don't think that, demented though I was by weeping, the irony of the situation escaped me. Don't think I didn't recognize that things had come full circle. Don't think I failed to realize that she was about the age I had been in my younger-woman days while I . . . well, I was old enough to be A Wife.

I remember the night I counted backwards on my fingers to figure out how old she had been when my former—her current—lover and I started living together. By my calculations, when my former—her current—lover and I started living together, going to the prom was one of her distant dreams.

I thought then of my counterpart, the wife I had supplanted. Had she too counted backwards on her fingers to see how old I had been when she got married? Could she picture me among the flower girls at her wedding, a basket of rose petals in my hands, a garland of ribbons in my hair, while she stood smiling at her handsome groom? Well, I finally knew how she felt, more or less, because of course I didn't have three towheaded children sitting at my feet while I counted backwards on my fingers, a distinction for which I was grateful. Still, I knew what it was like to watch the man you love walk off with jailbait.

When I first started crying I wasn't too worried. "Okay," I thought, "this is the really hard part and it lasts about a month. I'll cry endlessly for a month and then it will start to get better." So I cried endlessly for a month and it didn't get better. I cried for another month, and another, and another, and another. At the end of six months I felt just as bad as I had the day I found out about her.

"So," my friends said, "why don't you fight for him?" Now how do you fight for someone? What was I supposed to do—start wearing perfume? This man knew me. He knew whether or not he wanted me. And he had made it perfectly clear that he didn't. It's hard to fight for a man when he refuses to see you. My best friend had the best suggestion: "Hit her on the back of the head with a rock," she said.

My worst fear was that he would die loving her. I know that sounds pathetic—it *is* pathetic—but he certainly wasn't going to outlive her.

Thus I came to understand the difficulties people face in turning thirty or thirty-five or forty or whatever milestone birthday might be approaching. Thus I learned how unsettling such an event can be. My birthdays had had very little effect on me. I was perennially young. Everyone said so. "You haven't changed a bit," people who hadn't seen me in years would say. New acquaintances assumed me to be several years younger than I was. I was short, I was thin, I was elfin, so what was this business about aging, anyway?

Someday, perhaps, I would begin to look older. I might even begin to feel older. When that happened, I would accept it gracefully. My face, like those of the ancient and weathered Indian women whose photographic portraits are so admired, would be etched with the story of my life. It would be a strong face, a wise face, a face finally old, yet forever young. (Although I must admit I have yet to see anyone walk up to the Estée Lauder counter in a department store and say, "I'll buy whatever it takes to make me look like an eighty-five-year-old Navajo.")

If I had forgotten the power that comes with being nineteen, there were constant reminders. It's hard to get away from them if you live in Austin. One day, in a feast of masochism, I went to the University of Texas campus just to do a comparison. I wanted to make sure they were different from me. They were.

They were beautiful, those girls. Looking at them, I remembered the summer I was nineteen, when every man who met me fell in love with me. I remembered men turning to look at me, not because I was beautiful, which I have never been, but simply because I was nineteen. I remembered the power and the aura of that age, when you think a wonderful life lies ahead of you. You think everything will go just the way you want it to. You think that magical summer will last forever, and that all your life, men will turn to look at you. Watching those girls on campus, seeing them as competitors, I could have fallen in love with some of them myself.

Now I don't necessarily think that one day the man I loved looked at me and said, "She's too old." But when you get left for a teenager you have to conclude that if a man is interested in perfect muscle tone, there's not a lot you can do about it.

I tried to bring a bit of humor to the situation. I am, after all, known for my ability to bring humor to a situation. I told people I was going to make a tee shirt that said, "Old enough to be left for a younger woman." And I tried to stop crying. I tried very hard. I tried pulling myself up by my bootstraps, keeping a stiff upper lip, looking for the silver lining. I tried talking sternly to myself. "Oh, grow up," I said to myself sternly. "Would you rather have varicose veins?" And then I would start to cry again. I began to wonder if my eyes would ever not be bloodshot, if my face would ever not be swollen, if my nose would ever recover from facial-tissue burn.

Then one day I didn't cry. I cried the next day and for several days after that, but there had been that one day I hadn't cried. A couple of weeks later, I didn't cry again. Some days I was awake for five or ten minutes before I thought of him and her and how old I was, when of course I would start to cry again, but at least I didn't wake up crying, which is not an auspicious way to begin the day. Then there started to be more days when I didn't cry than days when I did, and now it's been a long time since I cried. Years.

I met her some time after all this happened, when it didn't matter anymore. (We worked together, she and I. Is this a story of the eighties, or what?) My friends had been right—she's not as attractive as I am. But what shocked me, what made me stare at her when she didn't know I was looking, was that there was about her nothing of youth. Where had she found that suit that a middle-aged banker would shun? And her graceless, lumbering walk—had that set his fingertips tingling?

She had, of course, gotten older. She was, at last, out of her teens. But she was still young. She was still a girl. So where were the aura and the power? I don't suppose I'll ever know, because it was hardly the kind of thing I could discuss with her. But it certainly left me wondering who was the May and who the December in their romance.

If I had seen her at the start, perhaps I would not have had to face the loss of my youth. I could have saved that crisis for my fortieth birthday. If I had seen her at the start, perhaps I would not have responded to an issue that didn't exist. But I mistook youth for the issue and I learned the wrong lesson. I learned that I was no longer young, when I could have learned that I'm a fool for love, or that my life was not to resemble Jane Eyre's. Or I might even have learned that it's not always best to be the one to leave.

I will tell you that, some time after I stopped crying, he came to see me. I was living in Travis Heights by then, growing my own cilantro and determining my moral stance on the Salvation Army's plan to move to South Austin. He sat next to me on the porch swing and watched while I snapped beans into a Tupperware bowl. Tapping a foot against the wooden floor I set the swing in motion, and as it carried us in and out of the shadows of the live oak trees, he told me how sorry he was and he asked me to come back.

Luckily I am a person of great emotional maturity and hence derived absolutely no satisfaction from this encounter. I simply stared into my bowl of beans and declined the offer in passionless language that did not include the words "nyah, nyah, nyah."

I don't mean to say it was easy for me. If I was no longer crying about the loss of love and of youth, I hadn't started laughing about it either. And I was glad he had not asked me sooner. I was glad he had not asked me sooner when I might have said yes and faced a lifetime of becoming ill whenever a woman 365 days younger than I approached.

I rose from the swing and watched as he walked down the steps—the curly gray hair that had lain on my breast, his darling neck where my breath had lingered, his artist's hands that would never again frame my face as he bent to kiss me—and I didn't yell "Shane!" and I didn't say "nyah, nyah, nyah." You do learn a few things with age.

I did finally have that tee shirt made. I wear it when I jog the Heartbreak Trail. People running toward me see a shirt that says, "Old enough to be left for a younger woman." Those who do a double take read on my back, "Young enough not to care."

The Legacy

LIANNE ELIZABETH MERCER

Alyce Ann Farnsworth had heard the word from Doc
Sullivan on a hot July day when the squash was baking on
wilted vines and even the large gray cat that occasionally
wandered through the yard lay in the shade of the crepe
myrtle with its tongue hanging out.

"Second hardest thing I've ever done, Alyce Ann. I hate
to tell you this," the doc had begun.

"From the look on your face I'm going to hate to hear it. Don't be a
sentimental old coot, just get on with it. Then I can drown my sorrows in
a cup of tea at the café," Alyce Ann had said.

"It's breast cancer and it's already spread to your back. That's why it
hurts when you weed your beans."

"How come it's never hurt in my breast, even when Harold gets to
loving on me, but sometimes it hurts so bad in my back that I cry just
standing there?"

"Nature has her ways." Doc stroked his scraggly mustache.

"Shit, Maurice!" Alyce Ann had always called him by his given name,
beginning in third grade when he'd washed her face with snow and she'd
told the teacher. "I don't want mumbling about nature's ways. I want to
know what's going to happen to me."

Doc sank onto his stool. "I don't know if I can stand by and watch you
die, Alyce Ann."

"Are you listening, Maurice? There won't be any standing by and pretending it isn't happening. I need you with me, especially at the end because Harold won't be able to take it if I get yellow and hollow-eyed like
his mother did before the Lord snatched her up."

"I needed that toughness in a woman, Alyce Ann." The doc grabbed her hand. "I needed you."

Alyce Ann pried his hand off hers. "No need to bring that up now. I want answers, not what-ifs."

Doc sighed.

"You will lose weight. If you choose chemotherapy, your hair will fall out. Your skin will become the color of clay that's been left too long in the sun. And you'll hurt. I'm going to give you stronger pain medicine, beginning today."

Alyce Ann dressed, staggered to her car, opened the door and got in, closed the door, rolled down the windows, gritted her teeth (the windows weren't electric and it hurt her back to reach across the seat to roll down the one on the right), started the engine, burst into tears, shifted into reverse and backed out of the parking space. She narrowly missed Emmaline Hodspepper, who was driving past with a load of chicks in her truck.

Alyce Ann didn't stop at the café, but she brewed herself a good strong cup of camomile tea at home. As she set the Wedgwood cup onto its saucer, the saucer chipped.

"Shit!" she said again.

Alyce Ann didn't tell Harold what the doc had told her. She had always planned to make it to their fiftieth wedding anniversary.

Alyce Ann weeded, lied, hoed, gritted, harvested, cried, snapped and canned until an evening in early September when she couldn't get up out of the beans. Harold found her there, tears running off her muddy cheeks into the earth, her legs waving back and forth like forlorn semaphores.

He dropped the bird feeder he was carrying and tried to pick her up.

Alyce Ann screamed.

Harold eased her into a sitting position and squatted beside her.

"Alyce Ann, what is it? What's the matter?"

"The matter is, Harold, that I'm dying and I hurt and the beans are going to be tough and too big and dry up on their vines because you won't pick them when they're ready."

"I pick the beans whenever you tell me to."

"I'm not going to be around to tell you. Are you listening, Harold?"

"No one dies from arthritis."

"It isn't arthritis, Harold. It's cancer. No need to tell you until now. Besides, I hoped Maurice was wrong."

"I don't like you going to him, Alyce Ann. I haven't trusted him ever since he charmed you out of the notion of having hives right before we went to the hinge classes in Chicago."

"He hypnotized me so I wouldn't scratch during the lectures, Harold. I wanted to stay home and take oatmeal baths, but you wanted me to go. Harold, are you listening to me?" She scooped up a handful of dirt and slowly crumbled the rich black loam into Harold's hand. "*I am dying.*"

"And the doc can't charm you out of it?"

"No."

"Well," Harold said. He piled the dirt back into the hole and patted it down. He flexed a bean on the nearest plant, picked it and threw it into the nearby dishpan. "Well, then."

"Help me up and get me into the house."

Tentatively, stiffly, Harold held out his arm. Alyce Ann kept losing her grip on it. "I'm no ghost yet, Harold Farnsworth! Hold still."

Harold did.

Later that night, from beneath the finely stitched quilt she'd made that long-ago Christmas just before Bonnie had been born dead, Alyce Ann looked up at Harold.

"I don't want to go to the hospital and die like a porcupine with tubes sticking out of me everywhere. I want to die at home."

"What will become of me?" Harold asked, kneading his hands. Harold always kneaded his hands when he was troubled, when he was faced with something bigger than he could handle. Alyce Ann knew he was remembering the peaceful days when he was ten and his only chore was milking Lady Belle each evening. It didn't take coaxing or strategy or strength; it just took sitting there and doing it. Harold was good at doing it.

"I'll ask Mabel and Lottie and Charlene to take care of you, Harold. You'll be my legacy to them. Let's see, Mabel on Monday and Thursday, then Lottie on Wednesday—she gets her hair done Wednesdays, so she'll look nice."

"Alyce Ann, hadn't you better check with them first?"

"You're right. I should see if they want to . . ."

" . . . want to skip days in between, or want me one day right after another. I'm good at leftovers."

Alyce Ann never got dressed again. Instead, she wore the pink chenille robe with the satin sash that Harold had brought her two years earlier from the hammer convention in Little Rock. In two weeks she took to her four-poster bed because she couldn't move her legs. A week after that, while crickets made noises outside the open window and whirrings and trills came from the bush where Harold had hung the hummingbird feeder, Lottie Lomax came to see her.

"I don't want Harold on Wednesdays and Sundays, Alyce Ann," Lottie said.

"Did you close the library early just to come and tell me that, Lottie?"

"It's Wednesday. We close at six."

"Here in this bed the time has gotten bloated, and I don't know one day from the next. Well, we can figure out Harold's days. And I'm leaving you this Wedgwood cup and saucer you've always admired, too. I'm sorry it's chipped."

"Alyce Ann, you can't will one person to another like china!" Lottie's voice rose an octave. "I don't want Harold. Period. No offense meant."

"None taken. Why are you here, then?" Alyce Ann asked. She brushed at her sweat-damp hair and remembered her manners. She offered Lottie tea and told her she was glad to see her.

"You never were a good liar, Alyce Ann," Lottie said. "I'm here to talk."

"About what?"

"Your dying, for one thing."

"How do you know I'm dying?"

"You're looking for a shelf for Harold. Besides, Doc told me you were dying. And Harold told Clarence, who told Charlene, who told me."

"Shit," Alyce Ann said.

"I should think now you're getting ready to meet your Maker you wouldn't talk like that," Lottie said.

"He understands I've had to live all these years with Harold."

"I'm sure He'll take that into account. But I believe He wants a clean slate. So I've come to explain about that night after the prom."

"What do you want to explain?" Alyce Ann stared at Lottie until Lottie looked instead at the dusty nightstand where the Bible lay open to Hebrews 11.

"Has Harold told you anything?"

"You've been at the library too long, Lottie. You're using words to try and buy time. That's one commodity I don't have."

Lottie fussed at her frizzy hair, sat on the edge of the chair, and finally looked again at Alyce Ann.

"We were down by the lake—most all the seniors except for you and Phillip Winston. Harold had been drinking, and he said he wanted just one thing from me before he married you. I had the biggest tits in town, he said, and he wanted to hold them in his hands and taste them. He said it would be like a secret wedding present from me to him."

"That sounds like Harold."

"It makes me nervous to talk about this." Lottie glanced toward the doorway.

"He's off at the store counting bolts."

"A month earlier, Doc had been home on a weekend leave just before he left to go to the war. I cried because he couldn't take me to the prom."

Alyce Ann watched Lottie's fingers crease and release the edge of the sheet. They picked at a thread on the blanket. Four inches of binding frayed loose. "So you sat home and sulked," she said.

In a quick motion, Lottie slid from the chair to the edge of Alyce Ann's bed. "I'm going to tell you something, Alyce Ann, that no living person knows. You can't even tell your flowers. Promise?"

"Yes." Alyce Ann hitched herself up to get more comfortable and her robe fell open. She clutched at the tie and pulled it tighter, but not before Lottie turned her eyes away from the wrinkled, lumpy mass that lay on her chest and crowded into the space where her breast once had first claim.

"Cross your heart and hope to die?"

"Lottie!"

"I'm sorry, Alyce Ann. I've never told this to anyone."

Alyce Ann tugged her right leg from where it was caught in the sheet. "You're making *me* nervous, Lottie. Just spill your guts without all the dramatics. I won't tell a soul."

"I had a child that next February," Lottie said. She looked like she'd been caught with three overdue books.

"I figured *that* out."

Lottie stared at Alyce Ann. "How?"

"You left town the day after Harold and I got married and once in September you were back looking mighty peculiar, bundled up in a coat when it was ninety degrees in the shade. I felt sorry, that's why I wrote to you, but you never wrote back. And then in the winter you came all skinny and pale to work in the library."

"So what are you thinking?"

"What am I thinking about who the father is or what am I thinking about what happened to the child?" Alyce Ann asked. She was beginning to tire, just like she used to when Lottie lectured the Friday afternoon Coterie Club on new book-lending policies, or on why the Eskimos didn't read novels. Lottie took forever to get to the point. Usually the coffee got cold and the cake got hard.

"Well, it's obvious the father is Doc." Lottie hugged the bedpost as though it were her date to the senior prom.

"Why didn't he marry you, then?"

Lottie poured herself into the chair and picked up her teacup once more. She took a long sip of tea and stared at Alyce Ann over the rim of the cup.

Alyce Ann stared back. Confession was so time-consuming and tiring, she thought. She wished Lottie had written her a letter. Or kept a journal, like Mabel Henderson. She could have read it faster and skimmed over the boring places.

Lottie glanced around and then whispered, "After he was injured, he came back with—with this problem. He'd just die if he knew I was telling you. You see, he couldn't have children, and he told me he didn't want to burden me with that. He knew what a strong sex drive I had." Lottie blushed.

"Then I should have thought he'd have wanted his own child all the more."

"I put her up for adoption," Lottie said.

Alyce Ann stared into Lottie's gray, guileless, childlike eyes. "Clarence and Vinnie Hodspepper adopted Emmaline that same year, if I recall right, Lottie. Emmaline may have hair the color of Vinnie's, but she drifts when she walks, just like Maurice does."

"In the city, Alyce Ann. I adopted her out in the city. You've been lying here with nothing to think about but your dying and taking care of Harold, and you're letting your mind wander." Lottie patted Alyce Ann's hand.

Alyce Ann shook Lottie's hand away. "Whose slate are you trying to clean, Lottie, mine or yours?"

"Both. I figure it will do me good to get forgiven, and you good to forgive me for letting Harold feel my breasts, and because I can't take care of him now. And besides that, you can die in peace because I am putting the kibosh to any rumors you may have heard during the last forty years that my child was fathered by your Harold because of what went on at the lake after the prom."

"Just a friendly little pre-graveside chat, eh Lottie?" Alyce Ann lay back on the pillows. Her back felt as though it had been pierced by a six-inch nail. She shut her eyes.

"That's sick, Alyce Ann," Lottie said. "How long have we been friends?"

Alyce Ann opened her eyes. "Since fourth grade, when you copied my penmanship papers."

"And we usually say what we think, don't we?"

"*I* do. And I think you *think* you're saying what you think, but it's usually disguised somewhere in chapter fourteen, like all the sex scenes in those dime novels we used to read under the hedge in your yard." Alyce Ann laughed. "Hell, Lottie, there's probably pages and pages of passion buried beneath the left third bush from your front sidewalk."

Lottie frowned. "I didn't know you thought I beat around the bush, Alyce Ann. And here I thought we were friends."

"We *are* friends, Lottie. That's why I can tell you what I think."

"Well, I just thought you'd appreciate clearing the air before you go. I've heard that the more you clear up while you're alive, the less you have to do in heaven."

Alyce Ann forced herself to sit up. She took three deep breaths, willed the nail in her back into a tiny carpet tack and pointed a shaking finger at Lottie. "It wasn't just a feel, Lottie. I know Harold when he makes up his mind. He loved up on you, didn't he? And that gives you a sort of proprietorship. You'll just have to get used to hardware conventions."

"I'll do nothing of the sort."

"What *will* you do?"

"I'll cook for him once a week. Wednesdays, most likely. I get my hair done, so I'll look presentable. Yes, Wednesdays—that's when I make spaghetti. He can have more than one helping."

"Does your slate feel clean, Lottie?"

"Yes."

"I'm tired. Would you mind going?"

"You never told me how your slate feels, Alyce Ann."

"Chalky—full of the dust of too many words. Tell me again why you didn't marry Maurice," Alyce Ann whispered.

"He wasn't whole and I couldn't see myself living happily ever after with him."

"Were you ever sorry?"

"No."

"Good-bye, Lottie."

Alyce Ann never heard Lottie let herself out the front door. She was dreaming of babies who looked like Maurice and Harold and Lottie and herself. When she woke up as she usually did at 2:30 A.M. and took her pain pill, she realized that she didn't believe what Lottie had told her about what had happened to the child. She also realized there was nothing she could do about it.

A few nights later, Alyce Ann lay in bed in her robe at midnight watching Harold grimace as he read the paper to her. He slouched in the big overstuffed chair they'd bought the summer after the prom, right after they got married. Alyce Ann had re-covered it four times. Once more the maroon-striped velvet was threadbare on the arms where Harold rested his elbows while he read. Alyce Ann had it in mind to redo it in a sort of a peach brocade to match the flowers in the wallpaper.

"'An additional tax of point-oh-one-tenths of a percent will be added to manufactured items,'" Harold read. "This is in addition to the taxes already slapped onto the steel when it enters the country."

"Harold, I don't want to hear any more about taxes and manufactured items."

Harold threw the newspaper to the floor and shook his finger at Alyce Ann. "Damn it, Alyce Ann! They're taxing foreign steel, they're taxing what we make out of it and they're taxing it when we sell it. I say there's a limit to the amount of blood you can get from a nickel screw."

"Damn it yourself, Harold. In the time I have left I want to fill my mind with something pleasant. Screws isn't it."

Harold looked startled. "I'm sorry, Alyce Ann. I just wasn't thinking."

"*I've* been thinking, Harold. About who's going to look after you when I'm gone."

"I don't like to think about you being gone, Alyce Ann." Harold looked away. "Where did you get the pansies?"

"Charlene brought them. I don't like to think about being gone either, Harold. I don't like to think about you being here alone. I talked to Charlene, but she's waiting for Eddie—still believes after forty years he's going to come back from the war. Lottie will cook for you only on Wednesdays. And Mabel is busy with her journal and her daddy."

"I don't want Mabel. She can't cook worth a damn."

"But I'll have an easier time of it if I know you're eating regular."

"The Village Restaurant on Sunday, and on Tuesday when they have sausage and sauerkraut. Kiwanis on Monday. Lottie's on Wednesday. Maybe on Thursday that new restaurant on the highway where they got enchiladas on those plates that are so hot you can't touch them. Friday I'll go to the church supper and Saturday I'll eat popcorn."

"I mean someone living here," Alyce Ann said.

"In sin?"

"A wife, Harold. Another wife."

"No sirree, Alyce Ann. I found you pure and simple and I'll find me another woman the same way. No sirree bob."

"I can't help but think about it, Harold."

"Think about this instead. I have been, ever since last night when I sat outside after you finally got to sleep." Harold smiled at Alyce Ann and it was a hopeful smile like the one he'd smiled at her after he'd asked her to the prom.

As Alyce Ann put up her hand to brush back her damp hair, she felt her rings twist on the skinny flesh of her fingers. She wished Charlene could come to the house and do her hair. She wished that Harold could say flat out what he was thinking. It never helped to rush him; he had to say things in his own good time. She fiddled with her sash. Finally, after she'd tied it into three bows-on-top-of-bows, he went on.

"Are you up to going outside?"

"You know I can't walk."

"I'll carry you, Alyce Ann. All right?"

Alyce Ann had had her last pain pill two hours before. She calculated that this might well be the last time she got outside.

"Bring me another pill and I'll go."

Harold brought it and she took it with the lukewarm glass of water that had been on her nightstand all day. Harold rummaged in the cedar chest, picked out the featherbed that had been his grandma's and scurried outside with it.

He returned, picked her up and slung her over his shoulder like one of the cement sacks at the store. She didn't like the indignity of it, and it hurt her chest. But she was too busy breathing upside down to complain, and then she got into the rhythm of Harold's stumbling walk and her pain lessened. The smell of the damp earth hit her when Harold stepped onto the porch. She bit her lip to keep from crying.

"Where are we going?"

"Just here in the yard," Harold wheezed. "See, there's the featherbed under the clothesline."

"Would you put it near the garden? I want to see how the zinnias and marigolds are doing."

"I swear, Alyce Ann, a few minutes after you get to heaven you'll probably be making suggestions to God about His gardens."

Harold kicked the featherbed to the garden's edge, rousing the stray gray cat from beneath a large zinnia. He set Alyce Ann down onto the featherbed like she was a carton of light bulbs.

Alyce Ann tugged at her legs, one of which had folded beneath her.

"Here, let me help," Harold said, grabbing her ankle and pulling her leg free. "Well, what do you think?"

Alyce Ann hitched herself over to the flowers. Their bottom leaves were crackling. There were dead blossoms on some of the plants. "I think the flowers need rain."

Harold squatted beside her. He picked a large zinnia and thrust it into Alyce Ann's hand. He cleared his throat.

"Alyce Ann, you know what you do has always been pretty much all right with me. You helped me out at the store and got so you could mix paint and sort screws nearly as good as me." Harold picked another zinnia and shoved it at Alyce Ann. "Hell, that isn't what I want to say. Do you know what I want to say?"

Alyce Ann saw his face glistening in the moonlight. Beyond him, the grass looked like a gray Swedish rug she'd seen once in a catalog.

"I might, Harold, and I might not. Since I've been sick, there've been a bunch of surprises, most of them handed me by my own body. So I've learned to be patient and wait to see what the message is. I think I'll do that now."

"You mean you're not going to help me out."

"Nope. You never gave me a flower before in your life, except the wedding bouquet, and Mama and Daddy bought that so it doesn't count. You've given me two flowers in fifteen seconds. I can't wait to see what you do next."

"Damn it, Alyce Ann." Harold jumped up, walked over to the birdhouse on the clothesline pole, peered into it and returned. He perched awkwardly on the featherbed, then took Alyce Ann's hand in his and kneaded it.

"It was the moonlight, Alyce Ann. Last night I watched it fill up the yard and hide the bare places. It even made the garbage cans look like little robots. Well, I got to remembering how it was when we were in high school. I wanted to do it once more with you out here in the moonlight, like we did that time after we left Charlene's and split the beer and started Bonnie."

Alyce Ann didn't say anything right away. She was remembering how it was with the grass on her bare skin, at first worrying about ants that might be hurrying through the grass and worrying about if they would find an easier path on her smooth buttocks, then becoming more interested in what was being done at her breasts and between her thighs.

In the chilly night air, now, she felt hot. She touched the palm of Harold's hand in their secret signal of desire. "I'd like that, Harold, but I don't want to get naked out here because you can see the lump in the moonlight, and my legs don't look like they belong to me since I can't feel them or move them anymore."

"You can keep your robe on, Alyce Ann," Harold said, tightening the sash.

Alyce Ann did.

Afterwards, they lay close together and watched the moon. Alyce Ann sifted through her fingers the dirt that the gray cat had used for a bed.

"Are you hurting, Alyce Ann?" Harold asked.

"No."

He sighed.

"There's one more thing."

She waited.

"I don't want to tell you this, Alyce Ann, but even more I don't want you finding out when you get up there." Harold waved his arms toward the stars. "The thing is, that me and Lottie, well, we did it. It was after the prom and you remember you got sick from drinking Charlene's rum and Coke and went home and went to bed for a few hours but you told me to go on ahead and go to the lake with the others? I did because I felt good about you saying you'd marry me and I didn't want to go to sleep yet." He kneaded his hands together.

"Lottie was there and she had on one of them skimpy tops and her tits was so big I thought they would split the seams and I watched her play volleyball and they bounced up and down— Well, the moonlight was so bright it was like a new penny, the old ones that was all copper, remember? And I thought, well, I can do anything and so I asked her and by God she did it and I haven't never even so much as checked a book out since. Alyce Ann, didn't you wonder why I wouldn't go look in the encyclopedias when I took a notion to build that airplane in '57? I didn't want to put myself in temptation's way."

Alyce Ann linked her dusty fingers with Harold's.

"I'm glad you told me, Harold. I've always appreciated how honest you are."

"I kissed another girl once or twice in the storeroom when I first started at the store, but there never has been anyone else like Lottie, swear to God, Alyce Ann."

He fell silent.

Alyce Ann watched the patterns the stars made with the moon. She never had been able to find all those creatures Lottie had lectured about once to the Coterie Club—the creatures that told you who you were supposed to love and whether or not you would be a good actress or secretary or doctor. Alyce Ann saw trees sometimes, or birds, or flowers. She wondered if when you were up there among them, they looked the same, or did you lose the pattern.

"Well, you ready to go inside?"

"Yes, Harold," she said. "I'm ready to go."

When Alyce Ann died three weeks later, Doc was with her.

Harold had gone to the city to pick up six gross of roofing nails, eight gallons of paint, and five squares of shingles for Clarence Hodspepper because there was a trucker's strike and Clarence told Harold he couldn't wait any longer to finish the roof on the feedstore addition, and he might have to do business with young Johnny Mason at the new discount hardware store out on the highway.

"You sure you'll be all right while I'm gone? I can ask Mabel to come in and stay with you."

"No," Alyce Ann said. Mabel had come a week ago and insisted on rubbing her dry skin with oil, then dressing her and combing her hair and putting on makeup. It had tired Alyce Ann, and when she looked at herself in her hand mirror while Mabel had her back turned trying to find a barrett in the top drawer, she thought she looked like a clown with her dark-circled eyes and too-red lips.

"Why is Clarence in such a rush to finish the addition?" Alyce Ann had asked Harold.

"He's hoping he can get Emmaline interested in starting up a little shop and teaching things. Churning butter, he told me, and tatting and stomping sauerkraut."

"Give Emmaline a discount, will you, Harold?"

That afternoon Doc stopped by as he had every afternoon for a week.

"My skin's getting these little blisters and I can't find a comfortable spot," Alyce Ann told him. "And sometimes I hurt so much I can't breathe. Lucky it happens when Harold's at the store because it would scare him. I just sit real quiet until it gets better. But what you've been giving me works quicker."

"Let me give you some now," Doc said.

"It makes me feel almost like I can fly and that's the truth, Maurice," Alyce Ann said, shoving up the sleeve of her robe.

He gave her the shot, then let his hand rest on her arm while he watched her with concern.

"Lottie was here the other night talking about truth," Alyce Ann murmured as the drug coursed through her veins, making her arms and her legs feel leaden.

"We each keep the truth that comforts us," Doc said.

"What the hell does that mean to a dying old woman?"

"It means I wish you'd been my wife," Doc said.

"I never told Harold," Alyce Ann said.

"Hardest thing I ever did in my life was take my dead child out of you," Doc said, putting his syringe into his black bag.

Alyce Ann tried to answer, but her tongue felt thick and her mouth was as dry as the beans she had quit looking at through her window. She sucked at the ice water Doc had brought her and thought about hummingbirds drinking.

"I wanted her to live, because of you and me," Alyce Ann said through cracked lips. "But I was glad she didn't because she would have been a constant reminder."

"How did you know she was mine?" Doc asked.

"Her birthmark. Not like Harold or me. You had one."

Alyce Ann took another sip of water.

"Why didn't you write to me when you knew you were pregnant?"

"Afraid to. Afraid you wouldn't believe me, or would think I'd done it on purpose to take you away from Lottie."

"Lottie and I were friends. That's all we ever were. I wouldn't have believed ill of you, Alyce Ann. Couldn't have believed ill of you. What I *did* find hard to believe was you marrying Harold."

"He needed me. I thought he would make a good father."

"Did you love him?"

"I learned to."

"You are an elegant woman, Alyce Ann. The truth is, I would have been proud to be your husband."

"Found out I was pregnant a week before the wedding . . . couldn't hurt Harold. So I lied. And he and I loved on each other once in the back seat of his car, if he ever got to figuring the time. When did you know Bonnie wasn't Harold's?"

"It was the first thing I thought of when I returned and saw you pregnant after my injury. And then you avoided me except for when she was born. When I pulled her out of you and saw the birthmark, I knew."

"Have you hated me all these years?"

Doc kissed Alyce Ann's hand.

"If you'd married me, you wouldn't have chapped hands and dirty nails."

"I couldn't have made it without the garden." Alyce Ann sighed. "You know what I hate most about that bonnie little girl being born dead? I didn't have a chance to tell her who she was."

Doc looked away.

"Cry with me," Alyce Ann said.

"What?"

"Lottie didn't cry with me. Neither has Harold."

Doc bolted into the bathroom and returned with a box of tissues. With moist eyes he sat on the edge of the bed and stuffed a wad of tissues into Alyce Ann's hand. "Shall we start?"

Alyce Ann dropped the tissues and took Doc's hand. She twined her fingers in his and thought about Bonnie. She thought about Harold. And she thought about Doc.

What she really felt like was smiling. So she did.

"I thought we were crying," Doc said, blowing his nose.

"I was wrong, Maurice. There's nothing to cry over."

Doc hugged Alyce Ann. "Maybe you were thinking you had to get something off your chest."

Alyce Ann's ribs hurt. "The only thing I want to get off my chest is this weight."

She sank back onto the pillows.

"Hasn't that medicine begun to work yet?" Doc managed a grin. "Aren't you ready to fly?"

"I'm ready to sleep, like when I used to spend the afternoon working in the garden in the sun."

Alyce Ann shut her eyes and leaned into the downy pillows. The feathers felt soft and strong. She picked up a handful and threw them into the air above her head, then watched them swirl into wings which attached themselves to her shoulders.

Alyce Ann flew. She reached for the satin sash, to tighten her robe around her. It wasn't there. In its place was a thin silver cord that seemed to be bound by something. Alyce Ann tugged on it. It came loose and she fastened the cord around herself. Suddenly she could breathe better.

She didn't need to breathe at all. The sun's bright light was all around her. She didn't feel sleepy. In fact, Alyce Ann felt better than she had for months.

From beyond the light, Alyce Ann heard a child say, "Mother will be here in just a minute. We're going to water the beans."

Alyce Ann flew toward the flute-like sounds of the child's voice.

This One's for Linda Joy

BOBBIE LOUISE HAWKINS

 It was on Good Friday just after five in the afternoon when the phone rang.

I was living in my barn then, in the ragtag of leavings from my whole life that had come crashing down around me. Everything was musty and damp and cold. Northern California. I started every morning by making a wood fire in the stove.

But the latest rainy season had passed. Spring was here. The days were getting longer. Things were in the yearly turnaround that blesses humankind.

And the telephone rang.

"Hello?"

"Hello, Molly?"

"Yes."

"This is Linda Joy!"

"Linda Joy who?"

"Your *cousin* Linda Joy! How many Linda Joys do you know?"

It was true I didn't know that many.

"Where are you?"

"I'm here. I'm in San Francisco. That is, *we're* here. I'm traveling with a *male* companion."

She said it in a teasing tone that left it to me to make something of it if I was going to. She knew I wasn't going to ring any Texas Baptist bells in on her. Not with my history and inclinations.

"That's the best kind," I said, and then, "Are you staying in a hotel?"

"We just came for the weekend so we started out in a hotel but by the time we'd been here that long we knew we wanted to stay so I've rented an apartment."

"You have an apartment in San Francisco?"

"I do."

Linda Joy was forty-four years old. She'd lived her whole life on the flat Texas plains within an hour of Lubbock. So far as I knew this was the first time she'd ever got as far as California.

It stood to reason that she was traveling with somebody. The story of Linda Joy's life was that somebody else owned it.

First there had been her mother. Linda Joy's mother adored God and knew for a fact that God adored her back. She had God's ear even on things as trivial as whether Linda Joy was minding her manners. It must have been intimidating to know that any difference of opinion with her mother was going straight to heaven on the nightly prayer hotline.

When Linda Joy was sixteen she swapped her mother for her husband. She was sucked into it that both of those people loved her and wanted the best for her. They both doted on her, at length and remorselessly. Her payoff for sitting still and being the object of their affection was that she got to be "spoiled." Her daddy had a few square miles in irrigated cotton and her husband had a few square miles in irrigated cotton plus a few herds of Black Angus cattle, so being spoiled meant Linda Joy had just about anything she wanted if it could be bought.

It looked like her life would be spent in an uncomplicated and pro-vided-for fashion, but she started having what got called *nervous break-downs*. Cars and clothes and appliances and a new brick house with air conditioning were apparently not answering all her needs. Every so often she'd try to kill herself and be hospitalized, then she'd come out looking fragile and her mother would fuss over her and her husband would fuss over her and her psychiatrist would double her appointments. One of the gauges for her being "cured" was that she would regain her natural opti-mism. The people taking all that care of her would relax back while there she'd be, in the same place.

People who have "everything" usually ask for more.

"Every time I saw you when we were growing up you were walking around with a book in one hand and an apple in the other looking for a place to sit," she accused me once. And she said, "Jack and I have joined a reading club. Every month we all read a good book and then we get to-gether and talk about it. I told Mama, 'Now I know what Molly was up to all those years.'"

"That sounds worthwhile," I said.

"You always had the advantages," she said wistfully.

"I don't see where you figure that," I said.

I don't want to go into my childhood at any length, but in a nutshell my father was brutal and a woman chaser, and there was never enough money. Shoes and doctors and winter coats were a large problem. We moved from one town to another every four or five months. Whenever we went into a new place my mother would wipe down the mattresses, getting into all the crevices with turpentine or kerosene. Whole nations of bedbugs snugged in and waiting for their next meal were dispatched by my mama's righteous hand. When my father was home there would be more money, paid for by fear and violent scenes, things crashing and broken, a lot of noise.

Linda Joy, on the other hand, went shopping with her mother every late summer for the coming year's school clothes: five new dresses so she wouldn't be shamed by having to wear the same dress twice in the same week, plus skirts and sweaters, school shoes and dress shoes, school coat and dress coat. And when she was in high school she had her own car.

I envied her. It looked like heaven to me to live all your life in the same house with your own bedroom and with ruffles around the bedspread.

All I really had to call my own was that book and that apple.

"I know you never had much money but you had the *worthwhile* things. You had *books* and *Art*," Linda Joy said, and smiled.

In addition to her book club she was learning how to paint in some women's group. She was convinced that we'd agree on the value of Art.

"Damn, I hate Texas," I snapped back at her. And of course it hurt her feelings. How could anybody hate Texas?

I wasn't talking about Texas at all. I was reacting to the squirm I felt around my kinfolks when I was invited to appreciate their latest sortie into *Art*. I loved my people but I hated that squirmy feeling.

When I hit puberty, me and my folks went at such tangents that they never again took me as normal. Whenever I'd visit they'd haul out their Art as a kindness, like talking to an Eskimo about ice.

Take the last time I visited my cousin Lonny and he showed me a rooster in profile, made by gluing different kinds of beans onto a ma-sonite board. He pointed it out to me that it made a difference whether the beans were glued down flat or whether they were turned on their edges.

I just went along, a compliant hypocrite, discussing bean technique like I was protecting him from some horrible further knowledge, resent-ing it all the while that at my approach those damned products of the paint-by-number kits came out.

I couldn't help noticing that the rooster looked a little mangey. There was a soft fuzz around some of the edges. Some kind of mealybug had seen those beans for what they were and the rooster was being eaten away.

"So when I made one for Mama at Christmastime I varnished it. Nothing's got into that one," Lonny said.

There we stood, them feeling happy and sure of themselves and me being the one who was out of place, telling Lonny and his wife and his mother that it was wonderful, that rooster, and what a shame the worms had got into it, and what a good thing he'd known enough to varnish the next one that I hadn't seen yet but would see at my Aunt Eubie's house.

However many books Linda Joy read, however many canvases she covered with copies of landscapes she would never see and Indians she had never seen, her nervous breakdowns kept pace. And she kept on thinking that having just about anything she wanted when she was sane enough to ask for it meant she was leading a good life. She took her breakdowns to be occasional interruptions in the best of all possible worlds, like having the hiccups.

Her psychiatrist told her when she was in her mid-twenties that she "suffered from pre-menopausal depression."

"If you had been in your teens he would probably have said your depressions were *pre*-pre-menopausal," I said.

I hated it that she took everything he said as gospel truth, but she never had been encouraged to question bosses.

"Billie Sue *likes* Jack," she told me, a twitch of disgust at the corners of her nose.

"Well, I should hope so," I said. "He *is* her daddy."

"No, I mean she *likes* him, like she's a woman and he's a man."

"Is that more of that psychiatrist you're going to?"

Bille Sue was about ten years old. I hated to think of the damage that fool of a "professional" was doing.

While Linda Joy's history kept repeating itself, her life, as lives will do, went right on ahead, with or without her.

Her kids grew up.

Her husband fell in love with his secretary.

There was a divorce.

Linda Joy moved into a condominium in Lubbock.

And now here she was, having just made the first long-distance call she had ever made in her life without putting it through the operator. Of course she gave Blue, her "male companion," the credit. He had told her how to dial me direct and she had done it.

"Well, where *is* your apartment?"

"It's right downtown. I'm right downtown." She named a street that I've forgotten now and added, "I'm on the eighth floor."

"When do you think we're going to get to see something of each other?" I asked her, and she started telling me about her bank.

Her bank was supposed to stay open late on Fridays, and that afternoon she had taken a little nap.

" . . . and I had plenty of time, according to when they *said* they'd stay open until, but when I got there they were closed."

"So you're calling me because it's Good Friday and the bank's closed and you're out of money and you can't cash a check until next Monday?"

"I got there in *plenty* of time according to what they said their hours were."

"I guess I owe it to the bank that I got to hear from you."

"I was going to call you this week."

"Okay, I'll tell you what. I'll drive in tomorrow morning and pick y'all up and bring you out here for the day . . . that is, if you'd like to come?"

"We'd like that."

"Do you have money to eat on tonight?"

"Oh Lord yes. I'm not completely helpless."

"Then I'll come in and pick y'all up in the morning. You can spend the night here if you want to and go back into the city on the bus Sunday. We can get a check cashed for you at the grocery store." I added, "It's going to be good to see you, honey," and I meant it.

"Me too. I'm looking forward to it."

I hung up the phone and no time at all went by before I thought that if Linda Joy was living here she was going to find out that I was a writer. And if she found out, everybody in Texas would get to know about it. Everybody meaning all the relatives I'd managed to keep it secret from.

The first book I ever wrote was about my relatives in Texas. I wrote down some of the stories I had heard all my life, from when I was little and the stories were being told after supper by the light from a coal oil lamp in the middle of the cleared-away table, through later on when I was big and the light was electric. The technology changed but the stories stayed the same. When I wrote them down they went onto the paper word for word, like automatic writing.

Then I started to worry about whether I had got it right, whether I had turned their talk into some kind of half-baked dialect. I didn't want them to sound like Hollywood hillbillies because they weren't.

So when I took a trip back to Texas with my mother I took along a small tape recorder in my purse. My reasoning was that whenever I meant to write on the book I could listen to the tape first, listen to their real voices and get the right tone and tempo into my head.

Once the tape recorder was there, there were all the new stories as well, a bonus, like my cousin Lonny talking about how worshipping the devil could give you the ability to turn newspaper into dollar bills.

All along, my notion of those stories was that later on I could improve on them. It was a lesson in humility to learn that they were better left alone.

I finished that book and somebody decently undertook to publish it. As the publication date drew near I started stewing about what I had wrought. I started waking up out of nightmares at three in the morning.

I'd lie in that damned damp bed in that damned cold barn and stare into the dark and think about how much my relatives were going to hate finding themselves in this book and how much they were going to hate reading what the others had said about them. In the course of driving around and visiting, it had naturally happened that people talked about whoever wasn't there. And there I had been, a natural fool with a tape recorder.

I could go on at length about why I felt guilty but instead I'll just tell you some of my late-night justifications.

Everybody in the family had already heard those stories dozens of times, that's where I had got them.

Nobody was being made public to their friends and neighbors because I had changed their names and I had changed the names of the nearby towns and even the counties. I had left the state as Texas but I couldn't think of that as a giveaway.

It still wasn't enough. I decided that I just had to keep the book a secret from my kinfolks unless I wanted my relations with them to get even more complicated.

Then I decided I had to tell my mother. I owed it to her for her years of believing I'd accomplish something someday. I called her on the phone and said that in about a week I had a book coming out and it was all about all of us.

She said, "Oh Molly, everybody's going to be so pleased."

I said, "Well, that's what I wanted to talk to you about. I think it'll be better if they don't know about it."

"Why not, honey?"

"I tell about stuff like when Uncle Odie was in the vets' hospital and Evelyn took his money and spent it."

And my mother said, "Oh."

The book came out, time passed, it looked like I had got away with it. And here, with one telephone conversation as its messenger, came Discovery.

The next morning I got into my beat-up old VW and drove in to the City.

Glorious sunshine was making a showpiece of one of the world's truly beautiful ocean coastlines. The bright sails that proliferate in good weather filled the bay as I crossed the Golden Gate Bridge.

Once, when friends of mine were halfway across that bridge, they saw two men in evening dress seated on either side of a folding table covered with a white cloth and set with candles, a wine bottle in a silver cooler, and wine glasses; two men having an elegant glass of wine, toasting the San Francisco skyline.

The address Linda Joy had given me was right downtown.

Every car parked in the vicinity was about fifty feet long. I didn't have any trouble parking right in front of the building. I just fitted into what they all thought was throwaway.

The building came fully equipped: a striped awning out to the curb; a doorman dressed like a foreign general; an elderly woman in a short mink cape looking like all she ever did was sit in the lobby waiting for the limo to be brought around.

A soundless elevator with wall-to-wall carpet carried me up so smoothly that when the doors opened at the eighth floor I thought I hadn't started yet.

I had called before I left to ask Linda Joy to be ready because I didn't know whether I might have to double-park. She opened the door and we gave each other a big hug. She introduced me to Blue, very blonde and good-looking. He was almost twenty-two. They'd met when he sold her a pair of shoes. I'll bet it was in a high-flash store. Whatever else he might be, Blue was not tacky.

We took one quick turn around the apartment and we were set to leave.

To come out to stay with me for one night Linda Joy and Blue were carrying a packed medium-size Samsonite suitcase, a garment bag with half a dozen hangers showing, an overnight bag, and a large cosmetics case.

On the way down in the elevator I told Linda Joy, "Honey, you're in for a culture shock."

I've never felt at home in California. It is too beautiful; the senses grow calloused in self-protection.

One evening I was sitting on a wooden bench at sunset watching the colors change and the pelicans fly in long lines from the right to the left, toward the lagoon. Below me the waves foamed in soft rhythms on the sand, and I thought, "That's why Californians get so laid back. They're perpetually besieged by the landscape."

But on that trip across the bridge, through Sausalito, over Mount Tamalpais, I felt like a proud parent whose child was being both beautiful and well-behaved.

I have, after all, lived here more of my adult life than I've lived anywhere else. Perhaps there will be a time when the air comes to my nose with the sweet smell of home.

We arrived at my barn, the poor half-derelict building I sometimes think of as my Irish solution.

It had two rooms, the main room large, maybe thirty feet by forty feet, with beams across at high-ceiling level and a pitched roof above. Wooden shingles showed between the rafters, and of course the roof leaked. The second room, long and narrow, where the milking stalls had been, ran the length of the back wall and farther. There was also a shed room I had turned into a sauna with a tin wood stove, and a bathroom with a toilet raised over a fifty-gallon drum which was regularly emptied by the local septic tank man.

I've never been overjoyed by the distance between me and the American Way of Life. I don't take delight in being hardy, as if it proves other values. It's just that when I cut the coat to fit the cloth it didn't include a flush toilet.

When we had brought all the luggage into the main room Linda Joy smiled at me and said, "Well, Molly, do you mind if I have a look around your house?"

I had forgotten that.

Among my kinfolks whenever you visit somebody the first time the convention is that you get shown around. You stand in the kitchen while you're told, "This is the kitchen." You stand in the bathroom doorway and get told it's the bathroom. And on and on.

And you're expected to be complimentary and interested as you go.

"What a nice idea to make every bedroom a different color."

"I just love it that your boys' rooms are so rugged and your girls' rooms are so feminine."

"Wherever did you find all those little animals made out of glass?"

Linda Joy was undertaking to do her part in carrying on that tradition. It was an act of courage, there wasn't a glass animal in miles.

I didn't intend to walk her through my three rooms so I just said, "Honey, help yourself."

She wasn't gone long.

Now it was up to her to say something complimentary. You have to know that I would never have put her on such a hook.

She said, "Mama always did admire your lack of love for material possessions."

"I don't know how in the world we're going to make do unless Jack gives me more money," Linda Joy said. "He took three of the farms and I took three of the farms. And I get half of the co-op cotton gin money. But I never had any idea that San Francisco would cost so much."

"Linda Joy, you don't *have* to hire a limo to go out to dinner. You can call a taxi and the driver'll buzz your apartment when he gets there, and when you're finishing your dinner you can have the waiter call another one to take you home."

She took a cigarette out of the pack, tapped it on the table, put it in her mouth and sucked in. By the time she was sucking, a gold lighter was in Blue's hand and he had a flame at the tip. It was all casual, effortless, gracefully choreographed. Who did I think I was anyway, offering advice to a duo capable of that kind of style?

"It just makes me feel so secure, knowing he's out there waiting," she drawled.

Linda Joy was smoking the longest cigarettes I'd ever seen. What she stubbed out and left as butts were longer than most people start with. Their length made them a natural menace. They would rest at an angle in the ashtray, accumulating ash and getting top-heavy. When enough of the tip had burned away, the cigarette would demonstrate some commonplace theorem of physics by tilting out of the dish and onto the table.

"And they're going to sue me over my lease in Lubbock. I just told Jack to take care of it. *Somebody* has to get all my furniture out of my apartment there and send it to me here. And I told Jack I have to have my car."

"How does Jack's new wife feel about him dealing with your problems?"

"She doesn't have anything to complain about. She's already got my house!"

"He's going to send you your car?"

"He said it should be here by next Thursday. It's a powder blue Cadillac. I got it when I went to Lubbock to live. I turned that maroon Oldsmobile in on it. After I get my car we can drive out here whenever we want to. I just *love* this little town." She gave me a big smile and took another cigarette out of the pack.

"We made out our wills so that if I die Jack gets my three farms, and if he dies I get his three farms. Now if I had *all* the farms we'd be just fine for money."

"Don't hold your breath waiting, honey. Ex-husbands don't die. They thrive."

That night the three of us went downtown to have a few beers and listen to some music.

Linda Joy's style, her wig and full-face makeup complete with artificial eyelashes, her "casual" garb from Neiman-Marcus, and Blue's natural elegance and ready cigarette lighter made them instantly interesting. They drawled their way through conversations telling everybody everything. They were charming. People I'd never had any particular reason to talk to would come over to me with their faces glowing. "I've just been talking to your *cousins!*"

"Well, you wouldn't think at *his* age that he has a *plastic* anus." Linda Joy bobbed her head in Blue's direction. The person she was talking to agreed that it hadn't occurred to them.

"That boy has had a very hard life," Linda Joy said sadly.

It seemed to be the case. He had the same history of nervous breakdowns that Linda Joy had, half as many but then he was half as old.

"We go to bed at night with half a cup of pills and we wake up in the morning with half a cup of pills."

Also, Blue's sexual inclinations had been a problem to him while he lived his life ass-deep in cotton fields.

"Oh yes," Linda Joy said. "It isn't just the *girls* I have to worry about with Blue, with Blue I have to worry about the *boys* too!"

Whatever their age and sex differences they were more like each other than they were like anybody else in the room.

Linda Joy would come over to tell me about somebody she had just been talking to. "That's one weird old boy," she'd say and shake her head.

It never occurred to her that she and Blue qualified as rare. She did notice that she might be a little overdressed.

"I can see that I'm going to have to have a whole new wardrobe that's just for when I'm in California."

I still had the problem of the book I'd written on my mind and it was proving true.

I'd introduce Linda Joy to somebody: "This is my cousin Linda Joy."
Their eyes would light up.
They'd say, "Oh! Really?"
She was bound to notice.

I had a letter from my mother: "Linda Joy has told Myrtle you wrote that book and she really wants to read it. If she gets a copy then Alma will want to borrow it and she'll get her feelings hurt when she reads that part about Evelyn taking Odie's money and spending it. So if you give Linda Joy a copy to send to Myrtle take that part out."

I come from a family of Irish-Cherokee-Fundamentalist-Baptists. They believe in miracles.

Linda Joy's Cadillac was drastically electric. If you had the bad luck to be in the damned thing with the doors and windows closed when the battery went flat you could die there.

Linda Joy and Blue liked to park downtown, walk away from the car and have somebody tell them they had left their lights on. The car had a timer that let it turn its own lights off. That car resisted visiting my town. It wouldn't turn off its lights the way it was supposed to. They'd come back and find a dead battery. By that time the garage would be closed. Then they wouldn't be able to open the trunk because it only opened electrically. They'd spend the night at my place in borrowed pajamas.

By the time they decided to get married they had made a lot of friends. We were in the bar and they told somebody and the word got around quickly. Everybody, however much they liked Blue, figured it was him marrying Linda Joy for her money. He strolled around the bar with a glass of wine in his hand, chatting and smiling, while Linda Joy sat at a small table enjoying the attention, and one by one the various friends they had made tried to dissuade them. Blue would just say, "Linda Joy wants it and I want to make her happy."

Linda Joy asked me if I would go with them to the Civic Center north of San Rafael and be their witness.

"I'd like to have somebody there that I'm related to," she said.

"Linda Joy, I'd be proud to be there, if you're sure that's what you want."

It was a busy day at the Civic Center. The nearest parking places were all filled. I was early, to be on time. I stood next to my car so they'd be sure to see me. Blue stopped the Cadillac long enough to let Linda Joy out and went on, looking for a parking place.

"Are you sure you want to do this, honey?"

Linda Joy was sitting sideways on the front seat in my car, her legs poking out through the door, high heels pressing into the warm tartop. She leaned forward, looking at me. "I'll tell you one thing, Molly. I never want to be alone again."

Theme songs from the past, catchphrases: *Who was that masked man* who stayed for his fixed hour of allotted time, climbed on his horse, rode away, a fading "Hi-yo, Silver . . ."

Hi-yo?

I've never in my life met a man who meant to stay.

I watched Blue come walking toward us, dropping the car keys into the pocket of his jacket.

It's all too bitter, the taste in our mouths, what passes for solutions.

The county clerk didn't approve. He wasn't sure what was going on but he didn't like it.

Well, I didn't know that I approved either but I knew I took sides if he was on one of them. I was the relative, the solid citizen, member of the wedding, and I snubbed him as firmly as I was able.

After the ceremony the three of us went to a restaurant in San Rafael for a wedding lunch.

Linda Joy rented a house for them and her furniture on the hill over Sausalito.

"I've always wanted to live in the mountains. And I just *love* that little village!"

She paid the whole year's rent in advance.

"Linda Joy, with that much money you could have made a *down-payment* on the place. Then if you decided later you wanted to leave it you'd probably make money on it."

"Molly," she said, "you just make my head hurt."

I make my own head hurt, as often as not. All I was doing anyway was what I had always done, acting like *practical* mattered, and Linda Joy was doing what she had always done, what she wanted to.

There was another phone call, late at night, in November. The rains had started up again. I was sick and coughing. My car was on the blink.

And the telephone rang.

"Molly, could you come over here and stay with me?"

"What's the matter, Linda Joy?"

"I've thrown all of Blue's clothes on the floor and when he gets home I'm afraid he's going to kill me."

"Where is he?"

"I don't know. He stole my car two days ago and drove off with one of his friends. *I've* got the keys. I guess he went into the dash panel and hot-wired it. I didn't know he knew that much about cars. And these Cadillacs are supposed to be thief-proof."

"Doesn't he have his own keys?"

"No. There *is* an extra set but I've got them too."

"He probably had some made."

"How could he do that?"

"Didn't he ever take the car out on his own?"

"Oh yes, he did that."

"Then he stopped somewhere and had some keys made."

"I don't think he'd think of doing something like that."

"So he's on his way home now?"

"I don't know. He hasn't telephoned or anything."

"You mean you want me to stay with you for as long as it takes for Blue to decide to come home?"

"He's really going to be mad."

"I don't want to do that."

"I was *afraid* that was what you'd say."

"It'll cost about fifteen dollars for a taxi to bring you here, Linda Joy. You leave a note and say you're here and for him to telephone when he comes home."

"I want to wait here for him because I want to get my car back. When I hear him drive in I mean to get ready and when he goes into his room I'm going to run downstairs and get in the car and drive it off."

"You think that's a good idea?"

"Well, I'm just torn between my car and my furniture. I know that if I drive off he'll tear up my furniture.

"I've called Jack and he's going to come and get me and my car and drive me back to Lubbock. But he can't get here for two days. Blue's afraid of Jack."

"Linda Joy, how worried *are* you about him being violent? Do you *really* think your life's in danger?"

"I just know that he's going to hate it that his clothes are on the floor."

"It sounds to me like the first thing you'd better do is pick up Blue's clothes and hang them back in the closet."

"That *would* give me something to do."

"Then tomorrow call a mover and tell him to come get your stuff. That way when Blue does get back all you'll have to think about is yourself and your car."

"Well, that does make more sense than just waiting for him to come home and have a fit about his clothes."

"Now, Linda Joy, I want you to think about how safe you are there. If you're not safe you get a taxi and come here."

"If I hang his clothes back up he won't have anything to be mad about."

My Aunt Myrtle called me when she learned about Jack's plans to come get Linda Joy and drive her back to Texas. She was worried that the night they would have to spend on the road Jack would try to "take advantage" of Linda Joy. I proved my immorality once again by saying that if Linda Joy was afraid for her life what mattered was getting her to somewhere safe. I think Aunt Myrtle had hoped that I might go along to act as chaperone for the ride.

The next day Linda Joy and Jack dropped in for a quick visit. We didn't talk about Blue or about Jack's new wife. They left the next morning. I'm sure that the night they were on the road wasn't spent in separate beds.

I get depressed at the approach of Christmas. Me and all the world, it seems. On the television and in the newspaper there are all the stories about desperate people, the mental wards fill up. The world is at its darkest.

In my barn, in the dark, the rats were back. That meant I'd have to go to the hardware store and get poison. The stuff is effective. Putting it down meant that the smell of rats rotting under the floorboards would be around for a while.

I had been writing in my bed and crumpling the papers that were to be thrown away so I wouldn't waste time by checking them out again. A pile of crumpled paper lay on the floor next to my bed. I was wakened by the rustling. Something in the papers. I turned the lamp on and looked square into the face of a piebald rat, its eyes flamed red with reflected light. We froze, looking at each other.

This was the first time I'd ever actually seen one of the things. I hadn't known rats were that big and I had assumed they'd be brown like mice. This thing looked more like a vicious mutant guinea pig. I made a move and with a fast scuttle it was gone.

Now I was fully awake. I had things to worry about, now I could worry.

I worried about money.
Then I worried about all the things I'd done wrong with my life.
I worried about love, my lack of it.
And health, my lungs and sinuses, cancer.
My car, rusting in the rain.
It was about 3:30 A.M. I had plenty of time to worry about everything.
And in the dark cold room the telephone rang.

I'll never know why Blue called me at that time of night to tell me Linda Joy was dead.

It might have been that I was the only one who would treat him like he'd lost a wife. I had been the only family at the wedding.

None of that explains the time of night he called. Anyone who sleeps badly knows the paranoia that settles onto whatever wakes you up. It often feels like malicious intent: he meant to wake me up and he meant to give me bad news.

Linda Joy had tried to kill herself with sleeping pills. Again. They had never worked before. Maybe that was what had been proven, that she could suicide herself over and over again with sleeping pills and always live to tell the tale.

But this time in the hospital she got pneumonia. And she died.

I thanked Blue for letting me know. I told him I hoped he was all right.

I got out of bed and added a wool sweater to my night clothes, put a bathrobe on top of it all. I took off my houseshoes and put on wool socks, then put the houseshoes on again.

I started a fire with the crumpled paper the rat had been walking around in, some kindling, some slightly larger pieces of wood.

I put the kettle on.

I was up.

In the morning I telephoned my mother. Then I telephoned my Aunt Myrtle.

"Hello?"
"Aunt Myrtle?"
"Yes."
"This is Molly."
"Nora's Molly?"
"Yes, it's Nora's Molly."
"Where are you?"
"I'm in San Francisco."

"Oh, are you? Did you hear about Linda Joy?"

"I heard about Linda Joy. I'm calling to tell you how sorry I am."

"Well honey, she's better off. She's at rest now. Her life was so tore up."

"Would you rather not talk about it?"

"I can tell you. She took some pills, you know. And they took her to the hospital. She was unconscious. And she come through and seemed to be doing good. We thought she was going to be all right. Then she took pneumonia and her lungs just give way so she passed away. But she called for prayer before she died and they had prayer with her and the chaplain said he felt like Linda Joy made her peace with God. So that gave me a great comfort."

"That's good, Aunt Myrtle."

"Yes, it really is. How are you? How have you been?"

"Well, I've been sick. And I always tend to get depressed at Christmastime."

"You know when Henry passed away . . . he was buried eleven years ago today . . . he was buried on Christmas Eve day. Christmas sure don't mean anything to me. Nobody's doing anything about Christmas this year. But Linda Joy did have such a nice funeral and everybody's been so sweet to me."

"Mama thought Linda Joy and Jack were getting back together."

"Naw, they weren't. He separated from that woman but then he went back with her. I think that's what caused Linda Joy to do what she did. She was tore up over him. If she had lived I think she'd just have tried to kill herself again."

"Well, I just hope this is not too hard on you."

"It's not. I'm relieved that Linda Joy's at peace. But I miss her. I have some of her paintings and that's something of her for me to keep. That's as much as I need of her. Blue's mama was at the funeral. And he sent some flowers. Poor little thing, he's all mixed up."

If I didn't laugh I'd cry gets said in every language everywhere.

Most of the stories I write are as funny as I can make them. Partway through, this story stops being funny.

For a long time I'd tell people the first part of this story. It was like I could overlook what came later, and like Linda Joy was still alive. But sometimes whoever was pleased and laughing about it would ask, "Where's Linda Joy now?" And I would feel obligated to tell the truth. "She killed herself." It would be like the words had killed her then and there.

After a while I decided I didn't have to answer just because somebody asked the question. From then on I'd just say, "She's in Texas," and let it go at that. Finally I stopped telling the story in any form.

But the story hovered.

So here it is. For Linda Joy.

Someday My Prince

HERMINE PINSON

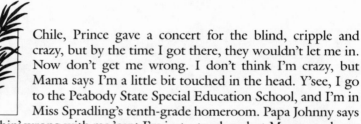

Chile, Prince gave a concert for the blind, cripple and crazy, but by the time I got there, they wouldn't let me in. Now don't get me wrong. I don't think I'm crazy, but Mama says I'm a little bit touched in the head. Y'see, I go to the Peabody State Special Education School, and I'm in Miss Spradling's tenth-grade homeroom. Papa Johnny says ain't nothin' wrong with me 'cept I'm just a tomboy, but Mama sends me to day school anyway, cuz she says I like to fight too much and she can't afford to keep buyin' me new clothes every time I tear 'em up rollin' round in the dirt with some hardhead who happens to call me a bitch or just talk about my mama real funky. Anyway, when Miss Spradling announced that Prince was showin' for free at the Music Hall for all special education kids, I almost swallowed my bubble gum. Chile, I started gettin' ready that day. I got some money from Papa Johnny to buy a dress. He so sweet, part Choctaw Mama says. Gave me twenty-five dollars, so you know that meant Lerner's for sure. I found a dress at the one downtown. That's where I catch the bus every day on the way home. Plain purple dress with a high collar and a black patent leather belt. Me and Mama bought some sequins at Sears Sewing Center and put 'em all over everywhere. Looked like stardust dropped on my dress when we got through.

On the day of the concert I missed the school bus that was supposed to take all of us over to the Music Hall, cuz I had missed Mr. Johnston's third-period class so I could go home and put on my dress. But I had to do it that way cuz I didn't want to wear my dress to school and get put out for bein' indecent before I even got to the concert. So I had to skip on over to Metro and let them get me there in their own sweet time. You know I was outdone, but then what could I do? And by the time I got there, they'd closed and locked all the doors tighter than Dick's hatband. I didn't see anybody from Miss Spradling's class. I pressed my lips to the smeary glass doors with all the others. I screamed and cursed, clawed, slobbered and cried for that Creole-lookin' boy until the blood had risen to my eyes, but nobody would let me in.

Then it came to me all of a sudden. There was a way to get in, but I had to give a little to get a lot. That is, I had to give a little lovin' to Meatloaf, the security guard. Me and Meat go way back, as far back as Fourth Ward, when my family lived next door to his on Robin Street. Meatloaf busted my cherry right under the stairwell when I was fourteen and just gettin' full o' myself. We even went together for a hot minute. They usta call me Sweets, short for Sweetmeat. But I didn't see Meatloaf much after we moved to Sunnyside. See, Fourth Ward bloods and Sunnyside boys do not get along in no form or fashion. I was surprised to see Meatloaf had got himself a respectable job. He was workin' at Burger King when I was goin' with him. I could always make him do what I wanted. He ain't too bright, but he's sweet, and he'll do when ain't nothin' else happenin'. So I went into my act.

I cried salty tears and squinted my baby browns at Meatloaf, who was over in the corner tryin' to look cool. See, he was older than most of us— thirty-three, same age Jesus was when he died to save all kinds, Mama says. He saw me lookin' at him but he sorta shifted his johnson and frowned at me cuz he knew that I would be by his house when Prince was long gone, and he just couldn't see through his genuine Michael Jackson curl in the middle of his forehead why I was makin' sucha fool of myself over this here Creole-lookin' boy with the slender hips and the lustin' eyes. Meatloaf says, "If anything, he looks zactly like my cousin André, in Opelousas, and he a fag." But, chile, I didn't care. I only knew that my whole sixteen-year-old body ached when he sang, "I would die 4-U." There, through the doors, I spied his slivery shadow dartin' cross the stage, his lapels makin' smoke trails in the haze. I beat on the front doors, I stomped, I kicked the glass.

Meatloaf shifted on over to me like he saw Clint Eastwood do in *Dirty Harry.*

"Girl, what's wrong wich chu, huh? Act like you ain't never seen no rock freak before in yo' short sweetbrown life. Need to slide by my crib tonight after the concert and lemme show you what all the shakin' is about. Girl, don't chu remember how sweet my lovin' usta be? It's even better now, cuz I got my own place right off West Gray."

"Well, I just might do that, Meatloaf sugah. I know a little bit 'bout shakin' even at my tender age, and I'll show you my brand after the concert if you let me in now."

Meatloaf fingered his johnson some more and looked at me all over out the side of his eye. "Come on over here by this exit," I whispered, "and tell me 'bout what chu got to show me later on." I didn't want to blow my chance to see Prince on this fool, so I walked him over to the exit and gave him an absolutely seven-day kiss in all of fifty seconds plus or minus a few slow and low grinds and groans.

"Are you free after the concert?" I fairly crooned. "Okay, Meatloaf sugah. Later!" And I was gone like the wind.

I stumbled to a seat in the back. Oh, shit! It was his last song, "Purple Rain." I cried until my makeup was runnin' all into the collar of my purple sequined dress. It was him! It was really him, struttin', slidin', splittin' and glidin' all cross the stage, all those women and otherwise would-be women screamin' his name till the blood rushed to their eyes.

"Prince! Prince!" they cried. Chile, next thing I knew, I was steppin' to the front. I don't know how I got there, cuz my legs had already gone numb from stompin' so hard on the floor. I almost got knocked down when these two sisters got into a fight over who was gonna take home the plastic rose one of Prince's bodyguards threw into the audience. Chile, what they do that for? All hell broke loose, and here come the police!

While they were draggin' those two out, I saw my chance. I didn't run backstage. Naw, honey, I'm too slick for that. I kinda sorta eased back there when I noticed one of the bodyguards rubbin' his hands all over some groupie in a purple mohawk, can't say whether it was man or woman. I tipped, then slid, then tipped on in. And there I was, "standin' in the shadows of love," chile, "waitin' for the heartbreak to come," like Mama say. I was sweatin' so hard I had to take out a tissue and wipe all under my arms and 'tween my legs. Didn't want to smell like I'd been jumpin' up and down and screamin' and hollerin' all night even if I had been. They were down to the last chords, Prince on his knees now, throwin' a kiss to Melissa on the front row. She in my class, blind in her left eye and can't hardly see out the other, y'know. After all, it was somethin' wrong with everybody out there. That's why Prince was showin' in the first place, for all of us.

Chile, then he did an about-face, y'know, like in the army, and walked off stage. Sweet Jesus! My heart felt like it belonged to somebody else. I sucked in my gut for all the good it did and tripped over a coil of rope before I could get to my prince. I came up on him so sudden he didn't even have a chance to change his mind, much less duck out. Just before he drew back I touched his shirt and cried, "Prince, I love you, even if I am crazy. I'm in Miss Spradling's class, and I skipped third period just so I could go home and put on this purple sequined dress for you. Melissa and DuShaundra won't believe I saw you in person. Would you please sign your name on my dress? Just gimme somethin' to take back. Jesus!"

I couldn't see for the tears in my eyes, but seem like he took a step toward me, then thought about it and pulled back again like he was afraid of catchin' somethin'. He whispered somethin' to the guards, but all I could hear was "crazy child" and "back door." Whatever he said was enough for those guards to start movin' toward me. Can you imagine? Three husky men comin' at me like I was John Hinckley or somebody! Before I could put my hands up, that big one who'd been feelin' up the mohawk groupie shook me hard enough to knock my earrings off. Screamin' in my ear, "Bitch, you crazy? Don't you know who that is you're messin' with? Come on here before I handcuff you and take you to jail myself!" You could sure tell he was a local guard. They get so important when somebody bigtime comes to town.

Prince didn't even look at me until he got to the door of his dressin' room. Then he stared at me real strange, his eyes wide like he was dreamin'. He kissed his index finger and pointed at me and said, "God loves you and I do too." Then he snapped his fingers and one of the other bodyguards handed him a plastic purple rose. He threw the rose at me just like you throw peanuts to a monkey at the zoo, but I couldn't catch it, cuz I had two bodyguards on either side of me darin' me to breathe hard. One of 'em picked up the rose and stuck it in the bosom of my dress, which by this time was tore in three places. My jheri curl was hangin' all in my eyes, and by the time I put my hands to my face to push my hair back and say a proper thank you, he was gone. Closed the door behind him.

The bodyguards marched me right on out to the parkin' lot in the back of the auditorium, gave one hard push, and I was outside in the August night, sweatin' and sore. Seemed so quiet outside. I could hear crickets cryin'. Now was that any way to treat somebody, 'specially if you weren't quite sure if they was blind, cripple or just plain crazy like myself? I know people won't believe me when I tell 'em I know two Princes, the one on the record and the one backstage, but I swear it's true. I remember once Miss Spradling told us a story 'bout a frog who was a prince in disguise. She called that a fairy tale. Well, this wasn't a fairy tale. This was "Believe It or Not!" and everybody who watch that show knows "the truth is stranger than fiction." Amen, Mr. Palance, I hear ya, bro', cuz I was feelin' mighty strange right 'bout then.

Well, least Meatloaf didn't know nothin' 'bout this and I needed some comfortin', even if I couldn't get much in the way of decent conversation. Chile, I went home, washed my face, combed my jheri, and took off that smelly purple dress and put on my jeans and a sleeveless tee shirt that had Bob Marley's picture on it. That's the one Meatloaf had gave me in the first place. I don't know if he liked Marley or just liked to see me in a low-cut, sleeveless tee shirt. I told Mama, Prince pulled me from the audience and kissed me on the cheek. That's how my dress got tore. I couldn't tell her the truth. 'Sides, she wouldn't believe I let somebody tear my dress and didn't punch 'em out.

When I told her, she thought the tears in my eyes was cuz I was so proud. I didn't tell her no different. I asked to be excused to go gossip 'bout the concert with my girlfriends, and she let me go, cuz she understood 'bout those things. Didn't she catch some of Jackie Wilson's sweat when he showed at Booker T. Washington High School in 1962? I left her huntin' through that old cedar chest in her bedroom for the bottle she'd saved it in.

So I even got to Meatloaf's before he got back from the concert. If I'm lyin', I'm dyin' and if I'm dyin', I'm flyin', chile. Oh yeah, and I left that plastic rose in the ditch with the bullfrogs and the cryin' crickets.

The Pact

JAN EPTON SEALE

 Wayna Sue stood with her hand on the oldest tree in Whitall County. A plaque at the base of it said so. "Put your hand on top of mine," she said to Becca. "Then we'll both say the words."

Becca scanned the softball area. "I can't, silly. Mrs. Fulsom is looking."

"Then put your hand beside mine, like you're leaning against the tree. But hurry."

The 1952 Vacation Bible School picnic of the First Baptist Church was almost over and the fire truck would be there soon to take them back to the church. The two girls had chosen to be different this year. They had hardly participated in any activity. Mrs. Fulsom, their teacher, was probably wondering what was up. What was up was a pact between the girls to have their first periods at the same time.

When the twirpy little fourth grade girls had run over to get them on their team in the boys-against-the-girls softball game, Wayna Sue and Becca had said no. "Because we said so." They turned away with mysterious smiles and chose a long walk under the giant Texas elms. They needed to talk.

They were twelve. Last year their physical ed teacher had given them a book called *Confidently Yours*. Now they could quote whole passages from it. "Some girls, especially in other countries, begin their periods at ten or eleven." Well, they hadn't done *that* but Wayna Sue and Becca were taking no chances. You could be hit in the stomach with a ball, or mess up your clothes and not know it and all the boys would see and then you would rather just die than go back to school, and so forth.

Besides, it was fun making everybody wonder. But then maybe their hair didn't look oily enough. Nobody's mother would let them wash their hair during their period. Sometimes girls with their periods had dark circles under their eyes. They sat around with their arms folded over their cramping stomachs and made frequent trips to the bathroom, always with their purse. If they were Texas girls, they whispered to their best friend that they had "started." If they had moved from somewhere else, they said they had "got" their period. There were things to cultivate and be careful about.

This was Wayna Sue and Becca's last Vacation Bible School. Next year they would be too old. The girls had been friends since kindergarten. They saw each other every day of the week at school and on Sundays in Mrs. Fulsom's twelve-year-old-girls' class.

The Junior Department at Sunday School was beginning to get on their nerves. For one thing, the nine-year-olds were such nincompoops in opening assembly. Wayna Sue and Becca could hardly wait to be promoted in the fall to the Intermediates—"Inter-idiots"—Becca's father, who was the superintendent of the Sunday School, was fond of calling them.

Even this week in VBS, by Wednesday they had played every card of Bible Bingo and memorized all the required Bible verses on love. Thursday they buckled down and learned the four youth choruses they had to sing with the group on Sunday. Friday there was nothing left to do but make two more dumb potholders.

Wayna Sue Bagley was bigger than Rebecca McGehee. Wayna Sue had already been to a fat camp this summer. It was too bad that she "had the tendency," as her mother put it, but it helped a little that her father was rich. Her hair was a wild goldish red and her mother bought most of her clothes at Ample Girl. Wayna Sue was the first one in her class to wear a training bra.

Rebecca's dark brown hair hung uselessly to her stooped shoulders. She wore tortoiseshell glasses and the belt on her pedal pushers was in the tightest notch. She was two months younger than Wayna Sue and her father was a grocer. When Rebecca entered sixth grade, she had officially listed herself as Becca and thought she noted an instant increase in popularity. Anyway, *Rebecca* was so old-fashioned, especially the way Mrs. Fulsom pronounced it.

"Okay, okay, that's good," Wayna Sue said when Becca kept moving her hand, hunting for a comfortable place on the tree. "Now repeat after me: I, Rebecca McGehee, do solemnly swear that I will have my first period when Wayna Sue Bagley does, not before and not after."

Becca withdrew her hand from the tree. "You mean on the very same day?" She was a stickler for details.

"No, crazy." Wayna Sue smiled her indulgent, upperhand smile. "Just close together—like the same week." They hadn't actually talked about that part.

So Becca put her hand back and said the words. Then Wayna Sue said hers. It was official.

The idea had been born on Tuesday when Mrs. Fulsom left the class making potholders. "I know I can count on you all to behave," she said to the five girls and three boys.

Wayna Sue and Becca had immediately moved to a corner to be alone. They couldn't *stand* the others. All they needed was each other. Best Friends. After a whole Sunday on David and Jonathan with the memory verses of "A friend loveth at all times" and "A man that hath friends must shew himself friendly," Wayna Sue had asked Mrs. Fulsom if there were any girlfriends in the Bible.

"Oh my!" Mrs. Fulsom said. "Oh, honey, let's not talk about girl-friends and boyfriends today."

"But—"

"You have plenty of time for that later on."

Becca spoke up. "She means were there girls in the Bible who were best friends."

Mrs. Fulsom shifted her weight. "Well, of course there were," she said. "Of course. Let me think."

Everyone looked at a floor tile or a corner while Mrs. Fulsom thought. At last she said triumphantly, "Naomi and Ruth."

"But they were women, not girls," Wayna Sue whined.

Mrs. Fulsom had had enough. These youngsters were soul-trying at times. She straightened her bosom. "Girls turn into women," she said. "It's all one and the same."

But of course it wasn't. Wayna Sue and Becca knew grown women couldn't possibly be Best Friends like girls could be. Besides, being Best Friends was necessary now. Changes were coming all around them this summer, sneaky things they couldn't always put a name to.

For one thing, there was suddenly more awfulness. A lot more awful things were happening—teachers and parents saying stupid things and just acting weird and awful right and left. Classmates were jerks. Food tasted yucky. Their clothes didn't fit, or if they did, they looked creepy.

So it wasn't just something to do, making this pact. It was making sure neither of them would grow up first and treat the other one all snotty and leave her by herself.

They would work out the details later. Maybe they would wait until after Christmas and then mark the same date on their calendars and concentrate on it at the same time. Would the one who started first be wrong because she had started early, or would the one who didn't start be mean for holding back? And what exactly would they do if it didn't work out, say, within a month of each other?

They hadn't been able to come up with any appropriate threatening alternative. Neither wanted to kill herself, or never speak to the other again, or run the length of the alley completely naked at a slumber party.

The illogic of their body rhythms being in total harmony haunted them only slightly. Their bodies were Best Friends too.

It was probably enough that they would suffer sin if they didn't keep the pact. The one who started first would be full of pride, and they'd learned all about the sin of pride. "Some people just ride on pride," Mrs. Fulsom had said, staring all around the circle, waiting for admiration.

The girl who didn't start would be full of ugly thoughts about the one who did, and that would be envy. Envy was more than jealous. Envy was hating somebody because they were smart or rich or had something special, and wishing they were dead. Or as Mrs. Fulsom put it, "If you wish you had your friend's new blouse and she had a wart on her nose."

But the pact wasn't going to get broken. Becca had found a good idea in the chapter of *Confidently Yours* entitled "What Every Girl Should Know." After it talked about how wonderful it was having a body, then a female body, then being on the verge of growing up, then how wonderful it would be as a wife and then a mother, it backed up one step and said how, for growing girls, all this wonderfulness meant that "the womb cleanses itself each month in a unique way.

"Of course, many factors enter into determining *when* this wonderful event will take place for the first time." Becca had figured they could put starting at the same time under "many factors." She had read an article in the Sunday supplement about a man in Russia who bent spoons by thinking about them. It wouldn't be *that* hard. Thinking together could be a factor.

Becca was brainy. She was a bookworm. If she thought something, it was probably so.

All right. They would wish hard. They would agree to pray at the same time every night. "Seek and ye shall find. Knock and it shall be opened unto you." Mrs. Fulsom said to call on God whenever you needed something—anything. "Don't ask Him just for big things, like world peace," she said. Then she told about her constant and unceasing prayers that ships would appear at a southern port to take the Negro population back to Africa. "I firmly believe He will answer my prayer," she said, her lips tight and thin and severely red. "Maybe not in my lifetime, but in God's own good time." They squirmed uncomfortably and wished she would not give so much personal testimony. They fought looking at her.

One morning in early October, Becca met Wayna Sue on the walkway outside Calvin Junior High. "I started," she whispered.

Wayna Sue was busy unwrapping the first piece of gum for the day. "What?"

"You know," Becca said. She wasn't about to say it out loud.

Wayna Sue stopped, cocked her head, and stamped her foot. It was an effect she had recently learned. "If I knew, would I ask you?"

Tears sprang to Becca's eyes. She felt a little nauseated and headachy. Now everyone was looking.

"Well, never mind," she said, hurrying up the walk.

Wayna Sue knew when she had overplayed her hand. She came along quickly beside Becca. "What? What?"

Becca opened her purse. There were two sanitary napkins.

"So?" Wayna Sue resumed her walking.

"Remember," Becca said, "we weren't going to get mad."

Wayna Sue slung her hair and adjusted her purse strap. "Who said I was mad?" And she marched off to English alone.

At noon they had to sit at a table with two shrimpy sixth grade boys. When the boys had finished, popped their sacks and headed for the ice cream station, Wayna Sue looked around. There was no one within earshot.

"How does it feel?"

Becca twisted a strand of hair. "It's not as fun as I thought," she said. "You feel kind of weird all over and have to check yourself between every class."

Wayna Sue tried again. "I mean, how does it feel . . . *there*?"

"Like a paperweight," Becca said and the bell rang.

Wayna Sue would wait until Halloween. That would be a month. After that she would decide what to do about Becca's breaking the pact. That was the limit.

Meanwhile, she massaged her stomach each night. She prayed without ceasing, as Mrs. Fulsom had suggested, but ran into a problem the first night because you couldn't pray to a *man* for something like this, especially God. She finally solved it by praying, "Dear God, help me to grow up this month." That seemed properly vague.

Finally she dreamed of paperweights, round heavy snow scenes she took from under her Ample Girl skirt and shook violently into blizzards.

Halloween came and went, and a few days later, as they shivered out-side the school in the wind of the first norther, Becca announced a repeat of her performance.

Wayna Sue looked toward the street. "You don't have to rub it in."

"I'm *not* rubbing it in!" Becca said. "You'd be mad if I didn't tell you." She was quiet for a moment. "The pact didn't work, is all."

"Are you saying it's my fault?" Wayna Sue snarled.

"It's not any—"

"Everything was my fault, I guess. Thinking up the pact and—having us say it at the tree, and—and then not starting right when you started." Tears began in her eyes.

"I didn't say—"

Wayna Sue whirled around. "Listen, Mary Poppins. For your informa-tion, I don't want to see anything in your magic purse."

Wayna Sue became obsessed. She hung a calendar beside her bed and, not knowing what else to do, marked a tiny *x* on the twenty-eighth day of each month. She studied the ads in the magazines carefully and then asked her mother for white pants.

"Why white pants in the wintertime?" her mother asked.

"I want to look fresh," Wayna Sue replied, putting special emphasis on "fresh."

She began tying her sweater around her shoulders, European bicycle-tour style.

"Why do you bother to wear it if you don't put it on?" her father asked at breakfast one morning. "Your mother and I pay good money for a sweater and you make it into a rope."

"It's warm this way," she said. "And besides, it's the style now."

She bought daisy earrings and a daisy bracelet and got a poster for her room showing a field of daisies. All of a sudden she was crazy about daisies. Daisies were fresh.

The day she answered roll in P.E. with "Sitting out" thirty girls in white blouses and blue shorts turned to look up the bleachers at her. Let them think what they would. Maybe she'd had strep throat, or maybe it was something else . . .

And she avoided Becca. She joined the annual staff so she could stay after school. She began getting to the cafeteria earlier than usual and buying her lunch. She made friends with the girls in her math class and sat at the table with them. By the time Becca got there, Wayna Sue had gulped down her green beans, meat pattie, and canned peach and was on her way to the annual-staff workroom. And she was extra sweet to Becca.

"Sorry I can't eat with you anymore," she said the third day of her new schedule. "I'm just soooo busy right now."

"That's okay." Becca put a whole corn chip in her mouth.

In the spring, Becca did the final hateful thing: she got saved. They hadn't exactly considered a pact on that but they had talked once about fourteen being the right age to have collected enough sins to be saved. Becca wouldn't be fourteen for eight more months.

Mrs. Fulsom was ecstatic. "One of my own brought into the fold," she trilled. "Girls, if you could know the joy that's in my heart today . . ." It was the Sunday morning before Becca would be baptized that night. She was to have been baptized the week before but her period came early so her mother had called the church secretary and reported Becca "ill." Then Becca couldn't go anywhere all weekend because someone might see her.

"She probably got saved on purpose," Wayna Sue told Marva, her best friend now, before Sunday School. "To call attention to herself." They cast private glances at each other when Becca entered the room.

"Rebecca McGehee, you arise to walk in newness of life," the minister intoned as he drew Becca from the depths of the watery grave. Her hair clung plastered to her face and water dripped off her nose. The outline of her bra showed under the white robe.

"Traitor!" Wayna Sue whispered.

After the service, Becca joined the crowd in the spring air on the cobblestones of the entryway, her wet clothes rolled in a towel under her arm. Her hair was done up in a little bun and she stepped like a budding ballerina.

"Well, how was it?" Wayna Sue said, not wanting to congratulate her.

"Wet," Becca answered.

Just then Mrs. Fulsom descended. She squeezed Becca hard, grinding Becca's glasses against a large green brooch on her jacket. "We're just so proud of you, my dear," she said. "Aren't we, girls?"

The circle of girls nodded carefully.

"Rebecca." Her mother was beside them. She was a thin, plain woman. She turned to Mrs. Fulsom. "We've got to get Rebecca home, wet hair and all, you know."

No one noticed until after Becca and her mother had gone that Mrs. Fulsom's hug had jarred Becca's bra and underpants from her bundle. They lay sprawled, white against the red cobblestone.

"Oh!" Mrs. Fulsom said. "Oh dear!" Her hand went to her throat and she looked around desperately. "We can't have this."

Her eyes fell on Wayna Sue. "Wayna dear," she said, "be a good Christian friend and pick up Becca's things."

Wayna Sue looked around. The boys would be here any minute to see what everyone was looking at. She couldn't do anything about becoming a woman but she could get a start on sinning.

"No ma'am," she said. "Get somebody else to." And she walked away heavyhearted and proud, carrying her refusal like a giant paperweight.

Neighbor Ladies

LILA HAVENS

 "Another lousy night," I remark to my neighbor Quince, trudging past her up the stairs. She knows I haven't been sleeping well lately, and she's concerned. Still, I'm surprised when she drops the bag of garbage she was taking out and guides me into her apartment by the elbow.

"Fantastic," she says. "Did you hear anything? It happened in the middle of the night."

I guess a long day of data entry at Big State Insurance has blunted my wits. I'm an underwriter, which always gives me this image of Michelangelo lying on scaffolding, scribbling on a ceiling. "The only thing that happened to me last night was that I watched *East of Eden* and finished the golf club covers I've been knitting for my father."

Quince gawks up at me from where she sits crosslegged on her meditation cushion. "Didn't you know? Mr. Roebuck was murdered last night. Come on, Janice—the old guy across the courtyard on the first floor. The one who grows jalapeños in his window box. He was shot through the head. Actually, the chin."

"Wow. He seemed like a nice old guy. I guess I did go to sleep around three."

"If you ate right, you wouldn't have that problem."

Quince is a vegetarian, and she lectures me regularly about my eating habits. She contends that all aberrations, including sleep disorders, are linked to diet and that there would be no cancer, divorces, rapes, murders, or molestation of minors if everyone was vegetarian. Once after I'd had a particularly bad night, I took her out for breakfast. She almost fainted when I ordered eggs and sausage.

"Are you on one of those carrot juice fasts again?" When she nods, I say, "I thought so. You're turning orange."

Quince actually looks like a carrot. She is tall and tapers from broad shoulders to trim hips to bony legs. She wears her hair cropped close with a fringe of bangs over her forehead, and her long face has a perpetually mournful look. In San Francisco she could live underground, but here in Houston she's always being forced to look life in the eye. The funny thing is how she's embraced it: she's the most dedicated newshound I know. She reads both of the bad local papers every day, cover to cover. She can't get enough of the freeway shootings and bar brawls.

"I've taken a big step forward," she declares. "Only fresh food, nothing cooked—just fruits, cereals, and veggies. Cooked foods make you burn out faster. And no more cheese because aged things age you. I feel better already."

"There *was* one thing last night. While I was looking out the window, I saw a cat pass under the spotlight above the gate. It was dragging a black snake between its legs."

"Now if that isn't an omen and a half," Quince says. "Get it, Janice? Meat eaters."

"I knew you'd like that one."

Quince shows me every article, reports the latest gleaned from the local newscasts and from gossiping with the neighbors, and I pass along the speculations of the claims adjustors at work, who know practically as much about crime as the police do. Everybody's excited about the case except Merton. He just doesn't think it's worth all the hooplah.

He is standing by the kitchen sink draining my orange juice pitcher, legs braced, one hand on his hip. He looks like a conqueror helping himself to the spoils. Finished, he smacks his lips for effect. "A mugger followed him home and got carried away."

"He'd been home for hours. He was in bed."

"I guarantee it was a botched burglary. Why else would somebody kill a poor old guy who worked in a dry cleaning shop? You and Quince just want to make it into some big drama. You watch—it'll turn out to be simple bad luck. The wrong guy broke into the wrong apartment. Fate."

Merton pulls out a chair and straddles it, resting his chin on the back. Merton is my lover between 5:00 and 8:00 P.M. on Mondays, Wednesdays, and sometimes Fridays. He comes over straight from his warehouse job, showers, eats, tumbles, and then goes to rehearsal. Three nights a week Merton is my lover and the drummer for a band called Johnny Eck;

the other four nights he is the live-in lover of Sheila, a fast-rising executive with Southwest Power and Light who, at forty-two, is thirteen years older than Merton. I don't pretend to understand.

"Mmm," Merton says, rubbing his chin. He's trying to grow a goatee, and he says it itches. He already sports a little Hitler mustache, but he's tired of the reaction it draws and is letting the sides grow out. He is going prematurely gray; if he had pointed ears, he'd look like a skinny Schnauzer. "You've made quiche once a week for the past three weeks. Does this mean something?"

"It means I got a new recipe a month ago."

He gets up and sits down normally. "If you're trying to impress me, forget it." When I scoop a slice of quiche from the pan, a long strand of spinach strings out and dangles from the server. Merton groans. "I can't eat that. It looks like a booger."

I flop the quiche onto a plate and shove it toward him. "I see you so little, I'd appreciate it if you'd try to act like an adult while you're here."

He hunches his shoulders and blinks. "Gee, Mom, sorry."

"Maybe I should move."

"Nah," he says. "Lightning doesn't strike twice."

"There's a man in Oklahoma who's been struck by lightning five times."

He is quiet for a moment, swirling the burgundy in his glass. I try this too, and am disappointed that the wine doesn't cling to the side of the glass the way a good wine should. I blew twelve dollars on this bottle—so okay, I *am* trying to impress him—but Merton doesn't seem to notice. "I know how *I'm* going," he says. "No, seriously, Janice. Spontaneous combustion. Some night when we're playing in a club, just like that, I'll flare up. Every once in a while I get the feeling I'm about ready then it passes. But my time will come. You wait"—he is wagging his fork at me now—"when I'm a stinking pile of bones and ashes, you'll be sorry you didn't let me be immature. Fair warning."

Nights when I can't sleep, I sit by the window with the lights off and watch the front gate. If the killer returns to the scene of the crime, I don't want to miss him. I've noticed that everyone in the building seems nervous. My neighbors sneak in and out the gate, dodging the light, peering over their shoulders. The woman who lives next door to Mr. Roebuck's apartment hasn't opened her curtains since the murder. She and Mr. Roebuck were about the same age, and they sometimes took walks together, the woman's ragamuffin toy collie in tow. Last night she was wearing a black shawl, and when her dog stopped to sniff under Mr.

Roebuck's window, she yanked his leash hard and dragged him out the gate.

Even Quince, who's fascinated with the murder, has gotten spooked by it, I can tell. Usually she spends her evenings alone researching astrological charts to supplement her income, but for the past week she's been passing a lot of time in my apartment under the pretense of counseling me about Merton and my health. Because of my insomnia, she's got me off coffee altogether. I have three glasses of spring water and a bowl of fresh fruit for breakfast, a cup of Sleepytime and four magnesium tablets before bed. So far, it's not working. Come midnight, I bolt upright, heart thundering, certain I've heard someone at the door.

Tonight Quince is slouched at the table, brooding over a cup of jasmine tea. "I never wanted to ask, but the guy's a meat eater, right?"

I nod without looking up from my embroidery hoop.

"See?" she says without satisfaction. "I can tell. He's got that look about him. That's why he's getting old so early."

"He told me the other night he's going to die from spontaneous combustion. He was serious. Friday he brought this book and showed me a picture of some relative of his who died that way."

"Wouldn't surprise me," Quince says. "He lives on the charred flesh of animals and smokes the weeds of the earth. Fire unto fire."

"Please."

"What are you making there anyway?" she asks.

"A petit-point toaster cover. I guess I have an urge to hide things."

"Mr. Roebuck now," she continues, "undoubtedly a meat eater. That's how it goes. The meat eaters battle it out."

"Not much of a battle if he was shot in his sleep."

"Well, he must have been involved in some kind of aggression or they wouldn't have killed him." Quince rises and dumps her tea in the sink then moves to the door. "That's karma for you."

"Listen, thanks for coming over. I guess I've been sort of freaked out since the murder."

"Yeah, me too, a little. But really, I don't think we have to worry," she says. "Haven't you noticed? It's the men. They're killing each other off. I say, Let them."

"What if I asked you to leave Sheila?"

It's Monday evening, and Merton is just emerging from the bathroom wearing my flowered kimono, beneath which shows a lot of long fuzzy leg. His wet hair is wrapped turban-style in a white towel. His goatee, which, unlike his hair, is still black, is almost a quarter of an inch long now. He falls onto the couch and swings his legs up on the back. "Really," he says, "you wouldn't want me to make a sacrifice like that. I live in a great house with a VCR and an endless supply of old movies."

"And an old woman."

Merton frowns. "You could hurt my feelings that way. I hardly see Sheila, but she's been very good to me. You know what she bought me last week? A nickel-plated saxophone. She's that kind of thoughtful." He takes my hand and pulls me down beside him. I can smell my cologne on the kimono when I lay my head on his chest. Secondhand, it's disturbing, like the smell of chrysanthemums at a funeral. "You're a wonderful girl, Jan: somber, obsessive, freckle-faced. It would probably ruin your disposition to be around me all the time."

"Try me." It's meant to sound cocky, at worst valiant, but even to my ear it rings pathetic. I push away from him and rise, tugging my sweater down over my hips. "Well," I say brightly, "what do you feel like eating—chicken, fish sticks, a big, greasy taco salad?"

"You," he says, coaxing me back. "Delicious Janice McCall."

Thursday night Quince doesn't appear until almost nine o'clock and when she arrives, she's obviously excited. She rushes in barefoot, wearing a voluminous red caftan.

"I know this will sound odd to you, Jan, I know you're skeptical, but really, just listen. I flashed on the murder tonight while I was meditating. It literally came out of nowhere, this vision of the killer. For real! He looked like Robert DeNiro, and I think now I know what happened." She strikes a stance and pushes up her sleeves. "Here's how it goes. Mr. Roebuck was into some kind of underworld thing, I don't know exactly what. Like maybe the dry cleaning shop was a cover to launder money."

"Is that supposed to be a joke?"

"No." She looks puzzled but only misses a beat. "So it was something like—I'm not clear—but like he squealed or something and the hoods offed him. It's just a sense I got: bad people, bad shit happening."

"A murder's pretty bad shit."

She looks crestfallen. "You don't buy it."

"Well, I don't know, Quince. I guess I've never put a lot of stock in intuitions. Of course, in some ways it makes sense. He was shot through the chin, execution style, so that seems to point to organized crime. I've got two problems with it. One, how did the killer get in? The door hadn't been jimmied."

Now she looks disgusted. "Come on, Janice. This is the Mafia we're talking about. They know how to do things like that. They probably have a passkey to every house in America."

"Two, Mr. Roebuck was a regular old guy. He worked thirty-five years for Western Union then retired and worked at a dry cleaners just to keep busy. When he was home, he pottered around in the courtyard in shirt-sleeves and suspenders watering his peppers. You're going to tell me that sweet old man was a criminal?"

"You take a lot for granted," she says dryly. "People aren't always what they seem."

"I don't know, maybe you're right."

She waves her hand in dismissal. "No matter. The main thing is that I feel a lot better now. I'm certain Robert DeNiro wouldn't kill without good reason."

On Friday, I say, "Tell me why I put up with you."

Merton steps into the towel I am holding for him. Smiling, he says, "Easy. You love me." He scrubs his pale skin, raising his arms and lifting his legs to dry the crevices.

I back up and sit down on the lid of the toilet. "I never said that."

He is looking at the side of his face in the mirror. He's seeing himself through the kohl-blackened eyes of a crowd of hip teenage girls and try-ing to decide if he should shave. The band has a gig tonight. "Okay, I assumed it."

I wasn't invited. Sheila's going. My only pleasure in the situation has come from imagining Sheila wearing a tailored dove gray suit and sturdy pumps to Rudyard's. She'd look like the den mother. My great fear, of course, is that she has black boots and a jean jacket tucked away just for occasions like this. That's why I can't sneak down there tonight. I might find out.

"Merton, what if I said I had another lover?"

He has decided not to shave; he is looking at himself for pleasure now, trying out different smirks. "When you do, let me know."

"I had another lover."

"Had?"

"Alright, *have*."

He wraps a towel around his waist and saunters into the bedroom. "Lucky gal."

I follow him through to the living room and huddle at the other end of the couch, hands clasped around my knees. When he tosses his head, water flecks my arms and calves, and I shiver. "I never said I wouldn't see other people. It's miserable sitting around here every night wondering what you're doing. I'm not built for it."

He wipes his hair back from his forehead. "I never asked you to stay alone. We took no vows to be true blue, not that I remember. Where's my lighter?"

I push it down the coffee table toward him. "Quince thinks you're right, she thinks you'll go up in flames."

He squints through the smoke. "When it happens, you won't be laughing." He turns toward me, legs crossed in a half-lotus. With a flick of his fingers, he taps the ash and brings the cigarette back to his parted lips. He's taking his time. He knows I love to watch him.

"It's not that lesbian, is it?" he says at last. "If it was Quince, I'd know you were just trying to make me jealous."

"Are you asking?"

"No. It's your business." He waves his hand. "Live it up. Have a good time. I do."

Someone has driven an icicle into the base of my spine. "You don't enjoy it with Sheila. That's what you said."

He shrugs, smoke spiraling from his nostrils. "Possibly I lied."

"You'd rather be with me." I try to look positive.

"That too," he says, "is possible."

I let my eyes travel from his feet, delicate as hands, up his legs, over the draped green towel, up the heartbreaking line of black hair that bisects his belly, over his smooth chest, around shoulders, up neck, past beard, lips, and nose until I meet his eyes, which are dark and thoughtful.

"If you love me," he says gently, "you'll get down on your knees and ask."

And finally I do.

I wake abruptly at the sound of a door nicking shut. With the sort of absolute clarity possible only in the dark, I am sure it was the door to Quince's apartment. The clock says 3:38. A vision of Merton sidling up the stairs after the gig and into Quince's apartment flashes across my mind like a bulletin. I remember seeing Merton and Quince talking in the courtyard last week, remember the slyness of his smile, and I can imagine him slipping into houses all over town at all times of the day and night like the fabled milkman, a love bandito. For all I know, there is no Sheila.

In the seven months of our relationship, I've never been to his home. Striving to be the perfect paramour, I've never even asked the address, although I have the phone number, to be used only in case of national emergency. And of course I don't have huge crises, I have small continuous ones, the kind that wake me at night, that cause me to gnaw my cuticles, that have made me a compulsive needleworker. For all I know, Sheila is simply a projection of the woman I will be in a few years—conventional, successful at business, lonely, a woman who writes chatty letters to her mother once a week without fail, who watches television because it's company for her while she stitches away at a teapot cozy that will end up relegated to the rear of a drawer in some relative's kitchen, a woman who waits for a feckless lover to add the grace notes to her monotonous life. When I lie back, heart chugging, suddenly I'm Susan Hayward, I'm every woman done wrong, and the gun in my grip as I stand over the dead man's bed is the warmest thing I've ever known.

Saturday, Quince is moping in the doorway of her apartment when I come home from the grocery store, evidently waiting for me. She couldn't look more morose if someone had just force-fed her veal. I'm sure I look worse. At four o'clock in the afternoon, I'm still wearing the tee shirt I slept—or didn't sleep—in last night, and I was halfway to the store before I remembered I'd never brushed my hair today.

"It's unbelievable, Jan."

"What's wrong?"

"I am seriously bummed." She follows me into my apartment, stepping out of her thongs by the door. "They solved the murder."

As soon as I set the bags on the counter, there is a knock at the door. When I open it, Merton is there, holding a liquor-store bag aloft and grinning. I'm not. "What's up? It's not your day."

"Sheila's gone to Shreveport to visit her mother." He steps past me but comes up short at the sight of Quince languishing in a silk pajama top and stirrup pants on the couch. "If you're busy, I'll split."

"Oh, not busy, just about to hear the latest on the Gardenia Courts murder. Join us."

Merton sighs. "Don't we have anything more interesting to talk about? I already know what happened."

"Oh, really?" I say.

"I told you." He pours a clear liquid from his bottle into three shot glasses and passes one to Quince, who takes it without looking at him. "Somebody broke in, thinking no one was home, but the old man was there so they shot him. Read the papers—stuff like this happens in Houston every day."

"I did read the papers. The door wasn't broken in, it was unlocked and then left standing open," I tell him. "And he didn't surprise a thief: he was in bed asleep when he was killed."

"And nothing was stolen," Quince murmurs.

I knock back the shot, which scalds a path to my stomach. "Right. You're so certain it's just the luck of the draw, and Quince thinks it's crime and punishment, the Mafia as the hand of God."

"Sometimes I get intuitions," Quince explains. "It came to me while I was sitting, just a feeling about the guy being involved in a double cross."

"So I heard," says Merton.

"I think the double-cross part is right," I say. Merton's taken a chair at the table, but I'm still on my feet, commanding attention. "My theory is just as basic as the ones you've put forward, maybe even more so. I guess you'd call it betrayal and revenge. I think Mr. Roebuck had a lover— maybe the woman who lived next to him, the one with the little dog."

"Wow," Quince says, sitting up on the couch. "That's good, Jan. Bernice Hanks, the neighbor lady. How did you figure that out?"

"Two lonely people. They take walks, they make plans. It's the best thing that's happened to her in years. She can't believe her good fortune—a man who really makes her happy, gives her something to look forward to. She'd lost faith, thought she'd never have anything good again." I'm pacing now, and I can feel Quince and Merton watching me, astonished. "She and Mr. Roebuck are back and forth to each other's apartments, they cook together, watch television, they share the quiet pleasures of life. It's the only thing she's been able to count on in years except boredom.

"Then one day she finds out there's another woman. Maybe she's doing his laundry and finds a note, maybe she overhears a phone call or just sees him talking to someone and knows. At first she doesn't let on. She'll wait, it will pass, and everything will be the same again. But gradually she understands that it can't be. His voice doesn't sound the same to her anymore, he doesn't look the same. She knows the truth, and she can't bear it. So one night she takes the gun she'd bought for protection, lets herself into his apartment with the key he gave her, and ends it. To her mind, it's almost a mercy killing."

Merton has slid off his chair and lies sprawled on the rug near my feet, comfortable as a cat. "Elaborate, melodramatic, and lots of human inter-est," he says. "It'd make great television." Deflated, I sink onto the floor and tongue the last of the liqueur from my shot glass.

"Fantastic," Quince says excitedly. "I almost wish I didn't know the real story."

Merton says, "You want to fill us in?"

"Well, you were partly right," Quince begins, leaning her elbows on her knees. "Mr. Roebuck *did* have a friendship of sorts with Bernice. They did take walks and cook together and all that. Then Mr. Roebuck found out that he had cancer. He got really depressed. His wife had died of cancer years earlier and he knew the expense and how hard it was on everyone, so he decided to kill himself, but he didn't want to deprive his kids of the insurance money so he set it up with Bernice to make it look like a murder. Of course she tried to talk him out of it, but he was firm and they were best friends so she said okay. She was supposed to wait in the kitchen until she heard the shot and then open the window so it would look like whoever had come in that way, then she was supposed to take the gun, lock the door behind her, and the next day go out and throw the gun in the bayou. The only thing she did right was taking the gun. She forgot to open the window; after she got a look at him, she grabbed the gun and ran out, leaving the door open behind her; and then she kept the gun. The police thought she was acting strange so they searched her apartment and found the gun in the bottom of the clothes hamper, so then she spilled the whole story."

"No insurance money," Merton says, shaking his head. "Janice, aren't you ashamed?"

Quince raises her glass. "What is this stuff anyway?"

"Ouzo," Merton says. "You like?"

"Mmm," Quince purrs, closing her eyes. "It's yummy, the way it burns going down."

"I've never seen you drink before," I remark, studying Quince. "I thought alcohol was bad juju or something."

"Well, special occasions," she says, smiling. "Since Merton was a sweet-heart and brought it for us."

"Janice doesn't think I'm a sweetheart," Merton says. "Do you?"

I lay one finger on his nose and press a little too hard. "No."

"Your scenario's a lot better than what really happened," Quince says. "I mean, I can identify with it more. I used to be a very big drinker, and I'd get violent. I actually beat up my husband one time, gave him this gorgeous black eye. I could probably kill somebody else, but I could never kill myself."

Merton turns to her with interest. "I didn't know you were married."

"It was a long time ago," Quince says. "I'm probably older than you think."

"That's an intriguing question," Merton says. "If you had to make a choice, which would you rather do, kill yourself or someone else?"

"I haven't slept well for weeks," I tell the side of Merton's face. "I've been sitting and staring out the window every night until my eyes feel like flannel. I tried to pretend I was watching for the killer, but that was a lie. I was looking for you, but you never come over after rehearsal anymore."

"You know that's not practical," he says. "We both have to get up so early."

"Well, I can't take it anymore, only seeing you a couple of hours a week. It makes me nervous and then I don't sleep, and lack of sleep is really getting to me. It's turning me into a paranoid. I've been getting wild ideas, imagining things."

He laces his fingers behind his head. "You knew the situation from day one, Janice. I never misled you."

"Young women are very insecure," Quince announces from the couch. "They always want some kind of guarantee."

"And what about older women?" Merton asks. "What do they want?"

Quince has one long leg extended across the floor so that her foot is inches from Merton's elbow. She wiggles her toes and smiles at him. "Depends on the woman," she says coyly.

At first I figure she's got to be drunk—this is Quince, who has a higher regard for cows than she does for men, who talks about non-vegetarians like me and Merton as though we're raging dinosaurs strewing behind us a bloody path of fur and bones—but we've only had one shot, and I can tell by her face that she knows exactly what she's doing, and so does Merton. Something that feels like a heavy stone drops to the bottom of my stomach.

"Some older women are terrific, I hear." I sling my leg across Merton's chest and straddle him. He looks surprised. "Some are generous and long-suffering." Leaning forward, I put my hands on his shoulders and pin him with my weight. "Some are killers."

He begins to stroke the sides of my thighs, his eyes narrowed with pleasure. "Come here, I've got a surprise for you," he says. When I lean down, he whispers, "I can stay all night tonight."

Still grasping his arms, I pull back enough to kiss his goatee. Under my breath, I say, "Pow."

Glossary

English translations appear here in the order the Spanish appears in the text.

Federico y Elfiria

Pos
Well

no le hacía—que era muy ranchera y nunca había visto más que su casa
it didn't matter—that she was such a bumpkin, and didn't know about
    nothin' beyond her own backyard

se vestía muy galán
was a real dresser

a lo mejor
they'd bet

a las escondiditas
secretly

de todos modos
anyway

como estaba ella media llenita
since she was a little plump

flacas
skinny

"La Gorda"
"The Fatso"

Elfiria estaba lavando el piso
Elfiria was scrubbing the floor

nalgas
buttocks

y también esas cosas
and also those thingamajigs

Pos, que se reventó el globo
Well, the dam just broke

pos estaba viniendo
well he was coming

una desas
one of *those*

cosa de viejas
old women's stuff

quitó los zapatos
took off his shoes

esa ingrata
that ungrateful so-and-so

¡Cabrona!
Damn broad!

¡ya le calaba!
it was really getting uncomfortable!

misa
Mass

que ya era tiempo
that it was high time

y ya le andaban las moscas y el polvo
and the flies and the dust were getting to him

hasta las 2:00 de la tarde, y lo único que vió
till 2:00 in the afternoon, and the only thing he saw

sobras al gato vecino
leftovers to the neighbor's cat

sufriendo del calor
suffering from the heat

"Amor de Lejos"
"Love from Afar"

sin decirle nada
without saying anything to her

Y ella se portó bien también, nomás que
And she behaved herself too, except that

e ¡híjole! pregnant y todo, qué desgracia
and golly, pregnant and everything, what a disgrace

y se mió allí, a chorros
and she peed all over, right there

le regañó
he scolded

viejito . . . Hijo
old man . . . Son

como si había comido algo
as if he had eaten something

Su hijo. Claro que era su hijo
His son. Of course it was his son

y pataleando
and kicking

pa' estar con él
to be with him

muy compañero
a real buddy

M'ija'ta más chula
My daughter's so-o-o cute

Υ ni le dieron
And they hadn't even given him

Hace mucho tiempo.
It's been a long time.

muy caballero
being the gentleman

¡Ya para con estas tonterías!
Cut out all this foolishness!

¡Ya olvídate de esas cosas!
Just forget all that trash!

Sabor a Mí/Savor Me

despacito, pianissimo. Υ me hablas en español.
slowly, very quietly. And you speak to me in Spanish.

palabras de amor
words of love

la morena más guapa y tú eres mi Pedro Infante
the loveliest brunette and you are my Pedro Infante

rebozo
shawl

La güera más morena. Bésame, bésame mucho.
The darkest blonde. Kiss me, kiss me a lot [also the title of a popular Mexican romantic song].

bolillos
Mexican-style French roll with an elongated shape

conchas
Mexican pastry often associated with the female genitals. *Concha* also means "seashell."

son tus pelitos acá, son rubios?
are your little hairs there, are they blonde?

Soy la más morena, la más guapa, envuelta en mi rebozo.
I am the darkest, the loveliest, wrapped in my shawl.

Puta, me dice. Sinvergüenza, sucia, cabrona, ya no vales nada.
Whore, she says. Shameless, dirty bitch, you're worth nothing now.

cuaresma
Lent

duerme, duerme negrito
sleep, sleep little dark one [from a lullaby]

que tu mamá está en el campo, negrito
that your mother is in the fields, little dark one

duerme, duerme moreno
sleep, sleep, brown one

Enedina Pascasio

No faltaba más!
Definitely!

Notes on the Authors
and the Stories

The contributors to Common Bonds *were invited to comment on their stories, and the comments of those who chose to do so immediately follow their biographical notes.*

Born in Graham, Texas, GAIL GALLOWAY ADAMS graduated from the University of Texas at Austin, where she later completed an M.A. in American Studies. Her poetry and short stories have been published in *American Voice,* the *Georgia Review,* and the *North American Review.* In 1987 her story "Inside Dope" was cited among one hundred distinguished stories of the year in *Best American Short Stories,* won the Texas Institute of Letters Award for Best Short Story, and was selected for inclusion in *Editor's Choice: Volume IV.* Adams was the Helen Wieselberg Scholar in fiction at the Bread Loaf Writers' Conference in 1987, and a collection of her stories won the Flannery O'Connor Award for Short Fiction in that year and was subsequently published by the University of Georgia Press as *The Purchase of Order.* She lives in West Virginia with her husband and son and is an adjunct faculty member in the Department of English at West Virginia University. She has completed one novel and is at work on a second collection of short fiction—and a dissertation in American Studies for Emory University in Atlanta.

"As one of three sisters with a large extended clan of aunts and female cousins flung all over Texas, I am in the privileged position of witnessing a variety of lives. One cousin is a welder, another a wild-animal trainer, but most of their jobs are not so exotic. They work as secretaries, helpers in the school cafeteria, child-care workers, clerks at department stores. We are all drawn together through things common to women. One of my cousins says, 'Let's talk a long time—but first let me borrow that lipstick you're wearing.' Then she hands me her baby. At any gathering we have the babies: Jesse, Austin, Travis, and Clay—good Texas names all.

"Lou Maxey could be one of my kin. This story began as a straight chronological narrative which emphasized Lou's strictly proper upbringing in a small Texas town, and how her love for Marlon Maxey pulled her away from what should have been an ordered life. Because there have been so many moves in my own life, I wanted to use 'The Purchase of Order' as a way to examine and understand what it is that remains constant in a life of what could be termed 'forced mobility.' I still have reams of notes on the characters in this story. Someday perhaps they'll move again, this time into a novel."

ADELA ALONSO was born and raised in Mexico but has lived in Texas now for nearly a decade. In literary competitions she has received an honorable mention for a collection of her poetry, another for a personal essay. She has published poetry in various journals; "*Sabor a Mí*/Savor Me" is her first published short story.

"Writing, like sex, is a frightening and exciting process of self-discovery, full of contradictions and mixed feelings, but well worth it. We change ourselves, we change those around us, until nothing is ever the same.

"Pedro Infante was a popular Mexican actor, a romantic hero with the gallantry of a Clark Gable and the cowboy roughness of a Clint Eastwood. He was also a famous mariachi singer. I grew up watching him on TV, and remember him in his vaquero or mariachi outfit, serenading a beautiful, dark woman. He was always handsome and seductive. Famous for being a drunk and a ladies' man, he is reputed to have left behind dozens of children when he died, young, in a plane crash.

"The lullaby at the end of the story sings affectionately to a 'negrito', which in Mexico and Latinoamerica means anyone with a dark skin, not necessarily black. The mother of the 'little dark one' is away in the fields, working."

Born and raised in Waco, KAREN GERHARDT BRITTON moved to Houston in 1966 and earned a B.A. in Spanish from the University of Houston in 1971. Since 1977 she has written book reviews for the *Houston Chronicle*, which she credits with giving her her first writing "break." In 1984 and 1985, she worked as a staff writer for *Houston Woman Magazine,* interviewing Houston-area businesswomen and educators. Britton has taught creative writing for the Houston Community College system and has worked with writers at the Southwest Writers Conference. She has published a number of articles and short stories and is presently writing a book about cotton ginning for Texas A&M University Press.

"'Infections' is loosely based on the events of the last years of my great grandmother Henrietta, a gentle woman who left her family in Mississippi to join my great grandfather as he homesteaded on the blackland prairie of Ellis County. I never met my great grandmother, but the stories of her abuse were whispered among the women of my family with great sadness and even greater rage. It is true that my grandfather Owen and his 'new wife,' my grandmother Elsie, heard of the mistreatment and went to the farm to try to save my great grandmother. They were turned out with such venom by Owen's sister that a schism was created in the family, a schism that never healed.

"Because abuse of the elderly is also a contemporary problem, 'Infections' seems to me to speak to all generations of Texas women, the inheritors and caregivers of family and tradition. And because of the close bond between mothers and sons, I dedicate the story to my son Seann (1969–1985), who left behind the lyrics of his songs and the poetry of his life, and to my son Richard, who keeps me looking ahead."

LEE MERRILL BYRD was born and raised in New Jersey, but has lived in El Paso with her husband and three children since 1978. Her work has been published in *North American Review, Quarry West,* and *Puerto del Sol,* and most recently one of her stories was included in a Danish anthology entitled *American Signatures: Nine New American Writers and Their Stories.* With her husband she runs Cinco Puntos Press.

"In 1981 our two youngest children, our two boys, were badly burned in a playhouse fire. Several stories came out of that most important event. In this one, which is not strictly autobiographical, I was working at recalling a particularly difficult part of that time, which was the realization that both boys would be scarred. Because burned skin doesn't manifest its permanent scars for a long time after the actual fire, it's not easy to understand that scars must, in fact, necessarily follow. The boys were in the Shriners hospital in Galveston for three months; for the first two of those months, I held tenaciously to the idea that my own children would not scar. It didn't matter that all around me I saw other children who were scarred. They were other people's children, not mine."

PAT CARR was born in Wyoming but has lived most of her life in Texas. She has a B.A. and an M.A. from Rice University, a Ph.D. from Tulane, and has taught in various Texas universities, including Texas Southern and the University of Texas at El Paso. She has published eight books, among them *The Women in the Mirror,* winner of the Iowa Fiction Award, and her short stories have been published in such places as the *Southern Review, Southern* magazine, and *Best American Short Stories.* In addition to the Iowa Award, Carr has also received a South and West Fiction Award, a Library of Congress Marc IV Award, a National Endowment for the Humanities grant, the Green Mountains Short Fiction Award, and the Texas Institute of Letters Short Story Award. She is currently teaching fiction writing at Western Kentucky University in Bowling Green and is completing a Civil War novel set in Arkansas and Texas.

"This is one story I did write for a definite purpose. I wanted to illustrate a kind of situation women face more often than most of us realize. I tried to focus on the emotional and visceral responses to fear, and I would like men to understand the terror that women actually experience in circumstances like these."

ELIZABETH DAVIS is a former school counselor with degrees from the University of Texas and the University of Houston. Presently she is completing her studies in the Graduate Creative Writing Program at the University of Houston, where she also teaches English. Davis is the mother of two sons.

"I am a second-generation native Houstonian whose maternal grandparents moved to the city in 1918 in the wake of the oil boom. My grandmother often told the story of how when she was born her mother died, and in the same breath she would recall how she, a premature infant, survived her mother's death by being kept warm in a shoe box surrounded by hot bricks. 'The Hawk,' which later sprang into a life entirely its own, was generated by this kernel of family lore. One of my other foremothers came to Texas from Louisiana after the Civil War in an ox-drawn wagon. Pregnant, she was widowed in transit; yet she established a homestead in East Texas with the help of her six other children and a former slave.

"Such stories of Texan endurance and heroics were told to me with reverence by my father and his mother, and I am sure that the vitality of their telling animates my writing impulse.

"'The Hawk,' which won the Houston Festival Prose Award in 1986, is an excerpt from a novel in progress."

Born and raised in Houston, LISA FAHRENTHOLD received her B.A. in English from the University of Houston in 1979. "Roberta" is her third published short story, the previous two having appeared in *Kansas Quarterly* and *Mississippi Mud.* She was awarded a Dobie-Paisano Fellowship in

1985. Her play *The Skin Trade* was produced as a work-in-progress at Capitol City Playhouse in Austin, and she has also written and performed a one-woman show of five monologues about women, *Conversations in the Dark*, at Chameleons Coffeehouse in Austin. Fahrenthold lives in Houston and is working now on a book of short stories.

"In writing 'Roberta' I wanted to share with others a rhythm—for lack of a better word—I remember feeling as a girl growing up in Texas in the early sixties. I don't know if that feeling was unique to me, or what everyone feels as an adolescent. In any case, I felt it as a kind of expansiveness, in an interior way, as though the landscape itself gave plenty of room to imagine. That's why the narrator of my story, I think, runs into a kind of shock, a boundary of that imagination, when she meets the journeyman. It is the finite world of maleness that she encounters and which, it seems, her friend Roberta dealt with by going mad. Maybe growing up Texan and female makes those kinds of real-world shocks come late, I don't know. I do remember feeling the boundlessness of things as a girl—and then the boundaries and confusion of emotions of bumping up against the world in which men are no longer daddies or brothers but are the Other, with all the fearsomeness and seductive strangeness that that implies."

MARY K. FLATTEN grew up on the south side of San Antonio. She attended Catholic schools and graduated from the University of Texas at Austin. Flatten works for an Austin advertising agency. Her tongue-in-cheek campaign for vice-president, with its slogan "More Men in Clerical Positions," and her promotion of Deb-Aid (theme song: "We Wear the World"), bringing aid to the financially beleaguered families of debutantes, have been featured on National Public Radio.

ROCKY GÁMEZ was born and raised in Pharr, in the Lower Rio Grande Valley. She graduated from Pan American University in Edinburg. Her stories have been anthologized in *Conditions, Cuentos: Stories by Latinas, Politics of the Heart,* and *Wayward Girls and Wicked Women*. At present Gámez lives in Albany, California, near Berkeley, and teaches Spanish in a high school in San Francisco.

Born in Galveston, S. E. GILMAN came of age in Austin. She moved to northern New England in 1980 and is a graduate of the Vermont College M.F.A. Writing Program. She has worked as a bookstore clerk, cook, copywriter, security guard, mental health counselor, and paste-up artist. Her writings have appeared in such small-press magazines as *Interstate* and *Stone Drum,* and her work has been nominated for both the Pushcart Prize and the O. Henry Award. Gilman is the author of a play, *Dedicated to Sheshat,* staged by Noumenon Productions in Austin in 1976, and the founder and editor of the short-lived literary magazine *Hubris.* "The Idle Time" is her first anthologized short story.

"The upheavals of the sixties took a little longer to sink into the soil of my native Texas, or perhaps it was I who was too young to notice how deep or how long. I still prefer to believe we can change the world.

"My story is written from the end of that decade, but the struggles continue for girls like Deb who reject the passivity of the traditional role for women, or for those like Callie who yearn for a life of the mind. As women, we are defining our place in a game which keeps changing. Inside, we reel between the pull of the passion for connection—and the distance necessary for understanding."

Born in Houston, DIANE PAYTON GÓMEZ was raised in the Rio Grande Valley and, except for three years in Alaska and one year in Omaha, Nebraska, has lived in Austin all her life. She attended Texas A&I University, Austin Community College, and the University of Texas at Austin and at present is a freelance writer living in Austin. Gómez has taught creative writing classes sponsored by the City of Austin at the O. Henry Museum. Her articles, stories, and poems have appeared in numerous publications. Restaurant critic for the *Austin American-Statesman,* she is the author of *Dining with Diane: The Austin Restaurant Cookbook.*

LILA HAVENS was born and raised in Conway, Arkansas, earning a B.A. in psychology at Hendrix College in 1975. After that, she "took up moving as a hobby," living in twelve cities (including two in Europe and one in Africa) in eight years and working a variety of jobs—grocery checker, insurance underwriter, short-order cook, psychiatric technician, mail clerk, Peace Corps volunteer, bartender—along the way. Havens started writing in 1979, and in 1983 entered the Creative Writing Program at the University of Houston on scholarship. She has published two stories, "Baby Moon" in *Arkansas Times Magazine* and "Safe Driver" in *Equinox,* and an interview with Bobbie Ann Mason in *Crazyhorse,* which was reprinted in the book *The Story and Its Writer.* She lives now in Berkeley, California, where she works as a secretary and freelance proofreader.

"Willfully footloose for most of my adult life, I came as close to settling in Houston as anywhere I've lived. I went there for the Writing Program at the University of Houston, intending to stick it out for two years at most; I stayed four. Houston was a surprisingly rich location for my writing because of its confusion of styles. Within blocks of my apartment in Montrose were Frenchy's Fried Chicken, the Rothko Chapel, a produce stand selling Pecos cantaloupes, the Ball Park Adult Bookstore, and bars called Wet-and-Wild and Boobie Rock. Tall buildings shot up in the midst of bungalows. Cowboys drove Cadillacs and, on weekends, kids cruised Westheimer like the main drag of any small town. The contrasts were jarring and yet somehow similar to ones I found in myself.

"I started writing 'Neighbor Ladies' soon after my move to Houston. It draws on three sources in my life at that time: a very quirky and manipulative neighbor who talked to me for hours about meat eaters and Jesus and enemas; a friend's apartment in an old building with a courtyard, which caught my imagination because of its potential for voyeuristic involvement in other people's lives; and, most important, my sense of being overwhelmed by the amazing and bizarre place I had come to. I don't think I would have written this story anywhere but Houston."

Raised in West Texas, BOBBIE LOUISE HAWKINS has studied art in London, taught in missionary schools in British Honduras, attended a Jesuit university in Tokyo while acting on radio and stage, and has had two one-woman shows of paintings at the Gotham Book Mart in New York. Her published books include *Own Your Body, 15 Poems, Frenchy and Cuban Pete, Back to Texas, Almost Everything, One Small Saga*, and, most recently, *My Own Alphabet*. In 1979 Hawkins was one of one hundred poets from eleven countries who attended the One World Poetry Festival in Amsterdam, and she was awarded a fellowship from the National Endowment for the Arts. From 1975 to 1983 she toured regularly in the United States and Canada with singers Terry Garthwaite and Rosalie Sorrels. The trio reunited in April 1989 at the Great American Music Hall in San Francisco, and has plans for further touring. At present Hawkins teaches in the M.F.A. Creative Writing Program at Naropa Institute in Boulder, Colorado.

Born in Marion, Kentucky, SHELBY HEARON lived for many years in Austin before moving to Westchester County, New York, where she now makes her home. Her novels include *Armadillo in the Grass, The Second Dune, Hannah's House, Five Hundred Scorpions, Group Therapy, A Small Town*, and, most recently, *Owning Jolene*, published in 1989. Hearon has taught at a number of universities, among them the University of Texas at Austin (American Studies), the University of California at Irvine, and the University of Houston (creative writing). She was awarded an Ingram Merrill grant in 1987, a National Endowment for the Arts Creative Writing Fellowship in 1983, and the John Simon Guggenheim Memorial Fellowship for Fiction in 1982, and has five times won the NEA/PEN Syndication Short Story Prize and twice the Texas Institute of Letters best novel award. From 1979 to 1981 she was president of the Texas Institute of Letters.

Born in Brownsville in 1930, MARY GRAY HUGHES was raised in South Texas but lived in Austin for two years in the late 1940s before going east to finish college. She has published short stories and poems extensively, been a State of Illinois Writer-in-Residence for three years, and won a National Endowment for the Arts Creative Writing Fellowship. Two collections of her stories have been published: *The Thousand Springs*, in 1971, and *The Calling*, in 1980. She is currently finishing a novel. Hughes lives in Evanston, Illinois, but says that her "life and writing continue to be entangled with Texas," where she returns regularly to visit family and friends in Austin, Houston, and "that marvelous valley without hills culminating in Brownsville."

"'Luz' was very much a gift of a story for me. The beauty parlor was one from my Austin days. The physical Luz was from there also. I saw her and went to that beauty parlor when we lived in Austin during my last year of high school and my first year at the University. The essential 'big city' surroundings stuck in my mind from visits to Houston; also that neighborly quality and tone that one finds in large cities and that I felt in Houston's downtown area. Still, I did not know where the story 'Luz' would end when it began. I believe there is much in it almost inexpressible, but true, about what exists, or can exist, between women across age, ethnic background, and class differences in Texas, and everywhere."

BEVERLY LOWRY was born in Memphis, grew up in Mississippi, and has lived now in Texas for more than twenty years. Her most recent novel, *Breaking Gentle*, was published in 1988. Her third and fourth novels, *Daddy's Girl* and *The Perfect Sonya*, won the Texas Institute of Letters Jesse Jones Award for Fiction in 1981 and 1987. Lowry's short fiction has appeared in *Playgirl, Viva, Southwest Review*, the Sunday *Boston Globe* magazine, and elsewhere. Her nonfiction has been published in *Vanity Fair, Rolling Stone*, the *New York Times, Southern, American Way*, and the *Philadelphia Inquirer*. She lives near Martindale, Texas, with "a number of animals, a husband, a garden, and a lot of music."

"'Class' is a city story, written in the time before VCRs, when people actually went out of the house to take class. In our need for enlightenment and a spiritual life we—not just women but maybe women more than men—sometimes attach ourselves to a guide. The guide becomes our ideal; our precious other. We end up pursuing not so much enlightenment as the need to please the guide. We do lose track, but at least we find out there is one."

Born in North Carolina, ELIZABETH McBRIDE has lived in Houston for nearly thirty years, earning her B.A. from Rice University in 1964 and her M.A. in Creative Writing from the University of Houston in 1983. A freelance writer, she has published poetry, fiction, personal essays, art and architectural criticism, book reviews, and literary criticism. McBride is a columnist for the magazines *Sculpture* and *Artspace* in Houston, and a panel member of the Cultural Arts Council of Houston and the Texas Commission on the Arts.

"I came to Texas to go to Rice, and the stimulation of my education plus the open Texas land made me feel for the first time that anything was possible. There is a tendency in my work to explore the fringes of potential which I feel is directly related to the land's invitations.

"'Whooping Cranes' was inspired by a photograph by Annie Leibowitz of the writer Robert Penn Warren in old age, sitting on the edge of a hospital bed with his shirt off. I was surprised to see that his body looked old only at the neck and hands, and it was that surprise, combined with the affection I had always had for old men as father figures, that led to this story."

NJOKI McELROY grew up in Dallas. She received a B.S. from Xavier University in New Orleans, and an M.A. and Ph.D. from Northwestern University in Evanston, Illinois. She now teaches Interpretation of Black Literature at Northwestern and, each fall semester, in the Master of Liberal Arts program at Southern Methodist University in Dallas. McElroy is president of Black Fox Enterprises, Ltd., a hair care and cosmetics firm, and founder/director of The Cultural Workshop of North Chicago. As a storyteller and lecturer she has performed throughout the United States, Africa, and the Caribbean. Her published works have appeared in *Essence, The Speech Teacher, The Theatre Bulletin, Black World,* and various newspapers and scholarly journals. She is the mother of six children.

"In May 1930 my grandparents were among those Sherman residents who lived through what has been designated by some historians as one of the worst race riots in America. 'The Ninth Day of May' is a story based on some of the oral and written accounts of the riot that I have been familiar with for a long time.

"The young voice in 'The Ninth Day of May' could have been my voice or the voice of my foremothers. Besides the ordinary stresses of Texas women, my foremothers as well as myself have spent much of our lives dealing with an oppressive reality of indignities, injustices, and terror. However, despite these almost unbearable realities, my foremothers and other Texas women of African descent have reared beautiful children who became successful, productive adults. Like 'Mama' in my story, they maintained loving and caring family settings on meager budgets while participating in their churches and in community activities. As a fifth-generation African American Texan, I feel the constant presence and guidance of my ancestors' spirits, and I give tribute to these strong, enduring women who kept things together so well for me and for the generations to come."

JOYCE MEIER was born in Minnesota and moved to Dallas with her husband, Rodger, in 1949. She has had poems and short stories published in numerous literary magazines, and is former editor of *Sands,* a literary magazine published in Dallas. She has recently completed her first novel.

Originally from Michigan, LIANNE ELIZABETH MERCER has lived in Houston for fourteen years. A psychiatric nurse, Mercer writes fiction, poetry, and nonfiction. Her stories have appeared in *Plainswoman, Dark Starr,* and *Fiction 1986,* an anthology published by Exile Press. Her poetry has appeared in *Calliope!, Negative Capability, Blonde on Blonde, Concho River Review,* and *The Dan River Anthology.* Mercer also has taught business and technical writing for Booher Writing Consultants in Houston and has written a correspondence course on writing for the National Independent Study Center in Denver, Colorado. She is co-author with Hal Persons of the book *The How-To of Great Speaking: Stage Techniques That Tame Those Butterflies,* to be published in the spring of 1990.

HARRYETTE MULLEN grew up in Fort Worth, graduated from the University of Texas at Austin, and has lived at various times in Houston, Galveston, Beaumont, and Mount Pleasant. She is the author of *Tree Tall Woman,* and her poetry has been included in the anthologies *Washing the Cow's Skull* and *In Celebration of the Muse.* Her short stories have appeared in *Her Work, South by Southwest,* and *Lighthouse Point.* Mullen presently lives in Ithaca, New York, where she teaches in the Department of English at Cornell University.
"Although in my family of preachers and teachers a girl was expected to grow up to be a lady, I was fascinated by those black women in the community who had no interest whatsoever in ladylikeness. They were

absent from the piano recitals, club meetings, teas, and fashion shows that my sister and I were required to attend, but we caught glimpses of them on shady porches, in corner groceries where they purchased small tins of snuff, or at work in their modestly impressive gardens. I salute them whenever I take off my shoes to walk barefoot in the rain—or when I stroll past a beauty shop, grateful not to be under the hot comb, and nostalgic only for the intimate voices of the women inside.

"'Tenderhead' was written in honor of all the girls and women who are uninterested in becoming ladies."

SUNNY NASH grew up in Bryan, and lived for a time in Houston. She received a degree in communications from Texas A&M University in 1977 and at present is associate director of that university's Office of School Relations. Her essay "On Being Black in Houston" won first place in the Friends of the Houston Public Library Essay Competition in 1986, and she was named second alternate for the Dobie-Paisano Fellowship the following year. Nash has been editor, writer, and photographer for technical journals, magazines, and newspapers; producer and scriptwriter for commercial and public radio and for industrial video; and professional singer. "The Ladies' Room" is her second published short story.

"The material for this story came firsthand some thirty-five years ago (though, in reality, the mad dog that comes through the ladies' room floor burst through the floor of a friend's kitchen while she and I watched in terror). Survival on Candy Hill depended upon knowing what was going on around me at all times. Being keenly aware of my environment continues to provide me with more material than I can use in a lifetime of writing."

Born in Nashville, Tennessee, CAROLYN OSBORN has lived in Texas since 1946. She went to high school in Gatesville and earned a B.A. and an M.A. from the University of Texas at Austin. Osborn has been a newspaper reporter and radio writer and has taught English at U.T. Her stories have been published in many literary magazines. A frequent contributor to U.S. anthologies such as *Southwest Fiction,* edited by Max Apple, and *South by Southwest,* edited by Don Graham, her work has also appeared in anthologies in England, Belgium, and Peru. Two collections of her short stories have been published: *A Horse of Another Color* (1977) and *The Fields of Memory* (1984). She was a co-winner of the Texas Institute of Letters Award for short fiction in 1978. In 1985 she won a P.E.N. Syndicated Fiction Award. Osborn now lives in Austin.

Beaumont native HERMINE PINSON received her B.A. in English from Fisk University in Nashville, Tennessee, and her M.A. in English from Southern Methodist University in Dallas. At present she lives in Houston, where she is an assistant professor of English at Texas Southern University as well as a graduate student at Rice. Primarily a poet, she has published work in *Faces Anthology, The Poetic Conscience of African Souls, The Cultural Arts Review, Houston Poetryfest Anthology,* and *Blonde on Blonde.* "Someday My Prince" is Pinson's first anthologized short story.

Born in Cuero, Texas, ANNETTE SANFORD was a high school English teacher for twenty-five years before resigning in the mid-1970s to become a full-time freelance writer. Her stories have been anthologized in *New Fiction from New England, Her Work, Fiction and Poetry by Texas Women, New Stories from the South,* and *Best American Short Stories* of 1979, and she has received two Creative Writing Fellowships from the National Endowment for the Arts. A collection of her stories, *Lasting Attachments,* was published in 1989.

Sanford lives with her husband in Ganado, Texas.

SANDRA SCOFIELD was born in Wichita Falls and grew up there and in West Texas. She graduated from the University of Texas and earned a doctorate at the University of Oregon. Scofield has published in *Touchstone, The Laurel Review, Plainswoman,* and other literary journals, and stories by her have been included in the anthologies *Women and Aging* and *The Ploughshares Reader: New Fiction for the Eighties.* One of her stories was awarded a Katherine Anne Porter Prize in 1985. In 1989, Scofield received a Creative Writing Fellowship from the National Endowment for the Arts, and her first novel, *Gringa,* was published.

"'The Summer My Uncle Came Home from the War' was written at the crossroad of memory and imagination, and explores the balance of loyalty and grudges among women in a family that has known—that *is knowing*—hard times. It also is about how moving from country to city challenges generations of rules. I wrote this story and others after a brother I never knew I had appeared in my life, asking about our dead mother. I wanted him to know how it was . . . and I wanted to remember."

JAN EPTON SEALE is a native-born Texan who makes her home now in McAllen, in the Rio Grande Valley. She has two books of poetry, *Bonds* and *Sharing the House,* and eight children's books in print. Six of her short stories have been syndicated through the P.E.N. Syndicated Fiction

Project, appearing in such newspapers as the *Chicago Tribune, Newsday,* and the *San Francisco Chronicle.* Many other stories, poems, and articles by her have been published in various periodicals. Seale received a Creative Writing Fellowship from the National Endowment for the Arts in 1982. At present she teaches creative writing and is an Artist-in-Education with the Texas Commission on the Arts.

"There's sadness and there's joy at a girl's first menses, and I wanted this story to contain both. The event is far more meaningful in girls' lives than literature has ever shown.

"The story became funnier, more ludicrous, and more significant to me as I wrote. One detail led to another until I was recalling more than I thought I remembered about my own coming of age. As I shared the story with other women, I realized that it touched a lost, mute time in them too, and they laughed and added their own versions to Becca's and Wayna Sue's. So again the obvious but often historically neglected truth of women's lives: that in the shock of pleasure of shared experience we come to value better our own selves."

ALMA STONE sent along the following (auto)biographical note:

"Alma Stone is from Jasper in East Texas and lives in New York City with two cats, Evelyn and Martha, and a host of friendly roaches. She attended Southern Methodist University in 1925/26(?) and later Bradford College in Massachusetts and Columbia University. She has published four novels and a number of short stories, and is working on a novel about the homeless (she thinks, 'It could easily be me') in her Upper West Side neighborhood. Though only one of her novels (*The Harvard Tree*) is explicitly about Texas, each has substantial Texas underpinnings. She does not consciously write about strong women or unstrong women from Texas but some of them turn out that way and she expects they always will.

"She is eighty years old and thinks it's for the birds."

CARMEN TAFOLLA, a native of the West Side barrios of San Antonio, is the author of several books of poetry, seven screenplays, three chapbooks for children, and a textbook on racism, sexism, and Chicana women. Her latest collection of poetry, *Sonnets to Human Beings,* was the first-place winner of the 1987 UCI National Chicano Literary Competition. Presently, she lives in Flagstaff, Arizona, where she is at work on a novel, *La Gente.*

"While I enjoy many writing styles, from love sonnets to 'intellectual stuff' to comical children's rhymes, my favorite style and approach are to write in the voices of people, to let poetry or prose come in their words and thoughts, *and* to let it come in their language and accent, be that good-ol'-boy English or *my* native language, Tex-Mex. I like my works to understand, to *profundizar*, people—to reveal our strengths and our weaknesses, our struggles and victories and failures and flaws, and, ultimately, our beauty as human beings.

"'Federico y Elfiria' was born out of the small-town Texas experience—Eagle Pass, Texas, to be exact. But it could have happened anywhere, just by changing the names and the particular symbols for misinterpretation and stereotyping. Eagle Pass has lots of smart, accepting people. And then it has folks like Federico. But don't pick on Federico, or on Hispanic men, or on Eagle Pass. There's plenty of sexism and just all-around stupid behavior in all of our modern cultures. Maybe if we can understand, and just *see* ourselves, maybe then we can grow beyond where he was . . . pobrecito. Cuídamelo."

PAT ELLIS TAYLOR describes herself as a "writer, poet, dreamer, gardener, accordion player, used-book seller, and Texas traveler." Born in Bryan, she went to school at the University of Texas at El Paso, where she received her B.A. and M.A. Her books include an oral history, *Border Healing Woman: The Story of Jewel Babb;* a collection of poetry, *Tonics, Teas, Roots & Remedies;* and two collections of short fiction, *Afoot in a Field of Men* and *The God Chaser.* In 1978 Taylor was awarded a National Endowment for the Arts Creative Writing Fellowship, and in 1986 a Dobie-Paisano Fellowship.

A native Texan (and Baptist preacher's daughter), CAROLYN WEATHERS is the author of *Leaving Texas: A Memoir, Crazy,* and *Shitkickers and Other Texas Stories.* Her work has appeared in various little magazines and in the anthology *My Story's On: Ordinary Women/Extraordinary Lives.* Weathers lives now in Los Angeles, where she and Jenny Wrenn run Clothespin Fever Press. Together they are editors and publishers of *In a Different Light: An Anthology of Lesbian Writers.* Weathers writes that she is "currently at work on a novel that will be permeated with Texas and mixed with the West Coast (as I am myself)."

"Texas is deep in my bones, and in my writing, especially all that is explicitly 'Texas.' It's a rich deposit I dip into.

"'Cheers, Everybody!' was written as an evocation of a certain time and place and time of life. That 'certain time' is the early sixties, on the eve of the great social movements (including the Gay Liberation Front) of the mid- and late sixties—that hush of anticipation in the heavy, sticky heat, that had to break soon. The place, of course, is Texas, specifically San Antonio. If the story were set in some other city or state, it wouldn't be quite the same, but certain aspects—the wild youth in the big city, the early sixties gay/lesbian scene—would still bring flashes of recognition almost anywhere. (If there were such a thing as gay/lesbian race memory, the Orchid Bar and the Cave would be part of it.)"

S. L. WISENBERG has the same initials as her grandfather, who came to Houston during the Depression via Kishinev, Russia; New York City; Macon, Georgia; and Laurel, Mississippi. She was born in Houston in 1955 and left in 1974 for college Up North. (She learned later that she had arrived in an area known as the Midwest.) Wisenberg has published work in various genres in *The New Yorker,* the *Miami Herald, Calyx, Other Voices, The Progressive,* the *Chicago Tribune, Houston City Magazine, U.S. News & World Report,* and elsewhere. She teaches writing at The School of the Art Institute of Chicago.

"Everyone up here in Chicago says, 'Jews in Texas? I didn't know there were Jews in Texas.' I don't feel that Texan. I don't know if I ever did. I think of ancestors in the Old Country. Sure, I remember Fat Stock Show Day (whatever it was called) and country songs and bluebonnets, Sam Houston and the Battle of San Jacinto, but those were really for the Christians. Our customs were different from the Texans', and, on the other hand, we were quieter, more secretive (ashamed?) than Northern Jews.

"This story is about coming of age as a woman in a place where there's no room to explore your political or spiritual or sexual stirrings *on your own terms*. I hope it opens the door to the question: How could it have been better?"

SUZANNE COMER, editor of this volume, was born in Knoxville, Tennessee, but has lived in Texas since 1969, first in Austin, more recently in Dallas. She graduated from the University of Tennessee in Knoxville, earned an M.A. in English at Duke University, and completed all requirements but the dissertation for a doctorate in English at the University of Texas at Austin. She was acquisitions editor at the University of Texas Press for seven years. Since 1986 Comer has been senior editor at Southern Methodist University Press and co-editor, with Tom Pilkington, of that press's Southwest Life and Letters series.

BARBARA ELAM, whose art is featured on the cover of *Common Bonds,* is a Dallas artist concentrating on intaglio printmaking. Born and raised in Wichita Falls, she holds an M.F.A. degree from East Texas State University in Commerce. Her work has been included in numerous international juried and invitational exhibitions, and she has received more than twenty-three purchase and first-place awards. Elam's nine one-person shows include exhibits at the Galería de Arte Moderno in Guadalajara, Mexico, and the San Angelo Museum of Fine Arts. She has recently been awarded a Mary Ingraham Bunting Fellowship for 1989–90 from Radcliffe College.

I'd Trade All My Tomorrows is an original intaglio print especially created for this book.